a novel by Joel Gross

inspired by
Sir Walter Scott's "Ivanhoe"

SYLVAN COURT PRODUCTIONS

joel@joelgross.com

In 1192, a truce between Saladin and Richard Lion-Heart ended the Third Crusade. En route from the Holy Land, King Richard was imprisoned by Leopold of Austria.

THE JEWESS takes place in England, in 1194.

Main Characters

REBECCA, a healer, daughter of Isaac of York

IVANHOE, a heroic knight returning from Richard's Crusade

ROWENA, betrothed to Ivanhoe, ward of Cedric

BRIAN, Prince John's greatest tournament knight

ISAAC of York, a Jewish financier, loyal to Richard

GURTH, Ivanhoe's squire

ETHELREDA, Gurth's future wife

CEDRIC, nobleman estranged from his son Ivanhoe

PRINCE JOHN, Richard's brother, ruler of England in Richard's absence

RICHARD LION-HEART, England's Crusader king

PART ONE: ROTHERWOOD

CHAPTER ONE

Sometimes Rebecca felt the stab of happiness.

When her father Isaac's eyes fixed on her lovingly, when a memory of her mother, laughing, passed like a shadow, or even when sighting the moon emerging from clouds, she felt it: Happiness, penetrating like a suddenly too-bright light.

Now, despite the dangers of traveling through unfamiliar forest, birdsong distracted her from lingering despair, a sharp reminder of nature's blessings. Despite the long miles between Doncaster and Sheffield, the road wound through pristine marshland and woods, climbed easy hills, descended picturesque valleys. She couldn't help but see that the world was a thousand shades of green. Green, the color of life, gift of the Almighty, struck her heart with inescapable hope. Even the sight of a storm-blasted tree trunk, rotting on the ground, broke chinks in the armor of her gloom. It reminded her that death came to everyone. Rebecca knew this too was a gift of the Holy One.

The trail, flanked with oaks, beeches and hollies, allowed her room to ride alongside her father, to be with him in silence, allowing each their solitary thoughts. As shafts of sunshine came through a canopy of broad-headed trees, Rebecca thought of Zaragoza. It was only a matter of weeks before Isaac's business would be concluded, and they could turn their backs on England forever. France had killed her mother, England her cousins, and in Germany, once a bastion for their family, new strains of fanatical Jew-hatred were growing.

In Spain, it would be different. There her mother's family had lived for twenty generations. There her father, once a young man with honey-colored eyes, had met her mother, and told her tales of Northern countries: Saxony, Frisia, Brabant. Tales of kind Christian rulers, on whose behalf he traveled, raising funds for castles, lands, armies. Tales of thick forest, of white snowfields, of abundant game.

Tales, she thought, letting loose an infrequent smile. Her father, Isaac of York, was a storyteller who favored happy endings. Ever determined to find the good in a landscape of wickedness. Convinced that evil could not stand, that it must disintegrate in the light of reason. But she wondered what had become of his own reason. In the Northern countries, evil was not disintegrating; it was growing and growing, like a monster feeding on its young.

Had he forgotten that his own father had been forced to flee from Prussia for Silesia, then forced to flee again? Isaac had been raised in Bavaria and in Suabia, in Turin and Verona, his family forever packing up and setting forth one step ahead of angry mobs.

Somehow, that history hadn't soured him. Isaac picked up languages and friends wherever he lived. Maybe it was the honey-colored eyes, maybe the acumen with numbers, the daring that financed ships sailing to unknown waters, which lent gold to rulers of tiny principalities who hoped to be great kings. Isaac was a handsome dreamer, with a grandfather who had been a rabbi known throughout the world.

How could her mother Deborah not love such a man?

When Rebecca was born, they had been living in Mainz. Later they moved to Worms, then Strasbourg. When she was ten years old they established a home in France. A lovely home, near the synagogue, in a community of Jews five hundred strong. Surrounded by friendly Christians, or so her father had assured her.

The local baron was enlightened, could even read a bit, and played chess with Isaac when he was at home.

But Isaac was seldom at home. He was most often abroad, in search of opportunity. Perhaps he imagined some nameless business with some great prince would finally give his family the stability and safety that had never been theirs for more than a few years at a time. Perhaps if he'd stayed at home, he'd have had an inkling of the growing danger to the Jews of France. But probably not. Her father insisted on seeing the world as a joyous place.

Few Jews traveled to cold and treacherous England, land of the great massacre, but her father retained his old name, Isaac of York, without a shudder of irony. And when they were forced to flee from France, Isaac led his daughter to England without fear or foreboding.

"Don't let it go," said her father suddenly, turning his kind eyes to her. When she looked at him wonderingly, he explained: "You were holding on to a happy memory, but then you dropped it."

"I never let go of any memory, Father," she said. "But not every memory brings a smile."

Isaac didn't pursue this line of talk. In a
moment, she would be harking back to horrors he didn't
wish to hear. He turned his eyes to the road ahead.

Rebecca urged her thoughts back to Spain. In
Spain there would be safety, comfort, respect. To
live under bright sun, drink clean water, consult with
doctors with knowledge far greater than her own – this
might give her father years of additional life.

If only her father could be well again, could
live to a great old age! In warm Andalusia the cold
disease in her heart might burn away, allowing her
spirit to lift from mourning.

At this hope, Rebecca nearly smiled again.

But as their horses walked up a gentle rise past
a grove of beeches, the sight of a giant cross sunk in
the center of four intersecting trails banished all
joy.

Instinctively protective, Rebecca grabbed the
bridle of Isaac's easy-gaited palfrey, stopping both
their horses. Years had sunk the wooden cross to
little more than a cubit's height. Standing behind it
was a tall young man in filthy clothes and tattered
chain mail, marked with a Crusader's cross. The young
man's warhorse, laden with weapons, grazed nearby. He

hurried to meet them, pale blue eyes shining in his grimy face.

"There is nothing to fear," said Isaac to his daughter. But it was not fear that Rebecca felt, but hatred. Familiar hatred: For the sunken cross, for the cross on the Crusader's mail, for the warrior returning from murder, pillage, and rape.

The young man was shouting in his English language, not belligerent, but beseeching: "Doctor, this way, hurry! She is dying."

The Crusader jumped onto his horse, revealing golden spurs, a knightly mark of distinction at odds with his scraggly beard and disgraceful armor. "Why do you stop? You will be paid."

"I am not a doctor," said Isaac, speaking the young man's language with an indefinable accent.

The knight gripped the hilt of his sheathed sword, trying to restrain his temper. Rebecca understood that her father's dress and demeanor had confused the young man. Other Jews were obliged to wear the square yellow hat that marked their nation, setting them apart for special humiliation.

But Isaac, the fourth richest man in England, had royal permission to wear what he liked. Of course that permission, carried inside his writing case on a tiny scroll, could not be read by the illiterates who might take offence at this exception to the law.

Since the slaughter at York four years before, there were few Jews left in this part of the world. In Doncaster there was one family, in Sheffield, a single narrow street. Succumbing to Rebecca's entreaties, Isaac had finally agreed to soon vacate their own country house outside the village of Ashby. As most of the local people never strayed more than ten miles in any direction, few had ever seen a Jew, though all had heard about them: Money-lenders, black magicians, killers of the Christian god.

Rebecca knew that in russet cloak and fur-lined boots, her father would seem neither pauper nor warrior, churchman nor franklin, serf nor pilgrim. A nobleman would be more arrogant, a merchant would have sumpter mules and a retinue of servants. Isaac, at fifty, was already a rarity in a world where few lived past their fourth decade, and most died far earlier of plague, hunger, or warfare.

What else could Isaac be but the old doctor the young man had sent for, the only one for a hundred miles?

"You can have every zecchin in my purse, Doctor. Save the poor girl's life, and you can even take my stallion."

"I am not a doctor," repeated Isaac.

"Gramercy, do not lie to me. I have sent to Doncaster. You come from Doncaster. Do not let her die because you imagine me a pauper. She is more child than woman."

"What is wrong with her, Crusader?" said Rebecca, suddenly breaking her silence.

The young man turned from father to daughter. The hood she wore couldn't disguise her striking beauty, or that she could be little more than twenty years of age. Rebecca was used to the leering of Gentiles, amazed to find a girl of the despised race with an almost otherworldly loveliness.

Perhaps, she imagined, it was because she washed her face and hands daily, she cleaned her teeth with a cunning little brush purchased in Venice. The very cleanliness which left her skin unblemished, her teeth white and whole, her hair a mass of shiny curls, gave her an alien aspect in a world that had become filthy and mean.

Serfs never bathed, noblemen almost never. The world had forgotten the lessons of ancient Rome, and covered their unwashed bodies with dirty clothes. Even young people lost their teeth, had matted hair and blotchy skin.

Against such a human landscape, Rebecca's face looked like an angel's. More than one patient, waking to her touch, would blink back tears, staring into her enormous eyes with religious awe. Surely this could be no one but the Madonna, come down to earth to effect God's mercy.

But this reaction was less common than one of slow-building rage: Rebecca's flawless features bespoke an ideal of health and youth and promise that was denied to all but a few in this dark time. This incited not only lust, but envy and hatred. Not only the desire to possess her, but the desire to destroy her; her very presence a rebuke to all that was imperfect.

But the Crusader wasn't looking at her with lust or rage, but with a simpler amazement. Young women did not intrude themselves where they did not belong. They did not interrupt their fathers, or speak to strange knights.

"What is it?" she insisted sharply, continuing in an English touched by the same indefinable accent as her father's. "Broken bones? Snake bite? Plague?"

The young man, deciding to ignore the girl, looked to Isaac for help, insisting: "She has been beaten, Doctor, left for dead." The knight's voice sharpened to a vengeful tone: "Probably raped."

"My father is not a doctor," said Rebecca, intruding once again. "But I can help you."

"I'm sorry, Rebecca," said Isaac in Hebrew. "You cannot help… We must be in Sheffield before dark."

The young man's face lit up with sudden delight. "You are Jews," he said, his Crusading years in 'Outremer' allowing him to recognize their language. "Thank God. She will be saved."

Rebecca would learn that he had only loathing for drunken pillagers, on their way to the Holy Land, who had slaughtered Jews in a blood lust more notable than any warlike feat against the Saracens. And the young man could have had no idea that Rebecca's mother, Deborah, a gentle healer of the sick, beloved by Jew and Christian alike, had been murdered by a mob of French Crusaders three years ago.

His voice filled with respect, he told Isaac and Rebecca that Jews were wise, capable of wonders, that even Richard Lion-heart, fallen ill at Acre, had consulted the famous Jewish doctor Maimonides. That great Jewish sage had cured the King with a few magic words!

"Do you happen to know them?" said Rebecca curtly. "The 'magic words'?"

"No," said the knight, stung by her ironic tone. "I was not present, but the Hebrew words cured the King."

"Words don't cure," said Rebecca. "Sometimes they are not even capable of solace."

The young warrior turned to her, taken aback by the pain and anger in her eyes. He hated being reproached, but perhaps she had reason. In spite of the urgency, he couldn't turn his eyes from hers; he couldn't find words to speak.

Finally, it was Rebecca who turned away.

"Come, Father," she said in Hebrew. "This is an obligation we cannot refuse."

"All right, young man," said Isaac in English. "My daughter will help."

The young knight smiled at this, and his smile
was radiant. Rebecca was struck by the force of his
gratitude. For a moment, the fact of his unholy
knighthood, his association with everything she
loathed, vanished.

But as father and daughter followed the Crusader
down the narrowest lane leading from the crossroads,
Rebecca found herself worrying. She couldn't
understand what new, nameless fear had entered her
heart.

CHAPTER TWO

To staunch and clean the peasant girl's wounds had been a simple task for Rebecca. Comforting her had proven more difficult. Barely more than a child, she demanded to know how it could be God's will for five armored horsemen to drag her through muddy fields, to rape her one after the other, to leave her unfit for any decent future? What sin had she committed to merit so much earthly punishment?

"You must ask your priest," said Rebecca.

"I ask you, my lady," said the girl, gripping Rebecca with dirt-encrusted hands.

"Those men have committed sin, not you."

"Will God punish them?" said the young girl.

"I cannot speak for God," said Rebecca. "He is beyond human understanding. I do not understand what He is, only what He is not. And I know that He is not bad."

"God is good. God is great," insisted the young girl.

It was impossible to say whether Rebecca's mother had been raped before she had been murdered, as she had been forced into a hovel with fifty other Jews so that the Crusaders could set the thatched roof on fire. A filthy hovel much like the one Rebecca was in now, where humans shared a space with their animals, crowding together for warmth.

God wasn't bad, and He wasn't evil, Rebecca had been taught. There was a reason why He allowed crimes to flourish in his world, but His reason was outside human understanding. Whether He punished rapists and murderers on earth or in the World-to-Come was unknown to Rebecca or to anyone else. A distinguished rabbi had once told her that it was enough for God to have given man reason to know right from wrong. With reason, he said, wrongdoers are inevitably punished, as all evil must leave illness festering in their hearts.

"Those men will be punished," said Rebecca, thinking not only of the girl's assailants, but of her mother's. "Punished more terribly than we can know."

"Thank you, my lady," said the girl, her childish face bright with thoughts of hellfire tormenting flesh.

"Forgive me, Daughter," said Isaac. She had given the girl a sleeping potion, and rejoined her impatient father outside the hut. Nearby, the knight readied their horses, wondering what they were saying in their magic tongue. "I told you not to help, thinking our convenience more important than your sacred calling. Your mother would have been proud of you."

"Perhaps not, Father," she said. "That I agreed was an impulse. He had to ask more than once. He had to plead for help that should have been freely given."

"You say you hate every Gentile," said Isaac. "Yet you risk your life for them."

"Yes, Father. And for teaching me such behavior, you have only yourself to blame."

It was still light when the knight led Rebecca and Isaac back toward the crossroads, but the darkness was growing, and with it, a hint of coming rain. He kept his silence for a while, imagining that the Jewess had softened toward him. After all, in helping the young peasant girl, they had together accomplished a good deed. Glancing at her in the fading light, he thought her melancholy features were leavened by a spirit of fellow feeling. Suddenly he began to speak out eager questions, not so much to have them answered, but simply to hear the beautiful girl speak:

Who had taught her to heal the sick, where had she had come from, where was she traveling, what languages did she know?

Rebecca answered each question in his own tongue, but so curtly that the knight eventually silenced, stopped by her evident distaste. This was unwarranted, he felt. Unfair, unjust. He turned away brusquely, bitter with disappointment.

Only then did the beautiful young woman speak what was on her mind: "Who did this, Crusader?"

The young man instantly brightened. Her mood did not reflect on him, but on the terrible evidence of a girl's rape. He spoke harshly: "Warriors on the way to the great tournament."

"Knights?" she said.

"In King Richard's absence, many call themselves knights," he said, more harshly still. "The girl was under the protection of Sir Mark of Bainbridge, a true knight."

"The protection did her no good," said Rebecca.

"Sir Mark was old, and certainly outnumbered. I suspect the warriors he fought observed no rules of combat. I knew him. If these men had fought him one at a time —"

"Why did they fight him at all? What manner of knight rapes a girl, and kills her protector?"

"Sir Mark was, in turn, under the protection of Lord Cedric of Rotherwood."

"The protection did him no good either."

"You don't understand. Sir Mark was killed defending his serfs… Lord Cedric will soon learn the name of Sir Mark's killer."

"So that he in turn may kill the killer?"

"I will attend to that myself," said the knight.

"Killing begets killing," she said.

"Vengeance must be taken," he said, surprised at her vehemence. "It is my duty to tell Lord Cedric what crimes have been committed on his lands in the name of Prince John."

"What does Prince John have to do with it?"

"The villagers who survived the attack say the warriors wore his colors."

"Yes, you Crusaders like to wear colors into battle. Whether you are fighting each other, or simply burning down a village."

"Rebecca," said her father behind her. His voice was unusually sharp. He spoke in English for the benefit of the knight. "Not every warrior in England is a Crusader. Nor is every Crusader guilty of crimes."

"I must disagree, Father. We have seen it over and again, everywhere we traveled. Crusaders are cut from the same cloth. All they do is kill, pillage, and rape."

Now it was the knight who no longer wished to talk. She knew nothing of him, yet the Jewess had called him a murderer, a rapist. He pulled ahead on the narrow trail, burning with anger, leaving her alone with her father.

The path through the woods crossed shallow brooks, skirting bogs and marshes, but the knight always managed to find firm ground for their tired horses. The ride gave Rebecca time to regret her words to the young man. It was not his fault that her thoughts never ceased roiling with memories of her mother's death. Nor was it his fault that she worried about her father, that she wished them safe and free in distant Zaragoza, away from this cold and hostile island. It was entirely possible that the knight was blameless of any crime other than his natural tendency to return violence with violence.

Pouring salt on her wounds, Isaac voiced, in Hebrew, what she already knew: She had been terribly unjust to the young man. Rebecca wondered what had impelled the knight's kindness toward the peasant girl. Serfs were normally treated little better than animals by the warrior class. Apparently, this Crusader was more decent than most.

The young man reined in, waiting for Rebecca and Isaac to ride close. It had grown too dark to see the anger in his eyes, but his carefully controlled voice made it clear; there was fury in his heart. He addressed Isaac alone. "It would be wise to delay your journey to Sheffield, sir," he said. "You appear to be fatigued."

Isaac was more than fatigued; he was half asleep in his saddle. Rebecca was holding onto his arm to make sure he wouldn't fall. When Isaac didn't answer, Rebecca spoke in his place. "Please. Just get us back to the crossroads, as you agreed," she said.

"But that is where we have come." Rebecca could sense the hurt behind his words, and resolved to be more amenable, to choose her word with caution. It was so dark that the sunken cross was barely visible. Moonlight could scarcely penetrate the cover of trees.

An unseen animal made a guttural cry. Isaac stirred, sitting up tall.

"Father, we are again at the crossroads," she said in English, wanting to include the angry knight. "Sheffield is only a few hours more, and the moon is nearly full. We must press on."

"You are without an escort," said the knight, sharply disagreeing with Rebecca's plan. "The forest is not safe at night."

"Thank you for your concern, Crusader," she said, meaning no irony, but she could tell he bridled at her words. She added: "Wherever we find ourselves, we are always within God's hands."

"Sir," said the young warrior. "I hope you will be more sensible than your daughter and instruct -"

"Sensible?" said Rebecca. "What would have been sensible would have been to continue on our path to Sheffield without allowing you to interrupt us."

"Do you mean to say that you are sorry for helping that poor girl?"

"No! What I mean to say is that I am sensible and that I do not like being called insensible!"

Isaac raised a head, silencing the debate. He looked from Rebecca to the knight, and back again.

"It is blasphemous to imagine that the Lord is paying particular attention to our small concerns," he said, but without any odor of sanctimony. "I supposed the Lord God has more important matters to dwell on then what will happen to us in this dark forest." Isaac's religious pronouncements, like his quotations from Scripture, were delivered with lightness, and in the spirit of expediency.

"There is no alternative, Father. You are not well enough to sleep in the woods. To remain here would be just as dangerous as traveling."

"Rotherwood is nearby," said the knight.

"Rotherwood," said Isaac, brightening.

"You can find food and shelter there," said the knight. "And continue on to Sheffield in the morning."

"Rotherwood is Lord Cedric's home," said Isaac. "A man who remains loyal to King Richard."

"No one but you remains loyal to Richard," said Rebecca, not seeing the acid look this prompted in the young man. "And I'd put greater trust in the forest than in the home of a nobleman who owes you money."

"Forgive her, Sir Knight," said Isaac. "Sad experience has made her wary. I think your idea eminently reasonable. We will be happy to spend the night at Rotherwood."

"I will not be happy in a Gentile's home," said Rebecca in Hebrew. "Not until we are living in Spain."

Resuming their journey, the knight walked his horse down murky trails, unhesitating, as if he could see every step through the blackness. Isaac followed, with Rebecca at the rear, watching her father closely. In half an hour, they broke free of the brush.

Straight ahead was a low, irregular building thrown together without any aesthetic sense. A muddy ditch and two crude palisades with sharpened oak pillars protected the large edifice and its unseen courtyards from intruders. The only way across the ditch and through the palisades was by primitive drawbridge.

"Please wait here, my lord," said the knight.

Rebecca watched the knight ride off, trotting across the green, on a straight line to a gate in the outer palisade. "Beware of Gentiles who call you 'my lord,'" she said.

"We will be all right, Daughter."

"We will be all right when we are both in Zaragoza."

"I have told you time and again that I am happy to send you on ahead, accompanied by trusted men."

"Stop your nonsense. You know I will never leave you. Why do you offer what you know I must refuse?"

Across the meadow, the knight drew his sword, and banged its hilt against the gateposts with peremptory force. His warhorse was old, his armor rusty and broken, his wallet without a single gold coin. Yet the young man knocked on that gate as if he owned the world.

Rebecca knew that to be rich was not always to be strong. Though Isaac had obtained the King's permission to dress like a Gentile, he took care to avoid exciting the hatred of people who regarded Jews as followers of Satan, the killers of Christ. When traveling he had learned to do without servants to avoid exciting murderous envy. Isaac's wealth was not in land, or serfs, or herds of cattle. His wealth was ink on paper, indicating sums owed him by scores of noblemen, sums multiplying through interest that might never be paid.

Noblemen often mortgaged all they possessed to get their hands on the Jew's paper, paper that could be translated into gold in some far off place. With gold they could buy armor, weapons, they could pay warriors, they could aspire to glory in the Holy Land. And if the loans could not be repaid, there was always the time honored method of alleviating financial distress: Banishing the debt-holder, or better yet, killing him.

The great city of York, where Jews had prospered for a generation, had been the scene of a massacre four years before. Assured royal protection from angry, indebted noblemen, Jews took refuge in York Castle. But the noblemen had too much money at stake to care about the King's strictures. The Jews, moneylenders and artisans, rich and poor alike, were besieged, starved and finally murdered. All financial records were burned, all debts canceled amid a self-righteous cacophony against Jewish usurers. But with debts exposed to cancellation through intimidation and slaughter, how could interest rates be anything but high?

Isaac, traveling in Italy with his family, had received the news of the massacre with disbelief. He was certain that Richard was different from his venal brother John, different from a hundred petty monarchs. The King had great ambitions for England, and those ambitions included a place for Jewish financiers. After the calamity, King Richard promised Isaac that the crown would punish the perpetrators of murder; that Jews would never again suffer from the violence of debtor nobles or hate-crazed mobs.

But a few months later, Richard Lion-heart had gone on Crusade. No one had been punished. Talk of justice for the Jews was forgotten.

Rebecca felt that Isaac needed to believe in Richard. When the King found himself in desperate trouble, a captive in Austria, held for ransom that his own brother refused to pay, Isaac helped raise the needed gold.

York was an aberration, Isaac claimed. A monstrous evil never to be repeated. Restored to power, Richard would make good on his pledge. This would be the king who gave the Jews of England protection under the law.

"Father," said Rebecca, snapping out of her reverie.

A hulking servant was stepping through the gate, on guard, belligerent, brandishing a heavy cudgel. The young knight dismounted, moonlight reflecting on his tattered chain mail, hands at his side. The servant continued toward him, in a hurry, the cudgel raised as if to attack, but the knight held his ground, his hands at this side.

Suddenly the servant stopped, astonished. He was a young man, younger even than the knight, heavily muscled, with a thatch of red hair. Speechless, he dropped his cudgel, fell to his knees, and grabbed the knight's filthy hand, bringing it to his lips.

It was too far to hear what name the servant called the knight, or what either said by way of greeting. But a moment later the inner gate was thrown open, and the knight was back on his horse, riding fast toward Isaac and Rebecca. By the time he had drawn alongside, the drawbridge across the muddy ditch was being slowly lowered, revealing the flickering light of torches.

"You will be safe here for the night," said the young knight, directing his words to Isaac alone.

He knew that Rebecca had come this way reluctantly, obeying her father's wishes with trepidation. Not only against all her instincts of self-preservation, but because she wanted nothing to do with any knight, especially him.

Still, ignoring a hundred pressing concerns, the young man turned to her, forcing a promise into his eyes. "You will see that this is the best thing for your father. Out of the dark and damp. Warm, well-fed, and drinking the sweetest mead in England," he said. "Welcome to Rotherwood."

Perhaps the knight was doing what he considered best for her father, for strangers, for a pair of Jews, thought Rebecca. He was a Crusader, he wore their cross, but even she, angry at the world, could sense his innate decency, his kindness. For the first time since they'd met, Rebecca smiled.

But he had already begun to turn, and didn't see the troubled beauty's acknowledgment of his kindness. His thoughts were elsewhere, and anything but kind.

CHAPTER THREE

Over the drawbridge, relieved of their horses, Isaac and Rebecca were left standing in a muddy courtyard. "Gurth will look after you," said the young knight. And then, all at once, he was gone.

Rebecca could see torches lighting the way to numerous doors into the main structure, and to a warren of derelict outbuildings. Gurth, the redheaded servant at the gate, satisfied that his master had safely passed through a side door, now turned to father and daughter. His face glowed with happiness. Gurth didn't move, even as it began to rain, even as the wind picked up.

"Please take us inside," said Isaac finally.

"Yes, my lord," said Gurth. But he was unsure about where he must lead these two travelers, of unknown class, brought to him by his beloved master. "Where?" he said. "What quarters?"

As if in answer, Isaac pressed a coin into the big man's calloused hand. The servant stared at it, wonderingly. It was a foreign coin, reflecting torchlight. Gurth bit into it with powerful white teeth. "Gold," he said, amazed. "This must be gold."

The rain was coming down faster, but Gurth, astonished by the gift, took the time to grab the old man's hand, and bring it to his lips.

Soon they were inside one of the low outbuildings, in a small room, waiting for Gurth to bring hot water. There was a wood stool, and two bed frames stuffed with straw, covered with filthy sheepskins. In place of a window there was a slit in the plastered wall. Rain dripped through overhead thatch. The floor was earth mixed with lime. Wind whistled through every chink, and blew hard through the slit, sending torchlight dancing.

Reading her thoughts, Isaac said: "We have taken refuge in far worse."

"We would be approaching Sheffield by now," said Rebecca, reminding him of his insistence on following the Crusader to Rotherwood.

"Or we would be stuck in the mud, waylaid by bandits, or attacked by wolves," said Isaac, smiling into her eyes. Her eyes weren't as green as her mother's, nor were they honey-colored like his own; but an extraordinary mixture, like emeralds veined with yellow light.

Neither mentioned that if she hadn't stopped to help the peasant girl, they'd already be safe and sound in Naftali ben Mordecai's comfortable home in Sheffield. "You're absolutely right, Father," she said, forcing cheer into her voice. "This is a delightful place, and we should be glad of the hospitality of the country."

Thunder sounded, loud enough to rock the timbers, and Rebecca was suddenly glad for shelter, no matter how crude. She urged Isaac to sit on one of the beds, and when he did, began to remove his boots.

"'As is the mother, so is the daughter,'" said Isaac, quoting from the book of Ezekiel.

"That is kindly said," said Rebecca.

"Though you still have much to learn from her memory," said Isaac playfully.

"Indeed."

"Your mother was forgiving, willing to renew her trust in any man."

Rebecca finished pulling off his boots, none too gently. "'A wise daughter makes a father glad,'" she said, reworking the proverb to her favor. Then she added a personal adage: "And wisdom makes me wary."

"To spend your life being wary can be worse than living at all."

"All right, Father."

"We are safe here."

"So you believe."

"It is said that Lord Cedric is an honorable man. If he learns I am here, he will have to seat me at the high table."

"As he has never met you, Father, I suggest you keep your identity secret. We must sit at the low table, keep our eyes down, and restrict our talk to each other."

Gurth entered, preventing further disagreement. Rebecca pulled up her hood, modestly covering her hair. The servant had brought hot water in a large basin, carrying the great weight without effort, his thick hands impervious to the heat. Rebecca thanked him, showed him where to put the basin, then took dried flowers and seeds from a leather wallet, and crushed these together into the steamy water.

Gurth watched with intense curiosity. "What is that brew?" he asked.

"Lavender flowers and parsnip seeds," said Rebecca. The servant continued to stare as she

scooped a silver cup into the basin, and brought some
of the liquid to her father's lips. Gurth smiled,
eagerly telling her that his mother's mother had used
something similar when he was a child, sick with
fever.

"Black snakeroot is better for fever," said
Rebecca.

"And for headache," said Gurth, "she used to
sprinkle salt on my head."

"That will do no harm," she said. "But neither
will it do any good. Drinking cinnamon water is far
more effective."

Impressed by Rebecca's knowledge, Gurth suddenly
braved a question: "And for anger, my lady?" he said.
"Do you know a cure for a father's anger?"

Later she would understand the source of Gurth's
concern. But she had no remedy for anger other than
time and prayer, neither of which had worked for her.

While Isaac drank his brew, Gurth explained that
no one could leave Rotherwood until first light, when
the drawbridge to the outer world would be raised.
While they had their evening meal, Gurth said he would
look for additional sheepskins so they might enjoy a
comfortable night.

"Thank you," said Rebecca, surprised that the young servant lingered in their small chamber. "Is there anything you require from us?"

"No, my lady," he said, watching Isaac take the silver cup from Rebecca's hands and drain the precious brew. "I am ordered to remain here until you are ready to go to the great hall."

"Ordered?" said Rebecca. "By whose authority?"

Realizing that Gurth didn't want to answer this, Isaac interjected: "By the law of hospitality, Daughter. We should obey it by taking all its gifts with gratitude."

Isaac rested a few minutes more, then Gurth struggled with Rebecca to see who would help the old man on with his boots. Gurth -- stronger than three Rebeccas -- won the struggle.

Then Gurth led them to the dining hall. It had stopped raining, which was good, as the path to the great hall was both outside, skirting gardens and outbuildings, and inside, through a maze of narrow stone passageways.
Finally approaching a massive door, Gurth turned to them, his boyish face wrinkled with apology. They must, he told them, sit at the table reserved for

wayfarers and ordinary folk. They must not address Lord Cedric or Rowena, he continued, unless they were spoken to first.

"And please, my lord, my lady," said Gurth. "Do not speak out the name of the knight who brought you to Rotherwood."

"We do not know his name," said Rebecca.

Gurth, surprised at this, didn't volunteer to reveal it. "Well then," said Gurth. "All that remains is to wish you a hearty meal." He opened the great door without effort, to a cacophony of peasant and martial voices.

Rebecca followed her father inside, then heard the door behind them close, separating them from Gurth's comforting presence.

Pulling her hood more fully over her head, Rebecca worried about the sudden quiet in the large room. She looked neither left nor right, but kept her eyes on her father's back as he moved toward a bench at a low table occupied by a sallow man in Pilgrim's garments. She wondered about the Crusader's discretion, and hoped he had told no one that they were Jews. That knowledge could lead to far worse than a chill from wet weather. Eyes lowered, she sat

next to her father, with the Pilgrim on her other
side, trying to calm her racing heart.

Once conversation had resumed around her, Rebecca
raised her eyes. The Crusader was nowhere to be seen,
neither at high or low table.

The hall was low-ceilinged, cold, and sooty from
two enormous fireplaces. One wall displayed archaic
hunting spears of varying length. Two walls were bare
plaster. The fourth wall, behind the dais and the
nobles' high table, was covered with embroidery in
garish colors.

Three long common tables with rough benches, made
from unpolished forest planks, were peopled by men and
women preoccupied with their food. Trenchers were
filled with meat, fowl, bread, and cakes. Drinking
horns were filled with sweet mead and strong ale.
This was an occasion for feasting, and hungry people
were taking advantage of their lord's largesse.

But though the grandees on the dais took no
notice of Isaac and Rebecca, the lower tables' men and
women gradually found themselves staring at and
talking about the old man in the rich cloak, and the
young woman with the hood covering her hair.

Something marked them as different, alien. The pair's disinterest in the general talk of the table was odd enough. But their disregard for the food placed before them was impossible to understand. How could anyone not want to partake of Lord Cedric's fare: Hot flesh of swine, deer, hares, goats; steaming fowl brought in on spits by proud servants, waiting for each guest to tear away a succulent wing or a leg; even a fragrant mess of potage and seethed kid.

But father and daughter tasted none of these delights, restricting their food to morsels of bread, and kept their few words to whispers for each other alone. There were monks who were meant to be this quiet, this abstemious; though at Cedric's table, no one had ever seen a churchman hold back his appetite for the greater glory of God.

Something was peculiar about this old man; something stranger still about his daughter, whose necklace, though covered by a filmy shawl, reflected torchlight with brilliance.

Lord Cedric and his ward Rowena sat side by side on massive oak chairs at the center of the high table.

The Norman knight Sir Brian de Bois Gilbert sat at Cedric's left hand. Brian, a young man of martial aspect with almost pretty features, was accompanied by four Norman knights. All were smooth-shaven, young, and without scars; but square-shouldered, eager to prove themselves warlike.

There was a great difference between Saxon aristocrats and those of Norman descent, or so the saying went. Saxons bathed once a year, at Christmas, while Normans bathed twice, at Christmas and Easter. This was sufficient for Saxons to look down on Normans for unmanly prettifying; enough for Normans to turn up their noses at Saxon slovenliness.

Rotherwood was a Saxon stronghold, and Lord Cedric a vigorous old man of distinctive Northern type. Whether he bathed or not, his hair was long, his beard full, his green tunic furred with miniver. His arms, still muscular at sixty, were ringed with wide bracelets. His neck wore a gold collar thick enough to deflect the blow of a sword.

But Rebecca's attention was drawn to his ward. Not because of Lady Rowena's fair-haired beauty, or the luminous blue eyes that were less inviting than dangerous.   Nor was it because of the gemstones

braided into her hair, or the slender gold rings on
her shockingly bare arms. Eating with her fingers,
chewing and drinking and talking at the same time, she
was as primitive in her own way as her guardian, Lord
Cedric. Primitive with robust health, untrammeled
feelings; primitive too with the threat of physical
force.

This slender young woman contained, with effort,
a fury within her that threatened to burst free at any
moment. Rebecca had never seen this in a woman of the
higher classes. It was difficult not to stare as
Rowena brooded over the barbed insults directed at
Lord Cedric by Sir Brian.

Rowena's hand reached out to touch old Cedric's
forearm, not simply restraining his temper, but her
own. Not simply offering him the consolation of her
love, as Rebecca would have done with Isaac. While
Rebecca's hand on her father's arm completed the two
of them, joined them in whatever fate would bring,
Rowena's hand on Cedric was different. They were not
joined, guardian and ward, but separate. Rowena's
hand was not offering to share Cedric's fate, not
accepting it, but eager to fight against it. Rowena
drew strength from the old man, thought Rebecca,

taking in his martial spirit, the memory of his youthful prowess, and claimed it for herself.

How could Rebecca not be spellbound by a young woman, cosseted by rank and wealth and custom, with the will to wreak vengeance for those she loved?

Sir Brian laid down a knife into his plate of roast meats. He spoke louder, as if wanting everyone in the room, high and low, to hear. "Prince John has allowed your position to go so long unchallenged, only out of respect for your age," he said.

"My age has nothing to do with it," said Cedric. "If John has any respect, it's for his older brother's sword."

Brian's eyes turned from Cedric to Rowena's hand on Cedric's forearm. "Your allegiance to Richard is obstinate-"

"Of course it's obstinate. It's also stubborn, determined, and fixed."

"And futile," said Brian. "Richard is never coming back, which makes you… foolish."

Rebecca could feel a chill around the common tables. It was not just Isaac who loved their absent king, or resented Prince John's heavy-handed rule.

Rowena gripped Cedric's forearm more tightly. "Please, my lord," she said to him. "To be called foolish by a fool is of no consequence."

"You dare call me a fool?" said Brian to Rowena.

"You may address me," said Cedric. "But not my ward."

But Rowena hadn't finished, filling the hall with her Saxon accent and truculent manner. "A fool who knows nothing of knightly combat."

Brian raised his hands, signaling his men to remain seated. He looked into Rowena's bold eyes, warning her: "I have won every tournament in the kingdom for three years running."

"Heed my warning, sir: Do not speak to my ward again." Before Brian could protest, Cedric added: "And tournaments are not combat."

"Men die in tournaments," said Brian. "Just like they do in war."

"No. Not like they do in war," said Cedric.

Rowena added fuel to the fire: "He knows as much about war as I do."

Brian turned to her. "Have you not heard the fate of Sir Mark of Bainbridge?" he said.

Lord Cedric interrupted violently: "For the last time, Sir Brian: I have granted you food and lodging, but not the honor of addressing the fairest Saxon in England."

"Then tell the wench not to talk to me!"

Containing himself, Brian finally said what he had come to Rotherwood to say: "I have already told you what every man in England knows. Richard is never coming back. Even the rabble who survived his useless Crusade know it in their hearts. But now I will make it clearer, so that even a Saxon can understand. Richard is gone forever, because he is dead."

Men and women at the low table put down their knives into trenchers, let go of drinking horns, staring up at the master of the house for a response, a direction to follow, as Brian continued: "You would do well to acknowledge it, to accept the new order. Your King is dead."

But Lord Cedric had no response other than to wipe grease from his mouth, pick up a goblet of morat, and drink it to the lees. This infuriated Brian more than any words.

"There is no ruler in England but Prince John," said Brian. "This you must declare at the great tournament, in the face of the crowd. You must pledge allegiance and fealty to John, or I swear you will find yourself landless, homeless, without rank or power."

"I will not believe that Richard is dead," said Lord Cedric finally. "Not until you lay out his corpse before me. As to threats from a tournament knight who's never crossed swords in a battle… I scorn them, and I scorn you."

Rebecca could see that this was too much for Brian, that he was about to turn from violent words to violent action.

Many Norman knights stayed behind when Richard Lion-heart went on Crusade. While other men sought glory in the Holy Land, they prided themselves on having kept the peace in England, serving Prince John as deterrents to invasion or rebellion. For three years knights like Brian had risked life and limb in tournaments to exhibit martial skills that could be turned on anyone who stood in John's way.

But knights returning from Richard's great war, many maimed or broken-spirited, reminded the tournament knights that they were untested; that for all their murderous jousts and sword duels, John's men had never fought the Saracens, never been to war, that all their knightly deeds were nothing more than play.

Brian got to his feet with enough force to send his chair clattering over backwards. His four knights stood up, gripping the hilts of their swords.

"For saying much less, I killed a man today," said Sir Brian.

"You killed Sir Mark of Bainbridge," said Rowena with loathing, "who spent three years fighting to capture Jerusalem. A man as old as my guardian, sick and weary from years of holy Crusading. In single combat with you, with your men on every side. In case the old veteran proved too difficult for your heroism."

Brian drew his sword, and pressed the point to Rowena's neck, his hand shaking with violent agitation. Cedric stood, the tallest man at the nobles' table, and grabbed the boar-spear leaning against the back of his chair.

"Put down your sword, or I will stick this through your Norman chest," said Cedric. These days, the spear was mostly used as a cane when walking rough terrain. Raised over the old Saxon's head, it seemed almost possible that it could perform what Cedric threatened.

"There is no cause for worry, my lord," said Rowena. "Sir Brian is cow-hearted and craven, and won't have the nerve to scratch my throat."

Rebecca could see that Rowena wasn't feigning fearlessness. She wasn't afraid of Brian, of the sword at her throat, of death, of anything. Where this fearlessness came from was a mystery to Rebecca. She had learned to be resigned in the face of danger, to fight the outrages of the Gentiles with shut eyes and prayer. But how much better to live in Rowena's skin, to fight outrage with outrage, contempt with contempt.

"There is no need for bloodshed under your own roof," said Rowena, flashing her hatred of Brian and all he stood for. "Even a tournament knight draws the line at killing an unarmed woman."

"There will be no need for bloodshed," said Brian, "as soon as you agree that Richard is dead."

"King Richard is not dead," said Cedric. "As you will be if you do not lower your blade."

Brian moved the point of his blade from Rowena's throat. Gripping his sword with both hands, he faced

Cedric with violent intent. "All right, old man. If you insist on dying…"

"Richard Lion-heart is alive!" shouted a voice from the common table, and Rebecca's heart fell.

The defiant speaker rose from the bench: Her father.

Brian lowered his sword, looking from the dais to the common tables below. Cedric in turn lowered his heavy spear, squinting in the same direction as Brian.

Isaac continued harshly: "To demand an oath of fealty to Prince John while King Richard yet lives is treason."

Everyone stared at the old man of no rank, the alien with the strange accent. "What is the name of the man who dares call me traitor?" said Brian.

"My name is Isaac," he said. "Isaac of York."

CHAPTER FOUR

Isaac's name was curious enough to still the room.   Rebecca knew there was no stopping her father.   She stood up beside him, prepared to accept his fate.

Cedric started at the familiar name.   He had never met this man, to whom he owned money, and was surprised to see him in his home.   All business had been conducted for Cedric through an intermediary in London, a clerk who could read and write and even calculate interest.

Staring at Isaac, thinking over his name, Brian finally decided what he was.   "A Jew," said Brian.

Brian seemed less outraged then relieved.   This was an enemy who would accept his insults without daring to speak back.   One who could add to his indignation about Cedric's intransigence.

"A Jew," Brian repeated, turning to his host. "You Saxons invite me to share my meal with a godless Jew?"

For a moment, Cedric had no reply.   He was trying to remember if he had ever seen a Jew at Rotherwood, even in his father's time.   But all he could recall

was the great sums he owed the man, and his priest's
dark words about usury.

"No one invited you, Sir Brian," said Rowena.
"My guardian gave you shelter, according to our
customs." Turning to Cedric, she added: "We Saxons
honor our customs."

"Customs," repeated Cedric, taking Rowena's hint.
He looked to Isaac with deliberate welcome. "Customs
that welcome all strangers."

"Thank you, my lord," said Isaac. "I have
recent news from Austria, wonderful news," he
continued eagerly. "King Richard is alive, and he is
well!" The lower tables erupted in excited talk.

Brian banged the hilt of his sword on the high
table. "Silence, Jew!" His men drew their swords
menacingly.

Nonetheless, Isaac continued: "If not for his
brother's treachery, the King would have long ago
arrived in England."

"Silence, you dog," said Brian, stepping down
from the dais. The Pilgrim at Rebecca's side
swallowed his last mouthful of food, and slid along
the bench, moving as far as he could from the pair of
Jews.

Brian approached Isaac, and raised his sword to the Jew's chest. Rebecca grabbed Brian's hand on the sword hilt. "Please, Sir Knight," she said. "My father is old, and he is not well."

Amused by the young woman's plea, Brian moved his sword point to the fringe of her hood, then flicked it back and away. The startling features of Rebecca's face were suddenly revealed to the torch lit room.

Rebecca's loveliness transfixed Brian.

For a moment, he lost his train of thought. He did not hear Cedric's demands to leave his guests unharmed, even forgot his anger at Isaac's defiance and Rowena's invective.

"A godless Jew," was all Brian could say. "A godless Jew... and his she-demon."

But these words seemed wrong, inadequate. Hate grew bright in Rebecca's green and gold eyes, and this hate disturbed him profoundly; a tragic mistake. To be hated by a creature this perfect was like a knife in his soul.

Then the knife seemed to turn, as a voice from across the great hall shocked the entire company. "Sir Brian de Bois Gilbert! I call you coward and murderer."

Brian looked across the room at a stranger without armor or weapons. He could see that Rebecca, like everyone else, was staring at the intruder, but Brian could not have known that it was the young man who had led Isaac and herself to Rotherwood.

The knight had shaved his beard, changed from ragged chain mail into a white robe worn over a purple undertunic. Rebecca had seen men like this on Roman mosaics. He had become as handsome as a pagan god.

Rowena, in a state of wonder even greater than Rebecca's, stepped down from the dais, walking toward the newcomer with joy.

"No, Rowena," said Cedric. "I forbid —"

But there was no stopping Rowena. She threw her arms around the young knight's neck, pulling him close, pressing a hand to his cheek. For a moment, the Crusader forgot his purpose, looking into Rowena's eyes, touching her cheek the way she touched his.

"Rowena!" shouted Cedric angrily. "Let go of him, stand back."

But it was the young man who disengaged himself from Rowena's embrace, stood back, and met Cedric's burning eyes with his own.

"You are not welcome in Rotherwood," said Cedric.

"Apparently," said the young man. He turned back to Brian. "Does your fear make you deaf to my words? 'Coward and murderer' is what I have called you. I challenge you. How do you respond?"

"Who are you?" said Brian to the unarmed man.

"Who I am is not important. How do you respond to my challenge?"

"Are you even a knight?"

The master of Rotherwood answered for him. "He is a knight," said Lord Cedric.

"No more excuses," said the Crusader. "I am a knight, back from the Crusade, and I call you 'coward.'"

"Give him your sword," said Brian to one of his men. Stepping away from Rebecca, he could see that all her attention was turned to this stranger.

And that the hate in her eyes had vanished.

"No," said Cedric. "I will not allow it."

But Brian's man tossed his sword to the young challenger, who plucked its handle out of the air.

Cedric stepped down from the dais, getting between the two young men. "The rules of hospitality do not permit a duel between a guest in my house and --- and my own son."

Cedric grabbed the hilt of the sword in the young man's hand. Son decided not to contest father, and allowed Lord Cedric to take the sword.

Brian responded with mock surprise. "Your son? The famous Crusader -- in the flesh?" He spat out the name with scorn: "The great Sir Ivanhoe?"

"My son," said Cedric. "Whose name I haven't spoken in three years."

"I'm not interested in the family squabbles of low-born Saxons!" said Brian, turning with contempt from Cedric to Isaac. "Or to the fantastic tales of wandering Jews!" Brian felt his attention drawn inevitably from Isaac to his daughter. Staring at Rebecca, he could not turn away, until Ivanhoe spoke.

"I have called you 'coward,' you have called me 'low-born,'" said the Crusader evenly. "We shall surely meet at a more convenient place."

"There is a tournament at Ashby next week," said Brian. "If, among your decrepit Saxon treasures, you can find horse and armor, perhaps you will give me the pleasure of killing you at that time."

"You murdered an old knight, your men pillaged and raped our neighbors," said Ivanhoe. "Even if it is on foot, I will go to Ashby. Even if my armor is rusty, it will be no feat to best a man like you."

"If you best me," said Brian, who had never been defeated in a tournament joust, "you will be the first one in Christendom to do so."

Finished with his boast, Brian turned away, his eyes once again drawn to the beautiful Jewess.

Rebecca looked at him with hatred, but still his eyes lingered. Then, furious, Sir Brian led his knights out of the great hall.

Rebecca turned her attention to Ivanhoe, whose hand was now gripped by Rowena.

"Dear Cedric, you must rejoice," said Rowena.

"Rejoice at what? Normans plague my home, and insult our king."

"Grimace and groan all you like, but you know you prayed for your son's return."

"I do not have a son."

"Ivanhoe is a hero. A son whom you must forgive."

"No," said Cedric, turning from his ward to Ivanhoe. "The night is foul. You may spend it at Rotherwood, Ivanhoe, but at first light - be gone."

It was only after these words that Rebecca felt her father pulling her.

"Come, Daughter," he said, in a sharp whisper. Though the Normans had left the hall, their malevolence lingered. Isaac worried about the ravenous look in Sir Brian's eyes. "You were right. We should never have stopped in this place."

CHAPTER FIVE

The ornamental silver goblet was large enough for a giant. Hundebert, Lord Cedric's steward, remained outside the travelers' room, his liquid offering in both hands. Isaac stood in the doorway, blocking any view of Rebecca. She knelt before the room's wooden stool, carefully inscribing small letters onto parchment spread out on its flat seat.

"In the name of hospitality," said Hundebert, "and with sincere regrets for any indignities you have suffered under his roof, Lord Cedric offers you this sleeping cup." The officious steward had not called Isaac by name, nor had he addressed him as "my lord." There was little etiquette for this situation: A nobleman indebted to a man without recognizable class, a rich man who belonged to a despised nation.

Isaac took the cup from his hands. Hundebert added: "The offering is for the drink, not the silver cup, which has been in my lord's family for generations."

"Please thank your master," said Isaac.

"Lord Cedric asks that you give him a few minutes of your time in the morning," said the steward,

twisting his mouth into an awkward smile. "So that he
may discuss his payment of your loan."

"I'm afraid we must be on our way very early, and
will not have time to discuss such matters," said
Isaac, ignoring the astonishment in Hundebert's face.
A Jew did not reject an invitation from a Saxon
overlord. "But the matter is no longer of
consequence. I consider the loan repaid in full by
his hospitality, and by the courtesy shown to me and
my daughter by his son Sir Ivanhoe."

"I do not understand," said Hundebert, bewildered
at the notion that a Jew might forgive a large loan
without grievous penalty.

Isaac took the heavy goblet from the steward's
hands. "Kindly tell Lord Cedric that I honor his
support of our great king," he said. "And that his
obligation to me is at an end."

"'Obligation at an end,'" repeated the steward,
making certain he had gotten it right. He nearly
bowed before remembering that the old man at the door
was a Jew.

Isaac put down the sleeping cup and closed the
door. Rebecca, finished with her writing, was holding

up the parchment to the torchlight, checking the
Hebrew letters.

"You grow more charitable every day, Father," she
said, without a trace of humor.

"Cedric has no ability to repay the loan. And
his good will is worth more than gold."

"You spread good will everywhere, to Jew and
Gentile alike." She handed the parchment to Isaac,
continuing: "Our cousin Naftali will be happy with
your magnificent purchase on behalf of Cedric's son,"
she said. "I'm sure it's been years since he's gotten
so munificent an order. He will imagine you are
buying warhorse and armor for Richard Lion-heart
himself."

"Do you not see the value in supporting the party
of King Richard against that of Prince John?"

"No, Father," said Rebecca. "All have taken part
in the oppression of our people, if not this year,
then last. If not last year, then a generation ago --
or a generation hence."

"To believe all men so evil, will deprive you of
the chance to do good," said Isaac. "I tell you this
out of love."

"Buy them horses and armor, broadswords and battle-axes. Forgive their loans and lend them more gold," said Rebecca. "You are very, very good, Father. Good to men who know how to repay goodness with evil."

"Surely you do not imagine our young knight eager to do evil?"

"He is not 'our young knight!' He is theirs. No matter how much gold you give him."

"Since when do you care for gold?" said Isaac. "Your heart is as generous as was your mother's."

"What a short memory you have!" she said. "Have you forgotten our murdered cousins in York?"

"I will never forget the atrocities in York. But I will not allow them to make me fear and revile the entire English race."

"You needn't fear them. Simply avoid them. Stay away from meddling in their politics. Stay away from England altogether."

"Do you think that Zaragoza is the answer to everything? There are good and bad among the Spanish, just as there are good and bad among the English. We must learn to live among Gentiles -"

"Like our kinsmen lived among them in York?"

"There is no help for it. We must live among them. And do so with amicability, with generosity, with true friendship."

"How many dead Jews will it take to convince you that the English are no different from the French who killed Mother?"

"Every man in France did not kill your mother. We had good friends there, friends who were sorry to see us go."

"These Christians are all the same!"

"As all Jews are not the same, neither are all Gentiles. Lord Cedric has welcomed us to his home."

"Then why do we run?"

"Not because we are Jews pursued by evil Christians."

"Why do we run again, Father? This time in the middle of the night?"

"Because in all England, no man has a more beautiful daughter than me," said Isaac.

Rebecca hesitated to respond, hating to be reminded of any burdens she added to her father's cares. Forcing a modest smile, she said: "Even if that were true - which it is not -- it would hardly be a reason to run off under cover of darkness, like sneak thieves."

"Did you not see how the Norman knight stared at you?"

"Everyone in that hall stared at me, and at you as well. Because we are Jews. Always objects of fascination."

"I am talking about one man's fascination in particular. Brian de Bois Gilbert."

"I know, Father."

Isaac continued: "Such a man fears neither law of man nor God."

"In that," said Rebecca, "he is a true Christian knight."

"Do you honestly believe," said Isaac, "that young Ivanhoe, who helped save the life of a serf girl, is not a righteous man?" When she didn't respond, he added: "Do not our sages tell us that the righteous are 'bold as lions'? It should please your sense of justice: The armor we supply will help Ivanhoe fight Brian de Bois Gilbert."

An image of Ivanhoe passed through her mind, not fighting anyone - but holding the Lady Rowena's hand.

A fair couple, without worries, their courage and beauty matched against the ugliness of the world.

Having spent her youth at her mother' side, helping in Deborah's healing of the sick and wounded, Rebecca knew far more about the body than was considered proper for an unmarried young woman. Bodies male and female, bodies sick and strong, bodies old and young. She had seen death up close, as well as lust and passion. Ivanhoe, home from the Crusade, ecstatic to be reunited with Rowena. Rowena, blissful at the return of her betrothed.

How could Rebecca not recognize the intense attraction between knight and lady? How could she not imagine them even now, hidden behind a barred door, behind luxurious bed curtains, lying on a bed graced with silken sheets, finally, ecstatically in each other's arms?

"I am not interested in discovering a righteous Gentile in England," said Rebecca, pushing the sensuous image from her mind. "What I am interested in is leaving this cold, violent country forever."

Rebecca picked up the sleeping cup and sniffed at it. "Sour wine, and over-spiced. Certain to keep your belly roiling all night." She poured the contents of the goblet into a slop bucket.

"Only a few more weeks to conclude my business here, as I promised," said Isaac. "Even in distant Spain, it will be good for us to have friends in this country."

Isaac opened the door of their room, and looked toward where Gurth lay at the far end of the corridor, lying in front of a shut door like a faithful dog. He called to him softly, and Gurth woke at once. In spite of his great size, the servant got to this feet without effort, and hurried along the dark hall without noise.

"I have a gift for Sir Ivanhoe, Gurth," said Isaac, rolling Rebecca's parchment into a tight little scroll. Isaac explained what was contained within: A letter for Naftali of Sheffield. "It asks him to provide whatever Sir Ivanhoe requires for the tournament at Ashby."

"I do not understand," said Gurth.

"It is a letter of credit," said Isaac.

"What is that?"

"It means that I will pay the merchant Naftali for whatever he provides your master."

Isaac handed Gurth the scroll. The big man clutched it as if it were magic. "When you give this to Sir Ivanhoe," Isaac added carefully. "Please say these words: 'The lion returns.'"

The servant didn't know the meaning of this phrase, but he was sure they would add to his master's pleasure. Imagine the gift he was about to give him! A chance to compete at Ashby with proper arms and armor. Gurth smiled, anticipating Ivanhoe's joy at receiving wonderful tidings.

Then Isaac asked Gurth for a great favor.

Gurth surprised Isaac by refusing a second gold coin. The devil was already tempting him with the riches that might be bought with the Jew's first gift. A second coin might lead the big young man directly to hell.

An hour before first light, Gurth accomplished Isaac's favor without mishap: Saddling their horses, opening the palisades, lowering the drawbridge, quietly leading Isaac and Rebecca to the edge of the forest.

The rain had stopped, and the beginning of the trail to Sheffield could be clearly discerned.

Rotherwood slept under a dissipating fog. They would be halfway to their destination before anyone behind Cedric's walls awoke.

Isaac, from horseback, urged Gurth to take the second coin. "You have performed a dangerous act on our behalf," he said. "I must reward your courage -- as if you were a knight with golden spurs."

Gurth still refused the gold coin, declaring that he had done nothing dangerous.

Rebecca, gentling her anxious mare, insisted: "Do you not understand why we leave so suddenly, Gurth?" she said. "My father is afraid for me. Afraid of the Norman knights who might follow us in daylight."

Gurth, who had not been in the great hall during Isaac's confrontation with Brian de Bois Gilbert, was taken aback. Why, he asked, would knights threaten a good man without arms, and his innocent daughter?

Rebecca hesitated, then put it plainly: "To attack my virtue," she said.

At first, this statement confused Gurth. Then slowly, he began to understand what she had said; the awful nature of the threat, the disgrace and shame of its origin from a knight, even one of Norman descent.

All at once, Gurth was shuddering with anger. It took some effort to speak: "Though I am low born, I will kill with my bare hands any knight who would treat you or your father with dishonor."

"Please take the gold," said Isaac. But Gurth still refused, and Rebecca took the coin from her father's hand.

"As a seal of our friendship," she insisted. Gurth reluctantly took the coin.

"Our Lady's benison for your generosity," he said to father and daughter. Then turning his attention to Rebecca alone, he added: "My master will know of your goodness, and your fears."

There was a sense in the air that the sun was about to rise. The remaining fog lifted, fresh dew carried the scent of trees. As Rebecca and Isaac walked their heavily laden horses along the trail, she thought about the passionate indignation shown by Gurth. Though a Christian, he was a good soul, and would never hurt her. Not because of the gold, but because he understood right from wrong, as he understood light from darkness.

Glancing at her father, Rebecca did not need to admit out loud that Isaac was right - that there were righteous men among the Christians. She and her father were close in spirit, and usually knew each other's thoughts without speaking.

"You think better about Gentiles," he said. She smiled for answer. "We are free from danger," he continued, "and for that you know that we must thank Gurth."

"What else do I think?" she said.

"That you would have rather we remained at Rotherwood till morning. And that I am unnecessarily cautious."

"Hardly! If you were cautious, we would have left England last month," she said. An owl hooted from a gnarled branch of an old oak. Dawn began to tinge transparent air. "But that is not what I am thinking about."

"You worry, Daughter," said Isaac lovingly. "You think I have not had my breakfast, nor had enough rest." It was a game they played, imagining each other's thoughts. Yet for once, she was hardly listening.

In fact, she was not thinking about her father at all; but about the reception Gurth would get from Ivanhoe when he would thrust the scroll she had written into the young knight's hand. This Jewish paper, Gurth would explain, will get Ivanhoe a warhorse, weapons, armor, money for a squire and any attendants he might require. Astonished, Ivanhoe would unbind the scroll, unwind it, look at the strange Hebrew writing. Perhaps he would wonder at the shape of the letters, imagine what words they represented.

Perhaps Ivanhoe would ask whose hand had inscribed the parchment, the father or his daughter. Perhaps he would touch the tips of his fingers to the ink on the page.

The young knight would be filled with gratitude, she knew. Gratitude for Isaac, the source of this unexpected wealth. But gratitude for his daughter as well. Then Rebecca imagined how that feeling would be reflected in the serious lines of his face.

It was lighter as the path led them to an open space in the forest. Here ancient stones - two and three times the size of big men - were stood up on their narrow ends, arranged in a circle open to the sky. Several of the great stones had fallen over, leaving a break in the man-made symmetry, striking against the wild contours of the forest.

Isaac suddenly slowed, urging quiet. He pointed to the remains of a smoldering campfire at the center of the circle. Sensing something at her back, Rebecca turned round, just as three burly men stepped free of the woods.

"Cover your head," whispered Isaac sharply.

Rebecca pulled on her hood, as the men stepped closer, grinning their malice. They wore soiled jackets of torn animal skins, sandals with boars' hide thongs, and carried large oak staffs.

"Swineherders, by their dress," said Isaac, trying to reassure her. "On their way to work."

As he turned round to look for a way out, Isaac discovered two more men blocking their path. One of them carried a cudgel. The other, Isaac recognized with a sinking heart, was a man with a hungry look, his sallow face ghastly in a shaft of daylight: The Pilgrim who had sat next to Rebecca in the great hall. He must have ran off from Rotherwood the night before, his plan already set.

"Early to rise, these filthy Jews," said the Pilgrim. "I want a full share. If not for me, you would not have known they were coming."

His companion barked out an awful laugh, then turned his eyes from the Jews to the Pilgrim, and surprised his confederate with a skull-cracking blow of his cudgel. The Pilgrim opened his mouth, but no sound emerged. His hands clutched his head briefly. He fell like a puppet cut from strings, unconscious or dead.

Rebecca's blood chilled. If he would do this to his friend, what would they do to her father?

"He wanted his full share," said the cudgel-bearer to his fellows. "I gave it to him." The other marauders drew close, laughing, imagining the extra loot it would mean, and surrounded Isaac and his beautiful daughter.

"Not swineherders, I'm afraid, but swine," said Rebecca softly. Like her father, she spoke in Hebrew.

"Look at the horses they ride, these Jews," said a bandit. "While decent Christians walk about like slaves."

Isaac reached for a purse tucked inside his cloak, and held it out like a reward. "There is no need for violence," he said in English. "Though we travel under the protection of King Richard Lion-heart, I freely give you these coins."

Isaac started to open the purse, but before he could pour out its contents, a bandit grabbed it out of his hand. "Freely!" he said. "You'll give everything freely, Jew." Another bandit grabbed at the purse, and silver scattered in the road. Two men scrabbled in the mud for coins, but the cudgel-wielder had bigger game in mind. He grabbed the reins of Isaac's horse.

"You think you can buy your way out of this with a few pieces of silver?" said the cudgel-wielder, as another brigand used his staff to fling back Rebecca's hood, leering into her frightened face.

"Look at the Jew girl."

"First things first," said the cudgel-wielder.

"Never seen such white teeth, such clean skin," said the leering man. Savagely, he ripped away her shawl and cloak, revealing a diamond necklace. The gems sparkled, but the brigand's eyes fixed on her kirtle and undergown of pale silk. The cudgel-wielder took hold of the diamond necklace.

"Don't touch it!" said Rebecca. The necklace had been her mother's. For a moment, she had no other feeling than revulsion.

For answer, the cudgel-wielder yanked the necklace from Rebecca's neck with so much force that she nearly fell from her saddle. Revulsion gave way to fear.

"Let us pass," said Isaac. "In the name of all that is holy and just."

The cudgel-wielder grinned at the necklace in his dirty hand, then yanked Isaac from his horse. The old man fell hard, on his hands and knees, his forehead banging on the hard ground. For a moment, Isaac didn't move. Rebecca slipped off her horse, and got to her knees next to him.

"Father," she said. "Father!"

"That's not the way to wake a Jew," said the cudgel-wielder. He kicked into Isaac's side.

"Don't hurt him!" shouted Rebecca. "Take whatever you want!"

Isaac stirred, slowly raising his head.

"We will take everything," said the leering man, pushing past the cudgel-wielder. "Beginning with you." Clumsy with desire, he yanked at Rebecca's garments.

"No," said Isaac, stunned with horror. He got to his knees, and tried to pull Rebecca away from the leering man. But the swineherd hit him squarely on the side of his head, knocking him over, senseless.

"Now how am I supposed to ask him where he's hiding his treasure?" said the cudgel-wielder.

Rebecca tried to take hold of her father, but the leering man pulled her away, forcing her flat on her back. "There's treasure enough right here," he said to the cudgel-wielder.

Suddenly, Rebecca found the ugly face hovering over her, showing yellow teeth in a rapacious grin. He was straddling her, the heavy weight of his reeking body making it difficult to breathe. She struggled wildly, desperate to push him off, to get to her father. Rebecca shouted and cursed in French and Hebrew. She screamed and spat into his face. The leering man smiled at her terror, then slapped her viciously, bloodying her mouth.

The cudgel-wielder laughed, seeing that Isaac was getting back to his knees, trying to crawl to his daughter. "Careful, the old Jew has come back to life."

Rage overtook Isaac's frail body, and he began to stand, to come to Rebecca's aid. But the cudgel-wielder kicked into Isaac from behind, and threw him back on the ground. "Hurry up," he said to the leering man, keeping one foot on Isaac's chest. "I'll take her next. Then I'll make the Jew tell us where he's hiding every last gold coin."

Blinking back tears, Rebecca shouted against a terror that would not end. It was only the leering man's foul hand over her mouth that shut up her screams, that let her hear another sound -- hoofbeats.

The swineherd heard it too and began to turn to the sound. Rebecca could not see past his thick frame, but she could sense the forest-bandits' dread.

Then she heard another sound, louder than hoofbeats: A horseman's war-cry, ferocious, unforgiving, deadly.

CHAPTER SIX

The brigand hurried to get up from straddling Rebecca, freeing her to lift her head to an unimaginable sight: An axe blade driving halfway through the brute's head, spattering blood and bone.

Revolted, she scudded backwards on the ground, but unable to look away as the nightmare continued: The blade had affixed itself to the dead man's head. And now the leering man's corpse was being dragged away along the ground, improbably tethered to the axe.

Rebecca, blood-stained and wild, didn't realize that she was shrieking.

She got to her knees, staring at her unknown savior, who was bending low from the saddle, gripping the handle of the axe. He urged his horse faster, dragging the corpse at increasing speed, until finally letting go of the axe. The corpse slammed into two of the three other bandits, knocking them to the ground.

Isaac, back on his feet, tried to pull his daughter close, to turn her away from the horrific violence. But Rebecca rejected the chance to press her head to her father's chest. She needed to understand, to witness. She was not a stranger to violence, nor innocent of what the human body was capable of suffering.

The horseman, white tunic streaked with blood, unhelmeted, wheeled about, the features of his face obscured by the bright angle of the rising sun. Shouting, he spurred his horse past her, riding fast to where a large, redheaded young man stood, holding the reins of a horse laden with weapons and chain mail.

The young man was a familiar figure: Gurth, his face fixed with rage.

As she watched Gurth pull a heavy broadsword out of its scabbard and extend it hilt forward, she knew who the warrior must be.

The warrior bent low, and without stopping, grabbed the sword from Gurth's hand, and raised the killing blade high.

Turning, the horseman had the sun behind his back, lending a radiance to the pitiless features of his face. A handsome face Rebecca could finally see clearly: The face of Sir Ivanhoe.

Three marauders were still alive. One of them was running for the forest, another was racing in the opposite direction, toward where Gurth remained beside the packhorse. The third, the cudgel-bearer, crazily stood his ground, raising his blood-stained club as the knight rode directly at him.

"No," said Rebecca, quietly, barely loud enough for her father to hear.

Isaac forcibly turned her away. She didn't see Ivanhoe swing the broadsword into the cudgel-bearer's throat, nearly severing his head; but a moment later, she broke from Isaac's grip and took in the sight of the fresh corpse, pumping blood into the ground.

Ivanhoe was already raising his heavy blade overhead, turning his horse around, eager to kill again.

The bandit running toward Gurth was shouting threats, but the big servant stood still as a stone, waiting to release his violent anger. As the bandit raised his oak staff overhead, about to strike, Gurth pulled a lance from its saddle-sheath, and swung it into the staff with enough force to send it flying out of the man's hands.

As Gurth approached, lance extended, the bandit backed away, terrified, pleading. Gurth drove his lance completely through the man's belly and back, impaling him to a tree.

Isaac could not restrain his daughter. She hurried toward where Ivanhoe was galloping after the last living bandit. She was shouting now, "Enough! Stop!"

But Ivanhoe didn't stop. He rode into the trees where the last living bandit had vanished.

Rebecca felt faint, the world whirling, the fact of her rescue from rape and death forgotten, overwhelmed by the slaughter around her.

She had witnessed the aftermath of other slaughters.

Rebecca had not been in their village in France, when Crusaders had burnt fifty Jews along with her mother. Other Jews had been struck down with sticks and spades, and left to rot in the sun. When she and Isaac had returned, the corpses greeted them silently, but in their rigid faces she could hear the screams that had died on their lips.

The friendly baron, on whose land the massacre had taken place, had a mass grave dug for the dead Jews. His serfs filled the grave with ashes, bones, and flesh in various states of decay. But the close-packed earth couldn't stifle the screams. Even as her father intoned the Kaddish, Rebecca heard the dead beneath their feet. Even three years later, their shouts of terror woke her from deep sleep.

She was sobbing, trying to blink away visions of bodies burnt to black bones, confusing Ivanhoe's war-cry with sounds she had heard in so many dreams that they were as real to her as her father's embrace.

Isaac picked up Rebecca's cloak, and draped it around her shoulders. "Praise be to God," he said. She looked at her father, incredulous. "We must give thanks for being saved from a terrible fate," he insisted.

Gurth hurried to them. His anger still burned, growing hotter at the sight of Rebecca's tears.

"You will be all right now, my lady," he said.

At that moment, Ivanhoe emerged from the trees, his bloody sword high, eyes sweeping the field of battle for any signs of life. Slowly, the rage in his eyes began to recede. Ivanhoe dismounted, filled with the afterglow of successful battle. Proudly, he thrust his sword into the muddy ground.

"Are you all right, sir?" he said to Isaac.

"I thank the Lord in Heaven for sending you to our aid, Sir Ivanhoe," he said, holding Rebecca against his chest, waiting for her sobbing to end. "We will be forever in your debt."

"It is I who am in your debt, my lord," said Ivanhoe. "It is why I came riding after you - to offer my thanks." The knight exhibited the small scroll given him by Gurth. "I cannot read, but Gurth says if I bring this to Naftali of Sheffield, it will grant me arms."

Isaac interrupted: "Arms, armor, warhorse: Whatever you need to triumph at Ashby."

"And 'the lion returns?' Am I to believe that you have news of Richard Lion-heart?"

"This must be our secret, but I have confirmation that King Richard's ransom has been received by the Duke of Austria. He has been set free. I wait for news that the King has arrived on English soil."

Ivanhoe let out a whoop of joy.

This boyish exuberance sparked fire in Rebecca.

She pulled away from her father's embrace and faced the proud knight with her tear-stained beauty.

"Is he dead too?" she asked, with inexplicable violence. She could see that Ivanhoe had no idea what she was asking, so she explained: "The one who ran into the forest?"

"You needn't fear, my lady," said Ivanhoe. "My sword found its mark." He didn't understand why her words were sharp, her expression devoid of appreciation.

"Four men, killed by your hand," said Rebecca.

"Three actually," said Ivanhoe, perplexed by her hostility. He attempted a modest tone: "Gurth must be given credit for one. I will today make him my squire. The great fortune brought me by your scroll will also benefit so worthy a servant. I honor you and your father for the opportunity to fight at Ashby in the name of Richard Lion-heart."

"You had best be careful, Sir Knight," she said. "At Ashby, Prince John's knights will have better arms than the men you murdered here today."

Ivanhoe's face reddened, as if it been slapped.

"Rebecca, that is shameful talk," said Isaac. "If not for Sir Ivanhoe, we would be dead."

"Only God knows the moment and the manner of our deaths," she said. Rebecca turned to Ivanhoe, his eyes blazing. "You had only to show them your sword, and they would have run."

"I cannot let such men run," said Ivanhoe. "Such men need to be killed, as anyone with sense knows."

"Master!" said Gurth, alerting them all to an astonishing sight: The Pilgrim, head bloodied by the cudgel-wielder, was still alive. Not only alive, but had gotten onto his hands and knees, and was crawling toward the trees.

Gurth drew Ivanhoe's bloody sword from the ground.

"No, please," said Rebecca. "No more killing!"

Gurth looked to Ivanhoe, waiting for his command. Ivanhoe took the broadsword from Gurth's hand, trying to understand. Rebecca stepped in front of him, blocking his path to the Pilgrim. "Show mercy," she said.

"Was he not one of them?" said Ivanhoe, the sword shaking in his hand.

"He is a Christian," said Rebecca. "Like you."

"A Christian, perhaps," said Ivanhoe. "But nothing in the world like me." Then the young knight, compelled to curtail his anger, plunged his sword back into the soft earth.

The Pilgrim, dazed with pain, collapsed, once again senseless and still.

"Father, quickly, my herbs," said Rebecca. Gently, she turned over the Pilgrim, examining his head. She didn't understand why her experienced hands were trembling.

Isaac untied a goatskin bag attached to Rebecca's saddle, and brought it to her.

"My daughter was trained in the healing arts by her mother, of blessed memory," said Isaac. Rebecca reached under her cloak and ripped off a piece of her silk under gown. "She has made a vow to help all wounded and sick men, whoever they may be."

Ivanhoe watched Rebecca wrap the silk around a few herbs. She pressed the silk to the Pilgrim's bloody scalp, aiding the man who had conspired to murder her and her father.

"I've made a different vow," said Ivanhoe. "To kill without pity, any and all enemies of my king."

Rebecca looked up from the wound, stung in turn by Ivanhoe's righteous stare.

"You had best keep your daughter away from Ashby," he continued to Isaac alone. "I go there with savage intent."

The look in Rebecca's large eyes confused Ivanhoe. She was no longer cold or caustic, but exhibited some other kind of passion. A passion mercurial, deep, unknowable.

He did not understand that she was sorry for having rebuked him, that the words she had spoken were hollow and false, a cover for desperation.

That suddenly she understood she had as much murder in her heart as anyone.

Beaten to the ground, beset by villains, her father about to be murdered like her mother before him, it was force that had come to their aid, ferocious and just. How could she not be grateful? What she had yearned for was the very violence that Ivanhoe had unleashed.

Rebecca wondered if he could understand that there must be no anger between them - that what separated them was something far different. Something that violated her family, her history, her every belief.

She watched Ivanhoe turn from her, pull the broadsword from the ground, and walk away. She wished she could tell him something that would ease his troubled feelings, but could think of nothing to say.

For Rebecca was terrified.

She wanted something she must never reveal, must deny herself forever: To embrace the young knight, even for a moment, to feel just once his wild spirit close to her heart.

PART TWO: ASHBY

CHAPTER SEVEN

Forcing patience, Isaac watched her swirl the mixture of mashed poppies and alcohol into peppermint tea. The liquid was cloudy, but Rebecca was clear. She knew her father was hopeful, and that his hopes would be crushed. She knew her father was proud, and that he would be humbled. Naturally, in his fragile state of health, she did not want to let Isaac out of her sight. But still, she couldn't countenance his behavior by being his companion in folly.

Isaac waited for her to pour the fragrant brew into a silver cup before speaking. "Prince John has invited me," he said. "Naturally, that invitation must extend to my daughter."

"Drink it," she said, extending the cup.

Isaac took a sip, and grimaced at the taste.

"Drink it before it cools," she said. He made an effort to swallow, then put the cup down.

"I will be safe," he insisted. "The prince has outstanding debts, guaranteed by alliances through foreign kings. He will extend me every courtesy."

"The prince cannot read or write. Do you expect him to understand intricate financial alliances woven out of paper and ink?"

"John needs me alive," said her father. "And he needs me willing."

"All he knows is that you support his brother."

"Not only has he invited me, he has insisted that I take a seat in his own gallery. There will be no danger when we are so close to the Prince."

"No danger?" said Rebecca. "To be exposed to humiliation? To the shoving and spitting of the mob? If his rich Jew is trampled, do you imagine John will come to his aid?" She picked up the silver cup, and saw that most of the liquid was still there. "Drink this down!"

Taken aback by her vehemence, Isaac drank the contents of the cup. "Thank you," he said. "The taste leaves something to be desired, but the intention is sweet."

"Very charming, Father. The compliment will be a great comfort as I sit at home, waiting to hear whether you are dead or alive."

"Isn't it possible - just possible, I say - that you are wrong?" said Isaac.

"No."

"That it will be a day filled with joy and sunshine, celebrating valiant deeds? A day we could enjoy together."

"It is not just fear that keeps me away. Not just anger at your stubbornness. Even if Prince John was an honorable man, who could keep you safe, and treat you with dignity, the event will still be uncivilized, primitive. Did you not hear Ivanhoe?" She spat back the young knight's words: "'Savage intent.'"

That night, in the small house outside Ashby, Isaac's sleeping draught had proven no match for the sound of restless pacing from a nearby room. Two servants, Joseph and Margaret, shared their home, but he doubted either had left their bed. So it must be his daughter who marched back and forth, plagued by indecision. Eventually, the steady pace of her footfalls put him to sleep.

In the morning, sunlight woke Isaac. He sat up, surprised to see his daughter standing at the foot of his bed. Even before she said a word, he could see that Rebecca had relented.

"I will accompany you to the tournament," she said.

"I am very glad to hear it, Daughter," he said. Apparently, she was not about to tell him why she had changed her mind. She was twisting an unfamiliar fabric in her hands, and he asked her what it was.

"This?" she said. She opened her hands, revealing a turban of yellow silk. "It was a gift from that merchant you do business with in Venice."

He remembered the merchant, remembered the giving of the gift, but had no memory of her having ever worn the turban. "I shall be glad to see you wear it, Rebecca."

"I cannot very well sit among grandees with my head uncovered!" she said. The turban had been stuffed at the bottom of her traveler's bag, never to be thought of until last night. When she had finally ceased her pacing of the room, and slipped into bed, she had thought of the beautiful fabric and, unfathomably, found herself rising almost at once; opening drawers, taking a candle to look into every corner of her room, searching for the head-piece.

But why, she thought, did she care what she looked like to these Gentiles?

Isaac watched as she jammed the turban onto her head, the yellow silk striking against black hair. Lovingly, he pushed back a few stray hairs from Rebecca's forehead, holding back from telling her how much she resembled her mother.

She turned away, facing a tiny mirror set in a silver frame. Eyes blazing, she adjusted the turban, fixing it in place with a diamond clasp.

Ivanhoe would think her alien, no matter what she wore, so she might as well wear the finest silk. He would resent her wealth, so she might as well feed his resentment with diamond glitter.

"Gramercy, Master," said Margaret, who had entered the room. "Even when she's cross, there is no one in this world more beautiful than your daughter."

Margaret and Joseph were Christians, named for saints, and married to each other. Not much older than Rebecca, they had lost six children at birth, yet remained pious. Their priest had given them his blessing to go into service for Jews, and for five years they had attended to the little house and garden outside Ashby that Isaac had bought from a wine merchant, to make his business trips to England bearable.

The drafty castles and unclean food of the barons
who owed him money were not hospitable places to stay,
especially when traveling with his wife and daughter.
His cousin Naftali lived in nearby Sheffield, and had
told them about the opportunity to purchase the home.
Isaac's wife, Deborah, had fallen in love with it at
one glance. With its stone walls, tile floors, and
stained glass, it would be luxurious anywhere in this
country. But more than simple luxury had attracted
her. It was not very large, but it was cozy and warm,
with a well-kept garden. Best of all, it did not
stand out in the humble environs outside the village
with dangerous ostentation.

Isaac had given the merchant a better-than-fair
price. He had wanted good relations in this
community. When anti-Jewish riots had erupted at
York, it had little effect in the Ashby area, where
the only Jewish home was Isaac's.

Only one man had dared to attack the house, a
disgraced monk who had become a forest dweller, a
poacher. He had made it past the palisades around the
house, tramped through the garden to the sturdy front
door, and driven a knife under the mezuzah fixed to
the doorframe.

But before he could pry the golden object free, Margaret had pulled open the door from the inside, holding a heavy iron skillet. Joseph came at him from behind, carrying an even heavier spade. The poacher fled, and Joseph repaired the damage to the door frame.

Isaac, accompanied by Deborah and Rebecca, had been in Salerno at the time, and didn't hear about the servants' defense of the house for many weeks. Margaret and Joseph had defended their Jewish master's home, giving Isaac proof for his feeling that England could be a haven for their people.

What Rebecca remembered from the incident was an angry Gentile, tearing at the Jewish symbol on their doorpost.

A year later, after her mother was murdered by a mob en route to free the Holy Land, Rebecca narrowed her heart to the possibility of good Gentiles. Suddenly she could see few exceptions to the general rule of Jew-hating. Joseph and Margaret were well-paid servants who lived in a comfortable home, their only task to keep it ready for rare visits. That did not mean they loved their masters.

Joseph had hitched up a wagon, and Margaret had cushioned one bench with embroidered pillows for Isaac and Rebecca. Margaret sat next to Joseph on the unadorned front bench, as he drove to the tournament fields. The road was filled with walkers, wagons, carts, noble litters marked with coats of arms. Everyone wore holiday clothes, with holiday spirit. Many pretty girls competed for attention, but there was only one who captured everyone's eye: The striking beauty in the exotic head-dress.

"You must promise not to engage anyone," said Rebecca, speaking in Hebrew. "No political talk. Promise that you will simply sit still and watch the brutes hack each other to death."

"They are not brutes, but warriors who hope to bring back just rule to England. If no one opposed John's knights at the tournament, the people would imagine him invincible. They would lose faith in Richard's ever returning."

Why he put faith in King Richard – in any Gentile – remained beyond Rebecca's comprehension.

A month before her mother's murder, there had been an outbreak of fever in the French village where they had lived in peace for years. Isaac wanted them all to go with him to England, where he had urgent business. But Deborah, healer for both Jews and Gentiles, had refused to leave the imperiled village to the quacks selling useless charms and nostrums.

Rebecca's dilemma had been to stay behind and help her mother with the sick, or go abroad with Isaac, even then in a precarious state of health. Not much of a choice, when her mother had been so adamant: "Your father cannot be trusted on his own."

They were in Ashby when news of the massacre in the village reached them. It took six weeks to get father and daughter, escorted by English warriors, to France. The friendly baron was disconsolate about the murder of Deborah. He explained that there was nothing he could have done against so large a mob of Crusaders. The baron took Isaac and Rebecca into his home, and tried to console them with thoughts of the afterlife. They stayed only a few days.

After Deborah's death, there had been nothing left of hers in France. The synagogue and every Jewish home had been razed. Everything Jewish had been burned; books, prayer shawls, bodies. Everywhere were charred remains, open pits with blackened bones.

Only gold and silver had survived, but these had been taken away by the murderers.

When father and daughter had returned to Ashby, they had scoured the house for remembrances. But because Deborah had spent so little time there, there was not much to find, to touch where she had touched: The carved mahogany bed Deborah had slept in with Isaac, the only one in the shire stuffed with down instead of straw; medicinal herbs, a few garments, bed linens, and a silver comb purchased in London. Rebecca had searched the teeth for a single hair, but there were none.

Sitting in the wagon, Isaac recognized the silver comb in his daughter's hand. Rebecca turned it over and over, staring at it, instead of the colorful pageant of tournament-goers.

"I am very glad that you are with me," he said.

"You are all I have in the world, Father."

"It is ungrateful to imagine that I am all you have," said Isaac. "You are healthy, wise, and young. Your life is laid out before you like a long and joyous road."

Rebecca took little comfort from these words. She and her father had been on the same road for years. Along this road was bigotry, violence, murder.

The tournament grounds were gentle meadowland, bordered by forest on one long side, and a stand of oaks on the other. They were a mile from Ashby village, six miles from their country home.

At one end of the green fields stood brightly colored pavilions, flying a variety of fierce pennants: Slavering beasts, crossed axes, lightning bolts. Knights loyal to Prince John, wearing heavy body armor, clustered at this end, sure of victory. Among them were Reginald Front de Boeuf, a giant of a man, talking to the tournament's favorite: Brian de Bois Gilbert, handsome and proud, preening for admirers.

At the other end of the fields were a few tattered tents, flying the lion pennant of King Richard. Knights in chain mail marked with Crusader crosses stood around dilapidated battle tents, staring with loathing at the younger, better-armed knights they would soon fight.

"I do not see him," said Isaac, in Hebrew, as they followed Prince John's marshal across the grounds, to where two large wooden galleries flanked a jousting alley. He didn't need to say Ivanhoe's name.

"Is it possible that Naftali wasn't ready?" she said. "That the armor couldn't be procured?" Isaac assured her that this was not possible. "How can you be certain? There are so many knights at Ashby, surely some of them visited the armory. Possibly his stores were picked clean."

"No, Rebecca," he said, trying to understand her concern for the young man she had treated with such contempt. "Naftali sent me the bill this morning. The knight got what he needed: The finest armor, the best warhorse gold could buy."

On one side of the tournament lists the gallery was filled with Normans. These seats were spread with sumptuous tapestries and carpets, with servants pouring wine into silver flagons. Here, merriment was evident. On the other side, unadorned benches were filled with Saxons and those of mixed heritage. No servants were in evidence, and many seats remained vacant. Here, gloom was the order of the day.

The greatest nobles sat on the high tiers, with Prince John at the top level, sitting on silk cushions like a Saracen potentate. At John's feet was Hunter, a huge old mastiff, dark brown with striking white markings on chest and forehead. Hunter had been Richard's favorite dog, but left him behind when he went off to war. John had taken Hunter for his own, like he had taken everything that had once belonged to Richard. Yet Hunter never seemed to appreciate his new owner. At the moment the mastiff slept, feeling nothing of John's excitement.

Looking below, the Prince could see his marshal's scarlet tunic and Rebecca's yellow turban stand out among the crowd. As they approached the reviewing stand, John called out to Isaac in his high-pitched, imperious voice: "Isaac of York!"

Isaac looked up and caught John's decidedly unfriendly gaze. Ignoring his coldness, Isaac smiled, and made a ceremonial bow. "Good day, Sire," he said. "I thank you for your invitation to this tournament."

"Don't thank me, Jew," said Prince John. "Pay me!"

A fat courtier, elegant in embroidered tunic and draped in gold chains of office, was the first to burst out in great peals of laughter at John's wit. Great lords and ladies who traced their descent from William the Conqueror and his noble followers joined in.

Isaac held onto Rebecca's hand as the raucous mocking became general, laughter spreading like disease from one gallery to the other, where old Saxon warriors found themselves laughing at the common scapegoat, forgetting their gloomy concerns. Even Hunter raised his great head, opening tired eyes, sniffing the overwrought air.

Below both galleries, seated on large banks of cut turf, sat commoners: Servants, including their own Joseph and Margaret, along with serfs, cottage maidens, thatchers, eelers, cooks, bricklayers, fowlers. Workers, male and female, whose myriad occupations could be read in their hands, their clothes, their speech.

Children sat here too, every one of them used to hard labor, and as hungry for pleasure as their elders. Everyone rejoiced that at the conclusion of the combat, great tables would be brought out to the field, laden with food and drink for all - a celebration to mark the victory of Prince John's followers.

The commoners also laughed at the Jews standing before their prince. There was no shame in it, no sin to mock the killers of their Lord Jesus. Only Margaret and Joseph remained quiet, feeling their masters' abasement as their own.

Even when the laughter died, the humiliation remained. "As always, Sire," said Isaac, "my wallet is at your disposal." But there was steel in his tone, a lack of obedience in his stance, an unvoiced threat in his unblinking eyes.

"Excellent," said the Prince. "As I require two thousand gold byzants."

"Two thousand byzants could not fit in any man's wallet," said Isaac. "I shall have to send for them."

"That I doubt, you treacherous devil," said John. "We all know Jews keep their hoards close to hand." The prince looked around his followers for confirmation. Every face showed scornful agreement. Rebecca tried to shut her senses to the general distaste directed their way, and clutched her father's hand a little tighter.

It was at that moment that she saw Brian de Bois Gilbert, sitting on an enormous warhorse outside the Norman pavilions, turn toward the lists. Helmet in hand, his black hair shining in sunlight, he stared at her without pity; stared at her as if she had no right to exist.

This indifference was preferable to other looks father and daughter received. All around were active hate, resentment, an inchoate anger that only murder could satisfy.

Rebecca knew what they thought: These Jews could be useful, they could be accomplished, skilled in tasks necessary for the crown. But a people so universally hated must merit their pariah status. A people so loathsome must not be allowed to live among decent Christians.

"Before the byzants come," added Isaac with gravity, "I will need your signature on a bond of surety."

"No bond, no signature!" said John, standing in a fit of real anger. "You had neither from Richard to raise gold on his behalf - and he is no longer ruler of England." John stopped in the middle of this tirade, as if to see if anyone would dare contradict.

Isaac remained still, his bristling silence very far
from approval. "I want the byzants by the end of this
week," said John, his eyes turning from Isaac to
Rebecca. "Or I will take your house … your skin … and
your pretty little wench."

Isaac's fury could no longer be contained. "The
young woman before you is my daughter," he said,
disregarding consequences. "Even kings treat her with
esteem. If you hope to ever get a zecchin from me,
you will never again speak of her with disrespect."

This reproach to the reigning ruler of the land
stunned everyone within earshot. Rebecca watched John
pick up a ceremonial truncheon as if he would like to
use it to club the disloyal Jew to death before the
crowd. But perhaps her father was right: John needed
him alive, and needed him willing.

John raised the truncheon a little higher, then
lowered it to scratch the head of Hunter. The dog
didn't care for the attention, and quickly lowered his
head, shutting his eyes.

"Your 'daughter,' Isaac?" said John, with ironic
emphasis. "Why didn't you say so? I didn't know
Jewesses grew so fine!" He pointed his truncheon at

the marshal. "Take my honored Jews to their
distinguished seats."

If John had taken a step back from further
insults, this did little to lighten the feeling from
either gallery, or from the turf-sitters. Following
behind the mincing marshal, holding her father's hand,
Rebecca felt as if the entire world was relishing
their mortification. Commoners and grandees alike
sneered as they stepped toward the lowest tier of
seats in the Saxon gallery, within striking distance
of the turf-sitters.

"Sit," said the marshal, with a malicious lack of
ceremony. When Isaac and Rebecca hesitated, the
marshal snapped: "Sit down, Jews. Enjoy the
privilege of your prince's invitation." Isaac sat,
gently pulling Rebecca's hand, so that she joined him
alongside.

Instantly, a clutch of merchants and petty nobles
got up from their bench, too good to remain in the
repugnant presence of Jews. Looking up, Rebecca was
afforded a view across the lists to Prince John,
sinking back into his luxurious cushions, the soles of
his maroquin boots on contemptuous display.

"I'm sorry," said Isaac, whispering the Hebrew words. "I should never have exposed you to this."

Isaac's regard, his love, was constant. But the rest of the world hated her, she knew. It always had, it always would. Rebecca had never felt so despised. Now, perhaps because the immediate danger had passed, the tears came. Isaac tried to comfort her, but once started, the sobbing wouldn't end.

"Lady Rebecca," said a familiar voice. A female voice; willful, and unafraid.

Before her stood Rowena and her guardian, Lord Cedric, newly arrived, dressed in tournament finery.

Isaac got to his feet, but Rebecca remained seated, trying to compose herself. "Good day, my lord. My lady," said Isaac brightly.

Cedric, never a diplomat, did not know what to say. He simply thumped his boar-spear into the dirt, looking not at Rebecca's tears, but into the eyes of the man who had forgiven him so heavy a financial debt.

Isaac continued, as if the thumped spear required a response: "A fine day for jousting!"

"Be finer if we can knock John's men off their big horses," said Lord Cedric.

"John is due for it," said Rowena, a little less quietly. She extended her strong hands onto Rebecca's quaking shoulders, as if to prevent her from rising. "Would you mind very much, my lady, if I join you?"

Rebecca wiped her eyes, looking at Rowena's pale and fierce beauty. It took a moment to understand what she was offering. A moment more to answer.

"Please, Lady Rowena," she said. "It would be an honor." At once, Rowena took her seat next to the Jewess, and covered her hands with her own.

Everyone in the reviewing stand was staring below.

"You're sitting here?" said Lord Cedric, dumbfounded. Their own seats were in the highest tier of the Saxon gallery. These two were Jews, born to shame. But Cedric understood that Rowena was showing defiance to the Normans, and made no complaint.

"I will join you soon, my lord," said Rowena. "If you don't mind, I'd like to stay awhile with my friend."

Her guardian nodded his approval, and began to climb to his honorable seat. Isaac sat down, smiling at Rebecca and the lovely young noblewoman at her side.

Rebecca, dazed, looked from Rowena to Isaac and back again. "You are very brave, my lady," said Rebecca.

"Not at all," said Rowena, clutching the jeweled hilt of the dagger she wore in her belt. "If were brave, I would defend justice with more than words and gestures."

How could Ivanhoe not adore his betrothed, thought Rebecca? As fair-haired, blue-eyed, and ferocious as himself.

CHAPTER EIGHT

Rowena stayed but a few minutes before joining Lord Cedric. Rebecca could sense her presence only a few rows above them. That presence seemed to safeguard her father and herself against malevolence.

And indeed, Rowena's visit had worked magic. The Jews' status had been elevated by the regard of noble Saxons. Sitters who had earlier deserted their bench returned. Hostility aimed at the scapegoats had dissipated, replaced by familiar partisanship: Saxons against Normans, Richard's followers against those of John, Crusader knights against those who had never been to war.

Rebecca now had only to hold her father's hand, keep her eyes front, and wait for Sir Ivanhoe to arrive.

The tournament: Boredom, punctuated by violence, compounded by exhilaration she did not share. It seemed like it would never end.

The tournament alley was neither golden nor very long -- no more than a quarter mile of blood-soaked dirt. Here the passage of arms had been celebrated for hours. Contests with broadsword and battle-axe, spear and mace. Battles on foot and on horseback. Single combat, and combat between small groups of armored men. Heads cracked, blood flowed, horses collapsed to the delight of the crowd. There was a collective, maniac eagerness to see each clash lead to punctured skin, broken bones; injuries that maimed or killed.

Sir Brian de Bois Gilbert was responsible for much of the mayhem. A skillful warrior, with excellent armor and a tireless horse, the Normans cheered his every exploit. He relished the cheers. After each battle, riding up and down the lists, his eyes swept the crowd, feeding on the accolades.

Never once did those eyes pause on Rebecca, and for that she was glad. His unnatural interest had frightened her at Rotherwood, and she had no wish to be exposed again to his baleful regard.

The fact that Brian was a favorite of the people was of a piece with the day's awfulness. Rebecca usually felt alien, apart. Quiet where others were noisy, sober where others were drunk. Today she was appalled by all she saw, while the crowd was delighted, united by sharing deadly thrills presented for their entertainment. Naturally, their favorite was repellent to her.

Time and again, she had to hold herself back from jumping up from her seat to aid chain-mailed veterans wounded by Brian, Reginald, and other heavily armored Normans. Isaac pointed out that the Saxon warriors had their own doctor in attendance, and would not appreciate interference from a young woman, a foreigner.

She understood. These English derived from different nations, but whether Saxon or Norman, they would feel the same way about a Jewess who practiced the healing arts. Still, it was difficult to remain in her place when a bloodied warrior was being carried away right before their eyes, one arm bent at a dangerous angle.

English doctors were notorious for cutting off limbs as a first resort.

"Why are we still here, Father?" she said, in Hebrew. "Have we not seen enough blood to satisfy a lifetime?"

The last contest had been between a Crusader knight and the brutish Sir Reginald, his gigantic frame protected by thick armor plate. The Crusader's mail had been not only rusty, but frayed. Reginald's lance had driven over the older knight's shield, splintering through his lightly protected chest. The Crusader fell hard, howling in pain.

Rebecca guessed that the fall had dislocated the veteran's arm, and probably broken his legs. "What good do we accomplish watching John humiliate his brother's followers?"

"I have financed Sir Ivanhoe's armor, and am eager to see what he does with it," said Isaac.

It was the first time in hours that the young knight's name had been mentioned. For a moment she was shocked by a memory: The way Ivanhoe had stared at her so angrily; the way he had turned from her and walked away.

Her words came out more harshly than she intended: "For all we know, Sir Ivanhoe has collected his new warhorse, and ridden off to a safer country."

"You might be right, Daughter," said Isaac, attempting lightness. "Perhaps the young man is a coward, and hopes never to cross paths with your temper again."

Rebecca controlled herself with difficulty. Hours before, her father's life had been threatened, to the general amusement of the entire assembly. They were there because Isaac believed in supporting the cause of King Richard; and were endangered for that support. They were there because Ivanhoe was to fight on behalf of Richard's party. Yet Ivanhoe had never arrived.

"The armor must have needed some final adjustments," said Isaac, more seriously. "But he is surely on his way. Ivanhoe knows that his father, Lord Cedric, sits in the stands, desperate for Saxon glory."

Sir Ivanhoe's father, she thought. And his father's beautiful ward.

That Ivanhoe had not come was a disappointment to his fellow veterans, and to every Saxon at the tournament.

It was true that much of the poor and dispossessed in England were of Saxon origin, while many of the great lords of the land were of Norman descent. But a hundred years and more had passed since the Conquest. Intermarriage had gone on for five generations. Saxon and Norman dialects were becoming a single language. The great differences

between the supporters of Richard and the supporters
of John were not lineal.

After all, Richard and John were brothers, and
both Norman. The differences lay in the way they saw
the world.

Richard was a romantic, who had brought thousands
to fight an endless war in the Holy Land, and who
imagined England could be an empire as great as
ancient Rome. King Richard's men supported him out of
love, for allowing them the capacity to dream.

Prince John was a practical man, who wanted only
to control the island of Britain, to hold it in thrall
for his lifetime. John's men supported him out of
utility, for allowing them to grow rich in usurped
estates and subjugated serfs.

To Rebecca, these royal brothers were identical:
Christian rulers who frequently needed to borrow great
sums of Jewish money. A massacre, a blood-libel, a
mass expulsion, any evil against her people was as
likely to come from one as from another.

The lists were once again cleared of the wounded.
One of the Crusaders limped to his warhorse for what
appeared to be the long day's final joust. Rebecca

saw that the old warrior was helped to mount by a squire with one arm. Other veterans watched him with hopeless silence.

Brian de Bois Gilbert was so heavily armored that he needed the help of a stool and two beefy squires to mount his warhorse. Reginald Front de Boeuf, joking with Brian about the easy joust to come, was laughing hard enough to be heard across the field.

So far that day, not a single Crusader had defeated one of John's knights.

Across from Rebecca, the young Norman ladies were unveiled, braided hair laced with gems, slender arms peeking out from under rich cloaks. She could see how they watched every joust, took note of every clash and tumble. But they were not merely onlookers, there to cheer and rejoice. They were, Rebecca realized, in a competition of their own: On display for the victors, lined up like merchandise in a costly emporium. The greatest knights would have their choice of the prettiest maidens.

Every triumphant knight would follow his joust in the same fashion. Removing his helmet, he would look to Prince John with a humble bow, then eagerly turn his eyes, and examine each young noblewoman in turn.

Riding back and forth along the lists, while attendants carried away the Crusader he had beaten, the young Norman would search lovely faces with care and deliberation, wondering which candidate might be his favorite.

Almost bored by his task, Prince John got to his feet, and lowered his truncheon, signaling two trumpeters to blow their shrill notes for one more unequal contest. Richard's old dog flinched at each blast of sound, but remained where he was, eyes shut, resting in the midst of a chaos he didn't care to understand.

Brian and the Crusader knight charged at each other, quickly closing the distance between them, galloping without fear or restraint, until meeting at the center of the lists: Crashing lances into each other's shields. Hunter raised his big head briefly, then did his best to return to sleep.

The heavily armored Brian remained on his recoiling warhorse. The older veteran was lifted out of his saddle, flung backwards onto the ground. Norman aristocrats, commoners, and even a few Saxons cheered the day's greatest knight.

Brian pulled off his helmet, revealing his arrogant face. Easily controlling his restive horse, he wheeled it around, and rode past the galleries. Then came back for a second look, turning right and left.

His gaze rose above where Rebecca sat, to the highest bench of the Saxons gallery; apparently lingering shamelessly on the lovely Rowena.

Finally he turned away, his attention shifting to the Norman beauties across the lists. A sudden flourish of trumpets stilled the crowd.

Brian de Bois Gilbert rode back to the Norman pavilions, and made a little show of taking a fresh lance from a squire. He knew what was coming.

Prince John stood up from his high seat on the reviewing stand, his sable-lined cloak open to the breeze. The Prince didn't try to make himself heard to the entire assembly. His subjects would have to strain to listen to his irritating, high-pitched voice. Hunter paid him no mind.

Rebecca was close enough to clearly hear every word: "The end has come," said Prince John, smiling toward the tattered tents where old Crusaders milled about their wounded comrades. "My brother's veterans are willing and brave, but their skills are no match for my brave knights."

Here a few cheers rang out from the Norman nobles. John raised his hand. When it was quiet, he said: "Are there no more challengers? No more 'Lion-hearted' men to test my champions?" He turned to his courtiers, smiling with self-assurance. Almost whispering his contempt: "Apparently not."

Turning to the Norman knights' pavilions, Prince John called out Brian's name in a slightly louder voice. Brian trotted over to the center of the lists, halting his horse with flamboyant expertise, then looked up to his prince.

"Well done, Sir Knight," said John. "In three jousts, you have unhorsed three Crusaders. Sir Reginald has done nearly as well, having unhorsed two of three, with the third man certain to die. But unfortunately for Reginald, the old Crusader stayed on his horse to the bitter end!"

"I am sorry, Sire," said Brian, "that today provided so little sport. Your brother's men are apparently tired out from their adventures abroad."

"Better call them misadventures," said John, laughing at his own wit. "This year, there are fewer

of his supporters who dare join our friendly contest.
Just as there are fewer who dream of Richard's
return."

Rebecca gripped her father's hand, anxious that
after his earlier confrontations with John, he remain
silent. But Isaac was quiet, eyes looking toward a
figure approaching from far across the meadows.

Rebecca turned to look in the same direction.

She could barely make out a man, apparently on
foot, leading a horse toward the lists.

"It is difficult for a brother to accept the
truth," continued John. "But we must all learn to
accept the fact: King Richard is dead."

There were a few hushed comments from the turf-
sitters, mostly Saxons, but their loyalty to Richard
had been sorely tested by his three years absence, and
by the feast about to be given them by his brother.

John picked up a ring of green satin and
exquisite lace. "You have won today's tournament, Sir
Brian," said John. "And have therefore earned the
right to choose our 'Queen of Beauty and Grace.'"

Brian lowered his lance, allowing John to place
the satin crown around its sharp end. "Thank you,
Sire," said Brian. "For granting me the honors of the

day, and the privilege of selecting the fairest of the
fair from this noble assemblage."

The approaching man was coming from the west,
where the sun was brightest. He was still too far to
be clearly seen. But had he been wearing armor,
Rebecca knew, the sun would have reflected off its
surface.

So it could not be Sir Ivanhoe, come to answer
all insults on behalf of King Richard. The great
knight who had warned Isaac to keep his daughter away
from this tournament, where he would spill blood in
search of honor and glory, was nowhere in sight.

Rebecca turned from this distant figure, and
watched Brian walk his horse up and down the
galleries, pausing to stare at one after another of
the Norman beauties.

"Look," whispered Isaac. She turned again to the
approaching figure. "Do you not see the pennant?"

Her father had the eyes of a sailor. She stared,
until she too could make out a splash of colored
fabric, flying atop something held by the walking man.
Probably lances. Yes, certainly lances -- the man
held a clutch of them, their metal points reaching for

the sky. The pennant dancing above the metal was gold
and azure.

The colors of Richard Lion-heart.

Brian's sudden turning of his horse forced her
attention elsewhere. The brazen knight was again
looking above Rebecca, to the high seats where Cedric
and Rowena sat. Stillness reigned, as all wondered
whether the Norman knight would dare outrage protocol,
and choose a Saxon beauty to be the tournament's
queen.

Brian walked his horse closer to this less
exalted gallery, ignoring the turf-sitters, forcing a
few of them to get hastily out of his way.

Rebecca steeled herself not to turn around,
though she was desperate to look up at Rowena, to see
how she would react to this prize from a man she
hated. Rebecca kept her eyes down, ignoring the
snorting of the warhorse, and a sudden break in the
crowd's silence.

A whispering had started up from both galleries,
a locust-like buzzing that quickly infected the turf-
sitters. The whispering grew, coming from every side,
increasingly loud. Though the words were impossible
to discern, the sound was ominous, hostile.

For some reason, eyes seemed to be turned to Rebecca.

There could be no mistake: Even the turf-sitters were craning their necks, looking to her, sitting on the low bench. Rebecca's heart pounded with dread.

A ring of green satin came into her line of sight.

Had Rebecca been able to think clearly, she would have understood every whisper. But she was not thinking clearly. Even when she realized that the green satin was a crown resting on the point of a lance, even when she remembered that this was the crown given to Brian by Prince John, the fact that it floated before her now made no sense at all.

Rebecca slowly looked up from her lowly seat to Sir Brian on his richly caparisoned horse, the lance held in his metal-gloved hand.

The knight's eyes burned, as if the gift he was offering the Jewess was being forced on him against his better judgment, as if he'd just as soon drive the lance holding the crown directly into Rebecca's heart.

"Take it," said Sir Brian. "Take the crown."

CHAPTER NINE

Rebecca remained still, the blood pounding inside her ears, staring at the ring of satin and lace at the end of Brian's lance. Across from her, a Norman noblewoman said: "But that is impossible."

The buzzing of the crowd transformed into other words, perfectly clear, sharp as razors, coming at her from both galleries, from the turf-sitters: "Insult! Outrage! Infidel!"

Brian's horse pawed the ground. She could see the knight forcing a smile onto his too-pretty features. But he was not happy, caught in a passion that threatened madness. "I mean for you to take the crown," he said.

Her response was slow in coming. She hardly recognized her own voice, with its false gratitude, its quaver of fear: "No thank you, Sir Knight."

Brian could not imagine that he was being refused. He was a nobleman, handsome, rich; the champion of the greatest tournament of the land. And she was nothing, of no family, without class or rank. He explained: "You will be our 'Queen of Grace and Beauty.'"

"I cannot," she said.

"I have chosen you, Rebecca," he said, beginning to feel humiliation, struggling with rising anger.

"You cannot choose me," she said.

Pushing aside the offered crown, she stood, looking up at the mounted warrior with determination. But the ground beneath Rebecca's feet seemed to shiver.

Brian brought the point of the lance to her chest.

Isaac stood up next to his daughter, and gripped the shaft of the lance. Brian ignored him, his eyes on her alone. Crazily certain that if she could only understand the munificence of his gift, the distinction it conferred, she would take it -- she would be glad to take it.

"I am giving you an honor," he said.

"I am refusing it," said Rebecca.

Brian's anger, dangerous and wild, was suddenly magnified as her green and golden eyes turned away from him. They squinted at something behind his back, something wonderful to her.

Rebecca could see that the approaching man was leading a packhorse to the tattered tents of the

Crusader knights. That above the lances in his hand
flew a pennant, clearly identical to those on the
tents: A golden lion rampant on an azure field.

The approaching man was young, big and broad-
chested, with red hair. Gurth.

The ground beneath her was suddenly less shaky.

Gurth's horse was laden with shining weapons. He
was Ivanhoe's squire, of course, so these must be the
knight's weapons. That must be why the air above the
meadowland was suddenly changing, as if a storm was
about to break from cloudless skies.

That must be why the sound of hoofbeats was
growing. Why something more reflective than the
packhorse's weapons was emerging from the forest,
crossing the boundary of the tournament field.

The highly polished armor of a man on horseback,
riding fast, breaking into a gallop that made everyone
but Brian turn to look.

Brian was still watching Rebecca, as the pounding
hoofbeats drew to a sharp stop behind his back. The
wonder in her eyes infuriating him more than any
words.

Brian turned.

The arriving knight's armor was as heavily plated as any Norman's. It gleamed, fresh from the armory, radiating power. The helmet was designed not just for combat, but for beauty. Its magnificent facade completely hid the stranger's face. The warhorse was the largest Brian had ever seen. It too was draped with Richard Lion-heart's colors. The newly arrived warrior came to a halt in front of Prince John.

"State your name, your allegiance, and your purpose," said John, with loathing. Hunter stirred, deigned to lift his head, to stare through cloudy eyes at the newcomer.

The knight slowly removed his helmet, revealing his young and ardent face. Few knew him by sight, but all knew why he was there.

"I am Ivanhoe," he said. "Son of Lord Cedric of Rotherwood. My allegiance is to King Richard Lion-heart. I challenge Sir Brian de Bois Gilbert."

Cheers broke out from the common folk sitting on the turf, from the old Crusader tents, from Isaac, from the Saxon gallery. Everyone got to their feet. Rebecca could not distinguish Rowena's voice from the crowd, but knew she was shouting out her joy.

Only Rebecca and Richard's old dog remained silent.

Ivanhoe, in Naftali's armor, on the warhorse paid for by her father, was ready to do battle. This was why Rebecca had refused to come. This was why she was here.

"I accept your challenge," said Brian, riding so close to his adversary that Ivanhoe's horse reared.

Ivanhoe brought the powerful horse under control, then turned, finally looking at the Saxon gallery.

He looked high, to his father and his betrothed, his glance filled with love and pride. But his eyes didn't linger. Someone else caught Ivanhoe's attention.

Ivanhoe lowered his gaze to the bench just above the turf-sitters. A black-haired girl in a yellow turban stared at him without expression.

Rebecca could see no anger in his eyes, only the shock of recognition. A recognition of feeling that made him start with shame. Ivanhoe turned away from her suddenly, covering his hurt with defiance.

The shouts were louder, coming from every side, but Rebecca heard nothing. Once again, the ground beneath her feet was shaking, the world threatened to swallow her alive.

At least the satin and lace crown was no longer in her face. Why had Ivanhoe looked at her that way? Why had he turned away so suddenly?

Something – someone – was pulling at her hand.

Rebecca, still standing in place, turned to her father, and understood that he wanted her to sit.

"Daughter," said Isaac. "It will be all right. The knight has come, as he promised."

That was not all Ivanhoe had promised. He had warned Isaac to keep his daughter from Ashby, because he would come with "savage intent." Finally, she sat down, trembling. Would he have noticed that father and daughter were on the lowest bench in the Saxon gallery?

Isaac took her hand, tried to still her fears. "It will be all right," he said. "Have faith."

Rebecca touched the edge of his fur-lined gabardine, as if it were a talisman. Isaac watched her close her eyes, as she prepared to shut out the world.

CHAPTER TEN

The world would not, could not be shut out.

Rebecca found herself opening her eyes, taking in the sight of Prince John sneering down from the reviewing stand. The Prince joked with courtiers, waved his ceremonial truncheon, as if issuing proclamations of great importance.

Isaac could see that the Prince had claimed her attention, and added to her fears. "Pig on a high horse," said Isaac.

But the remark elicited no smile from Rebecca. To her right were the pavilions of John's triumphant Norman knights. To her left, the defeated gaggle of Richard's veterans. Fear roiled her blood.

Knights were about to clash again, as they had all day. This time, one of them would be Ivanhoe, a man who had saved her life, a man whom she had then offended. The other would be Brian, a man who had insulted her with his devouring looks, a man whom she had rejected.

The two men had ample reason for mutual animosity. Saxon against Norman; Crusader against tournament knight; a follower of Richard against a follower of John.

Ivanhoe's challenge to Brian in Cedric's hall had been shouted out while Brian's back had been turned to him. That evening, Brian had been staring at Rebecca, overcome with raging feelings. Was not today even worse? Brian demanding she accept his crown; Rebecca refusing the honor, even with his lance pressed to her chest. Only the arrival of Ivanhoe had pulled Brian's attention away.

Rebecca's refusal to take Brian's gift would be more fuel to feed his rage. Because of her, Brian would take the joust for an opportunity to murder.

A churchman climbed onto the bench one row behind them, banging his metal-shod staff, muttering to one and all: "Benedicte, mes filz, benedicte!"

Directly across from her, the enormous gold signet ring on Prince John's hand reflected sunlight. Incredibly, the Prince had decreed that Brian would not be fighting Ivanhoe after all. Enjoying his own ironic tone, the Prince said that the favorite of the Saxons would have his chance at Brian de Bois Gilbert only when - and if -- he had unhorsed three Normans.

"I am ready now," Brian had said, turning his murderous glare from Ivanhoe to Prince John.

"You are always ready, Sir Brian," said Prince John. "But we must follow protocol. You have already battled three of Richard's veterans to take the honors of the day, and cannot be expected to fight an untested knight."

"There is no need to test a man who has challenged me," said Brian. "He already merits my deadly rebuke."

"You will do well to follow the dictates of your Prince," said John sharply. "It is a concession on my part to allow Ivanhoe to fight at all. He is a latecomer. Let him fight three other Norman knights. If he manages to survive those jousts, you can have the pleasure of unhorsing him."

"I am ready to unhorse him now," said Brian.

"So you say," said Prince John. "But I say, sit down, and put aside your lance until I tell you otherwise."

In a fury of frustration, Brian rode across the field to the Norman pavilions, and dismounted. He watched, rueful, as Sir Maurice, one of the Normans' best jousters, was helped onto his warhorse.

Brian understood what John was doing, and took it as a further insult. The Prince, in spite of his admiration for his best tournament knight, was too cautious to allow Brian to fight Ivanhoe at once. The Crusader had a great reputation, and even Brian must be tired after his efforts that day. John wanted the Saxon hero to be knocked about by three good Norman knights. One of them must surely slam him to the ground. If not, Ivanhoe would be weary enough to be easily finished by Brian's lance.

Waldemar Fitzurse, John's chief advisor, had a voice louder than any trumpet. Standing next to John, he boomed out the Norman command, familiar to all: "Faites vos devoirs, preux chevaliers!"

Rebecca imagined that the combatants could see each other through the eye-slits of their thick helmets, from the ends of the bloody field. A second command followed: "Laissez aller!" Then the trumpets sounded, incongruously jubilant.

Rebecca's eyes fixed on the center of the field. She was too fearful to watch Ivanhoe's approach, though she anticipated his every move. Surely he had lowered his lance, he was placing it into its rest, he

was dashing his gold spurs into the flanks of his
warhorse...!

Galloping sounded from right and left. Vibrant
colors, from waving scarves and kerchiefs, flashed at
the corners of her eyes. Shouting exploded from
hundreds, then held back as the two knights closed in
the center of the lists with thunderous noise, lances
splintering against shields, horses rearing in twin
clouds of dust.

One knight went down.

Rebecca squinted through the dust. A man lay
sprawled on the ground, and the man was not Ivanhoe.

Squires rushed to help Maurice de Bracy to his
feet. In spite of the weight of his armor, Sir
Maurice refused their aid, and stood on his own,
helmet in hand. He stared hatefully after Ivanhoe, as
the Saxon whirled about, and rode proudly back to the
Saxon tents.

For the first time, Rebecca realized that Ivanhoe
was the only knight without a device on his shield.
As if he were without a family, a home.

Again, Rebecca refused to follow him with her
eyes, keeping her gaze focused straight ahead, as her
father chattered excitedly at her side. Above them,

noble Saxons were cheering as loudly as the turf-
sitters below, but there was little cheer in Rebecca's
heart.

Ivanhoe must meet two more knights before
confronting Brian… and Sir Brian de Bois Gilbert had
never been defeated in a tournament.

Rebecca became aware that her father was patting
her hand, as if her concern was of little consequence,
almost amusing. The eternal optimist, Isaac believed
that Sir Ivanhoe could not lose. After all, the young
knight not only had the best armor on the field, but
had moral right on his side.

Rebecca knew that optimism was of a piece with
delusion. No one remembered the past the way it
actually was. No one could see even one single moment
into the future.

Another knight, Philip Malvoisin, was shouting
truculent threats across the tiltyard. This was a
breach of etiquette. She was appalled at the
maliciousness all around her. Saxons, no longer cowed
by Normans, demanded Ivanhoe rip through steel and
into flesh. Normans shouted for Philip to tear
Ivanhoe from his saddle, to break his back, rip out
his eyes from their sockets.

Narrowing her concentration, Rebecca tried to shut out the hateful cacophony, to slow the beating of her heart, to empty the bit of tilting field in front of her any meaning.

But suddenly Waldemar Fitzurse's voice boomed: "Faites vos devoirs, preux chevaliers!... Laissez aller!"

This time the trumpet blasts came faster, the sound of galloping seemed instantaneous. The weight of the past pressed inexorably forward into a terrible future where Ivanhoe might die.

At the center of the field horsemen clad in shining metal galloped into each other with murderous intent. A deafening collision that raised dust, struck sparks. Time seemed to stop.

But there, before her astonished eyes, Sir Philip was on the ground, his horse slowly wandering away.

Ivanhoe remained on horseback, but his great warhorse was turning wildly, ripping up the earth beneath its hooves. "Look," said her father. "The boy is wounded."

It took her a moment to see the blood seeping through the chain mail covering his neck. Ivanhoe dropped the broken lance in his hand, as if it were suddenly too weighty. Retaining hold of his shining shield, he finally brought the warhorse under control.

But she would not follow him with her eyes. Until this useless violence was over, her eyes would see only the center of the field. As Ivanhoe rode back toward the Crusader tents, he passed out of her field of vision.

"Sir Philip's lance," said Isaac. "It must have penetrated."

Rebecca would not look to where the Saxons warriors gathered around their pathetic tents. She would not see whether Gurth would hand his master a fresh lance. She would not speculate as to how badly Ivanhoe was hurt, or whether Ivanhoe would insist on continuing to fight a third knight.

"Sir Reginald," said Isaac, concern growing to dread.

Rebecca turned away from center, looking to the Norman pavilions, despairing. Reginald Front de Boeuf, the largest of John's knights, who had almost won today's tournament, was mounted on his warhorse at the end of the Norman lists. Covering his brutish face with a spike-topped helmet, his metal-gloved hand grabbed a lance from a squire.

The Saxons were clearly subdued, expecting the worse. The Norman cheers grew louder. The voice behind her was Rowena's, beseeching Cedric, peremptory and loud. "He cannot even hold his lance, my lord! You must stop him!"

Slowly, against her will, Rebecca looked to where Gurth was holding out a lance to Ivanhoe. For a moment it seemed that the knight wouldn't take the weapon, that his spirit was weakening along with his strength. But this could not be, Rebecca knew. Ivanhoe had come to Ashby with "savage intent." Nothing would stop him. Gurth pressed the weapon into his master's hand, and Ivanhoe suddenly straightened up in his saddle.

Whether it was a prayer or a vision, she knew that Ivanhoe must rise to the occasion, charging his enemy, thrusting with lance, swinging battle axe and broadsword, felling the giant. Behind her, Cedric echoed her thoughts with gruff pride: "I would not stop him if I could," he said. "Even at the point of death, Saxon warriors never surrender."

"Faites vos devoirs, preux chevaliers!" shouted Waldemar Fitzurse. "Laissez aller!"

To Rebecca, the trumpets now sounded like a death knell. Isaac heard her mumble a familiar Hebrew blessing: "Please, God, let him survive this terrible encounter."

Father and daughter watched Ivanhoe's powerful horse charge forward with a will of its own. She feared for the knight, so weak that he clung to the neck of the horse like a drunken man. She tried not to watch the enormous Reginald, more rock than flesh, more beast than man.

Her eyes widened in wonder as some unknown force allowed Ivanhoe, half a moment before arriving at the center of the lists, to rise in his stirrups, to raise his faltering lance high overhead and drive it forward at an awkward, unpredictable angle.

At that same moment, Reginald's lance shivered to pieces against Ivanhoe's shield, throwing Ivanhoe backward, loosing him from his stirrups.

But somehow one of Ivanhoe's hands retained its hold of the reins. Looking up at the sky, Ivanhoe remained on horseback, as his powerful steed galloped to the very end of the lists.

There was silence throughout the tournament grounds.

Reginald, hit by Ivanhoe's lance in the joint connecting the left metal sleeve to his metal shoulder, did not at first seem to understand why pain was blinding him. But everyone else knew. Blood ran freely from where Ivanhoe's broken lance stuck out from the giant's flesh and bone. Sir Reginald suddenly took hold of the shaft, and ripped it free.

Ivanhoe forced himself to sit up in the saddle. Slowly, his feet found the stirrups. He reined in his horse, and turned around, dazzled by sun. Squinting, Ivanhoe watched his powerful adversary drop the broken lance he had pulled from his shoulder, and draw his enormous broadsword.

Ivanhoe, blinded by sun, heart pounding, drew his own sword, and faced Reginald. It took an effort to simply keep the sword from slipping from his weakening hand.

Reginald raised his broadsword high, about to charge, when Ivanhoe beheld a wondrous thing: With a clatter that shook the galleries, the enormous knight, gripping his great sword, fell from his horse, and lay flat on his back on the ground.

As squires rushed to attend to the fallen giant, Ivanhoe returned his sword to its scabbard, trying to

control his wild breathing. He walked his horse to
the center of the field. He removed his helmet, and
wiped his sweaty brow. Blood continued to seep from
the wound below his neck, but he smiled up at where
Rowena stood in the Saxon gallery. How beautiful she
looked, how proud. She was shouting at him, but he
couldn't make out her words against the backdrop of
cheers.

Ivanhoe turned, looking to where Prince John sat.
The distinctive white markings on the brown mastiff at
John's feet reminded him of something, but for a
moment, he couldn't remember what it was. There were
no cheers coming from the Norman gallery. He had
something to tell John, but he couldn't remember what
that was either.

Of course, thought Ivanhoe. That is Richard's
dog. Hunter. Asleep at the feet of the usurper.

"You are wounded, Sir Knight," said John. "Feel
free to dismount at any time."

"No," said Ivanhoe, remembering what he had
wanted to say to John. "I have fought three men,
Prince John." His voice was weak, and he hesitated to
continue.

"You were a lucky man to stay on your horse," said John, expecting him to fall. "But your luck will not last forever."

Suddenly Ivanhoe sat up straighter: "I have followed your wishes. I have bested all three. I am ready to fight Sir Brian."

John almost laughed. "I congratulate you on your Crusader courage," said the Prince. "To watch a man in your condition fight Sir Brian will indeed be a memorable joust."

Brian rode quickly from the Norman pavilion, and reined in alongside Ivanhoe without giving him a glance. "Good," said John. "I see that my champion is ready to fight."

"Sire," said Brian. "I will not fight a wounded man."

"Wounds are routine in the course of a tournament," said John. "If Sir Ivanhoe insists, we must allow him his pleasure."

"I do insist," said Ivanhoe. Brian turned to him. Blood ran from Ivanhoe's neck, through chain mail mesh, trailing across the shining breast plate.

"That is folly, Sir Knight," said Brian. "You must withdraw -- we will meet another time."

"Death before defeat," said Ivanhoe.

"There you have it, Sir Brian," said John. "A challenge you must answer."

"No," said Brian, coldly defiant. "This is a contest that promises no honor. If he will not withdraw, I will."

"I will never withdraw," said Ivanhoe.

"Then I withdraw," said Brian.

Turning about, Brian glanced at Rebecca, and saw something unfamiliar in her green and gold eyes: Respect.

Still incensed by the beauty's rejection of his crown, Brian rode away at a gallop.

All eyes turned to Ivanhoe, as the helmet suddenly dropped from his hands. There was a collective gasp from the Saxon gallery, but Ivanhoe remained on horseback, obstinately looking up at Prince John's scowl.

"I will be happy to give Sir Brian another opportunity," said Ivanhoe. "Whenever and wherever he desires." Not waiting for a response from the Prince, Ivanhoe wheeled his horse about, and rode directly to the Saxon gallery. His eyes found Rowena, standing on the top level next to a beaming Cedric.

Cedric addressed John in a stentorian voice, though his words were for the whole assembly, including his son. "Prince John," he said. "The tournament is at an end."

Everyone watched Ivanhoe's broad shouldered father gripping his boar-spear. "Two men have unhorsed three knights, but only one of them has withdrawn. You must decree the victor of Ashby: Sir Ivanhoe, son of Lord Cedric of Rotherwood."

Ivanhoe, happy to imagine forgiveness in his father's words, turned from Rowena to Cedric. But the move was too sudden for his wounds. Ivanhoe slid backward off his rearing horse, into the dust. He lay still on the ground before the lowest level of the Saxon gallery.

Senseless, at Rebecca's feet.

CHAPTER ELEVEN

Rebecca dropped to her knees, and pressed one
hand to the chain mail covering Ivanhoe's bloody neck.
A pulse could be dimly felt, but it was fading. She
brought an ear to his armored chest, but could hear
nothing but the shouting about her, the pressing
concerns of a mob of friends and enemies. She pulled
away a metal glove and grabbed his naked wrist.

His shadowy pulse beat against her fingertips,
faint, but insistent.

A dozen people crowded them from all sides, and
around that dozen, five dozen more. From horseback,
from the tops of the galleries, everyone tried to see
what the Jewess was doing, why she refused to stand
aside.

Rebecca called out to Gurth to help strip away
the armor, to her father to bring her goatskin bag
with its cache of herbs and potions. But she did not
shout, and maintained an aspect of utter calm.

Rebecca's eyes remained on Ivanhoe, flat on his
back, eyes shut, her fingers pressed to this wrist, as
if willing the pulse to grow stronger. Until a
Crusader knight grabbed her from behind, breaking her

contact with Ivanhoe's wrist; dragging her away from the wounded man's still form.

"Let me go," she said, but he was shouting something too, something about making way for the doctor, and he wouldn't let go of her shoulders. "Let me go," she said more firmly. And then she called for Gurth.

Instantly, Gurth pulled the Crusader away from Rebecca without effort, with sufficient force to make the knight hesitate to try the squire's temper. The doctor, none too pleased, voiced his displeasure, demanding that Ivanhoe be lifted from the ground and taken away.

"No," said Rebecca. "He must not be moved."

The doctor looked with hatred at Rebecca, her face, hair, and turban streaked with Ivanhoe's blood, her green eyes flashing with violent purpose.

The doctor wore black robes, faded and frayed. His breath stank from rotting teeth. But still he spoke with grave authority, "Will someone get this infernal woman out of my sight?"

"Leave her alone," said Gurth. "Lady Rebecca is a healer." Gurth stood next to her, prepared to defend her from anyone.

The doctor pointed his walking stick at the wounded knight and ordered two burly squires: "I said pick him up. Take him to the tent."

"No!" said Rebecca, throwing herself across Ivanhoe's armored chest. "In the name of all that is holy."

"Get that miserable Jewess away from here," said the doctor.

"Doctor, please!" said Rebecca. "He must not be moved! Not until he wakes. To do so before, is to put him in danger of dying."

The doctor raised his walking stick overhead. "Leave him, witch, or I'll crack your skull like an egg."

Before the doctor could strike, Gurth came at him from behind, pulling away the threatening stick, and sending it flying. Outraged, the doctor turned his wrath on Gurth, but found himself face to face with Lady Rowena.

"Let her be, Doctor," she said.

The doctor, like every Saxon at the tournament, knew her at once: Lord Cedric's beautiful, headstrong ward, and never to be contradicted. Still, he insisted. "The witch interferes, my lady," said the doctor.

"Do not call her 'witch!' And do not question my wishes!" said Rowena, getting onto her knees near Rebecca. "I said 'Let her be,' and you had better do so."

The noblewoman didn't know why the Jewess dared contradict a learned doctor; but she had heard the passion in Rebecca's worrisome words, and believed them.

"My lord," said the doctor to Cedric. "You must not allow a Jewess --"

"Silence," said Cedric, dazed by the fact that the son with whom he was about to reconcile lay dead or dying in the dust.

"She knows herbs, my lord," said Gurth, daring to speak to Cedric. "Potions, charms, and writing too."

Isaac approached, the goatskin bag in hand. "Thank you, Lord Cedric," he said. "My daughter has wisdom. Experience beyond her years. She might help your son live."

"Gurth, the armor," said Rebecca. Gurth pushed past the doctor and his attendants, and began to unclasp his master's armor. "Gently!" said Rebecca.

Cedric, with some difficulty, got to his knees to help Gurth. Like Rowena, Cedric did not understand how the Jew's daughter could be more helpful than an English doctor. But doctors did little but saw off limbs, and predict the moment of death. Perhaps the Jewess was cunning, perhaps there was magic in the goatskin bag held out for her by Isaac.

Nearby, the rejected doctor was voicing his opinion: The knight was either dead, or at death's door. To employ the black arts to bring the dead back to life was a grievous sin. Ivanhoe would do better having a priest at his side than a witch casting spells, certain to hurl him into eternal hellfire.

"Go away," said Rowena. "I don't want to see you, I don't want to hear you." The doctor looked to the Crusader knights hovering nearby for support, but none were forthcoming. "Begone!" said Rowena, and the doctor shuffled away.

Gurth, helped by Lord Cedric, pulled away gloves, greaves, breastplate, backplate, codpiece. "Is she really a witch, Isaac?" said Cedric. "Is it from demons that your daughter gets her magic?"

"Not from demons, my lord," said Isaac. "Her knowledge comes from her blessed mother, and from the wisdom of the ancients."

Even before the armor was completely removed, Rebecca could see that the wounds were worse than she had imagined. Instinctively, she began to intone the "Mi Sheberach" prayer, the Hebrew words tumbling from her lips with concern: "May the Holy One who blessed our patriarchs, Abraham, Isaac and Jacob, overflow with compassion and bless Ivanhoe, son of Cedric, and restore him to health and strength."

All listened to the incomprehensible Hebrew syllables: "Mi she be-rach avo-te-inu. Avram. Yitz-chak… Ve-ya-akov!"

Rowena caught Cedric's worried glance, and smiled at him reassuringly. "Gramercy, my lord. Lady Rebecca is praying," said Rowena. "There is no black magic here." Even if the strange words were a spell, everyone knew that there were white witches; witches not in league with demons, but dedicated to goodness, expert in the art of healing.

Rebecca ripped away a piece of her silk kirtle, and pressed it to Ivanhoe's bleeding neck, holding it there with the flat of one hand. Remembering her mother's teachings, she willed herself to be calm, and took careful inventory of his wounds. The head of a lance had pierced the edge of the breastplate, and remained stuck in his side. When this was removed, it would be a jagged wound, dangerously large and unclean.

"My lady," Rebecca said to Rowena. "Will you hold this?" Without hesitation, Rowena placed her hand onto the piece of silk staunching Ivanhoe's neck wound. "Firmly," said Rebecca. Rowena did as she was told, looking from Rebecca to Ivanhoe's shut eyes.

"He is cold as death," said Rowena with broken-hearted sorrow. Rebecca pulled out a slim glass vial and a few herbs from the goatskin bag. "Can your magic bring him back to life?" Rebecca poured oil from the vial into the herbs, then rubbed them together vigorously. A rank smell erupted, awful and penetrating.

"He is yet alive," said Rebecca. "And I will do all in my power to keep him that way." She thrust the herbs under Ivanhoe's nose. For a moment there was no reaction. Rebecca covered the knight's lips with her hand, and commanded him: "Breathe!"

There was no reaction, so Rebecca repeated her command more sharply: "Breathe!"

The nostrils twitched.

"Praise the Lord," said Rowena.

Rebecca said nothing, all her senses alert. Suddenly, a great hacking sound came from the back of Ivanhoe's throat. Rowena was so relieved that she almost laughed, but following Rebecca's example, she tried to remain still. All at once, a shiver ran the length of Ivanhoe's body; even his head shook, as if about to lift from the ground.

Rowena raised her eyes to Cedric, unable to restrain herself: "Do you see, my lord? Your son! Your son is alive!"

Rebecca pressed the herbs closer to Ivanhoe's nose, until Ivanhoe's eyes fluttered open, astonished with pain.

"Lord Jesus be praised," said Rowena.

The knight's hand swept away the distasteful herbs in front of his face, wild eyes steadying, turning from Rebecca, and focusing on his betrothed.

"Only now may he be moved," said Rebecca.

"Whatever you say, Lady Rebecca," said Rowena.

"He will need a horse litter," said Rebecca.

Rowena shouted out the order, echoed by Cedric to his steward, Hundebert.

Ivanhoe's gaze shifted. Rebecca could see that the knight had taken in her presence -- with displeasure. His lips parted, as if about to speak.

"You must not speak, Sir Knight," said Rebecca firmly. "Do not tax yourself in any way."

"I choose," said Ivanhoe, softly, but defiantly.

"What is it, Ivanhoe?" said Rowena. "What do you choose?" He repeated the strange words, turning his eyes from Rebecca to Rowena. Rowena leaned closer, their lips close enough to touch.

"My lady, please," said Rebecca. "He must not talk at all. He must preserve his strength."

"No!" said Ivanhoe.

"Please, you must listen to Rebecca. She has brought you back to life, and you must obey her every wish. Do not talk, only rest."

"Tell the Prince," insisted Ivanhoe to Rowena. "Tell John."

Lovingly, Rowena pressed a finger to Ivanhoe's lips. "I will tell him whatever you like. But for now, you must be quiet."

Ivanhoe could see that the stoic face of his father, Lord Cedric, had grown ashen with worry.

"I have won," said Ivanhoe, as much to Cedric as to Rowena.

"Of course you have won," said Cedric with pride.

"So it is my right," said Ivanhoe.

Rebecca understood his words a moment before the others. She saw him grip Rowena's finger, and make his wishes clear to all: "I choose you. You will be the tournament Queen. Not her, Rowena. You."

CHAPTER TWELVE

"Darkness approaches," said Cedric, standing behind Rowena. "There are bandits and rovers on the way to Wittold. We can delay no longer,"

Answering Cedric, Rowena kept her eyes on the fair-haired young man in the luxurious bed. "If that is true, my lord," she said. "You must bid goodbye to your son."

"He does not hear me, child," said Cedric, staring at the immobile Ivanhoe. "He has heard nothing for two days!"

"Lady Rebecca says we cannot know what he hears or doesn't hear," said Rowena.

"I know that he does not open his eyes. That he does not speak!"

Cedric felt his ward grab his hand. "But see how he breathes," she said. "Feel how his heart beats." Rowena placed Cedric's palm on Ivanhoe's chest.

Staring at his son's face, still as a mask, Cedric felt the steady pulse; until he could stand it no longer, and pulled free. "I will ready our retinue," said Cedric. "Be outside in five minutes."

Across the room, Rebecca dipped aromatic herbs in a clear potion, listening to every word. Cedric turned so abruptly that he nearly knocked her over. "Forgive me, girl," he said curtly. "This room grows smaller every minute."

Cedric picked up his boar-spear, and hurried to the door. He nearly stepped on Gurth, asleep on a bearskin, then rushed out of the sick room.

Rebecca approached the patient with her herbal preparation. She had wanted Rowena and Cedric gone almost from the moment they had come, but now that they were about to leave, a nameless dread began to penetrate her thoughts.

"Lord Cedric appreciates your kindness, Lady Rebecca" said Rowena. "Even if he has not said so in words."

While still at the tournament grounds, Rebecca's magic had proved fleeting: Ivanhoe had quickly slipped back into senselessness. But Rowena and Cedric had witnessed the knight's transformation from death to life, and Rowena had begged Rebecca to continue her healing.

Ivanhoe had been brought in a horse litter to Isaac's home outside Ashby, accompanied by Cedric,

Rowena, a dozen Saxon notables, and twice as many servants. Rebecca had Joseph and Gurth bring her own bed into the main room of the house, near a great fireplace. Here, lying on plush pillows, lit by candles and firelight, Ivanhoe slept for two days and nights, never responding to his father's forgiving words, nor to Rowena's loving entreaties.

The Saxon notables had left after a few hours. Joseph and Margaret had prepared food and beds for their two exalted guests, but Cedric and Rowena had little appetite, and refused Isaac's offer to retreat to comfortable sleeping quarters. Cedric had slept on the same bearskin now occupied by Gurth, while his ward hadn't slept at all.

Rowena's worrying presence had disturbed Rebecca, making it difficult to narrow her attention on Ivanhoe. Lord Cedric had been equally disturbing. Alternately fuming and regretful, anxious that his son's wounds would eventually kill him, Cedric had paced the sick room like a madman. Rebecca wished they would both leave her alone with the wounded knight.

As for Isaac, his concerns had bothered her more than either of the Saxons. "Why do you delay pulling the lance-head?" he asked her shortly after they'd arrived in Ashby. "I don't pretend to know as much medicine as you, but I remember how your mother was always quick to remove a foreign object from a wound, no matter how grievous."

Rebecca did not answer at once. She had been looking down at Ivanhoe's still form, hoping for some signs of improvement. "If Mother were here, I believe she would wait until he had grown stronger."

"And I believe she would not wait a moment longer!" he said. "To my eye, the boy is getting no stronger. The longer that lance-head remains embedded in his side, the less chance he will have to survive the day."

Isaac watched as his daughter pulled Ivanhoe's bloody tunic up and away from where the lance-head protruded above his lowest left-side rib. "I know you are grateful for his saving our lives, but that should not make you too cautious to do what needs to be done."

"I am preparing to do what is necessary," she said with unusual tartness, but Isaac did not see her do anything more than stare at the young knight's shut eyes.

"I assisted your mother more than once, and if for some reason you are wary of —"

"I am not wary!" she interrupted. Then more calmly, she added: "I am not reluctant. I am simply doing what I would do for anyone in this situation."

She turned to look into her father's honey-colored eyes. "Now, I would like to proceed."

"Good. I am glad," said Isaac. "I would like to help."

"No, thank you."

"I can be useful, handing you what you need, holding up a lantern —"

"No," she said with vehemence. "I don't want your help, or Rowena's, or Lord Cedric's. I want to be alone with this Crusader."

"Why?" Isaac said. But she was through discussing the issue, and finally, her father left her alone.

Neither Rowena nor Cedric were there when Rebecca finally pulled free the lance-head. She had demanded that they remain outside the room as well, as their feelings might hamper the work she must do. But she had allowed Gurth to remain by her side, and he had proven an excellent helpmate.

Gurth didn't flinch when she pulled free the lance-head with force, nor did he say a word when the wound opened, and blood flowed. He waited for instructions, and when she told him what to do, his steady hand had helped her stop the rush of blood with thick squares of soft cotton. Gurth watched her use silk thread to sew up the wound with a delicate ligature, her fingers swift and sure. He brought her gauze soaked in brandywine, and watched as she cleaned the wound, and stanched the blood.

"Bless you, my lady," was all Gurth said.

They were the only words said in that room for many minutes, and when Gurth spoke, Rebecca met his eyes as if coming out of a trance.

That even this operation hadn't waked Ivanhoe frightened her, especially after she had discovered a bruise on the back of his head, hidden by his thick hair. Ivanhoe's helmet had protected him from the sharp blades of battle axe and broadsword, but clearly the buffeting had taken its effect.

If Gurth hadn't been present - and Rowena in the adjacent room - she would have tried a special kind of treatment: Rebecca would have sat on the bed, placing her hands on both sides of Ivanhoe's head throughout the night, joining in the patient's struggle to come out of darkness and pain into light and health. But this might look too much like an embrace.

Rebecca had learned the technique from her mother. The touch of a healer's hands, the compassion in her heart, - this could be enough to turn around the direst of illnesses. Though Deborah had not known why the technique sometimes healed, but often did not, she had said it could do no harm; and it gave solace to patient and healer both.

Solace is a great healer, Rebecca thought. For a moment she thought she had said the words aloud. But she hadn't spoken at all. It had been Rowena speaking, turning her concern from her betrothed to Rebecca. She repeated her words: "Did you sleep at all last night?" she said.

"Did you?" asked Rebecca with a gentle smile.

"It was impossible, with Ivanhoe senseless in the next room," said Rowena.

"You have a loving heart," said Rebecca.

"I am sorry that Lord Cedric insists that we leave," said Rowena. She was watching Rebecca place her herbs along Ivanhoe's neck. "Saxons loyal to King

Richard gather at the great monastery at Wittold. My
guardian is old, and anxious, and I fear that I must
accompany him."

Do not hesitate, thought Rebecca. Go away with
Lord Cedric. Go away at once.

"Unless you were to tell me to remain," continued
Rowena. "For any good I might do here."

"You have done much good already, my lady," said
Rebecca calmly. "When Ivanhoe wakes, I believe he
will remember all you have told him: About the
tournament he has won, how his father has forgiven
him, how you are named Queen of Beauty and Grace!"

"When he wakes," repeated Rowena stoically. The
redness in her eyes was from fatigue, never tears.

"He will wake," said Rebecca. "He is getting
better. I am sensitive to these things, and I feel
it now."

"You are an angel," said Rowena. She lowered her
eyes to Ivanhoe's pale face, and spoke softly to him:
"I must go now, darling. You are a guest of Isaac of
York and his daughter Rebecca, in their beautiful
country house. You cannot imagine the luxury. All
the wonders of Araby are here. Silver, gold, rare
woods, luxurious carpets. You sleep on a bed fit for

a king. When you wake, I will return with your father. And take you home to Rotherwood."

Suddenly Gurth woke, rolling to his feet, gripping the sword lying next to the bearskin. "Horses," he explained, stepping to look out the door.

"It is only Lord Cedric," said Rowena, smiling at the burly servant. "We are leaving. But you must stay. I trust you will guard your master in our absence."

"Yes, my lady," said Gurth.

"You must also guard his healing angel," said Rowena.

"I will guard them both," said Gurth. "With my life."

Rowena took Rebecca's hands in hers, then leaned close and kissed her forehead. "Thank you, dear Rebecca," she said. "Thank you for everything."

Gurth followed Rowena outside, to help with the horses. Rebecca stood still, waiting for stillness to overtake the sickroom. But what she felt wasn't stillness, but growing fear.

Fear coming through the roof and walls of the house, fear that was amplified by her being alone with Ivanhoe.

Isaac was in his study, Joseph and Margaret in the kitchen. A silver lamp, burning fine oil, threw a steady circle of illumination around the knight's handsome face. Rebecca found herself stepping closer, sitting on the edge of the bed, watching his chest rise and fall.

The breathing wasn't shallow, neither was there serious swelling around the stitches she'd made in his side. She touched his forehead, which was warm, but not hot. She felt the pulse at his wrist, which was strong. She felt the pulse at his neck, which was stronger still. But still, he showed no signs of waking.

Suddenly, she took a deep breath, and placed her palms on both his cheeks, exactly as she had been taught by her mother, exactly as she had been longing to do.

His eyes remained shut, his breathing continued as before, but she could sense something coming from him, something quickening beneath his skin. She lowered her face until it was inches from his. Then she shut her eyes. In the darkness, the only sound was his breathing, and her own. As her mother had taught her, she regulated her breathing so that they matched his exactly; until they breathed together, as one.

She was aware that time was passing, but whether it was minutes or hours, she could not say. Deliberately, she imagined him opening his eyes, filled with strength. Sir Ivanhoe, standing tall, the pallor gone from his face. He would be well, he would be grateful, and she would send Gurth after Rowena to tell her the happy news.

Then Rebecca could leave this place with her father, leave Ashby and England for safety in Spain.

Prince John, in full view of his courtiers, had demanded two thousand bezants from her father, gold coins that must be paid within five days. Or else John would not only confiscate everything Isaac owned in England, but might go so far as to imprison him, torture him, execute him.

Two thousand gold coins could not easily be found, especially when no one was certain who would rule in a week's time. Isaac might produce a bill of exchange, festooned with Hebrew letters and sealing wax, but this might not be enough to satisfy John.

Events in the Holy Land had their effects in France, in Austria, in alliances and enmities across

the face of Europe.   That the Saxon overlord Cedric
had preferred the care of a Jewish healer - a woman, a
foreigner -- to a Christian doctor, added fuel to the
fiery scandals of the tournament: Sir Brian choosing
a Jewess to be his tournament Queen.   Sir Ivanhoe, in
King Richard's name, besting John's tournament
knights.   And John's best knight refusing his prince's
command to fight the wounded Crusader!

The foundations of the country were being tested,
changes that might lead to a cataclysm.   Prince John
had been insulted, and no one knew how he would take
vengeance.

She opened her eyes to a darkened room.   The day
was done, but she saw no change in her patient.
Ivanhoe must recover quickly, she thought.   He must
be able to mount a horse, and get away, far from this
place.

She worried that someone would come, meaning him
harm, eager to take advantage of his weakness.   They
would not let the insult of his victory stand.
Exhausted, she let her eyes close.   Somehow, she kept
her hands on his cheeks, forcing herself to stay awake
through the long hours.

But as she continued to hold him, continued to pace her breathing with his, as darkness pressed against the windows of the house, as night moved in its steady pace toward dawn, these logical fears dissipated. In their place a different sort of fear arose, an irrational insistence: It was neither Prince John nor Sir Brian whom she feared -- but Ivanhoe.

But what on earth could he do to her? she thought. Surely he would not wish to hurt the woman who had saved him from bleeding to death? Surely he would understand what she had sacrificed in caring for him without respite for two days, nearly three.

"You. Why are you here?" said a voice, sharply breaking into her thoughts. His voice. Rebecca opened her eyes, so amazed to find him awake that for a moment she imagined herself to be dreaming.

But the slant of early morning light that ran across his angry face was not a dream, but the beginning of a new day. "What are you doing here?" he said, trying to sit up.

"You must not sit, Sir Knight," she said, her tone as sharp and unfriendly as his.

"Do not give me orders," he said, grabbing her wrists, as if her palms were somehow fixing his head to the pillow. Rebecca pulled free and stood. He sat up, looking past her to the unfamiliar room. "What is this place?"

"You are in my father's house at Ashby."

"Why?" he said, suspicious and hostile. She was amazed to see him turn abruptly, swiveling his legs off the bed.

"No, you mustn't," said Rebecca, placing her hands on his shoulders, not wanting him to stand.

"What have you done to me?" he said, reacting to the pain in his side, touching his hand to the bandages.

"You were hurt, and needed care."

"Why would you give me care?" said Ivanhoe, placing the soles of his feet on the floor. "You of all people!" He brushed aside one of her hands, and tried to rise.

"Gurth!" shouted Rebecca.

Ivanhoe suddenly sat back on the bed, his face whitening. "What have you done to me?" Weakening, he felt the herbs clinging to his neck, and tore them away with violence. Gurth rushed into the room.

"Lord Jesus be praised," said Gurth, seeing his master awake.

"Look what this witch did to me!" said Ivanhoe, showing the herbs to his squire.

"Lady Rebecca is not a witch, Master. And whatever she does -"

"Silence!" said Ivanhoe. "Get me out of this room, out of this place."

"Gurth, please listen," said Rebecca. "He must not move from this bed. You must try and keep him quiet."

"Gurth," said Ivanhoe. "Get me away from this she-devil."

"I cannot do that, Master," said Gurth. "You must try and lie down now."

"What?" said Ivanhoe, stunned to see that Gurth was not only refusing his orders, but grabbing hold of his shoulders. "Get me out of this witch's den!"

"We will go, Master, but first you must get better." Ivanhoe started to struggle against Gurth's hold on his shoulders. But he was weak and Gurth was strong.

"We will go, the moment Lady Rebecca tells me you are fit to travel," said Gurth, pressing him flat on the bed.

"Has she put you under a spell?" said Ivanhoe. He was looking up at the squire, unable to understand his disobedience.

"Master, this great lady is neither devil nor witch. And she has saved your life," said Gurth.

"Saved my life?" said Ivanhoe, remembering no such thing.

Gurth explained how he had been wounded at the tournament, how Rebecca had brought him back from the dead, how she had pulled free the lance-head, had sewn up his wounds.

"Saved my life?" said Ivanhoe again, a little less incredulously.

"If not for Rebecca, you would be dead and buried," said Gurth.

"Well I saved her life, remember?" Ivanhoe's head fell back against deep pillows. His eyes found Rebecca's, staring at him with anger. "And got no thanks for it," he said.

"Do not be alarmed," said Rebecca to Gurth. "It is natural for a wounded man to be querulous."

Rebecca stepped close, taking hold of Ivanhoe's wrist.

"What are you doing?" he demanded.

"Attending to your needs, Sir Knight. According to the dictates of my calling."

"What is she talking about?" said Ivanhoe to Gurth.

"Lady Rebecca is a great healer," said Gurth. Ivanhoe kept his eyes on her as she touched his forehead. He grabbed her wrist in one hand.

"Let me alone!" said Ivanhoe.

Rebecca pulled her hand free. "Very soon you will be rid of my presence, Sir Knight. But for the moment, you must recuperate here. Lord Cedric and Rowena will want to know that you are out of danger."

Rebecca turned to Gurth. "You muster hurry after them, Gurth. Go to Wittold."

"No, my lady," said Gurth. "You must send a servant in my place."

"My squire says no to everyone!" said Ivanhoe, less truculent. Suddenly almost amused.

"I am sworn to protect my master, and you," said Gurth to Rebecca. "And will not leave either of you alone."

"That is a great comfort, Gurth" said Rebecca.
Ivanhoe was again trying to sit up. "For the moment,
you can keep your master in bed, while I give him
something to help him rest."

Gurth pressed Ivanhoe's shoulders to the pillow.
"Now what is she doing?" said Ivanhoe. Both men
watched Rebecca shred strange herbs into a goblet of
water, releasing a pleasant scent. "What is that
witch's brew?"

"If she is any kind of witch, Master, she is a
white witch, and mighty. Like my mother's mother, a
healer of the sick." Gurth let go of Ivanhoe's
shoulders, and helped raise his head, so that Rebecca
could bring the potion to his lips.

"No, I don't want to –" said Ivanhoe, the
knight's eyes flashing defiance, but Gurth held him
firmly, and Rebecca brought the goblet to his thirsty
lips. He stared into her green and gold eyes.

"Did you ever see eyes that color, Gurth? Those
are demon's eyes." But his voice was no longer
truculent. Staring at her, Ivanhoe finally took a
sip, then another, and suddenly, all the fight was
gone from him, and he drank a great gulp. "Why is she

angry? I saved her life," he said once again. "And got no thanks for it. No thanks…"

Ivanhoe sank back into the pillows, astonished at a feeling of calm rushing through his body. His eyes closed. He slept.

Joseph was sent to procure a mounted courier. Gurth took up his post in the front hallway, while Rebecca joined her father in his study. There she began to write out the glad tidings to be sent to Cedric and Rowena. "I can do that, Daughter. You should sleep."

"Your penmanship leaves something to be desired," said Rebecca, staring at the parchment, trying to bring the carefully wrought English letters into focus before her exhausted eyes. When she finished writing, the pen slipped out of her hand, and her eyes closed. Rebecca fell asleep, her head cradled in her arms on her father's desk.

Isaac took the parchment from her lap, and tried to wake her, to get her to lie down on a proper bed, but it was no use. Her sleep was too deep. He drew curtains over the sun-dashed windows, and left his exhausted daughter where she was, lost in dreams.

Five hours later, the sound of a dozen armored horsemen couldn't completely rouse her.

How could Rebecca imagine that her fears had come to life, that Sir Brian and a troop of Norman knights were outside the house, that a deep-sleeping Gurth was being struck unconscious by the shaft of a warrior's lance, that her unarmed servant Joseph was being murdered by a knight's sword?

The scuffle outside her front door sounded like distant thunder on the outskirts of her dream. Like the noise of a nightmare that would pass the moment she woke.

CHAPTER THIRTEEN

It was a scream that finally woke Rebecca, a
scream that thrust a shaft of despair through her
dreams. She woke at once, hearing its deathly echoes.

Rebecca raised her head from her father's desk,
trying to understand where the scream had come from,
why it had stopped, and why there were other sounds in
its place: Stamping horses, breaking glass, creaking
armor. And outside the house, the sound of sudden
galloping; clattering hoofbeats swiftly fading, until
they could no longer be heard.

Exhausted, her head heavy, the again silent room
so dark that Rebecca thought she might well be asleep,
imagining dreams within dreams, creating fears where
none need exist.

Then, all at once, pallid sunlight poured into
the room from behind her back. The warm radiance
created an instant chill of fear. With effort,
Rebecca stood up from the desk chair and turned to an
unfathomable sight: A helmeted knight was pulling
aside draperies from glass windows, his chain mail
reflecting brightness.

Even before he turned round and removed his helmet, Rebecca knew who he must be.

Sir Brian de Bois Gilbert put his helmet on the desk, and looked at her keenly, as if searching for a key to know how he must behave.

"I heard a scream," she said, holding onto the back of her chair for support.

Brian could see that her emerald eyes held nothing but loathing. He was determined to change that. "High time you got up," he said. "The day is almost done."

"I heard a scream, and horses," Rebecca insisted. "I thought I was dreaming."

"You were not," said Brian, approaching her slowly. She looked at his brightly colored shirt, covered with a vest of burnished mail. Behind him the late afternoon sun was beginning to sink into distant treetops.

"Who screamed? Was it my father? Where is my father?"

"No one has touched your father," said Brian. "He is asleep in his bed, as peaceful as he will ever be."

With one hand on the hilt of his sheathed sword, he took a step closer, close enough to touch. But he

didn't reach out his yearning hands. Behind the
arrogant, pretty features of his face was something
fragile, something that shamed his warrior's soul.
"It seems you Jews are like bats, sleeping through
daylight."

He was attempting a light tone, but it was having
no effect on her worries. "And Gurth?" said Rebecca.
"The big young man guarding the door?"

"You needn't worry," said Brian. "Redheads
always survive a conk on their thick skulls."

"I had better see to him at once."

"No," he said, standing in her way. "We have
important things to discuss."

"I heard a scream. If not my father, not Gurth -
who? I know I heard --"

"Your maid screamed."

"Margaret?"

"She was upset at the death of her husband."

"Her husband killed? Are you saying that Joseph
is dead?"

"The maid said he was her husband. She threw
herself on his corpse."

"You killed Joseph…"

"The slave attacked my knights."

"Joseph was a freeman. If he attacked your knights, it was to protect this household."

"Then he should have used a better weapon than a broom. When my knights finished him, his wife was stupid enough to attack them as well."

"Are you saying that Margaret is dead?"

"Such people are not worth our concern," said Brian. He had included Rebecca in this statement; neither one of them need worry about serfs, peasants, and slaves. But she had found no compliment in his words. The yellow lines in her green eyes grew sharp with hatred.

"You murdered Margaret and Joseph," she said.

"Not me, my men. I save my sword for nobler deeds."

"If they are your men, their murders will be on your soul. When King Richard returns —"

"Richard is never coming back!" he said, with savage conviction. "And when Christian servants defend a Jewish traitor they deserve worse than death," he added, but already the savagery was fading from his voice.

Her beauty continued to unsettle him. She was not only oblivious to his charms, but growing increasingly filled with hate. He tried again, his tone mild, even flirtatious: "But I have sent my men away for a few hours."

"Why? What are you doing in my home?"

"You and I have need of privacy," said Brian. If this was a romantic sentiment, it was marred by a martial glare. He couldn't help from bristling at her hostile indifference. "You know I cannot stay away from you."

"No, I do not! And I demand to know on whose authority you have come to my father's house."

"You have not the power to demand anything," said Brian, unconsciously gripping the hilt of his sword.

"Go away, get out of my sight," she said. After a moment, she added: "You revolt me."

"I know that it is not true." It took a great effort to keep his voice calm. "As I know that you are in danger, and must be protected. I will see to that."

"I don't want your protection! Just go away. I must attend to Gurth."

"No," said Brian, smiling at her with a confidence he didn't feel. "I can see beyond the anger in your eyes that you feel something for me. I

saw it when I refused to fight Ivanhoe at the
tournament. Something I could feel, that I know is
there."

"Look better, Sir Knight," she said. "Disgust
and loathing. That's all you'll ever see in my
eyes."

Rebecca turned away, and again tried to go toward
the door, but Brian grabbed her shoulders, turning her
round to face him. He was angry, and was about to say
something harsh, but touching her thrilled him in a
way he couldn't understand. It took him a moment to
continue.

"You need not fear," he said. "I am not like
those priests who hold Jewish daughters accountable
for their fathers' sins."

Rebecca stepped backward abruptly, deliberately
slipping out of his grasp, banging hard into the desk,
knocking over one of Isaac's philosophical scrolls.
It was clear that she was avoiding his touch, that his
handsome figure repulsed her.

"I offer you protection, Jewess. You would do
well to force a welcome into your pretty face."

Tired as she was, Rebecca knew she must pick up
the scroll. Written on it, more than once, was the

sacred name of God. As she bent to pick up the
tightly rolled parchment, Brian felt ignored. His
tone was furious: "Did you not hear me, girl?"

Gripping the parchment, she stood up fast. Dizzy
with exhaustion and dread, she reached out to hold
onto the edge of the desk, but missed, feeling the
floor crumble beneath her.

Now Brian was looking down at her, less with
concern than agitation. Rebecca realized she had
dropped the scroll on the desk, then had herself
fallen, to a pillowed platform on the floor.

Above her, his pretty lips moved, his words
emerging clipped and sharp and insistent. Threats
apparently, perhaps alternating with something
gentler; something insistent. But she had stopped
listening. It was all she could do to keep her eyes
open.

How could Margaret and Joseph be dead? she
thought. They were alive only a few hours ago. A
loving couple, who had brought children into the
world, who had died defending this home. Where were
Margaret and Joseph now? Where did Christians go
after death? A World-to-Come must contain more than
her own people. Decency and goodness worthy of

heavenly reward surely meant that Christians, Muslims, ancient heathens of Greece and Rome would surely people the land of Life-After-Death.

Had Sir Ivanhoe died on the tilting field, his soul would have left his body. But where would that Christian soul have gone? That is a question she would have to ask a learned rabbi, perhaps when she and her father would finally arrive in Zaragoza.

She remembered how she had thought Margaret and Joseph's love for her was suspect, how she had never truly reciprocated their feelings. Guilt settled on her heart like a heavy, jagged stone.

Suddenly, Brian grabbed her hands and pulled her to her feet, shattering all thoughts of murdered servants and Christian souls.

"Listen to me, and listen well," he said. "The Prince has sent me here, to arrest your father for treason."

Rebecca heard every word. Any last vestiges of sleep left her. It was daylight, but late in the day. Surely her father must be awake, aware of the murders of Margaret and Joseph, aware that Brian was in his study, threatening to arrest him. And threatening his daughter as well, threatening her with vile insinuations and repulsive looks. Isaac must be listening, waiting for his chance to help her to escape.

Rebecca pulled her hands free of Brian, forcing herself to remain on her feet. When her father came, she must be ready. "What treason?" she said, stepping behind a chair, doing what she could to keep away from his growing rage.

"John received word from France. Richard's ransom has been raised in England, and transferred through bills of exchange to Austria. Jewish bills, of course, signed by Isaac of York. Your father will be tried for conspiring to overthrow Prince John."

"Not my father, but your prince will be tried. For usurping King Richard's legitimate rule."

Brian kicked aside the chair that was between them, and backed her against the still bright window glass.

"Why do you want to vex the only man in England who can help you live?" he said. "There is nothing I can do for your father, but there is much I can do for you. Isaac of York cannot escape his fate. But you…"

"I have no fate without my father," said Rebecca. "My mother is dead. If my father were to die, I would gladly follow him."

"Brave words, but no one wants to die." Brian tried to soften his tone, but everything he said came out like commands to an inferior. "You are a Jewess, but I am willing to offer you safety. All you must do is renounce your false religion. This is a great boon for which you must be grateful. If you do not understand why I offer it, look into my eyes when I take your hand."

Once again, he gripped her hand, and this time the arrogance left his eyes, until she could see clearly that he wanted her to be his, and willingly.

Rebecca laughed crazily. He didn't fight when she pulled her hand free. Joseph and Margaret murdered, her father threatened with disgrace and death, and this knight was making love to her!

"How dare you laugh?" said Brian. "It is not a laughing matter. It is a matter of life and death."

It took her an effort, but she stopped laughing. There was a manic twist to her lips, a macabre smile. "You are right about that, Sir Knight. A matter of life and death."

"You were wrong to refuse the honor I offered you at the tournament. And the honor I offer you now is even greater."

"I will never want anything from you, but to leave me alone."

"Don't you understand that you are member of a despised nation? Only I can see to it that you are elevated, that you can become a Christian, living in a castle."

"I would rather be a dead Jewess, than a Christian queen."

Brian tried to convince her in an even, logical tone. But his words tumbled out like sharp rocks: "Don't you understand what I am offering? Because of you, I will never marry. I will have no other woman. You will be my lawful mistress."

"You offer me the chance to be your mistress," said Rebecca. "And all I must do is renounce my religion, my family, my nation! An appealing prospect, if I were a harlot raised on a dunghill. But far less appealing than dying before this day is over."

The coldness in her eyes humiliated him. Bad
enough that she was disdainful, and proud. Worse that
she was revolted by his attention.

Enraged, Brian pushed her against the wall.
Couldn't she understand he wanted more from her than
possession of her body? He could make her his slave,
but mere obedience would never appease his hunger. He
wanted her soul. Could she not realize that he
offered her more than a chance to live? He was
offering her honor, privilege. In so doing, his
career at John's court would be damaged, if not ended
altogether.

Could she not appreciate that he was sacrificing
all for the sake of her heart?

Giving in to wild emotion, he pressed his lips to
hers, lips and teeth trying to force their way into
her shut mouth. But Rebecca's lips stayed tightly
closed, her body growing rigid as a corpse. Brian
could barely sense her breathing. Until suddenly her
mouth opened, and she bit into his lip with great
force.

He pulled away, wiping blood from his lips. She
had not bitten into him because of an excess of

passionate love. Her passion was hatred. But he refused to accept this.

"You don't understand," he insisted, looking at her, imagining something that was not there. "All that feeling, it is the same for me." If she could acknowledge the truth of his emotions, her loathing would transform to love, like lead to gold. "You have bewitched me," he said.

It was almost like saying that he loved her. He stepped closer, gentle, beseeching.

Rebecca spit into his face.

Appalled, Brian took a step back. Then he slapped her cheek, with violence. "Not a witch, but a demon," he said.

Rebecca barely reacted to the blow, her astonished eyes looking past Brian to where her sickly father was entering the room, a clay vase raised high.

Brian turned, at the very moment that Isaac brought down the vase, shattering it over the knight's uncovered head. But Brian remained steady on his feet, ignoring a trace of blood appearing at the scalp line. "Not very sporting, Jew," he said, seemingly unaffected by the blow. Slowly, contemptuously, he drew his sword, threatening Isaac with the point of his blade.

"Leave him alone!" said Rebecca behind Brian's back. She grabbed her father's parchment scroll from the desk, gripping it like a club. "You will gain nothing by hurting him. If you hurt my father in any way, you will never collect Prince John's bezants."

"Do you think I care about bezants?" said Brian, still amazed at her rejection. He brought his blade close to Isaac's throat. "Even my Prince cares less Jewish coins, now that his brother is approaching English shores. He has only one care. When and where is Richard landing?"

Isaac remained silent. "Put down your sword," said Rebecca, her hand gripping the scroll tighter.

Brian tried to shut out his passion for the girl, and narrowed his attention on her father: "I have asked you a question, Jew. When and where? Answer me."

"How is it possible," said Isaac, "that a knight, sworn to obey holy vows to God and King, can stray so far from righteousness?"

"You must and you will tell me the names," said Brian, "of every traitor in England, Jew and Christian alike, who contributed to Richard's ransom."

"You speak illogically, Sir Brian," said Isaac. "No one who contributed to the ransom of our true king is a traitor. Just as anyone who supports the usurper John can call himself a true knight."

Rebecca could sense that the frustrated, incensed Brian was about to press the blade through Isaac's skin. So she swung the parchment scroll into the back of the knight's head with all her force.

Perhaps it was sacrilegious to use a scroll containing God's name as a weapon, but it was all she had at hand. Brian staggered a moment against this second unexpected blow, but continued standing.

Head aching, he turned to Rebecca, and pretended to be amused. "First the father, now the daughter," said Brian. "It's a good thing you Jews don't have better weapons."

Picking up a mahogany lamp, Isaac used his remaining strength to smash it into the back of Brian's skull. At last, Brian wobbled, but still remained on his feet.

"Fall down! Why doesn't he fall down?" said Rebecca.

Brian clumsily swung his sword into the broken lamp held by Isaac, sending fragments of glass and wood to the floor. Before he could threaten her father further, Rebecca drove the tightly-wrapped scroll into Brian's head one more time.

Brian turned, blinking against blood and lamp oil running into his eyes, to stare at Rebecca. "It will take more than a Jew and his demon daughter to…" began Brian, before suddenly silencing.

Looking past Rebecca, he stared at an impossible apparition entering the room: Ivanhoe, woken from his drugged sleep. Ghostly pale, weaponless, wearing only a tunic, approaching on bare feet. Each step an effort.

"My brave challenger," said Brian. "Your hero." Ivanhoe, ignoring the sword loosely held by the staggering man, swung his fist into Brian's jaw.

Brian watched his sword slip from his hand, and crash to the floor. He looked from Ivanhoe's fury to Rebecca's amazement. Then Brian dropped to both knees.

"A demon," said Brian, addressing his fellow knight. "She will bewitch you." Then Brian fell over onto his side, frustration and anger fading to blackness.

CHAPTER FOURTEEN

Ivanhoe, having exhausted his strength with the blow to Brian's jaw, stepped back, colliding with Rebecca.

"Careful, Sir Knight," she said. "I have given you a powerful sleeping potion."

Forcing himself to remain conscious, Ivanhoe bent over and picked up Brian's sword.

"No!" said Rebecca. "You must not kill him."

"I do not intend to kill him, not today," said Ivanhoe, fury in his eyes. "Not until he recovers his senses, and is a worthy opponent. Then I will kill him, regardless of your tender feelings."

Suddenly Ivanhoe lowered the sword, and fell back into the chair where Rebecca had slept. The sword slipped from his hand, banging on the floor. Ivanhoe tried to resist the closing of his eyes, but after a moment, he was asleep.

"Can you wake him, Daughter?" said Isaac.

"I must not. His wounds have not sufficiently -"

"Brian's men will soon return," said Isaac. "To linger here is to be murdered. Not only you and I, but King Richard has need of this knight. Wake him somehow. Wake him at once."

There was much to be done before Rebecca could try and wake Ivanhoe.

She found Gurth stirring near the front door, clotted blood crowning coarse red hair. As Rebecca helped him sit up, his dark blue eyes narrowed, trying to make sense of the pain in his head, the foreboding in his heart. "What is wrong, my lady?"

"You have been hurt, Gurth," said Rebecca.

"How could I be hurt?" he said, starting to stand.

She pushed down on his massive shoulders, preventing him from getting up. "Pray be still, while I attend to you." She started to wipe the blood from his hair with a wet cloth, but he would not stay still, insisting on learning what had happened. Rebecca told him that he had been struck senseless.

"But I was on watch," he said, getting to his feet with effort, ignoring the dizziness.

"You were struck from behind," she said. For a moment, he looked at her with disbelief.

"Do you mean that I fell asleep, while I was on watch? That I slept, and allowed intruders to come in?" he said. She tried to continue cleaning the blood from his scalp, but he took the wet cloth from her hand. Rebecca was forced to tell him the rest of it: Fighting the intruders, Joseph and Margaret had been murdered.

"Murdered, because I slept," he said bitterly.

"It was not your fault. No one will blame you. You were attacked, and rendered unconscious."

"And Ivanhoe?" said Gurth. "What of my master?"

"He is all right," said Rebecca. "In spite of leaving his sickbed to save me and my father from Brian."

"Why couldn't they have killed me?" agonized Gurth.

"God forbid," said Rebecca.

"Better to have driven a spear through my sleeping carcass," insisted Gurth. "I wish to Christ they had killed me, instead of leaving me to live in shame."

"I thank God you are alive. My father and I could ask for no better guardian."

"When Lady Rowena learns of my disgrace - when Lord Cedric is told of my dereliction of duty -"

"Stop it, Gurth!" said Rebecca. "You have been keeping watch for days. You have committed no sin by succumbing to sleep, or by being attacked while your eyes were shut."

She tried again to get him to sit, to attend to his wounded head. But Gurth wanted none of it: "I don't deserve your healing, my lady," said Gurth. "For these sins, I will never be able to atone." He turned from her, facing the wall in shame.

Rebecca touched him from behind. "Gurth, I need your help," she said. "One of the attackers is still in the house."

"Still in the house," said Gurth, turning to her, his massive hands balling into fists. Rebecca set the guilty man to work.

First, Gurth bound the still-senseless Sir Brian to a chair with enough rope to hang a dozen men. Rebecca was glad that Brian remained unconscious. She feared what Gurth would do had Brian been able to speak. Then Gurth found a pick and shovel, and began digging a single grave for Joseph and Margaret in the stony ground. Rebecca urged him to take a rest, insisted that undue exertion could make his head wound bleed.

"They wouldn't need burying," said Gurth. "Not if I'd done my job."

Isaac joined them outside, fretting over the fading daylight. "That is deep enough," said Isaac, worrying when Brian's knights would return.

"Let Gurth dig a little more, Father," said Rebecca. "Surely, the Lord will grant us the time we need to return them decently to the earth."

"Nothing is 'sure' where the Lord is concerned," said Isaac. "His ways are not only mysterious, but confounding."

He tried to help his daughter wrap the corpses in sheets, but she could see that the work made him breathless, and insisted on his returning inside. "You must rest. Gurth and I will finish here."

Isaac retreated inside, but only long enough to find a scroll of Psalms. By the time he found the passage he was searching, Gurth had lowered the wrapped corpses of the servants into the narrow pit. Gurth wanted no help filling the grave, but Rebecca explained that it was a blessing to participate, even with a single shovelful of earth.

She took the shovel from his hands, and shoveled some of the dug-up ground into the pit. Then her father took the shovel, and followed suit. Breathing hard, Isaac was about to attempt a second shovel-full, but Gurth took back the shovel from his hands, and finished the job swiftly.

Isaac began to read from his scroll, the Hebrew words all too familiar to his daughter. Rebecca translated the Hebrew into English for Gurth. "For strangers are risen up against me, and violent men have sought after my soul. They have not placed God before them."

"They will pay," said Gurth. "I swear before Lord Jesus, Brian's men will pay for their crimes." Gurth rammed a makeshift cross into the mound above the completed grave, and Rebecca placed a hand on his shoulder. "Forgive me, great Christ," said Gurth with passion. "For letting the innocent die."

"The moon is rising," said Isaac. "We must hurry."

"Before we do anything else, Gurth must eat and drink," said Rebecca.

"I require nothing," said Gurth.

"And he must allow me to dress his head wound."

"There is nothing wrong with my head, except that it is thick and stupid," said Gurth.

"Please, Gurth," said Rebecca. But Gurth was in as much of a hurry as Isaac. He had failed in his duties, but he would not fail now. His master Ivanhoe, their benefactor Isaac, and Rebecca must be protected, and Gurth was the only protection they had.

Isaac explained that they must leave before Brian's men would return, too many and too well-armed even for Gurth's anger. "You can pay them back," said Isaac. "But not tonight."

At Isaac's direction, Gurth went inside, lifted the sleeping Ivanhoe from his chair, and carried him to the stable.

"We must tie him to his saddle," said Rebecca. Neither Gurth nor Rebecca noticed that Ivanhoe's eyes were blinking open in the dim light.

As Gurth placed his master onto the back of his warhorse, and began to tie his wrists to the pommel, he continued to berate himself for his failings. "When I was small, bigger boys threw rocks at me," said Gurth. "For their amusement." Securing his master on the saddle, his tone was abject. "For my education, holy monks beat me with wood cudgels. For my discipline, an overlord had his men force me to my knees, so he could more easily slam the handle of his sword into my skull. My brainpan's been slammed by sticks, bricks, iron bars. But not once did it leave me senseless. This was the first and only time."

"No one blames you, Gurth," said Rebecca. "Not even your master will blame you."

But suddenly that master was speaking, softly at first, a low rumble that could not be understood. Then Ivanhoe lifted his head, and spoke more clearly: "Untie me," he said.

Isaac, Rebecca and Gurth stared in wonder at the awakened knight. The young Crusader pulled at his bonds, wildly impatient, and repeated: "Untie me!"

"I did not want you to wake, Sir Knight," said Rebecca gently.

"Why not?" said Ivanhoe suspiciously. "Gurth! What are you waiting for? Do what I say!"

Rebecca explained to him as gently as she could: Ivanhoe had lost a lot of blood. They were fleeing in the dark, along rutted back roads. He was still weak from his tournament wounds. To untie him would be unsafe.

"If I am less strong than usual," said Ivanhoe, "it is because of the potions you have forced down my throat." Before she could answer, he turned back savagely to Gurth. "Free me from your bonds at once."

"You would do well to heed Lady Rebecca," said Gurth.

"You take your orders from me, not from your white witch," said Ivanhoe.

"The white witch saved your life, Master," said Gurth.

"Untie me, slave," said Ivanhoe, "or I'll rip the skin off your back, then chop off your head."

Rebecca gave Gurth a brief, reluctant nod. Gurth, equally reluctant, began to untie Ivanhoe. "When I give an order, you follow it," said Ivanhoe. Pulling his hands free, Ivanhoe sat up straighter, trying to remember where he was, what had happened to him.

"If you would like to eat before we set out, or have something to drink -" began Rebecca.

Ivanhoe interrupted her furiously. "Sir Brian was here, was he not? Or have I lost my mind in this infernal place?"

"It is natural to have difficulty remembering violent events."

"Did I kill him?"

"No," said Rebecca. "But he would have killed me, and my father, if not for your -"

"Why didn't I kill him?" said Ivanhoe. "You stopped me, I suppose. So he could live to maim and slaughter another day."

"You stopped yourself," said Rebecca. "Out of knightly courtesy."

"I do not understand. If he came here, it must have been to kill me," said Ivanhoe.

"He did not come here for you," said Rebecca.

Isaac intervened, explaining that Sir Brian had come to demand the names of all those men who had contributed to Richard Lion-heart's ransom. And to arrest him for treason.

"Treason," said Ivanhoe, letting the word imbue him with violent energy.

"Prince John considers me a traitor for getting Richard's ransom to Austria. Sir Brian pressed his sword to my throat, threatening me with death if I did not tell him what he wanted to know. If not for Rebecca, he would have killed me."

"I only stopped him for a moment, Father," said Rebecca. "If Sir Ivanhoe hadn't come in, all would have been lost."

Suddenly Ivanhoe remembered stumbling into Isaac's study, remembered the look of pain on Brian's face. But the pain had nothing to do with Brian's bloodied scalp. Neither did the lust and longing in the Norman knight's eyes have anything to do with King Richard's ransom.

Turning to Rebecca, Ivanhoe said: "What did Brian want from you?"

Isaac took the question to be meant for himself. "The names of King Richard's supporters," said Isaac. "The place and time of his landing in England. That is why we must hurry, and get away before Brian's men return."

Ivanhoe slowly turned his attention from Rebecca to Isaac. "What did you tell him?" said the knight,

"Nothing," said Isaac. "I would gladly die before betraying my king."

Ivanhoe addressed Gurth. "My sword," he said.

"It is heavy, my lord," said Gurth. "Carefully stored on a packhorse."

"Fool! I am not engaging in idle conversation. My sword and my belt. Bring them."

Even in the stable's dim lantern light, Rebecca could see awareness and determination growing in the knight's eyes. Bending from the saddle, he grabbed his sword belt from Gurth and strapped it on. "Isaac," he said. "Please approach."

Isaac stepped toward the mounted knight. Ivanhoe drew his heavy sword.

"What are you doing?" said Rebecca, fearing for Isaac's safety with the volatile young man. "My father will never reveal what he knows."

"Closer, my lord," said Ivanhoe, his fierce tone directed at Rebecca's interference.

"No, Father!" said Rebecca, afraid the knight might have decided to kill the man who knew too many secrets. "Do not listen to him!"

But Isaac ignored her warning, coming directly up to where Ivanhoe now leant over the saddle, sword in hand.

"Your daughter does not trust me," said Ivanhoe. Suddenly, with a flourish, Ivanhoe slipped his hand from hilt to blade, extending the hilt to Isaac. "Take it, sir." For a moment, Isaac didn't understand. "Your hand on the hilt, my lord," said Ivanhoe. "For a pledge."

Isaac placed one hand on the sword hilt. "I will die before letting any harm come to you," said Ivanhoe. "To you or to any supporter of my king."

"My daughter Rebecca," said Isaac, raising his eyes to the mounted knight's. "My daughter must be a part any such pledge."

"That is not necessary, my lord. As your daughter, she is vouchsafed by any pledge given to her father."

"Rebecca will outlive me, and must be given safeguards that will continue after my death."

"Once you are gone, I care nothing for what will happen to me," said Rebecca.

"Come here, Daughter," said Isaac. Ivanhoe watched Rebecca's reluctant approach.

"You understand what this hilt signifies, Father? A cross. You are pledging on a Christian's cross."

"Silence," said Isaac. "You will respect the custom of King Richard's loyal knight." Rebecca looked from Ivanhoe to her father, then placed one hand over her father's on the sword hilt.

Isaac raised his eyes to Ivanhoe. "Go ahead, Sir Ivanhoe. We are ready."

"What about Gurth?" said Rebecca. "Shouldn't he
be a part of any such pledge?"

"I do not deserve -" began Gurth.

"Gurth is my squire," interrupted Ivanhoe. "What
I am sworn, he is sworn. I do not need his sweaty paw
on my hand to know that he will die for you."

Ivanhoe placed his hand over Rebecca's on the
hilt. His hand was warm, so warm that she feared he
was still feverish. On the contrary, he found her
hand cold as ice. He found himself staring at her,
struck by the intense color of her green and gold
eyes. An unnatural color, he thought. An alien
beauty, foreign to his world. No wonder she is a
maker of potions, a caster of spells.

Suddenly Gurth's enormous hand was placed over
Ivanhoe's. "Forgive me, Master," said Gurth. "But
Lady Rebecca wants it this way."

Ivanhoe held back from berating his squire. It
was almost amusing to see the way the big man doted on
the enigmatic beauty. "All right, Isaac," said
Ivanhoe. "As she is your daughter, I swear before
Christ and King, that I will die before letting anyone
harm the Lady Rebecca."

"And so do I," said Gurth, with furious intent.

The Jewish father and daughter withdrew their hands, and the Christian knight returned his sword to its scabbard.

"Thank you, Gurth," said Rebecca. "I feel much safer now."

Before Ivanhoe could let her thanks for the squire – and not the knight -- vex him, Isaac interjected: "Let us leave quickly, before Sir Brian's men return," he said.

"Indeed," said Ivanhoe. "Your daughter has delicate feelings. She would not like to see what I will do to Brian the next time we meet."

Gurth helped Isaac mount, while Rebecca got on her horse unaided. She addressed Ivanhoe with care. "Do you think you could accompany us part of the way, Sir Knight?"

"'Part of the way?'" said Ivanhoe, not comprehending.

"Lady Rowena gave me orders, Master," said Gurth. "I must guard not only you, but Lady Rebecca as well."

"Silence!" said Ivanhoe. "I am your master, and you will guard whoever I tell you to guard."

"It should not be very far," said Rebecca, as if she were beseeching a favor. "We are only going to the coast. I must find some means of passage for my father to leave the country."

"Nonsense," said Isaac, who heard every word. "I will not leave England until Richard has returned, and taken his rightful place on the throne."

"I will not take you 'part of the way,'" said Ivanhoe crossly. "Did you not hear my pledge? I have vouchsafed your lives. Until you are both safe and secure, I will not leave your side."

Rebecca ignored Ivanhoe's reassuring words, turning instead to her father: "If not to find a ship to leave this country of Jew-haters, where are we supposed to go? Hounded by Prince John, chased by Sir Brian, without a single friend in the countryside?" She turned back to Ivanhoe's handsome face. "With or without this Crusader's great promises."

For a moment, Ivanhoe realized he had no destination in mind. King Richard was far from home. Prince John's knights ruled the countryside, and they would do anything to press Isaac for his gold and his secrets. As for Isaac's daughter, he feared her beauty would leave her wanted for much worse.

But Isaac had done a great service for his king, and loyal men would honor that service. Even Ivanhoe's own estranged father.

"I will accompany you to Lord Cedric's seat," said Ivanhoe. "Lord Cedric will be your friend, you may depend on it. We go to Rotherwood."

CHAPTER FIFTEEN

In an hour they were en route on a narrow,
twisting track, lit by a half moon. The track was
shadowed by ancient trees, living and dead. A few of
the trees were cracked and hollow, beginning their
reclamation by nature's eternal power. Golden light
transformed branches into ominous, fantastical shapes.

Ivanhoe arranged the single file: Gurth in
front, on Ivanhoe's old stallion, followed by a
packhorse laden with weapons. Next was Isaac, on his
careful-stepping palfrey, followed by Rebecca on the
gentlest mare in England. Ivanhoe, mounted on the
enormous warhorse he'd ridden at the tournament, rode
directly behind her, trailed by the second packhorse.
For a few minutes, no one spoke.

But soon, he could hear the beauty speaking to
Isaac, not even bothering to whisper. Ivanhoe could
make no sense of the Hebrew words. "I would like you
to drink some barley water," Rebecca was saying, and
not for the first time. Her father was weak, but paid
little attention to her worries. "You need not
dismount. I will come alongside, bring the goatskin
to your lips."

"There is no room for you to come alongside," said Isaac, carefully turning around to face her.

"Then we will halt. I will dismount, and bring you –"

"I am not thirsty, Daughter," said Isaac, abruptly turning away, looking forward into the dark.

Behind his back, Rebecca's words rang loud and accusatory: "There are men who can die from lack of water, without once feeling thirst. As there are men who can die from treachery, without once feeling threatened."

"You have a poetic temperament, my dear," said Isaac. "Forever making allusions."

"I am far from poetic," said Rebecca. "Poets deal with fantasies and emotions. I deal with real events and logic. We should head for the shore, to begin our voyage to civilized Spain… instead of seeking refuge from an unlettered Saxon warlord who owes you money."

"My lady!" called out Ivanhoe sharply. Rebecca slowed, but did not turn round. Perhaps, he thought, she didn't like his annoyed tone. But how could he not be annoyed? Did she not understand the peril of dark woods? He spoke again, attempting a more cordial tone: "It would be wiser," he said, "to refrain from talking."

Rebecca turned around in her saddle, and looked at him with deliberation. There wasn't enough light for him to see the mischief in her eyes. "I'm sorry, Sir Ivanhoe," she said. "I didn't realize the dark made you nervous."

"Nothing and no one makes me nervous!" snapped Ivanhoe, leaving cordiality behind. "Do you not realize that the countryside is lawless?"

"Not just the countryside. Your entire country." She said it like an accusation; as if he and murderous brigands were of common mind.

"The perilous state of the country is why I have pledged my life to protect you and your father."

"But Sir Knight, we have Gurth with us. His mien is particularly savage. Simply the sight of his shoulders and forearms will be enough to scare any brigands into submission."

"Gurth is a thick-headed serf! And you -- you are a willful, rebellious female!"

"I object, Sir Knight," said Rebecca. "Gurth is your squire, not a serf. As to 'thick-headed' - that is an advantage, when riding through so dangerous a neighborhood. As to 'willful and rebellious' - thank you for the compliment."

"'Willful and rebellious' may sometimes be an asset," said Ivanhoe. "But what I said was 'willful and rebellious <u>female</u>.'

"I understand better now, Sir Knight. What you object to is my sex. In future, I shall try and conceal it from you."

"If your girlish chattering attracts marauders from the dark, you will have only yourself to blame."

"There it is again: Your fear of dark places," she said.

"For the last time, I am not afraid of the dark!"

"I hope not, Sir Ivanhoe, as I expect you are a God-fearing man." Rebecca paused, enjoying her teasing. She explained, like a teacher to a dense pupil: "To the Master of the Universe, darkness and light are the same."

"Quiet, woman!" said Ivanhoe. "No more clever talk, not till we are out of this dark place."

She turned away before he could see that she was grinning broadly, enjoying her triumph at his show of temper.

Isaac could sense that she was preparing another sharp rebuke. "Daughter, stop," said Isaac quietly, in Hebrew. "Another word, and you will make our poor guardian fall off his horse."

"That was not my intention, Father," said Rebecca, in the same language. "As a matter of fact, the entire reason for my talking has been in hopes of keeping him awake."

"You deliberately incense the man who has twice saved our lives," said Isaac in a grave whisper. "You would be wise to ask yourself 'Why'?"

Rebecca was silenced by her father's words, words that were less a question than a statement. Isaac made sure to clarify: "You are acting imprudently. You are displaying ingratitude. And if you thought about your behavior to this young man, you might understand something profoundly troubling."

Rebecca kept her eyes on Isaac's back, as they continued along the path that felt like a tunnel into a land of dreams. She did think about her behavior, and was on the verge of telling her father that it was simple to explain. It was the Crusader who was ungrateful, who repaid her gift of healing with sharp words. Naturally she must pay him back in kind.

But she knew that Isaac wouldn't have believed this for a moment, so she kept her thoughts to herself

Ivanhoe was gratified that father and daughter had stopped talking. Clouds drifted across the half moon, enveloping them in near darkness. The silence seemed to grow, punctuated only by the cries of night birds, the muffled clatter of weapons on the slow-moving horses, the sounds of scurrying animals in the forest green. He hoped Isaac had reprimanded his daughter for unmaidenly insolence.

Perhaps she would no longer be eager to mock his every word, and might even learn to appreciate what he was doing for her. How could she not understand the worth of a knight's pledge?

Even in silence he found her maddening. Ivanhoe determined to direct his wandering thoughts away from her. Certainly, Rebecca was beautiful, that was impossible to deny. But Rowena was a great beauty as well, and she loved him, and he loved her. He must think of Rowena and not Rebecca.

Rowena would be filled with joy to see him appear in Rotherwood, even accompanied by fugitives from Prince John's false justice. There would be no irony in her eyes, no condescension. Rowena was as simple as he was himself, and their love was straightforward and true. Seeing Rowena, his first and only love, his betrothed, his romantic partner since childhood, and holding her close; that had been a second homecoming, a true welcome back from the Crusade.

Even if that homecoming had been upset by the appearance of Brian de Bois Gilbert.

But upset even more by the appearance of the too-proud, condescending Jewess. Like a stone thrown into still waters.

Ivanhoe forced himself to turn from useless thoughts of Rebecca, to more practical matters: Safeguarding Isaac and his daughter, according to his sacred pledge.

Lord Cedric would not deny Isaac and Rebecca admission to Rotherwood and protection behind its walls. Isaac was loyal to King Richard, and one of the King's greatest benefactors. But would Ivanhoe be allowed to join them? He knew that his father had been proud of his feats at the tournament, that he had been concerned at the wounds he had suffered. But Cedric had never formally forgiven him for defying his order not to join Richard's Crusade.

Now that Ivanhoe was recovering, there was every reason to believe that Cedric would continue to disown him, continue to forbade him entry to what had been his childhood home.

Soon Ivanhoe found his heavy eyelids lowering. What did it matter if he slept? His warhorse's footing was sure, and Gurth knew the way to Rotherwood better than himself. Any disturbance would wake him at once. It would be better for Ivanhoe to rest while he could, even if it was Rebecca who had told him so. Ivanhoe would need all his strength when they had achieved their destination, and would again be face to face with his father.

The lingering effect of Rebecca's potion made it possible for him to fall asleep in his saddle for moments, then wake suddenly, then sleep again. The time passed in flashes of dreams, followed by brief moments of awareness. The dreams were heady with memories of Rowena the night of his return to Rotherwood.

When his father had banished him in front of the company in the great hall, Rowena had followed him to his chamber. Her urgent embrace, the rush of mutual feelings had almost made him forget the moral code they lived by. He had moved his hand from her face to her breast, had pushed her against the wall near his bed, had pressed his body against hers as if he was back in Jerusalem and she was an Arab whore.

Then he had stepped back, ashamed of his lust. "I'm sorry," he had said. "Forgive me."

"I have nothing to forgive you for," Rowena had said.

"I have lived too long with horror and shame. And now I offend your honor."

Rowena had seemed to ignore his words. Indeed, she had taken his hands, was pulling him close again, until she felt his body resist. He had tried to explain: "Our Crusade was just, but you cannot imagine the terrible crimes —"

"The war is over," Rowena had said. "We should have done this years ago. It might have kept you home."

"No," he had said. "Nothing would have kept me from my duty to my king. And nothing will keep me from my duty to you." It was only then that Rowena had let him go. In a gentler voice, he insisted: "I long for the day when we will be married. As God is my witness, I vow that we will be married as soon as Richard takes back his throne."

Remembering that night, how he had held back his wild desire, his heart raced. Now, on horseback, following the Jewess, the blood pounding in his ears brought to mind something entirely different: The clamor of battle, the flashing of swords, screams of triumph and pain.

He had flashes of fighting the Saracens at King Richard's right hand, the King impossibly confident, braver and bolder than anyone, inspiring a kind of madness in Ivanhoe. A joyful madness.

Waking from a fleeting dream, Ivanhoe felt himself smiling. Fighting alongside his king had left him hot, almost feverish with joy. A familiar joy, he suddenly realized. That same kind of fever seemed to be with him when he had opened his eyes to the sight of Rebecca hovering above his sickbed. Looking down at him with her enormous, preternatural eyes, speaking words he couldn't hear, not knowing where he was, whether alive or dead, or inhabiting a dream.

Then the joy had vanished.

He had understood that he was in his bed, that the Jewess was looking after him, caring for him, and that he was angry. He did not want to be helpless, immobile, in this beautiful witch's power.

The young woman riding before him sat easily in the saddle, close behind her father. His warhorse snorted, eager to quit this walking pace, to charge forward. Ivanhoe calmed the great horse. The slow pace eased his wild thoughts.

After a while, he could tell himself that he couldn't remember what Rebecca looked like, couldn't conjure the elegant hands, the haughty posture, the astonishing loveliness of her face.

But suddenly the young woman on the gentle mare ran one hand through the thick waves of her hair, and a shock ran through him. Ivanhoe had to admit that he remembered everything about her physical presence. The dark hair framing pale skin, the luminous eyes, the full, unsmiling lips.

What was it that Brian had said? "A demon… She will bewitch you."

Ivanhoe deliberately shut his eyes to Rebecca's back. Yet even with his eyes closed, his other senses were alive: The touch of the reins, the sounds of the journey, the smells of the forest, the strange taste of fear in his mouth. This fear did not come from dreams, but from something else, something alive in the real world.

But of what could he be possibly afraid? Even if Brian's men had returned to Ashby and freed their master, they would never be able to find four travelers on this dark, back road. Even if some magic circumstances could lead Brian to cross paths with him this night, Ivanhoe could not confess to being in the least fearful. He could only die once.

He had been bred from childhood to prefer death to dishonor, trained to relish great deeds. Besides, for all his martial prowess, Brian was an underling of a usurper, while Ivanhoe was on the side of the rightful king. When he fought, Ivanhoe knew, he fought with the aid of Providence.

So the fear in his mouth had a different origin than Sir Brian and his men. Perhaps it had something to do with the magical potions given him by the Jewess. A witch's brew that had dire consequences.

But he hadn't asked for her potions. He hadn't asked for her help. Who could prove that he had needed her help to heal from his wounds? Ivanhoe forced himself to sit up taller, eyes suddenly opening, banishing all dreams, no longer drifting in his thoughts.

The half-moon had emerged from its cover of clouds, lending shifting patterns of light to play with the helmet of Rebecca's black hair. Looking at her, the taste of fear in his mouth grew sharper. She must be the cause of these feelings, he thought, increasingly angry.

He allowed his great horse to move into a faster walk, pulling alongside Rebecca, dwarfing her nervous mare. Inadvertently, his foot brushed her knee through its cover of silk.

As usual, his tone was harsher than he had intended. "Make way, my lady," he said. "Make way!" He sounded as if he loathed the very sight of her.

Rebecca pulled her mare sharply to one side, practically into the brush, allowing Ivanhoe to pass her on the narrow track. In spite of her healing skills, her empathy, her experience in spiritual matters, the fact of his fear was completely hidden to her. Watching him disappear along the twisting path, the only fear she recognized was her own.

It was all she could to do to restrain herself from calling out, to beg him to stand still, as if he was the only thing standing between herself and some unstoppable danger. Isaac's palfrey, startled by the warhorse's too swift approach, nearly bolted. Rebecca could hear the knight ask her father's pardon, as he passed Isaac in a rush. She couldn't hear what Ivanhoe said to Gurth, but a few moments later, Gurth took up the rear position in Ivanhoe's place.

"There is nothing to worry about," said Gurth. "It is just that my master prefers to lead."

Her heart was pounding, as if a stab of terror, suddenly begun, was increasing moment by moment. She searched her memory for a line from Proverbs, and finally recalled: "Be not afraid of sudden fear."

Perhaps this meant that a carefully thought-out fear was more sensible, more worthy of attention. But fear that started up all at once was different -- illogical, irrational, able to be discounted.

However quickly it might have begun, this fear had taken hold of her and wouldn't let go. A fear not of the dark, not of the sounds of unseen beasts, but of something else. Something nameless, something unfathomable. Not of the handsome young knight she had nursed back to life, certainly not. Why should she fear her sworn protector?

In a few minutes, the path widened enough to allow her to pull alongside Isaac. He could sense how troubled she had become. "There is nothing to worry us, Daughter," he said. Isaac quoted Psalms: "'He makes the darkness, and it is night. All the beasts of the forest creep forth.' But the darkness is the Lord's. As is every beast in the forest."

"Beasts do not worry me," said Rebecca. "And I fear the light as much as the dark. I will fear everything until we are gone from this cursed island, and safe in a far country."

"The Mishneh says that the world is sustained by three things: Truth, justice and peace."

"Why do you tell me this, Father?"

"Because, my dear, you are the light of my life. And you are not being truthful to yourself or to me. We are in England, where Richard is the lawful king, and Ivanhoe his trusted knight. You must long for justice and peace."

"Justice for Gentiles? Peace for Englishmen? Why should I care what happens to any of these murderers?"

"It is not your responsibility to repair the world, but neither are you allowed to prevent such work."

"You promised we would go to Zaragoza."

"You know well that promise will be fulfilled only when King Richard has returned, and returned to just rule."

"'Just rule,'" she echoed, her tone bitter and mocking.

Isaac took hold of her hand, and she turned to meet his loving eyes. "You must examine your heart. When you understand the nature of your fear, you will be able to vanquish it."

"'The nature of my fear!'" said Rebecca. "I understand my fear all too well. I am riding into hell with a Christian who hates the sight of me."

"Only part of that thought is true, Daughter. You are indeed riding into hell. When you are truthful with yourself, you will know enough to turn away from such a hopeless journey."

"Apparently, Father, I am not the only one of us who talks in allusions. Why not tell me what you mean?"

Isaac reined in his still skittish palfrey, and his daughter followed suit. He was silent for a moment, ignoring the fact that Ivanhoe was pulling ahead, and that Gurth was crowding them from behind.

Finally, Isaac spoke. "Ivanhoe is uneducated and a Gentile, but he is brave and handsome."

"I haven't noticed that he's handsome," said Rebecca.

"Daughter, listen. The young man knows nothing of our people, and can never become one of us."

"I do not understand why you're telling me any of this," said Rebecca, her heart beating wildly.

"Rebecca," said Isaac, trying to interrupt.

But she would not be stopped. "If you mean to suggest that I have feelings for him other than gratitude for his service to us, you are wrong. In point of fact, I like his squire Gurth much more than —"

Ivanhoe wheeled around on the narrow track, and was riding directly at them. The track was growing wider, revealing the first glimmers of dawn. But still there was little room for the great warhorse bearing down up upon them. Isaac and Rebecca pulled to either side of the track.

"Warriors," Ivanhoe said, reining in the excited warhorse, so that he could address both father and daughter from his greater height. "Attacking a closed wagon with Saxon markings. I can see two outriders already struck down."

"Your father's wagon has Saxon markings," said Isaac.

"Gurth," said Ivanhoe, calling over the heads of Isaac and Rebecca. "My chain mail."

"How many warriors?" said Rebecca.

"My spurs," said Ivanhoe, continuing to Gurth. Gurth slipped from his mount, and began to pull mail from the packhorse.

"A lance," said Ivanhoe.

"How many warriors do you intend to ride against, Sir Knight?" said Rebecca.

"All of them," said Ivanhoe.

"How many?" she insisted. Gurth was already rushing forward, attaching Ivanhoe's spurs to the knight's soft boots.

"About a dozen," said Ivanhoe. He took the chain mail vest from Gurth, and slipped it over his tunic. "More than enough to slaughter two unarmed attendants on horseback, and capture a defenseless wagon." Gurth held out the chain mail meant to cover his master's thighs, but Ivanhoe waved them away.

"What about sleeves and gloves, Master?"

Ivanhoe was looking at Rebecca as he answered his squire. "This is not a tournament, Gurth. Just a little skirmish, quick and easy."

"What do I fight with, Master?" said Gurth

Ivanhoe told Gurth to stay behind, not to enter the battle, but have lances and battle axes ready for use.

"A dozen men?" said Rebecca. "Why must you fight a battle that cannot be won?"

"Surely a woman as versed in holy matters as yourself understands that it is not up to me where and when I fight," said Ivanhoe. "It is up to the Lord." His eyes remained on Gurth, helping to straighten his mail coat, and tighten the golden spurs.

"You can't even be certain that the wagon conveys your father and your betrothed," said Rebecca.

"It is enough that the wagon bears Saxon markings, and is under attack," said Ivanhoe, finally turning to look down at her directly. "Even your 'Master of the Universe' couldn't send a clearer sign of my obligations."

As Ivanhoe clapped on his helmet, Rebecca looked up and met his eyes.

Their fear was suddenly revealed to each at the same moment. A fear that had nothing to do with the coming battle. A fear of a growing, irresistible passion.

A mutual passion that must always be forbidden, must never be fulfilled.

CHAPTER SIXTEEN

The track through the forest ended on a rise of land between great boulders. It was as if a giant had set the stones to mark the way out of the woods. From here, Rebecca could see for miles, could take in what Ivanhoe had spotted moments before: A party of warriors, chain mail glistening, surrounded a wagon with Saxon markings. That the distance made them tiny in perspective, their features indistinct, did not lessen Rebecca's worries.

Two men were sprawled on the ground, limbs at crazy angles, perfectly still. Their abandoned horses stood nearby, as if hoping their masters might come back to life. Surely these men had guarded the closed wagon, and had been murdered for their pains.

An attacker's horse was tethered to the back of the wagon, with its rider now taking his place on the bench next to what appeared to be another corpse. As the warrior pushed the corpse onto the ground, Rebecca's fear grew. She marveled at Ivanhoe's slow, leisurely pace to meet the enemy. A pace that was nonetheless relentless, that would not be stopped.

Ivanhoe's estimate of a dozen warriors was clearly wrong; there were at least twenty he would have to face. Even if he were not still recuperating from his wounds, what could he hope from so unmatched a fight?

With only Gurth alongside, who rode Ivanhoe's feisty old stallion, and led a plodding packhorse, Ivanhoe continued to walk his charger down toward the cliffs. No one from the large war party had yet noticed his approach, but in a minute or less they would be certain to see him.

Rebecca and Isaac were on foot, hidden from view by dense foliage. Rebecca held the reins of the second packhorse, while Isaac quieted the nervous mare and palfrey. "What does he intend, Father?" said Rebecca. She spoke in an urgent whisper, though there was no way her voice could be heard by the men so far below. "What can his plan possibly be?"

"He has no plan," said Isaac. "He rides forward on faith alone."

"What 'faith'? What does faith have to do with it? Does he expect his God to swallow up his enemies on his behalf?"

Ivanhoe was a quarter of the way to the armored knights now, still walking his horse, his approach less cautious than casual. As if he couldn't be bothered to hurry. As if he had no need to surprise.

"He is a knight, Daughter. He has faith in his ability to follow the dictates of his order. Those dictates are clear. He must always fight against evil, no matter how overwhelming the odds."

"It is foolhardy to risk one's life without a plan." Rebecca turned to her father, insisting: "His death will serve no purpose."

"Perhaps the Master of the Universe is not prepared to let him die," said Isaac. "Look."

Rebecca turned, amazed to see that the bulk of the war party was on the move, fifteen men or more, leaving the scene before noticing Ivanhoe's approach. The horsemen rode fast, disappearing into the rising sun. Besides the warrior at the reins of the wagon, only five mounted attackers remained nearby, not one of them aware that they were being approached by a single knight and his redheaded squire.

"He is still incapable of fighting so many at once. Six men or sixty, what difference does it make?"

"A great difference," said Isaac.

Father and daughter held their breaths as Ivanhoe reined in his eager warhorse, and waited for Gurth to ride alongside. Ivanhoe looked below, where the warriors' chain mail reflected the growing light of dawn.

Light reflected off the white cliffs too, cliffs that overlooked a dark blue sea and a white ribbon of sand. Rebecca knew that much farther along this coast were wider beaches, where fishermen set off in tiny boats, and where larger ships battled their way to Normandy.

More than a hundred years ago, Normans had made their way to English shores, braving the wild currents with boats overladen with armor, weapons, and horses. That had been the beginning of the end of the Saxon domination of Britain, with Norman knights usurping not only the kingship, but the lands and serfs of Saxon noblemen as well. Only a few, like Ivanhoe's father, Lord Cedric, survived with their property and dignity intact.

Suddenly, following a command Rebecca couldn't hear, Gurth pulled a lance from the packhorse and handed it to Ivanhoe. Instantly, the knight began to ride forward, at a faster pace than before. He didn't see Gurth pull a battle axe from the packhorse's store of weapons and heft it in his powerful hand.

Dropping the packhorse's lead, Gurth, helmetless and without chain mail, rode after his master.

Ivanhoe spurred the warhorse and began to gallop down the slight incline, eating up the distance with horrifying speed. Rebecca imagined his confident grin.

The warrior sitting on the wagon bench suddenly turned, looking toward the fast approaching knight in amazement. He stood, shouting a warning she couldn't hear.

But the small figures of the five remaining horsemen obviously could hear the alarm. They turned about in wild disarray. Perhaps, thought Rebecca, the sight of a single knight and one burly squire, was less frightening than confounding. Where was the rest of this knight's party? Why was a single warrior charging toward the middle of their line? Was it possible that this lone man meant to attack all five of them?

Preparing to face Ivanhoe, the five armored Normans slowly and coolly formed into a formidable row.

"Dear God, Master of the Heavens and the Earth," began Rebecca, as she watched three warriors draw swords, one a mace, another a lance.

Behind her, Isaac completed the prayer, not in Hebrew, but in the language of the country: "Watch over the valiant knight, our friend Ivanhoe, son of Cedric, who ventures forth against evil."

Ivanhoe suddenly turned his warhorse sharply left, pointing his lance at a warrior at one end of the line. Then the Crusader let his raring warhorse go.

The Norman raised his shield, but not fast or high enough. Galloping at fantastic speed, Ivanhoe's lance tore through the man's neck, lifting him off his saddle and onto the ground.

Reining in the powerful stallion, already fifty yards past the confrontation, he heard Gurth's voice right behind him: "Master, look to the wagon."

Ivanhoe turned to see that the sixth Norman had jumped down from the wagon, and was beginning to mount his horse. And that Gurth, no longer leading the packhorse, was a few yards away. "You are too close to the fight. Stay with the packhorse," said Ivanhoe.

"I had better help you here, Master."

"Obey my command!" said Ivanhoe, turning around and drawing his sword, facing the attacker who had jumped down from the wagon. But suddenly Ivanhoe held back his charge, shocked.

Two figures from the wagon were clambering onto riderless horses: Cedric and Rowena.

The Norman from the wagon had mounted his horse, raised his battle axe, and turned to face Cedric. Rowena pulled up alongside, but Cedric held her back protectively; then drew his broadsword.

Ivanhoe prepared to charge, when Gurth grabbed the warhorse's reins. "No, Master," he said, indicating where the four other mounted attackers, riding shoulder to shoulder, were about to intercept his path, preventing Ivanhoe from riding to Cedric's aid.

"Let go," said Ivanhoe, pulling the reins from Gurth, and charging forward. The four mounted attackers closed their line, raising their shields. Ivanhoe slammed his sword into the center of the shields, and was immediately surrounded, forced to counter blows with his sword and shield from every side.

Skilled as he was, and ferocious, Ivanhoe could not withstand the simultaneous blows of four armored men. His shield was ripped from his hand. Standing up on his stirrups, flailing with his sword, a chance blow of a mace slammed the sword out of his hand. The warhorse reared, as if fearing his master's imminent demise.

But as the Normans moved in for the kill, from behind their tight circle a powerful young man swung a heavy axe, screaming maniacally. The blow cleaved helmet and skull of one of the warriors, creating a breach for Ivanhoe to ride through.

Freed, Ivanhoe's warhorse galloped wildly across the field. By the time Ivanhoe had reined in and turned round, he could see Gurth pulling his battle axe free of a dead Norman's head with one hand. Gurth's other hand held Ivanhoe's dropped sword. He grinned at his master, and began to ride toward him, not deigning to look at the three mounted Normans behind his back.

From the cover of trees, Rebecca began to mount her mare. "What are you doing, Daughter?" said Isaac, though her intention was obvious.

"There will be wounded," she said.

Isaac hesitated for only a moment. "Of course," he said, laboriously getting up on his palfrey.

"There is no need for you to come, Father," said Rebecca. But she said nothing further as her father followed her out of the sheltering woods, and down toward the battle site.

CHAPTER SEVENTEEN

One of the mounted Normans had pulled a horn from his belt, and blew three sharp blasts.

Ivanhoe looked wildly from him to Gurth to Cedric and Rowena. The armored warriors were forming another line, again preventing Ivanhoe from going to Cedric's aid. "My sword!" shouted Ivanhoe to the approaching Gurth, who had just saved his life. "Hurry."

The Norman who had been on the wagon bench turned his warhorse to face Cedric, surprised to see that the old Saxon seemed unafraid of fighting a man two generations younger.

Cedric charged, either oblivious to the man's raised axe, or unafraid of what it might do. Extending his broadsword like a lance, Cedric galloped directly at the young warrior. The Norman turned his horse sharply away, crossing the path of Rowena's stallion. The frightened horse reared, and though Rowena kept her seat, it galloped away, out of control.

Out of the corner of his eye, Cedric saw his ward disappear along the edge of the cliff, where the ground was littered with irregular stones.

Rowena's horse lost its footing, struggled mightily -- and slipped over the edge!

Cedric could only see part of Rowena's disastrous fall: Horse and rider sliding wildly down the steep incline from the top of the cliff toward the narrow beach below. Urging his horse to the edge of the cliff, Cedric could see that Rowena had been thrown from her horse, and now lay on the strip of sand, perfectly still.

Gurth, holding out Ivanhoe's sword, kept an eye on the Normans, again forming a line of defense. "If I attack, Master, you will have a direct path to your father."

"Get the packhorse," said Ivanhoe. "I will need more weapons." Ivanhoe grabbed his sword, turning his warhorse in a wild circle, trying to decide how to break through the knot of men separating him from Cedric.

But Cedric was not waiting to be saved. He would attend to Rowena, but first he must attend to the Norman dog who had driven her off a cliff. Shouting an ancient war cry, raising his sword high, his body alive with hatred, Cedric charged into the Norman.

At the moment before collision, Cedric leaned suddenly forward in a move he had performed in a score of old battles, extending his right arm in a straight line. His blade ripped through the young Norman's shoulder.

Ivanhoe, not seeing any other way, charged directly into the mace-wielding warrior at the center of the line of three knights. All three Normans converged on Ivanhoe, and the mace slammed Ivanhoe's blade out of his hand. For a moment it seemed as if the maddened Crusader would throw himself at his attackers with only his fists -- but instead turned his nimble warhorse about, galloping free to where Gurth waited for him, battle axe held high.

"I told you to get the packhorse," said Ivanhoe.

As if in answer to the rebuke, the plodding packhorse drifted back alongside Gurth. "Better take this," said Gurth.

Ivanhoe looked to where the Norman wounded by Cedric struggled to stay on horseback, then back to the other three horsemen. "Get me a lance," said Ivanhoe. But his new squire ignored the packhorse, and continued to extend the battle axe.

"Take the axe, Master. Help your father."

Ivanhoe turned wildly to find Cedric on the field, still facing a wounded horseman. Gurth meanwhile pulled free a lance from the packhorse - for his own use.

As Ivanhoe looked for a way to Cedric, still blocked by two mounted Normans, he didn't see the third attacker, charging at him from the back, a sharp, studded mace swinging toward his head. But Gurth saw, hefting the lance, its weight much lighter than the axe.

Then Gurth drove the old stallion into a wild charge. He bent forward, trying to imitate his master's form. Howling, he ripped his lance through the mace-wielder's chest armor as if it were made of butter. Man and mace fell to the bloody ground, Gurth's lance vibrating like a newly planted flagpole.

"Thank you," said Ivanhoe. "But when I say 'lance,' that means get it for me, not you."

"Of course, Master."

From a great distance, three blasts of a warrior's horn sounded, the answer to the attacker's summons. Master and squire knew well the distant horn meant help would be coming for the Normans, and soon.

Ivanhoe wheeled about, raising the battle axe at the two horsemen across the field. "They stand in my way. I will attend to them, while you remain with the packhorse," said Ivanhoe.

"No, Master. You must help your father," said Gurth. Gurth did nothing to hide the fact that he was now drawing a mace for his own use from the packhorse. "I will attend to these. Only two of them."

"You are more churl than squire!" said Ivanhoe.

"Your father," insisted Gurth, as Ivanhoe noticed what Gurth had already seen: The wounded axe-wielding Norman was resuming his fight with Cedric.

Mace in hand, Gurth charged the two Normans, who had never been attacked by a man without helmet or mail or any kind of knightly finesse. But they had seen the enormous redhead cut down their armored fellows like a monster from a fairy tale. Now Gurth's great bulk and ferocious war cry gave the two knights reason enough to ride away from his swinging mace.

His path free, Ivanhoe bore down on Cedric's antagonist, shouting, giving the Norman ample warning to turn. But the Norman turned only to see Ivanhoe drive his battle axe directly into his neck. Then he couldn't see anything at all.

Cedric didn't pause for thanks or congratulations. "Rowena," said Cedric, breathless. "She is hurt."

Ivanhoe followed his father's gaze, looking below to where Rowena lay motionless on the beach. "Wait," said Cedric, afraid that his headstrong son was about to ride off the edge of the cliff. "First we have men to kill."

Ivanhoe turned from the edge of the cliff, following his father's gaze to where the two remaining horsemen were being chased by a single huge man with a mace. "Who is that knight?" said Cedric. "And why doesn't he wear armor?"

"That man is not a knight," said Ivanhoe, raising his bloody axe, and charging toward the melee, his father riding alongside. They drew close enough to see the big man smash his mace into a Norman's shield with enough force to send both shield and man to the ground. Chasing after the last mounted man, the enormous warrior turned, revealing his face to Lord Cedric.

"Gurth?" said Cedric, astounded, and none too pleased.

Meanwhile, the Norman on the ground had gotten to his feet and drawn his sword, and was about to hack into Cedric's thigh, when Gurth returned, riding fast. Leaning from his saddle, Gurth swung his mace into the warrior's helmet, cracking through metal and bone.

"Excuse me, my lord," said Gurth. "I thought perhaps you didn't notice him."

At the same moment, the second mounted Norman met Ivanhoe, who blocked Ivanhoe's swinging axe with his shield, and thrust at him with his sword. Twisting his torso away from the blade point, Ivanhoe urged his warhorse forward, then into a desperate turn. Swinging his axe with all his strength, Ivanhoe severed the warrior's arm, leaving him clinging to his horse's neck with his remaining arm, screaming in pain.

"Give me that mace, churl," said Lord Cedric to Gurth.

"Certainly, my lord," said Gurth. He handed the much bloodied club to his master's father, and immediately wheeled about, riding across the field. Finding the warrior he had felled with a lance to his chest, Gurth bent low, and ripped the lance from the body.

"Why do you let a serf fight like a knight?" said Cedric to Ivanhoe. Before he could answer, father and son could hear the distant horn blow again. The sound was louder, the horn blasts seeming to drift up from the sea below. Looking in every direction for the source of the sound, Ivanhoe caught sight of something inexplicable: Rebecca, escaped from the safety of the woods, was riding directly toward the edge of the cliff.

Instantly, the sounds of struggle seemed to fade. Ivanhoe's ears strained to hear something past the silence. His head grew light. Rebecca was going off the cliff. The knight was dizzy with that same impossible fear, a confounding anger that stopped up all action.

Until Gurth shouted a warning.

Somehow the hideously wounded one-armed man had drawn his sword, and was raising it at Ivanhoe. Ivanhoe turned from watching Rebecca disappear over the cliff to where Gurth rode at the Norman from behind, driving his lance down and through the man's back. Gurth had again saved his master's life, but Ivanhoe didn't thank him.

"What is she doing?" demanded Ivanhoe.

Gurth, who hadn't seen Rebecca, now turned to watch. Rebecca had gotten off her mare, and was hurrying down the treacherously steep slope to the beach. Isaac, following his daughter's example, dismounted, leaving his palfrey to wander on the cliff. Frail as he was, Isaac clambered and slid down the slope.

Then, as if by magic, a horn sounded, much louder than before. "No, son!" said Cedric, worried that Ivanhoe was about to follow Rebecca over the cliff. "Look!"

Far below, a man rode along the strip of beach, quickly followed by another knight, then two more -- then a long double file of mail-clad warriors. The Norman war party had returned. At least twenty men, riding through sand and shallow water, approaching fast.

Ivanhoe, Cedric, and Gurth looked from the edge of the cliff to where Rebecca and Isaac had scrambled down to Rowena's aid. The Jewess was on her knees next to the young noblewoman, Cedric's ward and Ivanhoe's betrothed. Rebecca was taking hold of Rowena's lifeless hand, shouting something to her father. Isaac pulled free the leather bag hanging from the saddle of his daughter's mare.

"We cannot join them, my son," said Cedric.

"What?" said Ivanhoe, trying to determine if he could ride his great horse down the precipitous incline, or if he should simply make his way down on foot.

"There is nothing we can do on that beach but die."

"Not before I kill many Normans," said Ivanhoe.

"If we die, Rowena will die too."

"Run away if you want, Father," said Ivanhoe. "But I will not turn from my duty. The duty you taught me never to question."

"That is your justification for everything!" said Cedric. "I ordered you to stay home from a useless Crusade, and you defied me. Now I order you to retreat from a useless battle, and you defy me again."

The war party surrounded Rowena and Rebecca. One very tall and broad man, mounted on a great stallion, took pleasure in knocking Isaac off his feet. The huge, heavily armored knight, wore a distinctive spike-topped helmet. He raised his head, not so much to examine the three horsemen at the top of the cliff,

as to exhibit his face to them. As if to taunt them
to ride down to their deaths.

"That is Reginald Front de Bouef," said Ivanhoe
with loathing. "Where he goes, Sir Brian is sure to
follow."

Gurth dismounted, lance in hand, and peered down
from the very edge of the cliff, watching the clutch
of horsemen around Rebecca and the still Rowena. The
drifting packhorse ambled over to Gurth, and nudged
him with her head.

"I can go first, Master," said Gurth. "Lady
Rowena may still be alive."

"Silence," said Ivanhoe.

"I can fight the big knight," insisted Gurth,
brandishing his bloody lance. "The others will attack
me, and in the confusion you can free Lady Rowena and
her friends."

"No more talk, Gurth. You will do as you are
told," said Ivanhoe.

"You have more sense than your big slave," said
Cedric. "You know that he would never stand a chance
against Sir Reginald, much less the whole war party.
You are yet recovering from your wounds. And I am
old. But even if you were whole, even if Gurth was a

trained knight, even if I was twenty-five again, we would not prevail against so large a force. The only way we can help Rowena is to retreat safely, and come back with more men."

But Ivanhoe was not thinking of Rowena. "I made a pledge, Father," he said.

"Our pledge to follow the knightly code is less important than saving the kingdom for Richard."

"I made a special pledge to Isaac's daughter. And, of course, to Isaac as well."

"Isaac has shown his loyalty to Richard. Now you must do the same."

"Look, Master. I think she is praying," interrupted Gurth. "Lady Rebecca is praying over Lady Rowena's body."

From horseback, Reginald seemed to be examining the ascent. There was no way to ride up the cliff face, and to climb on foot would take time. The light was bright enough to see his overweening smile. Ivanhoe bristled, watching the big man walk his horse to where Rebecca was hovering over Rowena.

"Perhaps Reginald will agree to fight me alone," said Ivanhoe. "The man is a villain, but even he will honor the knightly code."

"I am ready, Master," said Gurth, looking to the remaining weapons attached to the packhorse. "What will you use? Sword, axe…?" Gurth held up the lance in his hand. "Lance?"

Fearing to lose the argument with his son, Cedric gripped Ivanhoe's shoulder, addressing him severely: "These are Normans. Normans don't share our knightly code. Your duty is not to joust with this gigantic champion. Win or lose, his knights will kill you."

"I am not afraid of dying."

"That is a boy's boast. Dying gloriously is always easier than retreating," said Cedric. "But your duty is first and foremost to King Richard. He was wrong to leave the kingdom to fight his Crusade, but even so, he remains our lawful sovereign. If our king still lives, he will need our help to secure the kingdom. For once in your life, think before acting."

"She is alive," said Gurth quietly. He repeated the words more loudly. "She is alive! Lady Rowena… sitting up. Look, look! Lady Rebecca has brought Lady Rowena back to life."

"Thank God," said Cedric.

"Yes," said Ivanhoe. If Rebecca was a witch, she was a white witch, just as Gurth had said. If she

practiced magic, it was not to harm but to heal.
"Thank God and every angel in heaven."

Reginald dismounted, and the horsemen around
Rowena and Rebecca made way. From the top of the
cliff, it was impossible to hear what Reginald said to
the miracle-working Jewess. But his actions were
clear. He yanked Rebecca to her feet, and roughly
pulled her hands behind her back. The giant, perhaps
afraid of her witch's powers, was tying her up.

"Look how he treats her, Master," said Gurth with
violent hatred, not understanding how Ivanhoe could
restrain from leaping into action. "Lord Jesus will
laugh with glee when you kill the big coward."

"Let us ride away, and fast," said Cedric. "They
must not be able to catch us. We must get the men we
need, and come back for Rowena."

"Master?" said Gurth to Ivanhoe, waiting for
different orders.

"I am your master, churl," said Cedric to Gurth.
"And the master of my son. You will both do as I say,
and do it now."

Ivanhoe didn't see where Rowena, still on the
ground, was raising her head. His eyes were on
Rebecca, who was looking up the cliff face, turning

until she could see Ivanhoe staring below. She was not looking to him for comfort or salvation. Beyond the sadness in her face, there was something else; a kind of relief.

This relief infuriated Ivanhoe. Rebecca was saying goodbye, and gladly. She didn't want him to come for her, she didn't want anything from him except to be left alone.

"All right, Father," said Ivanhoe savagely.

"What?" said Gurth. "I don't understand. If you won't go down, I will."

"No, Gurth. There is a hierarchy in this world. First God, then King Richard, then Lord Cedric -- then everyone and everything else."

"I have made a pledge as well," said Gurth, gripping his lance, looking down to the beach.

"It is a sin to die bravely, if it will prevent the return of our King. Get on your horse."

Gurth turned sad eyes to Ivanhoe. "I don't think so, Master. It will be easier to climb down on foot." Turning his back, Gurth began to take the first careful steps down the precipitous decline.

Ivanhoe didn't hesitate. Spurring his horse at Gurth, he lifted his booted foot and kicked with all

his strength into the back of Gurth's head. Gurth
dropped the lance, and fell, sliding a few feet on his
back, until stopped by a rock outcropping. Ivanhoe
dismounted, and slid down alongside his still
conscious squire.

"Master," said Gurth. "You kicked me."

"Not hard enough, apparently," said Ivanhoe. "I
hope you'll forgive me." Ivanhoe suddenly butted the
big squire's forehead – Ivanhoe's helmet against
Gurth's skull – and the big man fell, and unconscious.

It took all Ivanhoe's strength to drag him up the
cliff, and onto his old stallion. Then he tied Gurth
to this saddle, and fixed a rope from the saddle to
the packhorse. Only then did Ivanhoe mount his
warhorse, and turn to Cedric. "All right, Father. I
will do as you say. We will come back and kill these
men another day."

He didn't wait for his father's response.
Holding the packhorse's lead, Ivanhoe began to ride
away.

PART THREE: TORQUILSTONE

CHAPTER EIGHTEEN

Isaac's head moved slowly up and down, following the rhythm of the pack mule's steps. The heavily laden beast was foul smelling, but temperate, obeying the shouts and slaps of Sir Reginald Front de Bouef's horsemen without a hint of rebellion.

Rebecca knew that consideration for Isaac's old age was not the reason he was allowed to share the mule's back with sacks of provisions. Even Sir Reginald understood that exhaustion, illness, and the blow to Isaac's head had left him incapable of walking.

But Rebecca could walk.

Amid a sea of horses, she was on foot, sandals fraying, muscles aching. The Master of the Universe gave her strength.

She had never walked so far, on so rough a track. Rebecca stared straight ahead, forcing herself forward, step after step, mile after mile. Her hands remained tied behind her back, and a rope was looped around her neck, tethering her to the pack mule's saddle. Whenever Rebecca slowed her pace, or faltered, the rope around her neck tightened.

She wondered what would happen if she gave in to fatigue and just remained still. Would the rope pull her off feet, drag her by the neck, and finally choke her to death?

How would she recognize death, know that she had moved over to the World-to-Come? Would there be brighter light from God's Radiance, or would it be dark and quiet, the serene blackness of the grave?

Rebecca became aware that, once again, words were floating down to her from above, calming words, encouraging words. Lady Rowena had not forgotten her. The Saxon girl seemed heaven-sent, a guardian angel.

"Have courage," Rowena was saying. "They have no regard for their captives, but like all rovers and outlaws, will want to rest their precious horses."

"Where do they take us, my lady?" said Rebecca.

Rebecca was flanked by Rowena and a silent knight, both mounted on towering stallions. From the corner of her eye, she could see that Rowena's hands were tied in front, and secured to the saddle of her horse.

"Somewhere they think they can hide from Ivanhoe's vengeance," said Rowena. The voice was fearless and clear. She didn't care who heard. If

Rowena was a guardian angel, she was one who longed to wield a flaming sword.

"Why won't they let me attend to my father? He has barely stirred since Sir Reginald struck his head."

"They are afraid of you, dear Rebecca," said Rowena. Her voice grew suddenly harsher: "These great warriors are too frightened to let you out of your bonds."

"Afraid of what, my lady?" said Rebecca. She tried to raise her head to meet Rowena's eyes, but was held back by the rope around her neck. Rebecca wasn't so much asking a question, as expressing her frustration. She knew well of what they were afraid: Of her otherness, her Jewish rites and rituals, her magical powers. "I am not a sorceress," she said.

"But you brought me back to life," said Rowena fervently.

"You weren't badly hurt, only senseless from a fall. There was no magic. All I did was rub some Spanish herbs under your nose."

"You have great powers, Lady Rebecca. I know the power comes from goodness, not evil."

"You mustn't talk about 'powers,'" interrupted Rebecca. "That is why they call me a witch. That is why they threaten my father. That is why they persecute my people."

Rowena didn't care to dispute this. If Rebecca didn't want her to speak about her powers out loud, she would respect her wishes. But Rowena had seen her bring Ivanhoe back to life, and was certain he would have died without Rebecca's help. One moment Rowena's lover was lifeless, the next moment he lived. Whatever Rebecca wished to name it, how could Rowena not believe in her magic?

Like Ivanhoe, Rowena had been awakened from death to stare into Rebecca's green-gold eyes. The moment had affected her profoundly.

Rowena remembered being thrown into a deep cavern, falling, deeper and deeper, into a hole without end, until suddenly a voice had reached her through the darkness. The words were foreign, musical, but strangely comforting. And these very words stopped her fall.

Rowena had felt as if, in the darkness, spectral hands had taken hold of her, held her in check. Then the foreign words grew louder. Suddenly she had been floating up, ascending the same cavern, faster and faster, moving toward brightness, a light she could feel even through her shut eyelids.

Rowena had been told to open her eyes, and she had done so, bravely prepared to face anything.

It was at that moment that she had seen the Jewess's face, so close to hers, the lips moving caressingly, calling her back to life. Rebecca was surely a sorceress, but a good one, as benevolent as she was beautiful.

"Ivanhoe will find us," said Rowena. "Wherever they take us, no matter how far. He will come with my Lord Cedric, and every man loyal to the King. And Ivanhoe's vengeance will be savage."

"'Ivanhoe's vengeance!'" said a mocking voice behind the two women. Sir Reginald rode his gigantic horse alongside Rowena, pushing aside another knight. "Don't put a lot of faith in your Ivanhoe, Lady Rowena. He watched you from up on the cliff, took one look at me, and decided to run! A great champion! He has abandoned you. Ran off with his father to hide in the woods. A coward, like all Saxons."

Rowena tried to swing her tied hands into the big man's face, but tethered to the pommel of her saddle, they stopped short of her goal. "You call Saxons cowards, but are too afraid to let my hands free," said Rowena.

"I'm only afraid of the Saxon girls," said the big knight, leering. "Afraid you might make me forget my code of chivalry. If I let you loose, there's no telling what I might do to you."

"Let me loose with my dagger, and I'll make sure you adhere to your knightly vows."

"If I let you loose, pretty lady, it won't be with a dagger in your hand. It will be with a pile of pillows under your ass in the corner of my tent."

"Very gallantly put, Sir Knight," mocked Rowena. "You look at me like I'm a whore. You strike down a revered old man, bind his virtuous daughter like a runaway slave, and force her to walk while men ride. You know as much about knighthood as a Barbary ape."

"Isaac is a Jew and a traitor to Prince John," said Reginald. "His daughter is a witch, who brought you back to life with black arts and Jewish incantations. If it was my decision, she'd be burning on a bonfire."

"Then it's a good thing that Prince John doesn't allow his apes to make any decisions," said Rowena.

Reginald reached down and grabbed Rowena's mouth, nose, and chin in his enormous right hand, silencing her. "You are mistaken, Lady Rowena. We apes are given much discretion as to how we dispose of prisoners. If you continue to defy me, you will find this out for yourself." He removed his hand, and Rowena breathed deep, wild with anger. She refrained from spitting, or answering in kind; the defiance in her eyes was comment enough.

Not waiting for further argument, Reginald spurred forward to the head of his troop.

Low tide allowed the warriors to ride three and four abreast. In the distance, the sand gave way to a rocky shore, where a path led inland, toward sheltering trees. Rowena watched Rebecca stumble forward, one foot after the other, in a fog of exhaustion.

"It can't be much further," said Rowena. "We will certainly stop and rest very soon… Rebecca? Are you all right? Do you hear me?"

"What… What did he mean?" said Rebecca.

"What did who mean?"

"The big Norman… He has murder in his eyes. Murder and lust. Why does God allow such men to thrive?" Rowena had no answer to this, but was glad that Rebecca was able to talk. "He said if it was his decision, he would burn me on a bonfire," said Rebecca.

"It is not his decision to do anything but make idle threats."

"Is he not the leader of these warriors?"

"Sir Reginald Front de Bouef is overlord to these warriors," said Rowena. "But Sir Brian de Bois Gilbert is overlord to Reginald. As Prince John is overlord to Sir Brian."

"Lords and overlords, princes and kings," said Rebecca. "A lot of ceremony to pretend that crimes are righteous deeds."

"It is more than ceremony, dear Rebecca," said Rowena. "We know that Sir Reginald has committed crimes today. For that, not only he, but his overlord Sir Brian, will be punished."

"'Sir Brian,'" said Rebecca with loathing. "I pray to God I never see his face again!"

Rowena spoke in a quieter voice. "If you have bewitched Sir Brian, it is not through any sorcery, nor through any desire on your part. You cannot be blamed for the beauty granted you by our Heavenly Father."

Rebecca didn't answer. She believed that Rowena was a good woman, and kind, and so did not understand the hatred Rebecca incited in her fellow Christians.

At the tournament, when Sir Brian had demanded she take the satin crown of the "Queen of Beauty and Grace," Rebecca had felt the wildness of that hatred. Hatred for Brian's choice of an infidel. Hatred for the alien's strange clothes and manners. And when Rebecca had rejected the honor that no one but Brian had wanted her to take, the hatred only intensified.

That is because the hatred was without logic or reason. Her mother had cured Jew and Gentile alike, but that had not prevented her from being hated, accused of witchery. Her father had given fortunes to help princes and kings in half a dozen countries, but that hadn't saved him from resentment, suspicion and violence.

Rebecca wondered if it were possible for Rowena to begin to hate her as well. There was no logical reason for the golden-haired girl to turn against her, to join the other Gentiles of this land in wishing her and all her people dead.

Rebecca would never try and take what was Rowena's away from her. Even if she wanted it, she thought. Even if Rebecca wanted Ivanhoe for herself. But what on earth was she thinking? She didn't want him, Rebecca thought, she didn't want anything to do with him. Some things were impossible in this world. Some people were meant to cross paths, but never touch. Some feelings were evanescent, destined to vanish like fog hit by bright sun.

Reginald's deep voice suddenly boomed from the head of the troop: "Halt," he said, and Rebecca felt herself stumbling up against the odoriferous mule bearing her father's weight. All around her, horses were reined in, confused and nervous. Distant hoofbeats sounded, not from the hard packed sand, but from inland.

"Father, are you awake?" said Rebecca. "Father!" Isaac's head finally moved from its slumping position.

"Daughter," he said. But he spoke no more, as a dozen mounted knights rode out from the inland trail, joining their fellow warriors on the beach. Like Sir Reginald's troop, they wore chain mail with Norman

insignia. Three of them were out front, with one man
slightly ahead of the others.

This leader was the only one among the dozen
without a helmet: Reginald Front de Bouef's overlord,
Sir Brian de Bois Gilbert.

Sir Reginald rode to meet Sir Brian, but the
imperious knight barely acknowledged his greeting.
His eyes were elsewhere, searching the company, and
quickly stopping on the prisoner tethered to the mule.

Rebecca turned away from his cold gaze, and
forced her attention to the two knights who had been
flanking Brian, familiar to her from the tournament:
Maurice de Bracy, and Philip Malvoisin. Both had been
defeated by Ivanhoe, but now there was only triumph in
their eyes.

Yet there was little triumph in Brian's eyes. He
turned away from Rebecca and walked his horse slowly
among the troops, his eyes sweeping past Isaac and
Rowena, then turning back again to Rebecca. As he
rode up alongside Rowena, Rebecca moved her tethered
neck as much as she could, and was able to observe him
from the corner of her eye.

The knight's face showed no evidence of bruises,
though she had seen him struck in the jaw with great

force. There was no blood in his hair, though she had seen his scalp bloodied by the oil lamp that had struck his head. Somehow, after his men had come back and freed him from where Gurth had tied him to a chair in Isaac's study, Sir Brian had taken the time to wash the blood from his hair and change his shirt.

Rebecca listened to him talk to Rowena, his voice caustic, insinuating, hateful. "This is quite an unexpected pleasure, Lady Rowena," he said. "Prince John sent me to apprehend the Jewish traitor Isaac of York, and here I find you together with him. Another link in the great chain of conspiracy that we will defeat in Prince John's name. Apparently what they say about the Saxon nobility is true. No Saxon is to be trusted."

"No true Saxon," said Rowena, with satisfaction. "We cannot be trusted to curry favor with the usurper of the crown. Neither can we be trusted to leave behind conscience, dignity or honor. That is for Normans."

Brian raised his hand, but held himself back from striking Rowena. "Go ahead, Sir Knight," said Rowena. "I won't break. And you will be able to brag that you struck a Saxon lady with her hands tied."

Brian put down his hand. "It is unfortunate that you have been raised by a brute like Cedric. With proper upbringing, you'd have made some Norman a fine wench."

"I'd sooner bed with a screech owl," said Rowena. "But as you are not going to strike me, perhaps you'd be kind enough to release me. My friend needs my assistance. She is about to fall down."

"No, I'm not," said Rebecca. She saw Brian's eyes drawn to hers, and stay there. "The stench of evil has revived my spirits. If this great Norman overlord wants to discuss the finer points of treason, it would be better to do it with my father. After he's had a proper rest."

"There is nothing to discuss," said Brian. With effort, he turned away from Rebecca, addressing Rowena instead. "Prince John is the legitimate ruler of England. When the death of his brother is confirmed, he will be crowned king."

"King Richard is not dead," said Isaac, breaking out of his half-sleep.

"My Lord Isaac, we meet again," said Brian, quickly turning his Arabian around, again avoiding Rebecca's eyes. Reaching down from his horse, he grabbed Isaac by the scalp, and looked into his face. "Apparently, Jew, you have information about the whereabouts of Richard, or you would not be so bold with your statement."

"Let go of my father," said Rebecca. "You know he is not well."

"Silence, Jewess," said Brian. He could not help but turn to her again, and the sight of her silenced him for a moment. "I will deal with you later," he said, and turned away, tightening his hold on Isaac's scalp. "Listen, my treacherous lord: Do you remember my asking you a question that you were reluctant to answer?"

"You asked me several questions, Sir Knight," said Isaac, increasingly alert. "Where and when was King Richard landing on English shores? Who participated in the ransom that his own brother refused to pay? Strange questions from the envoy of a prince who insists his king is dead."

Retaining his hold on Isaac's scalp, Brian brought him close. "Do not defy me, old man," said Brian.

"King Richard is alive," said Isaac. "And he will return."

Brian slapped Isaac.

"Coward!" said Rebecca.

Brian found himself letting go of Isaac's scalp, and slowly, inevitably, turning back to Rebecca. It was maddening that her rebuke stung. There was nothing cowardly about him, and there would never be. Yet she continued: "Ivanhoe should never have treated you with knightly courtesy, as you are not worthy of your high station. He should have killed you like a mad dog." Exhausted as she was, her defiance strengthened her posture. In the dimming light, her eyes glowed.

"'Not worthy of my high station,'" said Brian. "Perhaps you are right. To refrain from killing evil when he sees it, to offer favors to infidels, to offer mercy to the murderers of our Lord Jesus – these actions are not worthy of a great knight. They are the actions of a man in thrall to a witch."

Brian drew his sword. "And there is only one way to deal with a witch."

"No! She is not a witch," said Rowena. "She is a healer, and good, and God-fearing. If you harm her in any way, you will be damned for eternity." Brian raised his sword, and Rowena shouted: "Stop! Your fears will make you lose all chance for eternal life."

As Brian hesitated, the sword held high, Rebecca looked into his eyes. For a moment, she forgot her fear of dying, her guilt at leaving her father behind. All that she saw in Brian's eyes was pain, all that she could feel in herself was the healer's instinctive passion to take that pain away.

Rebecca could not imagine that Brian would see the flickering of kindness in her eyes; or that he would take it as a mark of pity. All she knew was that his hesitation ended. He brought down his sword with force.

But the blade was not aimed at her head, but at the taut rope tethering her to the mule.

As the tether snapped, Rebecca staggered. The ground seemed to quake, the light dimmed as if a curtain had been suddenly drawn. It was all she could do to remain on her feet. She could hear her father and Rowena talk, but couldn't make sense of their words. Her heart pounded as she saw Brian's naked blade catch the dying sunlight.

Suddenly Brian sheathed his sword. "I have no fears," said Brian, looking at Rowena. "Not of any man or woman under the sun. And not of any witch!"

Leaning from his saddle, the powerful knight grabbed the slender Rebecca with one hand, and lifted her onto the front of his saddle as if she had no more weight than an infant. Sprawled painfully crosswise over the pommel, her wrists bound behind her back, she could feel Brian's blade slice through her binds.

"I simply know how best to treat a witch," said Brian, as if he was explaining his actions to a court of law, as if he had need of defending his honor. "You must hold her close."

Once again Rebecca felt herself lifted by the man's powerful hands, holding her high. Suddenly, she was facing front, her arms free, her legs splaying under her loose skirt, straddling Brian's Arabian horse. "Hold her close," Brian was saying. "So she cannot do any more harm."

At this unaccustomed height, her field of vision wavered wildly, like a vision seen through water: Her father slumped on the mule; Sir Reginald glaring from under his spiked helmet; Rowena, her ferocious eyes filled with worry; savage Norman warriors.

Everyone was looking at her, some with hatred, some with fear; all with amazement.

All at once, Rebecca felt herself moving forward rapidly, her back to Brian's chest. She blinked wildly. Her vision cleared. Horsemen restrained their steeds, as Brian and his captive galloped past, away from the beach, toward the dark expanse of dense trees.

With her newly freed hands, Rebecca gripped the pommel, though she knew that wasn't necessary. Brian did not intend to let her fall. He was overlord to a murderer; his own overlord was a usurper. Brian was a traitor, and had looked the other way when his warriors had plundered, killed, and raped. But of this Rebecca was certain: He did not intend to let her fall.

He did not intend to let go of her at all.

CHAPTER NINETEEN

Gurth's mother had sixteen children, the oldest ten years his senior, the youngest eleven years his junior. All but two survived infancy. He had eight living brothers, five living sisters, each one stubborn, and more than a little proud of their natural gifts of strength and fortitude. These traits derived from their mother. Their father was no longer around, having left their mother when she was pregnant with their last child.

Perhaps, as one of Gurth's brothers believed, their father had been lost while poaching deer on a lord's preserve. Or maybe he was lost in a storm off the rocky coast while fishing for the family's benefit, as his youngest sister dreamily insisted.

But most of his siblings believed as Gurth did. Their father had broken faith with his wife, had abandoned his family. No one spoke of him anymore. Whether he was alive or dead would never again be their concern.

Gurth's mother was very much alive, with all her teeth and all her hair. She had never been beautiful, but in old age, her straight back and clear blue eyes struck every observer: This was a woman who could endure anything.

Gurth's mother had been born into an equally large family. From her line, Gurth had far too many uncles and aunts to remember their names. As to the children of these uncles and aunts, his cousins -- there were at least a hundred, scattered about the countryside, healthy, lusty, long-lived. <u>This</u> is why the priests kept records. To wed your first cousin was a great sin.

Second and third cousins were something else.

Gurth's extended family was a veritable tribe, known to each other by their qualities and quirks. The men were big, thick-limbed, thick-necked. They spoke little, and kept their word. The women had spotless skin and large, capable hands. They spoke more than their menfolk, but were equally loyal to their promises. When possible cousins met, they would sit down and compare mothers, grandmothers, places of birth, trying to determine relationship.

One of Gurth's female cousins, Etheldreda by name, seventeen years old by most calculations, was now standing before Lord Cedric, Sir Ivanhoe, and Sir Kenrick, the Saxon lord of the manor house where father and son had taken refuge. Like Gurth, she was red-haired, but unlike his coarse, impenetrable helmet, her hair flowed in romantic waves. Ethelreda's pale skin was flawless, glowing with youthful health.

It was Gurth who had told his master Ivanhoe about Ethelreda's position – a kitchen girl in Torquilstone Castle – and Gurth who had sent for her in Sir Ivanhoe's name.

Their messenger had been Brother Mungo, a penniless friar living on Sir Kenrick's charity.

Brother Mungo had taken seven days to journey on foot to Torquilstone, through forest and bog. Every day had felt like an eternity. With begging cup and holy words, Brother Mungo had penetrated the castle's defenses, and had found Ethelreda laboring diligently in the kitchen, just as Gurth had promised.

The friar found Gurth's description of the girl to be accurate. Ethelreda seemed to radiate satisfaction at everyone and everything. To her, apparently, life was a blessing. Every morning was beautiful. Every night an opportunity for fantastic dreaming. Even when chopping onions and scrubbing pans, Ethelreda's smile was beatific.

"Your cousin Gurth has an urgent message for you," Brother Mungo had whispered.

"My cousin Gurth," she had repeated, as if happy to single him out from all her myriad relations.

The serious friar had come to the point at once: "He asks you to run away."

Ethelreda had looked at Brother Mungo, taking his measure. Though his eyes contained a hint of rebellion, the friar was a dour man with a sallow complexion. She had put down the pot she had been scrubbing, and had taken the friar to a quieter corner of the vast kitchen.

"My cousin Gurth has asked me to run away," she had said, smiling fetchingly. The friar had been surprised that she hadn't seemed at all worried or concerned about Gurth's message. To run away from your lord and master - Norman or Saxon made no difference -- was a grave crime, punishable by whipping and branding and worse.

The friar had continued: "You will have to undertake a journey on foot to the manor of the Saxon overlord, Sir Kenrick."

"A journey on foot," she had said, amused by the idea.

"You need not repeat every word I say!" Brother Mungo had said, exasperated by her complacency. "I can see that you hear me." The friar had continued: "The journey is not easy. It took me seven days."

"I can do it in five," Ethelreda had said.

The friar had frowned, letting her know that he was not a frivolous man, and that his message was serious. "If you run away, you will never be able to return to Torquilstone."

"If I run away…"

"If you are caught fleeing.."

"If I am caught fleeing," she had said.

"Stop that! Listen, do not repeat, merely listen. Then decide what course you will follow." Brother Mungo had collected himself. "If you are caught fleeing, you will be punished terribly."

"Are you trying to worry me, Brother Mungo?" she had said, entertained by his nervousness.

"I am trying to make you understand that this is an important matter, a serious matter."

"Of course, Brother Mungo. Even if it is not the first time someone - usually a cousin, I have so many -- has asked me to run away with him, it is the first time he has enlisted a holy man to help his plans."

The friar had gripped her elbow, looking around the enormous kitchen for eavesdroppers and spies. His pitted teeth were awful to behold. Then he had spoken with even greater urgency.

"It is not about running away with your cousin, but about talking to his masters. Important leaders of the Saxon nobility. It is dangerous for you to agree to their request, but if you do, you will be appreciated and rewarded. Gurth's master, Sir Ivanhoe, son of Lord Cedric of Rotherwood, will more than compensate you for your troubles, and Saxon lords will find you another and better position in Sir Kenrick's manor."

"Pardon me, Brother Mungo, but it helps me to repeat: "His masters. Important leaders of Saxon nobility."

"That's right."

"Appreciated and rewarded."

"Yes!"

"Sir Ivanhoe, Lord Cedric, Rotherwood, Sir Kenrick. My cousin Gurth seems to be well acquainted with these great men," the girl had said, her pale skin blushing with delight.

The friar remembered to include the last part of Gurth's message. "And your cousin gives you his solemn word," he had said. "You will never be sorry for taking the trip."

"But that is not possible," the pretty girl had said, anticipating the teasing and flirtation she would practice in Sir Kenrick's manor. "How could my cousin know what will make me sorry?"

"Enough, wench," Brother Mungo had said. "Do you agree to come with me, or don't you?"

After Ivanhoe deserted his betrothed at the white cliffs, after breaking his pledges to the Jewish father and daughter, it had taken Gurth more than a few long days to get past his disappointment. En route to Sir Kenrick's manor, Gurth had not spoken to Ivanhoe, not even to answer a direct question. But he had done whatever he was ordered to do without comment, and his master had let him be.

Gurth had understood why his betters had retreated from a confrontation they could not have won. But he didn't like it.

Arriving at Sir Kenrick's, Gurth had stayed with the other servants and squires of an assemblage of lords and knights, and had little to do with his master except for silently serving him at table in the great hall. Even when Sir Ivanhoe had commented on the big squire's surprising prowess at arms to the other knights on the dais, Gurth had remained silent. Even when Lord Cedric had remarked that from a distance, seeing the enormous Gurth battling without helmet or armor, he had thought the squire might be King Richard himself, back from the wars, Gurth had remained silent.

But when Gurth overheard the name Torquilstone Castle, he had listened more carefully. He hadn't known that Torquilstone was the seat of Brian de Bois Gilbert, and this was enough to excite his fury. When he had learned more, that Torquilstone was the place where Lady Rowena, Lady Rebecca, and Isaac had been taken, he had realized he would have to speak.

The assembled knights had been debating how best to attack the formidable castle, and whether an assault was possible at all. Gurth had put down the trencher he was bringing to Ivanhoe with a bang on the table loud enough to turn every man in the hall to him.

"I know a girl who works in the kitchen," Gurth had said. "At Torquilstone."

Gurth had convinced himself that Ethelreda was a sufficiently distant relation, a second or even third cousin. If on some future date he could persuade her to be his wife, the priest's records would not be an impediment. He had seen her only once before, at last year's harvest festival, when she had given him a radiant smile, then refused to turn his way again all evening. One look at his fellow redhead had been enough. He had never forgotten her. He had heard she was working at Torquilstone, but had not known that it was a Norman castle.

"Her name is Ethelreda. I can send for her," Gurth had said. "She is my cousin, and can tell us what we need to know about the castle."

"Listen to the serf talk about military strategy," Lord Cedric had said. But every man at the table was glad of Gurth's suggestion. Brother Mungo had been sent to Torquilstone that very night.

They had waited for the friar to get to Torquilstone, waited for the maid to arrive at Sir Kenrick's manor. Twelve days in all, and Gurth could see that the days had weighed on his master. "We will go to Torquilstone," Ivanhoe had said to Gurth. "And once there, we will not leave without Lady Rowena."

"And Lord Isaac and Lady Rebecca," Gurth had said. "I will not leave without them as well."

"Naturally, fool! Do you think I will break my sacred vow?" Ivanhoe had said, furious with Gurth, more furious with himself for having left them on the beach, captives of Sir Reginald Front de Boeuf, now locked away by Sir Brian de Bois Gilbert.

"No, Master," Gurth had said. "This time, you will not break your vow."

Ivanhoe held back from explaining yet again why he had acceded to Cedric's demands, and not sacrificed his life to no purpose. "Where is your infernal cousin?" Ivanhoe had said. "How do you know she'll even come to us?"

"She is young, eager, and will be wanting a husband," Gurth had said. "She will come."

Gurth had tried to calm Ivanhoe by telling him more. How his mother had said that when it came time for him to marry, he must seek out the maiden Ethelreda, and ask for her hand. When Gurth had asked what Ethelreda was like, his mother had said: "Strong

enough to bear you healthy sons." But then she had
added: "You will not be the only man who wants her
for wife. There is something about the girl that
makes grown men foolish."

"And my mother was right, Master. The one time I
saw her, she made me stammer and trip, along with
every other man in the house. But when I bested three
men at arm-wrestling, I could see that she was glad
for my victory. That she was interested. She will
come, you will see, and she will help us."

And Ethelreda had come, twelve days after Brother
Mungo had left. Weary, and dirty from the trail,
flushed face, and exhilarated. Having brought her to
these lords, Gurth stood right behind her, trying not
to be foolish. He was close enough to touch, waiting
for her to answer the question just posed by Lord
Cedric. As Gurth breathed in her scent, he found it
hard to follow Cedric's words.

His mind was busy with telling himself that this
girl was certainly not a first cousin. For one thing,
her hands were not that large, her limbs not quite as
thick as he was used to seeing in his cousins. And as
to her stubbornness, her pride - Gurth was sure there

were men and women throughout England who were both stubborn and proud and not related to him.

A second cousin, at the very least. Perhaps a third cousin, which would be an even greater blessing.

Besides, she had come, at his request, no one else's. Ethelreda had run away, had taken a chance merely at his say so. There could be no doubt she was interested in him, and not just as a cousin, but as a husband. Such feelings could not be unholy. For a moment, the possibility of their union overwhelmed Gurth with joy.

Lord Cedric's voice was suddenly loud enough to break through Gurth's sensual fog. "I ask again, you saucy wench -- how many men are garrisoned at Torquilstone Castle?"

Why was Lord Cedric calling his cousin "saucy?" thought Gurth. Had she dared to speak back to her betters, to answer without respect?

Gurth forced himself to listen more closely, as Ethelreda continued. "I haven't counted them, my lord," she said. "For one thing, I cannot count to so great a number. For another, I cannot be in every part of the castle at the same time. And these many men come and go all day and all night."

Ivanhoe interrupted. "We cannot expect you to have counted every man in Torquilstone, but perhaps you could tell us if there are more than twenty or thirty warriors inside."

"Much more than that," she said, dismissively. "I've heard tell there are five hundred soldiers in arms."

Ivanhoe turned to his father, and exhibited an unworried look. "We can ignore that. I am sure Sir Brian has no such large number of men at his command."

"You will always ignore what is convenient, my son. But if there are anything like five hundred men at Torquilstone, we will be forced to wait here longer than we would like."

"I have waited twelve days for this girl to come to us from Torquilstone with her precious information. No matter what she tells us, I am leaving for Torquilstone tomorrow."

Ivanhoe turned back to the girl, demanding to know who had given her that number. Ethelreda explained that she had heard the number from a scullery maid, and an even greater number from a stable boy, neither of whom could count higher than

twenty, whereas she could count all the way to one
hundred.

She had heard other numbers from other servants,
but had barely listened to them, as she gave them no
credence. "No one knows, my lord. How could they?
All we see is drunken louts in mail coats chasing
servant girls as if they were doing us honor. These
Normans all look the same. Tall and skinny, no
shoulders."

Ethelreda paused for a moment to turn to Gurth,
as if to share a silent comment about the robustness
of their own clan. Then she turned back to the
assembly: "I almost broke one boy's little wrist when
he wouldn't let go, but I took pity on him, and only
rammed my elbow into his fool head." She turned
again, so that Gurth could see how pleased she was
with her answer.

The lords were less pleased, finding her
information disquieting. That the lords were all
seated on the dais in Sir Kenrick's great hall and
looking down at her severely, didn't bother Ethelreda
a whit. That behind where she and Gurth stood were
two dozen Crusader knights seated on benches,

following her answers with impatience and vexation, was no concern of hers either.

She was not a prisoner here, but a guest. She had walked and ran through night and fog for five days and nights, sleeping under brambles and leaves, and had so far been offered neither food nor drink nor a place to sleep, not even from her broad-shouldered cousin. No matter how great were these lords, no matter how lowly her own station, it took all her self-control not to shout out loud: "Whatever became of Saxon hospitality?"

"It's not the numbers you'll be wanting to know," she said. "It's how to get in." Perhaps the only way to get a meal and a bed in this place was to empty herself of everything she knew about Torquilstone, and quickly. The lords stopped talking amongst themselves, listening carefully.

"The castle sits on rocky ground, high above the sea coast," she said. "There is no entrance from that side, only stone walls. Even if you could land a boat on the narrow shore, there is no way to climb up to the battlements from there. The only entrance is at the front of the castle, where there are two moats, outer and inner, but the drawbridge covers them both.

The bridge is very wide, and very long, and very heavy. They say the chains and gears it used were made in Sheffield, and cost the first Baron of Torquilstone half his fortune. But he made up the silver he spent. The Baron's men captured wayfarers wherever they could. If need be, they turned friends into enemies if they had family treasures at home."

"Enough with this long story," said Ivanhoe, getting to his feet. "How do we get in?"

Cedric ordered his son to sit, and to allow the girl to finish in her own way.

Ethelreda continue to relate how the castle has long been famous for holding prisoners for ransom, in the castle's dungeons. "They are deep, the dungeons," she said. "Deep and damp, and no one gets out without paying the price. Night and day, crossbow soldiers stand on top of the walls, looking down from towers and turrets. Once the drawbridge is up, there is no crashing through. The chief cook is a very old woman, and she says it has never been tried since she was there. Before her, she says, it was tried once or twice. She heard the story from the chief cook before her, many years ago. Invaders laid down a bridge across the moats, and tried to batter their way

through with a ram. Legend is no one ever made a dent
before they were shot through with a thousand arrows."

Ivanhoe stood again, ignoring Cedric's entreaties
for patience. "You said there is a way in. Tell us
what is."

"Oh, no, Sir Knight," she said. "I didn't say
there was a way in. I said you'd be wanting to know
how to get in." Ethelreda paused, weighing the effect
of her words on the great lords. "There is no way.
No one has ever escaped, or has ever been rescued from
captivity. Not from Torquilstone."

CHAPTER TWENTY

"And this, Father," said Ivanhoe to Cedric, about
Ethelreda's report. "This long disquisition leading
to a hopeless conclusion, is why we have waited twelve
more days."

"We have delayed not only for this girl, but for
our troops to arrive."

"They arrived yesterday," said Ivanhoe.

"Men weary of travel, and still wearier from
years of battling in Richard's Crusade. Would you not
allow them a few days of rest?"

"I go tomorrow, with whoever is ready to follow
me," said Ivanhoe. He was about to step down from the
dais, when Cedric stopped him.

"I have one last question to his girl," said
Cedric. Turning to Ethelreda, he said: "<u>You</u> walked
out of Torquilstone. Tell me how."

"The soldiers know me, my lord. We're servants,
not slaves, and I am permitted to visit my old mother
every Sunday." Here, Ethelreda's tone changed to
something like resentment. "She cooks me rabbit stew.
Not as good as what we get at Torquilstone, but it's
food from my mother's own hands. Tasty and warm."

Perhaps this talk of food, this reminder that she was a servant and not a slave, would remind these great lords of their obligations of hospitality. She turned her back to them suddenly, meeting Gurth's surprised eyes.

"I need to sit, cousin," she said.

Ignoring all protocol, Gurth brought over a stool for his cousin. As she sat down heavily, Ivanhoe spoke: "I also have one last question."

Incredibly, Ethelreda interrupted the knight, insisting to her scandalized cousin: "I need to drink."

As Gurth hurried to a lower banquet table, Ivanhoe continued: "You speak of captives, of ransom, of dungeons. Do you know of any --?"

"There is one only captive now," she interrupted, anticipating his question. Before she could continue, Gurth was back, with a brimming goblet. "One captive," she said. "An old man. Some say they hear his screams at night." She gripped the goblet of golden mead. "And I need something to eat, cousin. Bread, stew, anything."

"Only one captive," said Ivanhoe, watching her drink. "An old man… But what of the two women taken by

Sir Brian? Did you not hear of them? Two young
women, one fair, one dark."

Ethelreda waited to drain the goblet and wipe her
lips before speaking. "They are not captives," she
said. "At least, they are not in the dungeons, but in
the locked rooms where the knights keep their women."

Before his son could respond, Cedric demanded:
"Locked rooms for women? Do you mean bed chambers for
their wives?"

Lord Cedric bristled as Gurth returned, delaying
her answer by filling Ethelreda's goblet, and placing
a trencher of bread and meat before her.

"These men have no wives," said Ethelreda,
looking keenly at the meat. "And no religion either.
But they have women, some of them Saxons of decent
family, and tricked or forced into a life they lament.
These Norman knights keep them locked up."

Ethelreda paused long enough to put a chunk of
meat into her mouth, and wash it down with sweet mead.
Chewing and swallowing, she continued: "The new women
are in two of those locked rooms. I only saw one of
them. I had to bring her food, and leave it outside
the shut door. When I was nearing the end of the
corridor, a guard opened the door, to hand her the

tray. I got a glimpse. Thick black hair in great waves, the eyes of a madwoman. She was screaming something, I think about her father, and threw the tray back at the guard. He slammed the door, locked it, crossed himself, and saw that I was still standing there. 'Don't stick your nose in where it don't belong,' he said. 'That girl's a witch. If you even look in her face, you will burn in hell.'"

Ethelreda took a bite of meat, and a swallow of mead. This time she waited to swallow before continuing: "But she wasn't no witch. I've seen witches. They're old and ugly. This one is young and beautiful. Anyone could see why she why was there. These men are worse than dogs in heat. If she's gone mad, I'm thinking she has reason."

Ethelreda held out her goblet to Gurth. At first, he didn't react, preoccupied with her terrible news. Then Gurth took the goblet, and refilled it, as Ivanhoe continued with increasing urgency: Was this girl with black hair a Jewess? Had Ethelreda actually seen Sir Brian herself? Had any knight actually gone into the Jewess's room, and spent time with her behind a locked door?

Ethelreda answered between swallows of food and drink: How could she know what a Jewess looked like? Yes, she had seen the knight called Sir Brian, and he was very severe and handsome too, especially for a Norman. As to whether any knight had gone into the Jewess's room, she already told him that she didn't know what a Jewess looked like.

Gurth, furious with each new revelation, spat out a question of his own: "Has Brian or any other Norman knight gone into the room of the black-haired woman?"

Before Ethelreda could answer, Ivanhoe demanded: "Has any knight spent time with her behind that locked door?"

"Enough, son," said Cedric. "The girl doesn't know any more."

"If she keeps guzzling that mead, she'll know even less!" said Ivanhoe.

Cedric looked disapprovingly at his angry son. "That is not the way to talk about a girl who has done a brave service," he said. "The girl needs food and a warm bed. See to it, Gurth. At once."

Ivanhoe said no more, and Gurth brought his pretty cousin to the lowest table in the hall. He brought more meat, bread and mead to her, and watched as she ate and drank.

"Thank you for coming," he said. "You make our entire family proud."

"All the cousins, you mean?" she teased. "The first, second, and third cousins?"

"We are not first cousins," said Gurth. "Of that I am certain. My mother, and your mother were first cousins, once removed, and that makes us -"

"Related," she interrupted, smiling kittenishly.

"Ethelreda, I am glad you are here, because there is something I must ask you. Something personal."

"But Gurth, you are now a squire, companion to knights and lords. Perhaps you no longer wish to direct any personal questions to a mere kitchen girl."

Gurth place his massive hands on hers. "I will be going with them," he said.

"Going?"

"To Torquilstone."

"Haven't you been listening? There is no way to attack the place."

"With God on our side, we will find a way," said Gurth. "You must remain here. If I live, I will be back."

"Who do you think you are, to tell me where I must remain? And what is it to me, whether or not you come back?" But her tone was no longer frivolous. Gurth smiled, as if he had already asked for her hand, and she had already accepted.

No one at the low tables had paid them attention. All eyes were on the dais, where Sir Kenrick was trying to mediate an argument between father and son.

"Troops have arrived," said Cedric, "but there are more coming."

The eyes of every Crusader knight in the hall remained on their leaders. "It doesn't matter how many more troops are coming," said Ivanhoe. "It doesn't matter when they will arrive. I am leaving tomorrow."

"You have obligations," said Cedric. "To your king, to your father." Cedric had pulled his son back down to his seat, and now spoke in a confidential tone. "And to your betrothed."

"It is because of those obligations that I am leaving," said Ivanhoe, in a louder voice. "King Richard would be furious to discover what I have done, dishonoring my name and my knighthood."

Suddenly, Ivanhoe lowered his voice, bringing his head close to Cedric's. Sir Kenrick, on Cedric's other side, might have been able to overhear, but no one else. "To abandon the King's benefactor Isaac is crime enough. But to have left behind the woman I've vowed to marry… And the woman I've vowed to protect..."

"Just how many women is that, son?" said Cedric.

"Why do you ask such a question?"

"Because you don't ask it yourself."

"You needn't speak in riddles," said Ivanhoe. "If you have something to say to me, say it plainly."

Cedric spoke in a harsh whisper. Now not even Sir Kenrick would hear what he had to tell his son: "You cannot love a non-believer," he said to Ivanhoe. "The infidel daughter of an infidel gold-trader."

Ivanhoe looked at his father with fury. "I do not love Rebecca!" said Ivanhoe. "I hate the very thought of her." Controlling his temper, Ivanhoe continued: "Perhaps hate is too strong a word, though she has treated me contemptuously from the first day we met."

"Well then, son, I am glad to hear that you do not love the Jewess."

"As to Rowena – I love her," said Ivanhoe.

"I am glad to hear that as well."

"And I will marry her."

"Rowena is of the highest Saxon lineage. From the day I made her my ward, my only thought was to one day marry her to my only son."

"I will never break my vow to Rowena," said Ivanhoe, without a trace of joy in his eyes. Then he stood, suddenly prepared to leave.

But something held him back. His father still didn't understand something, and Ivanhoe needed to make it clear.

"Even if Rebecca had not saved my life, I made my vow to her as well," he said, clarifying his thoughts not only for Cedric, but for himself. "I have sworn before Christ and King that I will die before letting anyone harm the Lady Rebecca. With or without troops, I leave for Torquilstone tomorrow."

CHAPTER TWENTY-ONE

Gurth worked steadily in the dimly lit stables. He fed the three horses, talking to them in his kind, firm voice. After all, it was pitch dark outside, and this sudden work would be unexpected for them. He saddled Ivanhoe's old stallion, then saddled the knight's new warhorse, gift of the knight's patron, Isaac of York.

Then Gurth prepared the packhorse, lading it with armor, weapons, food and drink. Ivanhoe had been clear: Whether or not Cedric and Kenrick would release the Saxon troops made no difference. At the first glimmer of dawn, Ivanhoe and Gurth would ride out.

A door to the large stables opened from the outside, and Ivanhoe stepped in. He wore neither mail nor helmet. The knight stood straight, with shoulders squared, determined. Ivanhoe stepped closer to the lantern Gurth had lit, the squire could read exhaustion and disappointment in his master's eyes.

"The troops will not be coming with us," said Ivanhoe. "My father still insists on waiting for the rest of the troops to arrive."

"You knew that this evening, Master. There was no need to wake your father up in the middle of the night to see if he had changed his mind."

"Of course," said Ivanhoe sarcastically. "Why would I need a hundred Saxon warriors at my back when I have you?"

"I was only saying that Lord Cedric is a man of even temperament."

"The man threw me out of my own home for being loyal to our King."

"That is all in the past, Master. You are reconciled, are you not?"

"That is enough, Gurth."

"Reconciled with a father who thinks, plans, then waits for the right time to act."

"Silence, man! Do not dare lecture me about my own father! There is nothing about him that I do not know." Ivanhoe took a breath. "Nothing," he added.

"Yes, Master. A son knows his father." Gurth couldn't help but add: "As a father knows his son."

"It is all your Ethelreda's fault!" said Ivanhoe with sudden vehemence. "She has given my father and Sir Kenrick the idea that a thousand men or more are needed to take Torquilstone, when fifty would do the task."

"She has said no such thing, Master," said Gurth.

"Gurth! You are not to contradict nor defy me. When I say something, take it as an absolute truth, take it as an order!"

"Ethelreda has not given us any idea of the number of men behind the walls of Torquilstone, or how many Saxons it would take to vanquish them."

"Do you want to be flogged? I will not abide a squire who cannot obey."

"Perhaps you didn't understand her, Master. All Ethelreda has said is that there is no way to breach their walls."

"That is what my father heard! That is why they delay and wait for troops and siege towers and battering rams that may never come. Wait and wait and wait some more. We should have fought Sir Reginald on the beach."

"Yes, Master. That was my idea."

There was no irony in Gurth's tone.

If Ivanhoe had not knocked his squire unconscious at the cliff's edge that day, there is no doubt that Gurth, ignoring all perils, would have hurried down to the beach. Surely, Gurth would have been killed by the overwhelming force, but just as surely, Gurth would have remained true to his pledge to Rebecca and her father.

"You're right, Gurth. We should have both died on the beach. Is there anything else you'd care to add to my list of sins?"

As Gurth strapped two lances onto the packhorse, he said: "Yes. Don't blame Ethelreda."

"Why shouldn't I blame whomever I want to blame?" said Ivanhoe. "I blame her, and I blame Sir Kenrick, and most of all I blame my father! In spite of everything you say, I blame him with all my heart."

"But you mustn't blame Ethelreda."

"All right, Gurth. I understand. The pretty wench has you under her spell. I know all about such things!"

"No, Master. That is not the reason I tell you not to blame her. You must not blame Ethelreda, because she is wiser than you know." Ivanhoe held back from answering. Clearly, Gurth was besotted with the redhead, and there was no reason to antagonize him. They were about to undertake a difficult journey, to fulfill an almost impossible quest.

So the knight put aside thoughts about Gurth's saucy cousin, and tried to do the same about his father's procrastination. Ivanhoe centered his rage where it belonged: On Torquilstone, and its master, Sir Brian de Bois Gilbert.

Ivanhoe could not know that Rowena shared his rage at Sir Brian. If Ivanhoe's rage was hot, Rowena's was blazing. In the hour before dawn, she turned in a tight circle in the small locked room, around and around, burning. She had shouted, but that had done no good. She had cursed, had wished for dark powers, had even called down the powers of old pagan gods -- all to no avail. Forcing calm, she sank to her knees on the hard floor.

"Dear Lord Jesus," prayed Rowena, as gently as she could, looking to the single narrow window set in the stone wall where a twisted belt of stars could be seen. Perhaps, she thought, this was where heaven was located. "You are kind, wise, all-knowing. I beseech you, I beg you…"

But Rowena could not sustain her prayerful tone. Her gentleness was a sham. "Damn the guards for taking her below!" she said, jumping up, turning away

from the window and toward the shut door. Rowena had
to watch what she said in her prayers, because she
felt that it was as much Lord Jesus's fault as her own
for failing Rebecca in her time of need. She beat her
fists against the door. "Damn Sir Brian for ordering
her there! Damn him to eternal hellfire!"

Turning about, Rowena pressed her forehead to the
cold stone wall below the narrow window, breathing
hard, desperately trying to tame her violent temper.
She believed that a penitent heart could renew Lord
Jesus's compassion, could enlist His support. Perhaps
her prayers had begun the wrong way. In praying to
the Christian god, one must always remember the
hierarchy of things.

Rebecca was loyal to her father, Isaac. Isaac
was loyal to King Richard. The King was the first
Christian in the country.

She tried again. "Dear Lord Jesus, safeguard
brave King Richard, bless great lord Cedric, protect
and comfort my dear lord Ivanhoe."

The distant sound of waves slapping a rocky shore
drifted up intermittently, sometimes temperate,
sometimes savage. Rowena knelt again on the
unforgiving floor, her forehead chilled by its

pressure against the outer wall of the small chamber. For a moment, she was calmer, until suddenly imagining a scream from deep in the dungeons. Or one from the locked room on the other side of her wall.

Rebecca, calling out to her in terrible pain.

Above Rowena, the narrow window, in daylight, afforded a view of the wild seacoast a hundred feet below. Yesterday, she had watched waves smash an abandoned rowboat, again and again, against the cliffside. At low tide, the broken hull was strewn over the strip of sand, only to be washed away by the rising water of late afternoon.

"Lord Jesus, powerful and good, who can do anything, bring down vengeance on the Normans who have captured Lady Rebecca, and have thrown her father Isaac into a dungeon. Save Lord Isaac from torture and death. Save my Lady Rebecca from desecration. Bring Sir Ivanhoe to our rescue, speedily and with great force of arms."

This was better, she thought, more like the words she heard in the chapel at Rotherwood, more like the supplications of priests and monks. But the small solace didn't last. Why should Lord Jesus, who knew everything, believe her to be sincere? Lord Jesus knew her soul, knew the violence within, knew everything about her.

Lord Jesus knew that Rowena was not one to beg for help, not from anyone, not even from Himself.

Cedric had often remarked that Rowena behaved more like a warrior than a maiden. But what knight would have allowed Rebecca to trudge through the miles while Rowena rode on horseback? What brave warrior would have allowed Rebecca to be thrust onto Sir Brian's saddle, so that he could ogle and touch her at his pleasure?

Of course, Rowena understood that she was not a knight, but a female, a powerless ward of an old nobleman. Brave and headstrong she was, but she could never challenge a knight to a duel, would never have the chance to drive a lance through Sir Brian's black heart.

Here, in the demon's castle, Rowena had gone to her locked chamber with barely a struggle. She had allowed Rebecca to be separated from her in another room, where Sir Brian could visit her at will. A knight might not have succeeded in preventing this, but at least he would have had the satisfaction of dying while doing the right thing.

Rebecca had saved Rowena's life, and the life of
her betrothed. Yet what had Rowena done to help
Rebecca? Nothing, she thought. The frustration of
being unable to help was infuriating.

The outer walls of Rowena's chamber were
impenetrable stone, but the inner walls were thin.
Night after night, she could hear Sir Brian come into
Rebecca's room, shutting the door behind him. Brian
would speak with his hateful Norman accent, first
uttering promises, then threats.

Rowena would listen, enraged, as Brian dared tell
Rebecca to be kind to him. "Be kind," he would say,
again and again, until the word had twisted its
meaning into something entirely different. Until
kindness meant submission; and submission meant defeat
of everything that was good and pure in the world.

Rowena couldn't always hear Rebecca's responses.
Brian, obviously rebuffed, would continue doggedly:
Did Rebecca not want to live? Did she not realize
that a foreigner, a Jewess, the daughter of a traitor,
must be executed? Only Brian's intercession could
save her. Why couldn't Rebecca understand that he
offered her honor? That to be the official mistress

of a great Norman lord was a position only a fool
would reject.

When Rebecca's responses would grow loud enough
to be heard, Rowena would press her ear to the wall
between chambers. Two nights past Rebecca's words had
been perfectly clear: "What have you done to my
father?" she had said.

"Your father is alive," Brian had said. "But he
is beyond help. Treason must be punished. But if you
can learn to obey me, you can avoid his fate. I give
you my word --"

Rebecca had interrupted: "The word of a Gentile
cannot be trusted," she said. "Esau will always hate
Jacob."

This had been painful for Rowena to hear. Though
she had broken no promise to Rebecca, no oath, the
fact that she had failed her was as bad as a broken
promise.

Brian had continued, insisting: "I don't know
your Jewish Bible, but I know that the word of a
knight is sacred. I am a knight. And your only
chance of salvation in this world."

"You break the laws and commandments of every
nation," Rebecca had said. "You talk of salvation and

carnal sin in the same breath. Because you are more
beast than human. That is what I think of you.
Beast, animal, savage. The torturer of my father who
wants me as his harlot."

"Not my harlot," Brian had said. "Don't you
understand I want much more from you than that?"

"It is you who cannot understand. Rabbi Hillel
taught us that a brute cannot fear sin. But you will
be damned nonetheless. For harming my father is a
monstrous evil, and for that you will be tormented
forever in the pit of Gehenna. I would rather be dead
than your mistress."

Rejected by his prisoner, Sir Brian's voice would
grow increasingly wild. Rowena, shaking with hatred,
could imagine him grabbing Rebecca's thin frame, his
powerful grip leaving marks on her pale skin. Perhaps
he twisted her arms, perhaps he struck her face.
Rowena couldn't hear everything that was said, and
couldn't imagine everything that was done. But it was
clear that Brian's lust had stained his honor. It was
only a matter of time when he would give in to his
basest impulses.

Last night had been worst of all. Brian had
begun angry, and left angrier. There had been nothing

gentle about his promises, about his helpless
feelings.

"You would do best not to threaten me with Jewish
curses," Brian had said. "You sound like a witch.
That is why everyone believes I debase myself by
offering you gifts, instead of taking you as my right.
You are a witch, people say, and your false charms
have made me weak. But I am stronger than you or
anyone else thinks. I am not afraid to show you hell
right here on earth. A vision of flames. A bonfire
for a witch. Continue to refuse me, and I will chain
you to a stake, and watch a bonfire burn away your
beauty forever."

Rowena had listened as Rebecca's door had opened
and slammed shut, leaving behind only silence. She
had rapped hard on the wall between their chambers,
but Rebecca hadn't responded. Rowena had beaten
harder on the wall, until finally she could hear
Rebecca's gentle double tap.

"Listen to me, Rebecca," Rowena had said,
shouting into the wall. "You are not alone. I am
here. And Ivanhoe will come. He will come, I swear
it!" She had been saying this for days, too many days
to remember.

Rebecca had never disputed Rowena's contention. All she knew was that her father was being tortured, and would soon be dead, and that she must quickly follow. So Rebecca hadn't answered, and Rowena hadn't continued.

Her friend needed rest, thought Rowena. Sleep was a great comfort. Perhaps Rebecca would find hope in dreams.

But there had been neither sleep nor dreams for Rebecca last night. Rowena had soon heard unfamiliar footsteps in the corridor, followed by the unlocking of Rebecca's door. The footsteps in the corridor hadn't been Brian's, and the harsh authoritative voices had been unfamiliar. At least two men, maybe more. They were taking Rebecca out of her room.

Rowena had scurried to her own locked door, and shouted through it: "Rebecca, where do they take you?" There had been a response, but too quiet for Rowena to hear. "What do they want with you, Rebecca?" she had shouted.

This time Rebecca's response had been louder. "Goodbye, my lady," Rebecca had said. "Goodbye, dear friend."

"Answer me, Rebecca! Where do they take you?"

"To my father," Rebecca had said, her voice fainter, as she had been dragged away from Rowena's door.

"No!" Rowena had said, pounding on her door. "Don't take her down! She is under the protection of Lord Cedric of Rotherwood. You cannot take her to the dungeons. You cannot take her!"

The guards hadn't answered Rowena. She had heard their heavy footsteps grow increasingly faint, until the hallway was perfectly silent. Brian had sent Rebecca to the place of torture and death. There had been nothing Rowena could do. It was then that she had begun to rage and pray and rage some more.

But it was clear that prayer hadn't worked. Rowena suddenly rose to her feet. "Only tell me, Lord Jesus," she said. "Tell me a way to help my friend."

This was better, thought Rowena. Asking the great Christ for guidance, rather than begging Him to do everything for her on His own. The priests always said that God helps those who are willing to struggle for themselves. Rowena was more than willing.

She stared out the narrow window. A three-quarters moon hung below the belt of stars in the cloudless sky. Below, unseen waves continued to pound

the base of the cliff. What can I do, Lord Jesus? she
thought. I will do anything. Tell me.

Suddenly, without conscious thought, she found
her hand reaching for the jeweled hilt of the poniard
hanging from her belt. Sir Reginald had taken the
knife away when she had been captured, but Sir Brian
had returned it to her. She was a noblewoman, and
would be allowed to cut up whatever food they gave
her. Sir Brian didn't worry about the little blade.
He wasn't concerned that it was not just a knife with
which to eat, but a dagger with which to kill.

Rowena raised her eyes higher, beyond the moon,
beyond the stars, certain that this was inspiration
straight from the great Christ.

Another, louder crashing of the waves, lowered
her eyes to the black surf. Then she raised her eyes
slowly, until she could make out the thin ledge under
her window, a ledge narrower than her feet; a ledge
that ran along the cold stone all the way to the
window of the neighboring room.

Rowena's heart pounded, louder than the waves.
This was fear, she realized. All at once she was both
afraid, and surprised to be afraid. But she embraced
the fear, she tasted it with delight, she swallowed it

whole. Knights lived with fear, made it their
companion, their source of strength. So would she.

Rowena slipped out of her sandals. The fear
intensified. To slip through the narrow window, to
place her hands against the damp stone, and point her
bare toes to the ledge; this would be daring, this
would be frightful, this would be a heaven-scent
challenge. She smiled at the moon, at the stars, at
the unseen God who had inspired her fear, and gave her
courage.

"Thank you, Lord Jesus," she said, with a tone
more comradely than reverent.

Rowena crossed the room, and sat on the floor,
her back against the door, waiting. Slowly and
surely, daylight filtered into the room. Rowena
couldn't know for certain if Rebecca was even alive.
She might never be brought back from the dungeons, her
corpse might be left to rot in chains out of sight for
all time.

But no, Lord Jesus would not have sent Rowena
this brave idea, this warlike vision to save her
friend, if Rebecca was already gone.

Brian wasn't done with Rebecca, of that Rowena
was certain. Brian hadn't whipped and branded her,

hadn't broken her bones, hadn't burnt her alive.
Rowena had seen the lust in his eyes, had heard the
unholy passion in his voice. Few demons were as
strong as lust. Lust would force him to try to make
Rebecca give in, at least one more time.

Rowena waited for Rebecca's return, her hand
caressing the hilt of her weapon.

Rebecca must be alive, she thought. She would be
brought back to her room with its narrow window. A
narrow window connected by a tiny ledge to its
neighboring window: The window in Rowena's locked
room. The blessed opening to light and air, to the
heavens above, the earth below.

Brian would push Rebecca inside her room,
shutting the door after him. He would feel powerful,
unstoppable. There would be just the two of them in
the small, confining chamber.

Brian and Rebecca, victor and victim, knight and
captive, with Brian ready to break all his vows, ready
to leave behind his place in heaven in exchange for a
few moments of temporal bliss.

Asking for advice was better than prayer, thought
Rowena. "Thank you for advising me, Lord Jesus," said
Rowena. "Now, I know what I must do."

CHAPTER TWENTY-TWO

"Why did I listen to you?" said Ivanhoe. "We should never have taken the left fork. This way is much longer."

"It only seems that way, Master," said Gurth. "When you are in a hurry, everything seems to be slowing you down."

"Only you are slowing me down," said Ivanhoe. "I know this countryside as well as the route to Rotherwood, so don't be telling me 'left' when I mean to go 'right.'"

"You have been out of the country for so long, and do not know the roads as well as you used to."

"I know the roads perfectly well! Just as I know you are up to something! You, with your short cuts, your left forks, your tale of the river being impossible to ford!"

"You cannot expect a fully laden packhorse to swim."

"I should have tried the ford myself. But no, you insisted you were here at this same time of year, when two horses drowned trying to cross!"

"Three horses and a mule."

"Your story gets better at every telling. Soon that ford will have drowned an entire army."

"We didn't lose much time avoiding the river," said Gurth.

"Half a day following that muddy track single file! Maybe that's not much time to you, since you're not, apparently, in any kind of a hurry." As if in agreement with the knight's statement, Gurth slowed down.

Ivanhoe reined in beside him, wildly frustrated. "Now what are you doing?"

"I'm sorry, Master, but we need to stop."

"What? Again? No! We are not stopping for anything." But the squire had already jumped down from the stallion. "Why do you insist on taking every chance to delay our journey?"

"Perhaps you didn't notice," said Gurth, approaching the packhorse. "The poor old mare is dragging her foot."

Ivanhoe turned in the saddle, watching Gurth raise the packhorse's left rear foot. "At this rate, we will never make Torquilstone by nightfall."

"Night is a bad time to arrive in Torquilstone," said Gurth, poking a finger around the horseshoe.

"I never would have thought you would be afraid of what we will face at the end of our journey."

"I am not afraid."

"Because if you are fearful about what I will do when we arrive, that I will simply throw myself into a fight that I cannot possibly win - "

"I am not afraid," repeated Gurth, continuing to poke in and around the horseshoe.

"I do not intend to attack the castle, one man against an army of bowmen on the battlements. What I intend is to call out a challenge to the master of Torquilstone. Sir Brian is a traitor and a villain, but he is also a knight."

Gurth let out a breath of air, half-way between a laugh and a snort of contempt. Ivanhoe ignored it, continuing: "I will challenge Brian to single combat in front of the castle walls. He will not be able to refuse. When I vanquish Sir Brian, the rules of chivalry are clear. I will be given the keys to the castle, and be able to free Rowena."

"Thistle," said Gurth, breaking his silence. Letting the horse lower her foot, Gurth exhibited the prickly stem to Ivanhoe. "Caught under the horseshoe."

"Did you hear what I just said? I have a plan. I will set Rowena free."

"Perhaps you will also want to free Lady Rebecca and Lord Isaac," said Gurth, mounting the old stallion.

"'Perhaps'?" said Ivanhoe, furious.

"You didn't mention them, but I hope you mean to free them as well."

"Of course I mean to free them, fool! Do you imagine I have forgotten my duty or my oath?"

Ivanhoe spurred his horse forward. Gurth followed at a slower pace, leading the packhorse. In a few moments, Ivanhoe looked around, angry at having to wait for Gurth to catch up. As Ivanhoe reined in, he demanded: "For the love of God, you big oaf, try and keep my pace."

"I don't understand why are you so angry, Master," said Gurth, pulling alongside. "I only mentioned Rebecca and Isaac, in case you had forgotten that they have been taken as well."

"I have forgotten nothing," said Ivanhoe, moving forward, trying to set aside guilty thoughts. They rode side by side along a road shaded by ancient trees.

"Then perhaps you remember that Sir Reginald Front de Bouef will be in Torquilstone as well. He too is a knight, and probably knows all the customs and codes of chivalry. But I am certain that once you vanquish Sir Brian, Sir Reginald will instruct his bowmen to shoot you down. Shoot you until they have used every arrow in their quivers."

"Even if Reginald had been born a serf, he would have more decency than to give such an order," said Ivanhoe.

"Serfs have more decency than you imagine, Master," said Gurth. "As well as intelligence." The road narrowed, so that the two men rode very close together. Ahead lay yet another fork in the road, and Ivanhoe began to turn left.

"No, Master," said Gurth. "That is not the way." Without waiting for a rebuke, Gurth turned right, pulling the packhorse behind him.

"No, stop!" said Ivanhoe. Ivanhoe quickly rode alongside, and took hold of the reins to Gurth's horse. "You are wrong. I am sure of it. Torquilstone is to the left. This way leads to nothing but a clearing and a brook."

Gurth pulled free his reins, then looked his master in the eye. "Please, Master. Just follow me." Ivanhoe was astounded to see the rebellious Gurth move forward. There was nothing to do but follow. As Ivanhoe pulled alongside, Gurth again reined in. The squire was looking ahead, where daylight marked the end of the tunnel beneath the trees.

"You will soon understand, Master," said Gurth. "We are almost there." Gurth was smiling. "This is where I've been heading since we left Sir Kenrick's."

"Understand what? Understand why you have been taking me on a wild goose chase to nowhere?"

"Understand that there is a better way into Torquilstone than issuing a challenge to Sir Brian." Gurth continued to walk his horse toward the light.

Ivanhoe again caught up to the squire, struck by a new look of joy in his face. "What are you so happy about?"

"You will soon understand that too," said Gurth.

Turning from Gurth, Ivanhoe looked to a peaceful, sunlit clearing a few yards away, where a sprightly mare was tethered to a branch. "So you dare admit it? You brought me here by design?"

"Yes," said Gurth simply.

"Why? Whose horse is that? Why have you brought me to this place?" Ivanhoe controlled his anger, remembering what was most important. "And what did you mean when you said that there was a better way to Torquilstone?"

"Not 'to,'" said Gurth. "'Into.' Anyway, it would be better if she explained."

For a moment, Ivanhoe didn't understand what he was being told. But then a young woman, who had been out of sight, kneeling before the brook on the other side of the mare, got to her feet. Her red hair shined in the sun. Ethelreda was pleased to see that they had finally arrived.

CHAPTER TWENTY-THREE

Two guards had taken Rebecca below, pushing and
prodding her down steep stone steps, into darker and
darker regions.

Between flights of stairs were airless corridors.
Her bare feet recoiled from ghastly liquids on the
unseen floor. Torches cast horrific shadows. Rebecca
had willed herself to be calm. The night before, she
had begged Sir Brian for the chance to see her father,
and he had finally granted her wish. But cruelty had
shone through his eyes when he had said: "All right,
Rebecca. You grant me no favors, but I will grant you
one nonetheless. Tomorrow night you will see your
traitorous father one last time."

And the next night, just as he had promised, the
guards had come for her, to take her to her father.
She had heard Rowena's fury, knew that her Christian
friend was good and brave, and wanted to save her.
But Rebecca couldn't explain, couldn't let her know
that it was her own desire that was taking her to this
hellish place, that she wanted nothing more than to be
alone with Isaac one more time before crossing with
him to the World-to-Come.

More steps, more smoky torches, more menacing passageways, as the guards had hurried her along, one in front, one behind. Nearing an alcove, the underground stench had grown in strength, and she stared, horrified, at an old man in ragged clothes chained to the wall. The teeth in his mouth had been recently broken. She had stopped in her tracks.

The old man had raised his head briefly, to look at this strange newcomer to his underworld. He had smiled at her, as if the very sight of her had been a comfort, a respite in a world of pain. But he was not her father.

Rebecca had spoken to him: "Who are you, sir? Why do they keep you here?" Her guards had tried to push her forward, but Rebecca had resisted. Then she had spoken in Hebrew, loud and clear: "A man who is banished from the company of men, is never banished from the company of God."

The old man had smiled at these indecipherable words, but the guards had grown fearful. One of them had warned her: "Silence, witch! None of your devilish spells!"

Then Rebecca had added, in English: "May the Lord of Heaven and Earth bless you and protect you, even in this terrible place." The old man had allowed his eyes to close, his head to fall forward.

As the guards had hurried her along, she had demanded: "Who is this man?"

"A traitor," one had answered. "He resists just rule."

As they had brought her deeper into the dark and foul place, she felt terrible fear. The old man was not her father, but what would Isaac look like when she finally saw him? He had already been weak and ailing on the voyage to Torquilstone. And Brian had made it clear that her father was not answering his questions about the whereabouts of King Richard and the names of his supporters. That her father was a traitor, and would receive the fate of traitors. Had Brian allowed him sleep, given him food, kept him warm?

Light had revealed leather whips, metal presses, branding irons, a torture-rack. Coals had burned in a brazier, where a huge man with dead eyes stood, arms crossed, watching her near. Rounding a corner, she had been confronted with Sir Brian de Bois Gilbert, his immaculate clothing and handsome face an abomination in this unholy place.

"Leave us," Brian had ordered his guards, his eyes never leaving Rebecca.

As they had left, Rebecca had spoken: "Where is he?" Where is my father?" Chains that might have held a man's wrists had hung empty from the stone wall behind Brian. Torchlight had revealed stains on the walls and floors.

"He was here a minute ago," Brian had said. "Still lecturing me about loyalty." He hadn't meant to add to her fury, but so deep was her hostility , that he couldn't help but lash back. "Lecturing me between his screams."

Rebecca had thrown herself at Brian, her hands balled into fists. The knight had grabbed her wrists easily, and held her close, looking into her hate-filled face. "What did you do to him?" she had said. "You said he was alive. You swore I would see him before he died. Before you murdered him for doing his duty to King Richard."

"I will take you to your father," Brian had said. "Lord Isaac is not dead."

Brian had spoken truly. Rebecca's father had not yet died. The knight, gripping her wrist tightly, had taken her along another fetid corridor, where he had pulled open a heavy door revealing a man sitting up on a pallet, dimly lit by a guttering candle.

She had tried to pull away from Brian's grip, to go to her father at once, but Brian held tight to her wrist. "Not much of a father, so ready to make an orphan out of a daughter like you," he had said. "You had best get the traitor to tell me what I want to know."

Deep in the dungeon, there was little difference between night and day. It had been late at night when Brian's guards had come for her. Now that she finally saw Isaac's face, she wondered whether dawn would ever break again on the surface of the earth, high above this underground hell.

"Daughter," he said, filled with gratitude. "Thank God for answering my prayers. The Lord has brought you to me one last time."

She sat with him, taking hold of his dirty hands, kissing his sunken cheeks, looking into his honey-colored eyes. The flickering candle light was enough to see that he had lost weight, that his eyes burned with fever. But these simple markers of his struggle were of little moment, compared to what Rebecca sensed at once. Her father was not long for the world.

"Father," she said. "You owe nothing to the Gentile King. Isn't there something you can tell Brian that will set you free?"

"I am almost free right now," Isaac said.

"To seek your own death is an abomination," she said.

"I do not seek death," said Isaac. "But as an end to suffering, I welcome it."

"That is not the only way to end your suffering. Can't you offer Sir Brian money, arrange a ransom for yourself as you have arranged one for your King?"

"No," said Isaac. "His prince wants more than money from me. He wants me to help destroy the rightful king. I will not do that. Though I love life, though I love my daughter, I will not abandon my sacred duty."

Before she could answer, he smiled, and pressed a finger to her lips. A current of profound feeling ran between father and daughter. All the pain she had felt in his body seemed to vanish.

She understood that her father had made up his mind. Isaac was not looking for a way to survive his ordeal. He was looking for release. Whether or not King Richard would ever return to England, the names of his allies would go with Isaac to the grave.

"Daughter," he said. "Forgive me for leaving you alone in this place. You were right. We should never have delayed our trip to Spain. Now you must go without me."

"I will go nowhere without you!"

Isaac held her eyes with his own, saying nothing for a long time. When he finally spoke, it was to remind her of the words of Rabbi Shimon ben Gamaliel: How the world is sustained by three things only – truth, judgment, and peace.

Rebecca quoted the passage from *Pirke Avot*: "'Speak the truth to one another, render in your gates judgments that are true, and make for peace.'"

"We must make peace between us, Daughter," said Isaac. "And you must find peace for yourself. There is not much time."

"I have nothing to forgive you for, Father. But if you want to hear me say it, here it is: I forgive you and honor you and love you."

"Thank you, Rebecca. But now I am talking about something other than forgiveness. Peace."

She didn't understand what he was saying. Isaac had been forgiven, and so now she gave her oath that she would try and leave England and go to Spain. To Zaragoza, where her mother's family lived. The Cuheno family was large and prosperous, and would take her in, protect her as if she were their own child.

"To find peace, you must go to Zaragoza as soon as you are able," said Isaac. "Because I can see beyond all the terrors of this place, that you have a greater fear." His strength fading, he paused for breath. "That he will find you. Come for you. Ivanhoe."

"Do not speak of him, Father," said Rebecca. "Not now."

"There will never be another time for the two of us," said Isaac.

"I am not afraid of Ivanhoe," she said.

"I can feel the morning light coming. Somehow it penetrates into this dark place. When there is bright light outside the walls of Torquilstone, I will be gone."

"I am not afraid of Ivanhoe," she insisted.

"Then give me your word," he said. "That you will never abandon your faith and your people."

"How can you ask that of me? Ivanhoe means nothing to me! Nothing," said Rebecca.

"I forgive you, Daughter," said Isaac, the life fading from his eyes. "When your heart is so full, understanding is… impossible."

"Father, no! Don't go. Please. Only a moment longer. Only a moment." She held him close, muttering prayers, rocking back and forth, back and forth.

When Brian entered the room, she had no idea how much time had passed. It took him an effort, but the knight pulled her away from Isaac, then forced her to stand. Slowly, she turned her eyes from her father's corpse, to the handsome knight who had murdered him.

"Now you have no father, Rebecca. All you have in the world is me."

In the crushing sadness of the moment, Brian's words rang true. She had forgotten that there was family waiting for her in Zaragoza. Forgotten that Lady Rowena was her loving friend, and would risk anything to protect her. Forgotten that Ivanhoe had given his pledge to protect her. And not only Ivanhoe, of course, but his burly, redheaded squire.

Brian, gripping her arm in a jailer's hold, took her up winding stairs, higher and higher, to where daylight and air penetrated, to the high, locked room next to Rowena's, overlooking a turbulent sea.

Rebecca couldn't know that at that very moment, on the opposite side of the great fortress, a pretty young woman was crossing the drawbridge into Torquilstone. That she was accompanied by a solid young man, in peasant's clothes. Both of them strong, fearless – and redheaded. Ethelreda was holding Gurth's hand.

Two warriors, armed with spears, leered at her, stepping in their way. "It's about time you're back, wench," one said. "We thought you'd given up kitchen work for good."

"Don't call her 'wench,'" said Gurth, smiling proudly.

"And why not, you Saxon son of a whore?"

"My mother is not a whore," said Gurth. "And Ethelreda is not a wench. She is my wife."

"This is Gurth," said Ethelreda to the warriors. "We have been married for three days. I expect Cook will find him a job by my side."

The warriors stepped aside to let them past. "Listen, wench," said the warrior who had early spoken, ignoring Gurth's correction. "When your Saxon husband is too busy chopping onions to give you a proper bedding, you have only to knock on my door."

Gurth turned, already halfway inside the gate. "Very bravely said," said Gurth. "Put aside your spear and your mail coat, and come knock on my door. Bring as many friends as you wish. I will be happy to instruct you how Saxons defend their honor."

The warriors smirked as the big peasant, holding his young bride's hand, walked into the impenetrable castle.

CHAPTER TWENTY-FOUR

Sir Brian returned Rebecca to her locked room, and released his painful grip on her arm.

He watched her sink onto her knees, forehead pressed to the stone floor, her body racked with sobbing. The Norman thought about helping her back to her feet or onto the thin straw mattress against the wall, but decided against it. She had no understanding of what he was offering her, no gratitude. The Jewess blamed him for her father's death, though clearly the fault was Isaac's.

Brian was an agent of Prince John's will, and Prince John was the legitimate ruler of the land. Her father was a traitor, and by extension, so was she. In another man's hands, Rebecca would have been raped, killed, torn to pieces and burnt to ashes. He remained standing, hands at his sides, bristling with frustration at the display of her anguish.

"You think me a beast," said Sir Brian. "But I am not without comprehension of your grief. I will leave you alone until you are done crying." He stood there a few moments longer, realizing she had heard nothing of what he had said. In a harsher tone and louder voice, he added: "Do not keep me waiting

long." He doubted whether she had heard this either.

Then Sir Brian de Bois Gilbert left Rebecca.

Inside the adjacent room Rowena heard Brian pass

by, moving in a great hurry. She pressed her ear to

the wall separating her from Rebecca. Rowena heard

sobbing, great cries of pain, a muffled drumming that

might have been Rebecca's fists beating the floor.

Then suddenly the crying stopped. Now there were

words, foreign words, intoned in a dogged, unstoppable

rhythm. Apparently, Rebecca was reciting a prayer.

The prayer was repeated over and over. Every once in

a while, Rebecca would let out another sob. Then the

prayer would begin again.

Rowena didn't try to attract her friend's

attention by shouting, or banging on the wall.

Rebecca must be mourning. She must have learned that

Lord Isaac was dead. Perhaps she had witnessed his

last moments, perhaps she had seen the corpse.

There were no words that Rowena could bring up

that would console her friend. No words that could

assure her that all would be well, that they would

soon be free. If Rebecca could not bring Isaac back

to life with her Jewish sorcery, what help could
Rowena provide?

Rowena sat on the hard floor, her back to the
wall. No, she could not conjure the dead, but there
were things she could do. Actions that did not
involve consoling words. Looking out her window into
bright light, Rowena gripped the jeweled hilt of her
sharp little poniard. Then she gripped it harder.

On the other side of the wall Rebecca lifted her
head, staring toward the adjacent room she could not
see. She had felt Rowena's presence, and remembered
that she had a friend in the world.

Rebecca took in a great breath of air. Life was
the gift of the Almighty, and could be taken away at
any time. If she was alive, it was because the Holy
One, in his infinite wisdom, wished it to be so.

Sorrow rose up from her belly, to her throat,
into her mouth. She clenched her teeth, pressed her
lips together, refusing to let the grief fly free.
Carefully and painfully she swallowed the great lump
of sadness. Easing it down her throat, into her
belly. Rebecca knew it must stay there, not only as a
part of her soul, but as a part of her body. She must

not reject the pain of Isaac's absence, the misery of being left an orphan in the world, but accept it.

Mourning too was part of life. Did she not mourn her mother every day since she had passed? Was not that aching sorrow as much a part of her body as her heart and lungs? Now she would swallow up her grief for Isaac's passing in the same way. She would mourn her father the only way she knew how.

She returned to the words of the Kaddish: *"Yisgadal, ve yiskadash, shmei raba..." Glorified and sanctified be God's great Name through the world, which He has created."*

The Kaddish was the prayer for mourning, yet nowhere in it was regret for the dead. It was instead a hymn of praise for the Holy One. The Great Lord who had given everyone life, and now had taken that life away.

"May His Great Name be blessed forever and to all eternity." A hymn, not a lamentation, she thought. *"Blessed and praised, glorified and exalted, extolled and honored, adored and lauded be the Name of the Holy One, blessed be He."*

Again and again, Rebecca intoned praises to the Master of the Universe who had let her father be tortured and die in a dungeon. **"Beyond all the blessings and hymns, praises and consolations that are ever spoken in the world."** The Lord had His reasons for everything he did. Was he not omniscient as well as omnipotent? **"He who creates peace in his celestial heights, may He create peace for us and for all Israel."**

Peace, that is what her father wanted. Peace between them, and peace for her. On his deathbed, Isaac had insisted: "Give me your word. That you will never abandon your faith and your people."

But she had never given her word. It wasn't necessary. "Ivanhoe means nothing to me! Nothing!"

She had practically shouted the denial at her father, his honey-colored eyes filled with sadness. With understanding. Is it a really a lie, when you lie to yourself? **"And let us say Amen."**

She had held her father close, as the life force had left him, as his soul joined his ancestors, leaving behind nothing but the body that would soon turn to dust. **"Yisgadal, ve yiskadash, shmei raba…"**

She did not look up when the door to her room was unlocked, neither did she stop her prayer. A guard came close and placed a bowl of gruel on the floor beside her. He said something to her, but she paid it no attention.

"Yisgadal, ve yiskadash, shmei raba…"

"Sir Brian said you should eat," said the guard.

"B'almah devrah kherusei…"

The guard grabbed her hair and pulled her head back, so that she was no longer staring at the floor.

"None of your spells, Jew-witch," said the guard. "They may have worked for my master, but they won't work for me." He turned her head painfully, so that they were eye to eye.

Rebecca continued to intone her prayer, as if the guard was not in the room: *"V'yamlich malchusei. B'chayechon, oov'yomechon…"*

"I said none of your spells, witch!" said the guard, shaking her until she was quiet. He told her she had better eat, she had better rest, she wouldn't be worth much to his master if she lost her looks.

Rebecca looked at the guard's cold eyes, his fast moving lips, his rotten teeth. Then she continued: *"Oov'chayeh d'kall beis yisrael…"*

The guard let go his hold on her hair and stood, watching her lips move, listening to the language he didn't comprehend.

"B'agalah oo vizman khariv... v'imru Amen." Her green-gold eyes blazed, but they didn't seem to take him in. He could see how she had bewitched his master. Who would not be enthralled by so rare and wild a beauty?

"Better do what I say, Jew-whore. You will need your strength when your knight returns." The guard left, slamming the door shut and locking it.

She had not been listening to the man, but his angry words lingered in the confined space. Something about how she would need her strength. Something about how his master was coming back. He had spoken of her knight. She remembered that clearly. "When your knight returns."

What could he mean? No matter what foul wish he might have, Brian was not her knight. No one, good or evil, was her knight, and no one would ever be.

No knight, Christian or pagan, had any claim on her, any connection to her at all.

Rebecca looked at the shut door, then down at at the bowl of cold gruel, marked with greasy chunks of forbidden meat. She picked up the bowl and stood, walking to the window. A narrow window, but not too narrow. She hurled the bowl out of the window, knowing that it would fall all the way to the roiling waters below. Gruel and meat would be swallowed by the sea, just like she had swallowed her misery.

Rebecca stood still, breathing in the fresh air and bright light. But the air did not refresh her, and the light could not dispel the darkness around her. She turned from the window, sat on the thin straw mattress. Perhaps in dreams, she could find some happiness. Slowly, she lay her exhausted body flat, and closed her eyes.

CHAPTER TWENTY-FIVE

On another straw mattress on the ground floor of the castle, just behind the enormous Torquilstone kitchens, Ethelreda lay still.

Gurth was beside her, his powerful body as tight as a drum. His eyes were open to the low ceiling. They were in a tiny section of a room behind the great kitchen, their private space outlined by ragged sheets hanging on either side of the mattress.

The servants who shared the sleeping quarters had left at first light, at least an hour before, making no attempt to be silent. The clanging sounds of pots and pans from the adjacent kitchen would be enough to

wake the deepest of sleepers, but Gurth could not be
sure that Ethelreda was awake. What did he know about
the ways of women? He had slept at close proximity to
his sisters and mother, but that had been years ago.
And Ethelreda was neither sister nor mother.

"Ethelreda," he said. "Are you awake?"

"Of course not, my husband," she said. "No bride
sleeps on her wedding night."

"I wish you wouldn't joke about matters so
serious," said Gurth. She turned her head slightly.
Gurth moved in kind. They looked at each other. Her
lips were grinning at his great solemnity.
"Especially as my greatest hope is that one day we
really will be married."

"My greatest hope is that we're not murdered by
Sir Brian's men," she said, grinning wider. She
slipped off the mattress, and got to her feet. Like
Gurth, she was wearing only underclothes. She didn't
preen, but neither did she parade false modesty. He
watched, breathless, as she put on her much washed and
mended kirtle, a young goddess in homespun.

"If you're through inspecting me, you can begin
to breathe again," she said.

"Forgive me for staring," said Gurth, getting off the mattress, trying not to crowd her.

"Every man stares at me," said Ethelreda. She picked up a bundle of his outer garments, secured by an old belt, and tossed it at him.

"I am not like every man," said Gurth. "Not where you're concerned." Ethelreda watched him slip on his rough tunic.

"I don't mean this unkindly," she said. "But, cousin, every man is the same."

"Don't call me that! 'Cousin.'" He buckled on his broad leather belt, with its hanging wallet and knife. "We are only distantly related, and will remain that way until we are married."

"When did you ever hear me agree to marry you?"

"I heard you call me 'husband.' I heard you explain to Cook how we had decided to marry when you visited your mother. I heard you say it was Brother Mungo who had blessed our union before man and God."

"But Gurth, those were lies. Lies to get you inside this place. All pretense."

"Yes, Ethelreda. Pretense." Gurth took a great breath, then continued: "But marriage was your idea. A wonderful idea." Gurth took her hand, looking at her lovingly. "And we must soon follow your idea in every detail."

"You are holding my hand," said Ethelreda, but she did not try to take it away. "Very courteous. I suppose you learned such manners from your high-born master."

"I don't mean any disrespect," said Gurth, eyes on her pale hand in his massive fist.

"You are a strange sort of suitor," said Ethelreda.

For lack of anything better to respond, Gurth blurted out: "It was kind of Cook to let us sleep in."

"Courtesy, respect, kindness - these are strange thinks to receive from a man with red hair. A man who grew up in a hut just like me."

"I only mean to say that Cook was thoughtful… to allow us a little time together."

"It's not every day one gets married," said Ethelreda. "Cook probably thought we needed to make loud noises without everyone listening."

"What do you think she'll want me to do in the kitchen?" he said.

"Now you're talking about kitchen work! I hoped you had better things on your mind when you took hold of my hand."

"I'm not much use at woman's work. And it is important she allow me to stay until Ivanhoe can arrive."

Suddenly she withdrew her hand from his, and sat on the low mattress.

"Never fear," she said with sudden sharpness. "Cook is a great taskmaster. There is wood to be chopped, heavy cauldrons to be lifted. Perhaps she'll trust you with a butchering knife to carve up a few cows."

"Is something wrong?" said Gurth.

"Yes."

"What? Do you fear for our plan?"

"Your master must think a great deal of you, Gurth, if he imagines you will be able to open the doors to Torquilstone with one little knife."

"There are men with weapons throughout the castle," said Gurth. "When I want weapons, I will take what I need."

"You speak bravely, Gurth," she said, reaching up for his hand, and pulling him down on the mattress beside her. "When you speak bravely, you look almost handsome." Nearby, a bushel of onions sizzled in buttery pots. Hearty pies and puddings were being assembled by busy hands. Pleasant heat radiated through the stone wall. "But are you really as brave as all that? To take what you want, when you need it?"

"Yes," said Gurth. "But… What do you mean?"

Ethelreda laughed. "You have proposed marriage to me, have you not?"

"Yes," he said. "The moment we are free of this place, we will go to Brother Mungo and –"

"This is my answer to your proposal of marriage," she interrupted, smiling slyly.

"What is your answer?" said Gurth, amazed to find the young beauty placing her hands on his cheeks. She looked at his stunned, still uncomprehending face, then drew his lips to hers.

Ethelreda kissed him, gently at first, slowly, and Gurth tried to be as gentle and slow in turn.

But gently gave way to forceful, and forceful to ferocious. Slowly gave way to urgent. Gurth had never felt so much pleasure so near at hand. He had long desired Ethelreda, but until this moment, he had never realized how that desire could grow and grow, that it could become as impossible to resist as the life force itself.

Gurth thought it a terrible sin to have so much bliss without the bonds of wedlock. He thought it almost a crime to feel his great love returned with such passion, with such evidence of mutual joy. He thought it wicked to feel such ecstasy while Rowena, Rebecca, and Isaac were imprisoned, perhaps even tortured, somewhere in this vast fortress where he now made love with Ethelreda.

But soon, Gurth stopped thinking.

Ringing sounds of pots and pans, delicious smells of stewing and baking vanished. Gone were any thoughts of Ivanhoe, Brian, the life-threatening dangers to come.

There was only this moment on this thin mattress with this young woman who was his wife now and forever.

CHAPTER TWENTY-SIX

Time passed slowly in the locked room. Rebecca prayed, kneeling on the stone floor. The rhythm of the prayers, constantly repeated, slowly put her to sleep. She fell over, waked for a moment, then decided to remain where she was. She stayed on the floor, curled up, hugging herself like a child.

The next time she woke, it was still daylight. She stopped herself from wondering how many hours had passed. What difference did it make? An hour, a day, a week? Her father was dead. Rebecca's life was over.

She stood, feeling stiffness in her limbs, hunger in her belly. Suddenly dizzy, she pressed her forehead to the stone wall, recalling what she had promised her father in his final moments: She would leave England, she would make her way to Spain, to Zaragoza, to her mother's family.

But how could she have promised such a thing? She was a young woman, without protector, imprisoned in a fortress. She had no ability to leave this room, much less travel to a distant country.

"Rebecca, please," said a man's voice behind her. The voice was kind, insistent. "For your own good."

She turned to where Sir Brian de Bois Gilbert stood in the open doorway. The man she hated above all others held a leather bottle and a drinking cup, looking at her with concern. He closed the heavy door behind him, then stepped closer, forcing a smile.

Rebecca spoke in Hebrew: "May the Lord curse you and your descendants for a thousand years," she said.

Brian stopped, arm's length from the beauty, and poured a liquid from the small bottle into the cup. "Something to revive your spirits."

"May your bones break," she continued, in Hebrew. "May your flesh rot."

"You know I cannot understand your language, Rebecca. But the tone is clear enough. You hate me." Refusing to show anger, he extended the cup. "Drink. It will do you good."

She looked at the cup, desperate to drink anything, and grabbed it from his hand. If it contained poison, no matter, she thought. She caught his worried eyes, watching her drink.

It was barley water, a favorite remedy for nearly every ailment. Her mother had given it to her when she was sick with childish fevers. Rebecca had given it to her father in place of water or wine, knowing it would restore his strength.

Now she nearly laughed out loud. The Norman knight, her greatest enemy, offering her this pathetic attempt at an anodyne. What was he hoping to accomplish with this gift?

Brian took the cup, refilled it to the brim, and handed it back to her. He had shaved, groomed his long hair, and wore a fresh silk tunic. Brian watched as she drank the second cup, more slowly than the first. "That's better," he said. "You will be able to think more clearly."

She handed him the cup, without thanks. In fact, her expression was hardening into a mask of loathing.

In spite of that, Brian could not hold back what he needed to say: "I have not expressed myself properly before, but I shall try to do that now. I didn't want your father to die. I wanted him alive, to answer my questions. That he died was not my fault, but the fault of the men who tortured him, without taking care to keep him alive."

"His torturers will be punished," said Rebecca, in English. "You chief among them. You will all burn in Gehenna's flames."

"You blame me for performing my duties to my prince." In Hebrew, Rebecca interjected: "You are a horror, an evil thing."

"You blame me for your abduction, your father's death, your desperate position in a country hostile to your people. But what you do not understand is what I have done for you. Offering to name you the Queen of Beauty and Grace at Prince John's tournament, I shamed a dozen Norman beauties of the highest lineage."

"Cursed are you, a snake among men," she said, continuing in Hebrew.

"I keep you alive, when my best warriors have demanded your execution for witchcraft. Black magic witnessed with their own eyes."

"Upon your belly you shall crawl," she said, the Biblical words as familiar as mother's milk. "Dust you shall eat all the days of your life."

"Do you know why I keep you alive? Why I want to help you?"

"Let the day perish on which you were born, let that day be darkness," said Rebecca.

"Do you know why I've wanted to help you from the first moment I saw you?" said Brian.

"Yes," said Rebecca, surprising him by returning to English. "I know why." She took a moment before continuing. "I see it in your eyes, I hear it in your voice. It is why you have shaved your face, and brought me your precious barley water. You want to possess me like a slave in a harem, then have me thank you for it."

"No," he said, putting down the leather bottle and cup.

"You want to take me like a whore, and have me smile at you like a bride."

"I don't want to force you," he said, taking hold of her shoulders, bringing his face close to hers. Rebecca struggled to get free, but he was far too strong. "Please, don't make me force you." Rebecca, her shoulders caught in his hands, moved her head back and away until she was backed against the stone wall.

His lips grew closer, his eyes hot with lust. "Let me love you," he said, bringing his lips to hers.

Trapped, Rebecca once again bit hard into his lower lip, bloodying it. He let go of her shoulders, wiped his mouth, then slapped her across the face.

"All right," he said. "You hate me. But I will bend you to my will."

Brian grabbed her again, pressing her into the wall. "You are a Jewess, but I will allow you to convert to our faith, so that you may live in my home." He breathed deeply, taking a moment to continue. "But if you refuse my love, I will not waste it on you," he said. "You will be my harlot." His wild eyes drew closer, his lips parted, his breathing faster.

"You murdered my father. I'd rather make love to a jackal," she said.

For a moment, both seemed to hesitate. Her defiance was implacable; so was his desire. If they had anything in common, it was lack of reason. They were no longer thinking, no longer listening to anything but the rage in their hearts.

It was no wonder neither heard the faint scraping sounds from outside the room's window, a narrow opening in the thick wall.

Brave as she was, it had taken Rowena many minutes to step out of her own window, onto the tiny ledge between the two chambers, where her bare feet gripped cold, damp stone. Yet Rowena, ignoring

howling wind and churning waters below, never
hesitated to continue. Every step brought her closer
to what she must do, in the name of her God, in the
name of friendship.

"I am of noble blood," said Brian, gripping
Rebecca's wrists, and dragging her to the straw-
stuffed mattress. Rebecca struggled, but she was no
match for his strength or his fury. She flailed at
him, but he grabbed her wrists. She spit at him, but
he slapped her face until she was still.

"Look at me. Listen well," he said. "I am
celebrated and admired throughout the realm. Anything
I offer you, is an honor."

Brian forced her flat onto the mattress, and
straddled her. She was certain she was about to die.
God would not want her to live defiled by such evil.
Rebecca shut her eyes, prepared to leave the world.
His awful words seemed quieter, as if muffled by thick
cloth. In a few moments she would be away from Brian,
from everything earthly.

"You are a Jewess," he said. "And I am a
Christian knight."

"You are not a Christian," heard Rebecca. The
voice was a woman's, filled with anger.

Brian heard it too, though for a moment it had no more reality than words whispered in a dream.

"Christians fear for their immortal soul," said Rowena. "And you know you're going straight to hell."

Brian turned to the window, stunned to see Rowena coming through, and stepping into the room. But he stayed where he was, still straddling Rebecca, even as Rowena drew her sharp poniard.

"More proof that Rebecca is a witch," Brian said. "Witch enough to make you fly through windows." He stood, facing Rowena's knife without fear. "Witch enough to make you believe you can murder me."

Rowena raised her blade high. Brian, much taller, and fast as a lion, brought his hand down and tried to grab her wrist. But Rowena was faster. She stepped aside, avoiding his hand, and pointed the poniard at his heart.

"Witchcraft will have nothing to do with it," said Rowena. "Try me again, and I will send you to hell."

Brian stared at Rowena for a moment, then turned to where Rebecca had gotten to a kneeling position on the floor. "Be glad for this demonic intervention," he said to Rebecca. "You will have time to think

about my proposal. Talk it over with your Saxon
friend: Whether to live in luxury as my mistress, or
remain locked in this room as my slave."

Brian turned abruptly, leaving them, shutting and
locking the heavy door behind him.

"He killed my father," said Rebecca, incredulous.
"And then he tried to make love to me."

Rowena helped Rebecca get to her feet. "Our
Heavenly Master would never allow so vile a
desecration," said Rowena.

"God allowed the murder of my father!" said
Rebecca. "God allowed the murder of my mother! If not
for you, if not for your courage -"

"It was God alone who gave me courage," said
Rowena. "To step through the window, to walk along
the ledge to your room -- it was all God's plan."
Rowena pulled Rebecca close, assuring her that
Providence would save her, that all would be well in
God's hands.

But Rebecca wasn't comforted. Her faith in a
beneficent deity had been sorely tried by her mother's
murder. Her father's murder, too recent to
comprehend, was followed by swift prayers praising
God's Holy Name; but she knew her prayers had been

rote, meaningless, dulled by misery, devoid of religious feeling.

And now, if she was certain of anything, it was that Brian's attempt at rape hadn't been thwarted by her Jewish God. It had been stopped by a fierce Christian.

If all this had not broken Rebecca's faith, it had left her in mortal confusion. Was it possible that misfortune was leading her to completely abandon her faith? Was it possible that Isaac's loving daughter would forgo the sacred teachings of her people?

The Bible's words were clear: "The imagination of the heart of man is evil."

But, as her father had taught her, great rabbis throughout the diaspora had debated the meaning of the origin and purpose of evil for a thousand years. There was an evil inclination in man, yes, but it was balanced by a good inclination - the "Yetzer Ha-Ra" versus the "Yetzer Ha-Tov." Even though God knows everything -- the future as clear to Him as the Past -- the sages insisted that man has free will.

God knows what man will choose, but it is still man who chooses. It is always man's choice to follow

the good or the evil impulse: To choose righteousness
or wickedness; to do good or to sin. Despite all
sufferings, to believe in Him, or to let belief fade
away like a childish memory.

Was not this the war that was raging within her
at this moment? To be like Job, tested by God, and
accept every tribulation; or to let events shatter her
faith.

But without faith in God, what would she have?
thought Rebecca. For what purpose was her life? What
reason to stay alive? What reason to honor the wishes
of a dead father, and trek to Zaragoza?

Without faith, her father was nothing but a
moldering corpse, his wishes nothing but words shouted
into the wind.

"Ivanhoe," said Rowena. The name was not uttered
in answer to Rebecca's thoughts, but in response to a
faint commotion of noise outside the castle.

Rebecca heard the name, and wondered why Rowena
was voicing it. Her mind roiling, Rebecca stared at
Rowena, as she once again said the name of her
betrothed.

"Ivanhoe!" said Rowena. "He has come for us."

Though she now heard the same faint noise, Rebecca hesitated to respond. "Yes," said Rebecca finally, without joy or hope. "He has come." She spoke like someone acknowledging her greatest fear.

CHAPTER TWENTY-SEVEN

Rowena let go of Rebecca, went to the small window, and looked out. All she could see was the treacherous sea far below.

Because it was from the unseen front of the castle where the noise was growing. Where a mounted war party of Old Crusaders was gathering beyond the moat, hoping for a miracle that would let them vanquish the traitors of Torquilstone.

Rowena could not know that the miracle's name was Gurth. Or that Gurth had already killed three castle guards, and was even now beginning to release the great chains that would lower the heavy bridge across the double moat.

Just as Gurth could not know that in the three days he had kept his master waiting outside Torquilstone, Lord Cedric had finally arrived to join Ivanhoe, at the head of a small force loyal to their true king.

Just as Lord Cedric could not know that one of those veterans, a big man in black armor, his identity concealed by his helmet's face place, was more than an Old Crusader.

Much more: The stranger was the answer to all their worries, the embodiment of all their hopes.

And as would soon be revealed, he was not a stranger at all.

None of these unknowns mattered to Ivanhoe.

After three interminable days, he had stopped believing in Gurth's plan to open Torquilstone from the inside. If his father had not come today, he would have cast his fate to the winds, and shouted out a challenge to the castle's walls.

But his father had come, and with him a group of Old Crusaders, even older Saxon warriors, and the big stranger in black armor. Led by Lord Cedric, they would not seem much of a threat to the much greater number of young Norman knights inside the castle.

Ivanhoe knew most of these men from childhood. They would fight to the death. As Ivanhoe brought his warhorse alongside Cedric's, he could feel the righteous ferocity of the ragtag army behind them.

Soon Brian would assemble his knights, lower the drawbridge, and ride out to engage them. That was all Ivanhoe wanted. His rage would be enough to slay a thousand.

Now, as if in answer to Ivanhoe's prayers, the drawbridge was lowering, revealing the slowly opening mouth of Torquilstone Castle. He was certain that Brian, eager to prove his worth, would be the first one over the drawbridge.

There Ivanhoe would finally meet his nemesis in mortal combat.

"Not yet," said Lord Cedric. "Let them come to us."

But as the drawbridge continued its slow descent, the yawning opening showed no sign of Sir Brian or any of his knights.

Revealed instead was a familiar face, grinning triumphantly under its helmet of coarse red hair.

Gurth.

A moment later, the drawbridge's descent accelerated, slamming down with a great thud over the moat. Gurth was revealed in full. He stood alone, a bloody pike in hand, Three dead guards lay at his feet.

Ivanhoe understood: The Normans had not responded to the arrival of Lord Cedric's men. For all he knew, Brian's warriors could be asleep in their beds. The bridge had not been lowered at Sir Brian's order. It had been let loose by Gurth, exactly as he had planned.

Torquilstone had indeed been pried open from the inside -- and would be surprised.

Lord Cedric turned to the men at his rear, demanding caution, ordering everyone to hold back until Brian's men should come out, and make their intentions known.

"No, Father," said Ivanhoe. "Gurth has done his part. Now it is my turn."

"Wait!" insisted Cedric, gripping his son's wrist.

At that moment, they could see Gurth step away from a cluster of three mounted men behind his back: Armored knights, led by the enormous figure of Sir Reginald Front de Bouef.

"I'm through waiting," said Ivanhoe. "That giant is Reginald. He treated Lady Rebecca like a dog. I will kill him on the drawbridge."

"No, you won't, Crusader," said a commanding voice behind him. The voice sent a chill through Ivanhoe. He had not heard it for a long while, but he recognized it at once. It was a voice that expected to be obeyed.

But Ivanhoe didn't obey.

Shouting his war-cry, he spurred his warhorse forward.

As Ivanhoe galloped toward the drawbridge, Reginald spurred his horse forward.

Halfway across the moat, the two knights met in a thunderous clash of shields and swords. Both horses reared, threatening to fall off the narrow bridge into the moat's water. But the men controlled their great horses, then backed up carefully, eyes on each other; eager for more.

Moments later, huddled behind shields, swords held high, both again spurred their horses forward. Ivanhoe ducked, whirled, and twisted in his saddle, avoiding the towering Reginald's swinging blade. Reginald was rooted to his saddle, caring little for defense. The men's blades crashed and clattered, threatening to shatter.

Meanwhile, the big man in black armor had ridden his horse alongside Lord Cedric. This had not surprised Cedric. There were few men who could fill out that huge suit of armor. Cedric understood who this stranger must be.

Both men watched the battle without comment, until the stranger spoke: "Your son hasn't changed much, Cedric. Still likes to do things his own way."

It was hardly necessary for the big man to raise the face-plate of his helmet, to partially reveal his confident face to Lord Cedric. But that is what King Richard did.

Cedric said: "Maybe, Sire, his own way is best."

"I don't think so, Cedric," said Richard, looking to where Reginald's two knights had ridden onto the bridge, backing up their leader. "He's always been too quick to fight in hopeless situations."

Ivanhoe was tiring against the powerful battering of Reginald's sword and shield. Indeed, it seemed as if Ivanhoe might be unhorsed by the giant, until suddenly, he stood up in his stirrups, shouted –

--and with tremendous power let loose his shield!

Flung like a discus, the shield's edge slammed into Reginald's helmeted head.

Struck hard and off-balance, Reginald was thrown backward, and out of his saddle. Clutching sword and shield, the heavily armored giant fell into the murky waters of the moat.

"Not completely hopeless," said Cedric.
Remembering to add: "My Liege."

Not giving Ivanhoe a moment to recover,
Reginald's two knights charged. Gurth ran up behind
them, swinging his pike. The heavy pike-head slammed
across one man's back, sending him into the moat.

Ivanhoe, shield-less, dangerously exposed,
charged at the second man, extending his sword like a
lance.

Before Reginald's knight, protected by his
shield, could swing his battle-axe into Ivanhoe,
Gurth's pike drove through the back of his helmet,
penetrating his skull.

Impaled, the man fell off his horse and into the
moat, from where Reginald and his other knight
struggled to climb out.

"Mount the horse," said Ivanhoe, not taking time
to thank his squire.

"Which one, Master?"

"Choose one and mount!" said Ivanhoe.

Gurth chose Reginald's horse, and hoisted himself
up with a mischievous grin. "Forgive me, Master. I
suppose you wanted to kill one of them yourself."

"Hurry!"

Behind Gurth Ivanhoe could see a sudden massing of mounted warriors emerging from the inner castle. Far too many to count.

Ivanhoe whirled about, followed by Gurth. They clattered along the drawbridge to Cedric and the stranger in black armor; the disguised monarch he knew as well as his own father.

The line of Norman warriors stopped along the bridge. Warriors helped pull Reginald and his two knights – one dead, one wounded – out of the moat.

"It's hard to see them from here, Sire," said Ivanhoe to Richard. "But I saw. They're coming. Fifty, a hundred, two hundred…!"

"No wonder you look so pleased," said Richard.

Cedric turned to the men at his back. "Prepare yourselves. Die gloriously!"

"Like father like son," said Richard. "Stay here. Both of you."

"My Liege," said Cedric, beginning a plea that Richard cut short.

"Stay," ordered the legitimate King of Britain.

Then Richard Lion-Heart rode at an easy pace to the drawbridge.

Ivanhoe and Cedric disobeyed their king, and followed, just behind him. Father and son glanced at each other, acknowledging their mutual readiness for battle against overwhelming odds.

But the battle was about to be stopped, without force of arms, or even a word.

Richard Lion-Heart reined in, sitting tall in the saddle. Norman warriors watched as he removed his helmet, and tossed it aside. There was grey at the temples of the big man's golden hair. But to those who had seen him before the Crusades, the man was unmistakable.

Reginald Front de Bouef, wet and dazed, was sheathing his sword when he saw the face of a man he had hoped to never see again.

He hesitated. Reginald had a duty to Sir Brian, and to his Prince, but that lord and that prince were but parts in a heavenly scheme. Just as Sir Brian was overlord to Reginald, Prince John was master to Sir Brian. Just as Prince John was master to Sir Brian, John's brother was master to John. Just as John's brother was master to John, Lord Jesus was master to all.

John could say that Richard was dead, and that he alone was King, but here, right before Reginald's astonished eyes, was living proof that Richard Lionheart lived.

Sir Reginald bowed his head, and dropped to his knees.

CHAPTER TWENTY-EIGHT

Rebecca and Rowena could discern little from inside the locked room. Faint noises had grown louder, but their meaning was open to interpretation. Sounds that might be the rattling of a drawbridge's chains, or the thud of heavy wood hitting ground, might prove to be something else: Armored men in deadly battle, or a peasant's vegetable wagon clattering over the drawbridge; a line of manacled prisoners, or the felling of a great oak. Clashing of swords and shields might be nothing more than the clamor of scullery-workers' children at play.

"I am certain I heard horses on the drawbridge," said Rowena, who knew that the back of the castle overlooked a wild sea, where winds and waves never ceased to roar. "Sounds of metal crashing into metal. Shouts and screams. War-cries louder than the wind."

"It must be Sir Ivanhoe," said Rebecca, feigning happiness. "Your knight has come for you."

Rowena hesitated. There was another way to interpret the distant sounds. "I said what I hoped and prayed for. But hopes are not always fulfilled, and prayers not always answered. Those sounds could mean that Prince John has arrived."

"I do not think so," said Rebecca.

"Prince John with his retinue of warriors and courtiers," continued Rowena.

"Sir Brian's men would not meet Prince John with clashing swords and shields."

"We cannot be sure what we are hearing," said Rowena.

"It is not Prince John. Sir Ivanhoe has come," said Rebecca, with even greater certainty. "Come with an army to free his betrothed."

"Does your magic let you know what we cannot see with our own eyes?"

"There is no magic in what I say, my lady," said Rebecca. "Sir Ivanhoe loves you. That is why he risks life and limb to break into this terrible place. To take you into his arms."

Rebecca was partially right. The sounds of clashing steel were the result of Ivanhoe's assault on the castle. But she was not completely right. Ivanhoe was not risking life and limb simply to take Rowena in his arms. He had other motivations of greater moment: Making amends for a broken vow;

knightly honor; support of Richard Lion-heart.

And a passion greater than any of these, a

passion that he would not yet name.

Rowena would soon see Ivanhoe.

But Rebecca would never get a chance to see the

headstrong Crusader inside Torquilstone Castle.

The door to her chamber was once again unlocked,

and brusquely thrown open by Brian de Bois Gilbert.

Brian was in a great hurry, accompanied by two knights

with hands on the hilts of their sheathed swords. He

forced his gaze from Rebecca to Rowena. "If the Saxon

wench resists, cut her down," he said.

Rowena faced the three men, drawing her poniard.

"No, my lady!" said Rebecca. "Put that away.

Remember who has come for you."

"Cut the bitch down!" said Brian. As the men

drew swords, Rebecca stepped between them and Rowena.

"My lady, please," said Rebecca.   "You must

live.   Live for both of us."

"Better to die, than to live in disgrace," said

Rowena.

"You have taught me much, Lady Rowena." She

placed her hand on the handle of Rowena's knife.

"Neither one of us will live in disgrace." A moment passed, until Rowena decided to let Rebecca take her weapon.

Then Rebecca turned to Brian's men, opened her palm, and let the poniard fall to the stone floor. The men sheathed their swords.

"Take her!" said Brian. The two men grabbed Rowena from either side. She stood her ground, turning to Brian.

"If you hurt Lady Rebecca in any way, I will find you and kill you," Rowena said to Brian.

"Get her out of my sight!" said Brian.

Rebecca threw herself at Rowena's straight-backed form, wrapping her arms around her proud neck. Brian's men retained tight hold of their prisoner.

"Are you great warriors really too afraid to let me return my friend's embrace?" said Rowena.

The taunt had no effect. The men held Rowena, while Brian grabbed Rebecca from behind, forcing her to let go.

"Goodbye, my lady," said Rebecca. Feeling the Jewess's revulsion at his touch, Brian let her pull free.

At the door, Rowena dug in her heels, forcing her captors to stop. She turned to Rebecca one more time. "I will see you again, dear Rebecca," said Rowena. "As soon as these Normans meet their just fate."

Finally Brian's men took Rowena out of the room.

Though Brian quickly shut Rebecca's door, she could hear the booted tread of his warriors take Rowena to the adjacent room, its heavy door slam shut.

Wild with purpose, Brian approached Rebecca. "You will come with me now." The lust in his eyes had been replaced by something more urgent.

"You are frightened," said Rebecca. "Lady Rowena was right. Sir Ivanhoe has arrived."

"No man on earth frightens me," said Brian.

"There is more to fear in this world than mortal men," said Rebecca.

"I am not frightened by anything. Certainly not by a Saxon traitor," said Brian. "But your great hero has arrived with an unexpected ally. I must tell my prince with whom Ivanhoe travels."

Unable to make sense of his words, Rebecca insisted: "Is he really here? Ivanhoe? Is that the truth?"

"What is true is that you will finally do as you are told," he said. Rebecca backed away from him, until her hands touched the edge of the window.

"There is a hidden staircase that leads to the water at the castle's rear," said Brian. "And a boat that will take us to Prince John's court."

Rebecca turned from Brian, looking outside. The rush of wind reminded her of Rowena's courage. How she had stepped out, onto the narrow ledge, refusing to be afraid.

If only Rebecca could be as daring; brave as a lioness protecting her young.

"Come with me," said Brian, willing Rebecca to turn around, but holding himself back from again touching her. "There is no other way. You cannot live without my protection." It took him a moment to add: "And I cannot let you go."

Ivanhoe was here, in the castle, thought Rebecca. But he had not come for her. He had come for his beloved Rowena. What he felt for Rebecca was love's opposite.

From their first meeting, Ivanhoe and Rebecca were as unlike as sanity and madness, as antagonistic as life and death. They spoke different languages, prayed to different gods, looked at the world through different eyes. She was a healer, ready to bind the wounds of friend and foe alike. He was a warrior, eager to destroy every enemy.

Perhaps Ivanhoe would honor his knightly vows, and try to free the daughter of Isaac from this place. But duty to country and to Richard Lion-Heart was not why Ivanhoe had come, thought Rebecca. He had come for love of Rowena.

Rebecca could imagine him pulling Rowena close, holding her in his arms. They were two of a kind, beautiful and strong, destined for marriage and children. For a life without complication; with simple happiness.

No, Ivanhoe would not find Rebecca here. But neither, she thought, would Brian be spiriting her away.

Had she not just promised Rowena she would never live in disgrace?

Death was not to be feared. Death was the land where her parents lived. To join their world would be a blessing.

Heart pounding, Rebecca mustered all her strength to step up and through the window!

Outside -- onto the narrow ledge!

Brian was shouting at her to stop, that her life was precious, that to end it by her own hand would sentence her to eternal damnation.

Rebecca had no reason to answer Brian's words with a reasoned response. If she spoke aloud into the wind, he wouldn't be able to hear anything. And why would she respond to him at all? Wasn't he her greatest enemy?

There was no stopping Rebecca. I care nothing for life, she thought, feeling her mind grow quieter. Especially the life Brian wants to give me.

Appalled, Brian stood behind her, his hands holding the stone on either side of the open window. Terrified to get closer, to worry her off the ledge. "I do not want to harm you," said Brian. "I have never wanted to, nor will I ever…"

Rebecca looked below. It was a hundred feet to the wild water, crashing against jagged rocks. Fear assaulted her, but she swallowed it. She gulped down fear like a distasteful tonic that must be endured.

But the taste of fear brought something worse, a cascade of doubts that had until that moment been held at bay. Doubts that had been stifled after the

hideous murder of her mother in a burning hovel;
doubts that had grown stronger at the sight of her
tortured, dying father.

How dare he demand she never abandon her faith?
Did Isaac not understand that he had been abandoned by
God, as surely as her mother Deborah had been
abandoned, as surely as Rebecca herself had been
abandoned?

Life was shrouded in mystery, but this much was
clear: Their God had left them to their fates. Why
should she should worship and adore such a God?

Why should she believe in Him at all?

Gusting winds quieted long enough for her to hear
Brian's words: "Ivanhoe cannot help you," he said.

I know, thought Rebecca.

Miserable thoughts pulsed like a drumbeat in her
veins: Neither could her father help her, nor her
mother, nor her relatives in distant Spain.

Nor her faith.

Brian continued, nearly pleading: "No one can
help you now, no one but me."

Neither can you help me, thought Rebecca. She
shut her eyes, overtaken by a horrible idea, the

conclusion of all her fears: Not even God can help me.

Rebecca had relented to dark forces, allowing a shadow to pass over her belief.

If God could not understand her misery, He could not be omniscient. If God could not help her, He could not be omnipotent. If God had disappeared from her sense of the world, she was utterly alone. More alone than she had ever been, in life or in her dreams.

The wind picked up, howling at her new misery.

It didn't matter if she could no longer hear Brian. There was nothing Brian could say or do that would change the direction she was about to take.

"We must leave," said Brian. "Leave at once. The back staircase leads directly to the longboat. Let me help you inside before it is too late."

Urgent and fleeting as the moment was to Brian, for Rebecca it was just the opposite. The moment seemed to expand, to slow, to stop altogether.

She lived in a moment that waited for her, that let her remember the past, imagine the future. A thousand visions swept through her, memories of her mother's care, her father's love, dreams of a reunion

where all three would be forever healthy and young. A
vision of heaven. The moment didn't move. She could
stay here as long as she liked.

Rebecca knew this must be a miracle.

Nothing but divine power could have stopped time
- stopped it for her benefit. So that Rebecca could
stand outside this terrible event, letting her examine
it from every side.

Slowly, ineluctably, everything became clear.

She would not go back inside. To go back inside
meant slavery, dishonor, cowardice. On this narrow
ledge, she would be as brave as her Saxon friend.

Rebecca opened her eyes, not to the water below,
but to the world at large, the world she hated, the
world she was ready to leave.

But not yet.

If time had stopped, who had stopped it? If she
was experiencing a miracle, from where had it come?

Something nagged at the walls of her soul.
Something hissed at her, demanding attention. But
Rebecca was stubborn. She held onto faithlessness
like a convert to new creed.

Yet faithlessness is far more difficult to cling
to than faith.

Within this miraculous moment, understanding broke into her dark resolve like spikes of light.

Rebecca swayed, tears came, blood pounded in her ears. She felt her reason challenged, her heart break. Not assaulted by the stinging wind, but by a heaven-sent reproach. A reproach that shamed her, that cut to the quick, that illuminated her spirit with radiance.

The shadow that had come between her soul and her faith moved away, vanishing as quickly as it had come.

How could she have imagined that God wouldn't help her?

God is great, she thought. God is good, God is eternal. She had doubted this, and that doubt had left her broken. God, who sees everything, saw how she had been shattered on the wheel of misfortune.

God, who can do anything, removed doubt from her soul, as if an alien growth had been removed from a body.

Blessed are you, Lord our God, King of the Universe, thought Rebecca. He who rewards the undeserving with goodness.

He who has gifted me with the return of faith.

Doubt, fleeting though it had been, had broken her. But God had helped her banish doubt. She was whole again, part of God's world, God's plan. Faith had returned. Somehow, wondrously, sent by an angel or her parents' spirits, faith filled her soul with bright light.

Faith that was sure and certain, faith that would never again desert her, faith that gave her joy.

Misfortune had pushed faith away, but, thanks be to God, it had returned.

Faith that was stronger than despair, stronger than love or hate. Faith that answered every question, met every trial with triumphant force.

There was a God in Heaven, there was a World-to-Come where she would be united with her mother and father. There was justice and meaning in God's Providence.

Brian was still talking. As if he could only find the correct words they would make everything right. That Rebecca would finally see things his way.

He had never told her he loved her, but wasn't it clear nonetheless? In spite of her low birth, in spite of his noble lineage, he had fallen in love with

a Jewess. How could she not appreciate what he
sacrificed on her behalf?

Brian desperately wanted her to be still, to lean
toward him so he could take hold of her safely. He
longed to take her into his arms. To hold her close
without feeling her loathing. To keep her alive, and
with him.

So great was the strength of his concern, that
Rebecca could sense it, even in her reverie. A
concern that went beyond simple lust, a concern that
was far better than the man who had killed her father.
This was a revelation, and shocking, but Rebecca
batted away any sympathy.

Sir Brian de Bois Gilbert was the enemy of her
people, her enemy. Her father's murderer.

But now, thoughts of Brian evaporated. The wind
picked up with a vengeance.

Rebecca understood that the gift of stopped time
had come to a close. God had given her a chance to
retrieve her belief, to retain her faith.

Moments flowed, one after the other. Time had
returned in its natural rush.

Blessed be God's Name, she thought, at the very
instant that Brian reached through the window --

grabbing for her shoulders, desperate to pull here away from her fate.

But she was too quick, too determined. Nothing could stop Rebecca from stepping off the ledge, and into space!

She could not hear Brian's howl of despair. All she heard was the Name of God, blending with the rushing wind.

Before the sound of crashing waves obliterated all thoughts. Before a propulsive force hit her body, from the soles of her feet to the crown of her head. Before deep water, terribly cold, shocked her nearly senseless.

Rebecca understood that she was dead.

All was black, but soon there would be light. All was cold, but soon there would be warmth. All was mystery, ignorance, but soon there would be enlightenment.

She held onto faith. Faith supported her body and soul.

Bliss filled Rebecca's heart.

CHAPTER TWENTY-NINE

Rebecca could not know what was happening above the waters into which she had plunged.

She could not have imagined that Sir Brian de Bois Gilbert would climb through the window, and step onto the same narrow ledge!

Had she been standing next to him, she couldn't have heard his silent thoughts, as he searched below for any sign of her body: That Rebecca was alive, that she had to be alive… because her spell over him wasn't broken.

That nothing would stop him from pursuing her. That even if Brian had to break down the gates of hell, Rebecca would one day be his.

Had Rebecca been in the room behind Brian's back, she would have heard the commotion as her door was smashed apart by a heavy boot and the hilt of a sword.

She would have seen Brian vanish from sight of the window, as he stepped off the ledge - joining in her madness, following her into the void.

She would have seen first Ivanhoe, then Rowena, step through the hole in the door, and into her vacant room.

"Rebecca!" said Rowena, hurrying past Ivanhoe, her eyes sweeping the vacant room.

But even if Rebecca had been there, she could not have imagined the rush of events that had overtaken everyone in and around Torquilstone Castle.

Richard Lion-Heart had traveled incognito because he had good need to surprise his brother Prince John. A brother who had refused to ransom him, and had instead promoted the lie that Richard was dead, and that he, John, had inherited the rule of Britain.

Many nobles close to John knew the truth: That a secret group of merchants, spearheaded by Isaac of York, had raised the ransom money, and transmitted it via bills of exchange to the Duke of Austria.

What Prince John needed to know was who were these merchants who planned to replace him on the throne with Richard? Where and when would his hated brother land on British soil?

This was why Sir Brian, loyal to Prince John, had his men torture Isaac.

But the torture and murder of Isaac had been to no avail. Richard Lion-Heart had returned. Sir Reginald Front de Bouef would not be the only one who knelt before him. Still, Prince John's grip on Britain was strong. He had gifted too many nobles with land and serfs to be summarily replaced, when that replacement would leave those nobles penniless and disgraced.

Ivanhoe and Cedric had ridden up behind their king. But once Reginald had gotten to his knees, Ivanhoe didn't linger.

"Gurth!" he shouted. "Take me to her!"

Gurth spurred his warhorse forward, leading Ivanhoe directly into the courtyard of awestruck warriors, most already on their knees. Ignoring them, Gurth dismounted. "Hurry," he said to his master, making for a stairway. Ivanhoe slipped off his horse, running after Gurth.

Cedric explained his son's behavior to King Richard: "My ward Rowena, Ivanhoe's betrothed, is held captive in this place."

The King dismounted and stood on the drawbridge next to where Reginald knelt, his head still bowed.

Every one of Reginald's men were on their knees, along the drawbridge, and into the courtyard.

Richard looked from Reginald to nearby faces of the kneeling men: Reading their faces for signs of obedience or rebellion.

The King's many months in captivity had taught him to be less impulsive than was his nature. There was no point in starting a civil war. Richard would bring down his brother and take back the throne, but at the proper time and place.

Cedric stood alongside his king. "This is Reginald Front de Bouef. One of the men who captured my ward. As well as Isaac of York and his daughter, Lady Rebecca."

Reginald slowly raised his head. "It was your brother John's orders, Sire," he said. "They were traitors."

"Prince John's orders," said Cedric. "But Lord Isaac was no traitor."

"Isaac was a Jew," said Reginald. "And his daughter is a witch."

"Lady Rebecca is no witch," said Cedric. "She has helped both my son and my ward come back to life."

Reginald, still on his knees, nearly sneered. "A witch, like I said, Sire. And powerful."

A change had come over Reginald. There were men behind him, two hundred strong, men that had served John, not Richard. Men who would follow Reginald's command.

And any moment Sir Brian would appear, a man who would never forsake his prince.

Reginald suddenly stood, his hand on the hilt of his sword. He was pleased to see how much taller -- and broader – he was than the very tall and broad Richard Lion-Heart.

"A witch," insisted Reginald Front de Boeuf. "Whoever she brings back to life are her slaves, beholden to her Jewish purposes."

The King took a moment to absorb these words. Another moment to think what Reginald's getting up from his knees meant. Another moment to remind himself that he was not to be impulsive.

Perhaps this is what John would say when Richard reappeared: That the real Richard was dead. This figure brought back to life by witchcraft must be not only false, but demonic.

Behind Reginald, a few emboldened warriors were following his example, getting up from their knees. What had seemed like a surrender to the majesty of Richard's office, now threatened to retreat. Submissive men were discovering their greater numbers.

King or no King, it only required an order, an action, for them to turn into a death-dealing mob.

Richard forced calm into his words, though his impulse was to stop talking altogether. "Isaac of York has done me a service," said Richard. "Where is he?"

"In the pit of hell," said Reginald. There could be no doubt as to Reginald's tone. This was defiance. As if he had not just heard the King say the man had done him a service. "Where every Jew goes after death."

"How did he die?" said Richard, still calmly. Though his heart was pounding now, not in fear, but in anticipation of violent release.

"He died miserably, like he deserved," said Reginald. "It was his own fault. He wouldn't tell Sir Brian what he wanted to know."

Richard Lion-heart smiled. There was a joy in decisive action, a joy that he knew well. Reginald was warrior enough to sense what was coming. He began to withdraw his sword from its scabbard.

Richard drew his sword with the speed for which he had been famous, even among the Saracens. Assembled warriors held their breaths, watching with amazement: Reginald's sword wasn't fully unsheathed before Richard had sliced away the giant's hand at the wrist.

Horrified, blinded with pain, Reginald fell back to his knees, moaning.

"Finish him, Cedric," said Richard, with disgust.

To kill Reginald by royal hand was far too good for a traitor. Cedric drew his broadsword, and used the tip of the blade to flip off Reginald's helmet with contempt.

"I should have done this days ago," said Cedric. Then Cedric swung the sword into Reginald's neck. The Saxon overlord was not as strong as he used to be. It took him three more strokes to finish the job.

Behind them, every Norman warrior stayed in place; some standing, some remaining on their knees, some returning to kneeling position. None were advancing. Submission returned in a fearful wave.

Richard picked up the severed head by its hair, and raised it high. Behind him, Saxons cheered. Before him, the warriors of Torquilstone lowered their beaten eyes.

Their King had returned, and they would not defy him.

"Where is she?" said Ivanhoe to Rowena in Rebecca's room. Gurth had been sent below, to search the dungeons.

Rowena went to the open window, looking out to the ledge, and to the raging sea below. "She was just here," she said. "With Brian. He must have known you had come."

"I don't understand," said Ivanhoe. "Brian is not the kind of man who runs from a fight."

Rowena returned to looking below. For a moment she thought she could see something break the surface of the foaming sea. "Wait. Look," she said. But just as suddenly as the indistinct object had come into view, it disappeared beneath the water.

Ivanhoe came up behind her, following her gaze. "I saw something," she said.

"What?"

"I don't know," said Rowena.

Something broke the surface of the water, something that might be a human shape.

"I think I see it," said Ivanhoe. They watched the shape bob in the water. Showing no signs of life.

"It could be her," said Rowena.

"That's impossible," said Ivanhoe. "You said they were here together, in this room. How on earth-?"

"Because she is as brave as she is good," said Rowena.

Ivanhoe stepped back and away from the window, crossing the small room. "What is that supposed to mean? Are you saying Brian let her fly out the window to her death?"

"Brian could not have stopped her," said Rowena, proud of her friend. "She preferred death to dishonor."

Ivanhoe returned to the window, wild with anger. "I let Brian kill her father. Now I have let him drive her to her death."

"Perhaps not," said Rowena. They looked to where a second shape had broken the surface, near where a longboat was tied along the shore. This shape was moving on its own accord. Squinting, they could

almost see arms propelling it through surf.

"Two bodies," said Ivanhoe.

"Brian followed her," said Rowena. "She jumped,

and he followed."

"Why would he follow?" said Ivanhoe, amazed.

"You know why," said Rowena.

The second figure made its way to where the first

body floated face down in the surf. "She might still

be alive," said Ivanhoe.

"Yes," said Rowena. They watched as the moving

figure took hold of the still one. "If that is Brian,

he appears to be helping her."

The two figures, one still, one battling the

surf, made their way to the longboat. Ivanhoe and

Rowena watched silently as the tiny figure of a man

helped the still body of a woman into the boat, and

immediately untethered it.

"If she is alive, I will save her," said Ivanhoe.

"I know," said Rowena. "You must." They watched

the longboat, swept away on its urgent course by the

swift current, disappear.

"May Lord Jesus grant her life until I come to

her aid," said Ivanhoe.

Rowena could understand the hope and dread in Ivanhoe's voice. But she sensed something else in her betrothed's tone, something she could not understand: Despair.

CHAPTER THIRTY

King Richard repaid treason with violence,
loyalty with largesse.

Isaac of York had refused to give out the names
of the King's ransomers, even under torture, even unto
death. It was with gratitude that Richard ordered
Isaac to be buried with proper Jewish prayers.
Isaac's kinsman, Naftali of Sheffield, had been
summoned for the task.

It took three days for Naftali to arrive at
Torquilstone. But Naftali had brought more than
prayers. He had tidings of Prince John, of Sir Brian
de Bois Gilbert, and of Lady Rebecca.

Tidings of treachery, rebellion, witchcraft.
Prince John had promulgated lies, and many believed
them:

**Richard Lion-Heart was dead. The figure who
walked the earth in his form was inhuman, a slave
forced to do the bidding of his Jewish creator. To
believe in this "false king" was to be tricked by a
cabal of rich Jews who would subjugate Christians to
their rule.**

Nobles who laughed in private at John's falsehoods publicly supported his every pronouncement. They could never believe Lady Rebecca a necromancer who had conjured King Richard from bones and ashes, from secret potions and unholy spells. But they could make good use of John's fabrications.

The Prince's policies enriched great families at the cost of the peasantry. Noblemen swallowed up small households and farms. John's soldiers tramped through English villages, raping and pillaging as if marauding through foreign lands. Freemen unable to pay the Prince's taxes were reduced to slavery in all its insidious forms. Common people remembered a better time, under a better ruler, but harsh rule kept them quiet.

Beyond the quiet was a seething anger. Anger that must be suppressed, or channeled away from Prince John.

In times of trouble, what better scapegoat than a rich and beautiful Jewess?

King Richard was not surprised at Naftali's news. He had expected nothing else. Prince John was clever and sharp, saw fairness as an impediment to success.

Even as a child, Richard's younger brother had enjoyed cutting corners to win a contest, had gladly stabbed rivals in their backs.

No longer a child, John had usurped Richard's power, blackened his name, and was despoiling his kingdom. Wild with impatience, Richard had chafed at holding back. He wanted to confront his brother at once.

Lord Cedric, trying to keep his sovereign from precipitous action, engaged him by seeking royal judgments. There were men among the Torquilstone warriors who were identified as being too close to Prince John's treachery; Richard ordered that they be stripped of weapons, and banished. There were men who had participated in Isaac's torture; Richard sentenced them to death.

But a dozen traitors' heads on poles outside Torquilstone Castle was hardly enough to satisfy the fierce Crusader King.

While Richard had taken charge of Torquilstone, surrounded by fealty on every side, he knew there was a conspiracy against him. A conspiracy to hide secrets, a conspiracy to keep him from danger.

But danger had always been Richard's elixir. A challenge, no matter how daunting, was something to gulp down, to accept without hesitation.

Richard Lion-heart had never been one to shy away from risk. Whether it was a perilous voyage to Jerusalem to fight a horde of infidels, or a reckless battle against Prince John's superior numbers, Richard never hesitated. John ruled from his seat at Ashby, and Ashby was where King Richard must go.

"Not yet, Sire," said Lord Cedric. "We have sent couriers to every corner of the realm. Your veterans will come to you here. We must wait for them." The King had not asked for Cedric's counsel, but the Saxon lord kept offering it, night and day. "We must wait. Wait until the time is ripe. Wait until we are strong enough. Wait until we are sure to win."

Richard had brooded, longing for action. If not for his obligation to give Isaac a proper burial, he would already be on the road to Ashby. The moment Naftali finished praying over Isaac's grave, Richard Lion-Heart was through being patient.

Lord Cedric continued to offer every reason for delay. The two men sat on the dais in the great hall of Torquilstone, alone, without even servants to wait on them.

"I will not ask you to come, Cedric," said Richard. "You are not as young as you were, and we will be riding fast."

"I will go wherever you go, my Liege, and no man will ride faster," said Cedric. "But I implore you to wait."

"How is your son's fever?" said Richard.

"Ivanhoe is young, and will surely be well in a few more days, a week at the most," said Cedric.

This lie, Richard knew, was part of the conspiracy.

"Perhaps the fever will do something for his rashness," said Richard, with no concern in his tone. "Ivanhoe was the one man I could never hold back from battle, no matter how hopeless. It is a miracle he came back from our Crusade alive."

"Indeed, Sire. I thank Lord Jesus every day –"

"Even more of a miracle that he should catch a fever when I have need of his strong arm."

"Surely, My Liege, you do not imagine that my son would shirk his duty."

"No, Cedric. What I imagine is that he has plans to fight my brother all on his own."

Cedric paused long enough to silently confirm everything his king had said. "Ivanhoe is not a leader, Sire."

"Neither is he a follower," said Richard. "Or he might tell his king what he intends, without pretending to some fantastic illness."

"Every great leader must forego rash behavior, my Liege," said Cedric. "Must practice caution. Must never give in to impulse."

"Are you saying I should not have cut off Reginald's hand?" said Richard.

Cedric had no answer to the sarcastic tone, because he had been in full agreement with Richard's action.

"Perhaps you shouldn't have cut off his head?" added Richard. "Reginald might have lived without his sword-hand. Maybe we could have made him an emissary for peace negotiations with John."

"All I am saying, Sire," said Cedric, "is that John has been telling tales of your death for years. The people have come to believe those tales, so naturally we must be careful in how you are presented to them. To show up at Ashby and challenge John at once, is to risk being thought a ghostly impostor."

"They come," said Richard, ignoring Cedric's advice. "Finally." He was turning from Cedric to where Rowena had entered the hall from its far side. Cedric's ward was accompanied by redheaded Ethelreda, in servant's dress, their steps echoing on the stone floor.

While Rowena and Ethelreda neared, Cedric continued: "A month, six or seven weeks will make all the difference. We must wait, Sire."

"I am through waiting."

"Time for my son to get well enough to fight by your side."

"I am likewise through pretending to believe your son is sick."

"Time for Crusader knights to flock to your banner from all over the kingdom. You can lead a great army to Ashby, in triumph."

"Did you not listen to Naftali of Sheffield?" said Richard. Rowena was close enough to hear every word: "In another week, Lady Rebecca will be dead."

"God forbid, Sire," said Rowena.

"If not for her father, I would never have been ransomed," said Richard. "Do you think I don't know my duty?"

"Your first duty is to your country," said Cedric. "Lady Rebecca's fate will be avenged when you are returned to the throne. To go too soon to Ashby is to die."

"To go too late to Ashby is to ensure Rebecca's murder," said Rowena.

"Silence, girl," said Cedric to his ward. "Do not interfere."

"Rebecca saved my life, and your son's," said Rowena. "To do nothing to save her is not only cowardly, but sinful."

"I would give my life to save Lady Rebecca," said Cedric. "But I must not allow my King to do the same. Our King's life is more important than mine – or Lady Rebecca's."

Rowena was about to answer, when Cedric interjected: "No more, girl. This is not your place. I have private business with the King."

"Lady Rowena is here at my bidding," said Richard. "I asked her to bring Ivanhoe from his 'sickbed…'" Richard paused, as if to let them in on a secret joke. "But in case Ivanhoe was unable to come, I asked her to bring along his squire."

"It was all I could do to keep Ivanhoe in his bed," said Rowena. "Though he is weak and feverish, he was so eager to obey your commands…"

"I doubt Ivanhoe is weak or feverish," said Richard. "I suspect he is gone from this castle. And I am certain he is not eager to obey anyone."

The conspiracy was becoming clearer. The King continued: "I said that if his squire was not able to come, either from drunkenness or a sudden compulsion to travel to the town of Ashby – to ask his betrothed to come in his place."

Ethelreda, alongside Rowena, quickly corrected: "Gurth and me are more than betrothed, Sire. Married in every way that matters. If Gurth dies, I am his widow. Though I don't think he will die very easily, as he is so strong, and fortunate."

"Gurth is fortunate in having found so pretty a wife," said King Richard. Ethelreda had received similar compliments all her life, but never from so august a personage. She beamed. "Lady Rowena and Lord Cedric have been lying to me for three days now.

Perhaps you, Ethelreda, will tell me the truth. Where is Gurth?"

"Where he should be, Sire," said Ethelreda. "Ready to serve his master at a moment's notice."

"His master Ivanhoe," said the King. "The knight so unwilling to follow my commands."

"That is not fair, my Liege," said Rowena. "No one is more loyal to you than Ivanhoe."

"Ethelreda!" said Richard. "I ask you again: Where is Gurth?"

"I have told you, Sire. At his master's side," said Ethelreda. "And no knight could have a braver companion."

"And no squire a more hot-headed master," said Richard. He turned to Lord Cedric. "No more lies, old friend. Ivanhoe has run off, and you have covered up his absence."

Lord Cedric knew there was no longer any use in trying to keep the truth from his king. "I begged him to stay, Sire," he said.

"I have seen no diminution of our warriors here, so I can only hope he has assembled a force of men from outside the castle."

"He has not," said Cedric. "Which is why I begged him to wait."

"Apparently, to no avail."

"We are waiting for men to arrive, but as yet -"

"Waiting!" said Richard. "You ask me to wait, while letting your own son run off!"

"I could never control him, my Liege. My son has often acted without thought of consequences, but he is not the rightful king of Britain. I cannot see what he can hope to accomplish against John's army."

"The glorious death of a righteous knight," said Richard. Sudden anger forced him to his feet. "In the Crusade, there were men who valued their lives too highly to expose themselves to danger. Do you know what we called them?"

Richard didn't give Cedric time to answer. "We called them cowards."

Cedric stood as well. "Permit me to say, my Liege, that the fate of Britain is more important than any one man's glory."

"I am glad to hear what I have suspected for three days. Ivanhoe is not shut up in a sickroom, but following the dictates of his conscience and knightly code."

"Yes, Sire," said Cedric. "That is true. But no reason why the King of Britain must follow his example."

"Your son is en route to Prince John's court," said Richard. "One man against a multitude."

"No, Sire," said Ethelreda, daring to contradict. "Not one man, but two. Gurth is also a man, and he will never desert Sir Ivanhoe."

"Gurth indeed!" said Richard. He turned to Cedric. "Do you think me less a man than your son's squire?"

PART FOUR: ASHBY

CHAPTER THIRTY-ONE

Though standing, Rebecca was half asleep. The
green and gold eyes were open, but her notice of what
was before her was incomplete, confused with visions
of other times, other places. Young noblemen in fancy
dress in the room where she stood were interrupted by
memories: Her mother, treating her babyish bruise;
her father, instructing her on a point of moral law;
Lady Rowena, fearless and wild, stepping down from the
window in the locked room.

The images repeated, real and imagined, cycling
past in a hurried parade. The noblemen, her parents,
her friend.

And then, two knights, bitter rivals, also
appeared, intruding into the cascade of memories.
They appeared and disappeared, again and again,
dizzyingly. Sir Ivanhoe, angry at being castigated
for his good intentions; Sir Brian, angry at having
his evil intentions rebuffed.

Rebecca could make little sense of what she was
seeing. Sumptuous wall hangings, bright sun through
narrow windows, an enormous, familiar dog resting at
the foot of a great chair. Some kind of hall, with

stone floors. An open doorway, letting in garden
smells.

It was the fancy-dressed noblemen whose images
grew increasingly sharp. Broad-shouldered, scantily
bearded, foul-breathed, they closed in on her like a
waking nightmare.

Rebecca had neither rested nor eaten for a long
time. Light-headed, she felt like sinking to her
knees, lying down, embracing the oblivion of sleep.
But something was holding her up. Not only holding
her up, but making her turn around on faltering steps.

Turning around and around.

She remembered turning about in another place, in
another plane. Not standing, not turning with small
steps in a tight circle. Instead, head over heels,
falling through space into a realm of cold and
darkness.

A cold that had welcomed her. The darkness had
held no fear. Cold and dark had been a comforting
blanket, protecting her from a too bright world.

How could she have feared anything, when her
faith had returned?

She was going somewhere that would be safe,
something like home. Perhaps that is when she had

seen her parents. Surely they were beckoning her from the World-to-Come.

In the cold and darkness she had heard a sound. But it was a sound of this world, not the next. An urgent sound. Her name, spoken softly, insistently, then louder, then shouted out. "Rebecca!"

Her own name, again and again. When her eyes had opened there was sudden light, and behind the light the face of a handsome knight in sodden clothes, with wet hair, his eyes mad with despair. A knight she must never stop hating.

"Rebecca," Brian had been saying. "Rebecca!"

She hadn't time to understand where she was, and why he was there with her, when he pulled her close. Then suddenly he pushed her away, bending her at the waist like a rag doll.

Rebecca had found herself staring into raging water.

She was on a boat. A boat that heaved over wild waves. She knew if she looked up she would see the walls of Torquilstone Castle. She knew she had jumped to avoid a fate worse than death.

Rebecca felt her back pummeled. Brian continued to shout, and pound and press until she vomited up great quantities of water. The knight held her from behind, making certain she would not fall overboard. Making sure she would be safe.

That she would not die.

Rebecca had jumped, but she had not avoided her fate.

She had fallen deep beneath raging water, but had stayed alive long enough for Brian to grab hold, to pull her free of obliteration.

Her greatest enemy had saved her from death. Now she was in his hands.

But she was no longer on a boat. Neither cold nor wet, she was standing on a floor that didn't roll. And Brian de Bois Gilbert was nowhere to be seen.

Blinking wildly, Rebecca tried to separate the past from the present, to draw a line between memory and the room in which she now stood.

Men were surrounding her. She wasn't consciously turning to anyone, but somehow found herself looking from one to another of the men, three standing and two seated. So there were five of them. Strangers, though two looked familiar.

In the eyes of all of them the old hatred she had seen directed at her and her people in too many places to count.

Hatred accompanied by accusations, calumnies. By demands that could only be met by expulsion or death.

Prince John's tournament knights had that look of youth and arrogance, of inexperience bolstered by malicious intent. Perhaps the two who looked familiar might have been glimpsed at the tournament she had attended with her father. The tournament where Sir Brian de Bois Gilbert had presented her with a crown of green satin, resting on the tip of his lance.

Recalling the fear she had experienced at that moment, and the determination she had found to refuse him, something else came to mind. The present was again eclipsed by memories of the boat. She remembered being horrified to be alive. Brian was talking, his words kind, insistent, concerned. She had tried to understand the words then, and she tried to remember them now, but all was lost in her anguish.

Then memory retreated. There was someone talking now, not Brian. Some other man. Raging: "Black magic… Treason… Witchery."

The man's words came from behind her.

So there were six men with her in this sun-lit room. Before her five young men stood or sat in a semi-circle below a great raised chair. The familiar old dog lying beneath it. The chair was covered with red and gold pillows.

A throne apparently, and empty.

Her field of vision moved. Throne and dog disappeared.

The hateful faces came into view, then went away, then returned, as did the throne. Below the empty throne, the old dog laboriously raised its head, as if sensing something of interest. Then the dog disappeared, and the noblemen returned.

Finally she understood that she was turning, round and round. Or rather, being turned by the unseen man holding her shoulders from behind. The same man who was holding her upright, preventing her from falling.

She was not gently turned, but whirled around with deliberate roughness.

Rebecca was a captive, displayed before a group of young men. Worse, her wrists were bound together behind her back. The men could come as close as they liked, baring teeth in macabre smiles, enjoying their power over her.

The old dog came back into view, standing with difficulty. A brown mastiff, with white hair on its broad chest. Surely, she thought, the same dog that had sat at John's feet at the tournament. "Hunter," her father had told her. Hunter was the name Richard had given it when he was a young man. The dog he had left behind when he had gone off on his Crusade.

Some of the words behind her back became clearer: "Sir Ivanhoe brought back from the dead… Lady Rowena returned to life… Richard dug up from his Austrian grave…"

The man turned her about one last time, and let go, stepping in front of her, revealing himself. Glaring.

Prince John.

Rebecca steeled herself not to fall.

"Witnesses have testified to your magical powers," he said. "Powers that let you survive a jump of one hundred feet into a turbulent sea. Powers that let you enchant the Christian knight Brian de Bois Gilbert, to join you at the bottom of the sea."

As John spoke, she felt relief at no longer being turned. Her dizziness began to fade. Rebecca could look past Prince John to the five young nobles in what must be his throne room.

Why was Sir Brian was not among them?

Was Brian not the best of the Prince's tournament knights, one of John's inner circle? Brian had saved her from drowning, forced her to live, brought her to this place. That she was standing up, hands bound behind her back, could be attributed to no one else. Why was Brian not there to witness her on display for the pleasure of his Prince?

"Powers that let you conspire with Isaac of York and other traitorous Jews," said John. "Powers given you by Satan to usurp England's throne in the name of my dead brother."

Recoiling at John's words, another memory came to her: Her father smashing a lamp over Brian's head, followed by her own attempt to subdue the knight with a tightly wrapped scroll. Rebecca had slammed the scroll into his skull. Brian still hadn't fallen down, when Ivanhoe, having risen from his sickbed, staggered into their presence.

Ivanhoe had swung his fist into Brian's jaw, and
Brian had fallen to his knees. Managing to warn
Ivanhoe: "A demon. She will bewitch you."

The knight who hated her - Ivanhoe - knocked down
the knight she had "bewitched" - Brian. There was
almost humor in the memory.

Rebecca nearly smiled, when John grabbed hold of
her chin, demanding her attention, raising her face to
meet his eyes. "This Richard that threatens to attack
our just rule is not the Richard we knew and honored,
but an evil creation with no will of his own. A
rotting corpse brought to life for one purpose: To
give the rule of Britain to the Jews."

She noticed that a few noblemen were turning away
from her, looking to the entrance to John's throne
room.

Because someone was approaching.

"This is a trial, Jewess," said Prince John. "To
bring back the dead through sorcery is a crime."

Rebecca was hardly listening. She was waiting to
see who would come through the open door.

"You are required to answer charges," said John.
"Answer!"

Rebecca wouldn't have answered, even if Sir Brian de Bois Gilbert had not entered the room, his lovesick eyes finding hers at once.

Prince John slapped her across the face. "Answer the charges, witch-woman!" said John. "Plead guilty, and your death will be swift. Refuse to tell the truth, and your death will be slow."

John raised his hand to strike her again, but Brian had crossed the room and grabbed his prince's wrist, preventing the blow.

"No, Sire," said Brian. "You must not hurt her."

Prince John pulled his hand free. Every man in the room, save Brian, wore a sword. Two of John's nobles drew theirs.

"You go too far, Sir Knight. To defy your sovereign is a damning offense." John took hold of the jeweled hilt of his own sword, but left it in its scabbard. He turned to the eager young men who'd drawn their swords. "No," said John. "Let him be."

Brian met Rebecca's cold gaze. "I'm sorry," he said. "This is none of my doing." He drew a dagger. Prince John said nothing, as Brian quickly tore apart the rope binding her wrists.

"Not your doing?" said Rebecca. "Who has brought me to this place, if not you?" She turned suddenly, fixating him with her exquisite eyes. "Who has called me a witch, if not Sir Brian de Bois Gilbert? Who has murdered my father, if not you?" She raised her freed hand, about to strike him. Brian stood still, perfectly willing to take the blow.

But suddenly, with no one holding her up, Rebecca felt herself succumbing to fatigue. Brian took hold of her again, gently helping her into a chair.

"Prince John," said Brian. "Lady Rebecca is not a witch. I have not brought her here to stand trial, but to save her soul."

Rebecca looked up to Brian's troubled face. "You should not have saved me," said Rebecca, without a trace of gratitude. "I have no reason to live, and every reason to die."

"No," said Brian, getting to one knee before her chair. "I will never let anyone - be he knight or prince or king -- hurt you."

"Let me be," said Rebecca.

"You will convert to our faith," said Brian. "Then I will marry you."

"The earth will be swallowed by the sun before I abandon my faith," said Rebecca. "And I would sooner entomb myself in the vaults of hell than marry you."

"Rebecca, you do not understand." said Brian, pleading to her as if they were not surrounded by young knights anxious to prove their mettle to Prince John. "I am not the man you think I am. I will do anything to make you believe me."

"I don't want to believe you," said Rebecca.

"Have mercy on me," said Brian. "I am sick with love for you."

"If more proof was needed, we have it before us," said Prince John. "Sir Brian is bewitched by this she-devil."

"Love is not bewitchment. I am in love with Lady Rebecca," said Brian, standing up to face his Prince.

"Take hold of him," said John abruptly, and two men grabbed Brian from behind. "He is in the sorceress's thrall."

"You lie," said Brian. "And I challenge you –"

"I will not accept the challenge of a man crazed by deviltry," said John. "It is unfortunate you cannot look beyond the demon's beautiful face. You cannot see the monstrous evil beneath her skin."

"There is no evil in Rebecca!" said Brian. "The only evil in this room is what you have brought to it by this trial." Brian struggled to free himself, but the men held him tight.

"I declare our trial complete," said John. "This witch has brought a false, unnatural Richard back to life. She must be destroyed. I have given her the chance to plead guilty, so she might be quickly executed with one blow of the axe. But as she has refused to answer charges, I hereby condemn Rebecca to slow death… by burning."

Using all his strength, Brian broke free of the men holding him. Every man in the room but John drew their swords. Heedless of danger, Brian stepped close to Rebecca. "I will never let them kill you," he said.

"I don't want your death coupled with mine," said Rebecca.

Brian turned to her, his eyes filled with longing. For the first time, he thought her voice had a hint of sympathy.

"Sir Brian," said John. "You seem intent on proving the depth of your sorry enchantment."

"I will prove just the opposite, Prince John," said Brian, turning from Rebecca. "Our ancient laws are clear. With lance and sword, I pledge myself to support the truth. And will prove Lady Rebecca's sentence false by trial-by-combat."

"No!" said Rebecca. "No more bloodshed."

"I will fight any knight you choose to oppose my will," said Brian to John.

"I put my trust in God alone," said Rebecca. "My life is in His hands, not yours."

John turned from Brian, walked to his throne, and sat. Hunter, the absent king's old dog, raised his massive head.

"Any knight!" said Brian. "You have only to name your champion."

John finally answered: "Sir Brian, you know not what you say. You are a victim of a witch's charms and spells. Our wise rules forbid any victim of sorcery to fight on the witch's behalf."

Brian, ignoring the drawn swords, was about to throw himself on Prince John, when he was stopped by a challenging voice behind him.

"Then I will fight for Lady Rebecca," said a man dressed in a monk's habit, its hood covering his head.

Rebecca knew the voice at once. But she had nothing to say to him. Not to welcome him with gratitude, nor to repulse him with fear. Not even to say his name.

As if she were back on the boat, the floor beneath her feet began to roll. Dizziness returned. For a moment it seemed she had stopped breathing.

Brian knew the voice as well. The voice of a man who seemed to be always challenging him. The voice of a man he was destined to meet in mortal conflict.

"Clearly," continued the monk, "I am not bewitched by Lady Rebecca."

Beside this spurious monk was another, also hooded, equally spurious. Burly enough to test the fabric of his habit.

"Thank Lord Jesus, Master," said this second monk. "She is alive."

The first monk threw off his hood, revealing Sir Ivanhoe's ardent face. Rebecca tried not to stare, but it was impossible to turn away. It was a shock to see him, looking exactly like the memory she had tried to suppress. Ivanhoe had looked at her for half a moment, time enough for their eyes to meet like flint striking steel. Then he turned away, refusing to divert his attention from the task at hand.

"My status as knight and noble, and returning Crusader from the Holy Land, allow me to demand a trial-by-combat to prove the innocence of this woman," said Ivanhoe. He drew his sword. "I do so now demand."

"Demand what you like, traitor," said Prince John from his throne. "Arrest the Saxon."

The two nobles closest to Ivanhoe advanced, threatening with their drawn swords.

But the second monk moved behind them with uncanny speed. With brute force, he slammed the blunt side of his axe-head into the back of one man's skull, then whipped it back across the bridge of the second man's nose. Bones cracked, blood gushed. Both young noblemen went down, deathly still.

As the second monk grabbed a fallen sword, his hood fell off, revealing Gurth's red hair and vengeful face.

"Gurth!" said Rebecca, finally able to speak her heart. "I'm so happy to see you."

Gurth's face radiated absolute joy.

John had risen from his throne, sword in hand.
Hunter, at John's feet, looked up for a moment, then
lowered his great head, deciding to continue his
senescent rest. John's three remaining swordsmen
stood their ground before him.

They were still four against two, with an army
outside the door.

"What are you doing?" said Ivanhoe to his squire,
more amazed than angry. Gurth was extending a sword
hilt-first to Brian. "Brian is the man who abducted
her!"

"We all want the same thing," said Gurth.
"Justice for Lady Rebecca."

"Yes," said Brian. "The same thing." Brian took
the sword from Gurth, and stepped alongside Ivanhoe.

CHAPTER THIRTY-TWO

A courier on a fleet horse might ride from
Torquilstone to Ashby in two days; if the weather was
good, his horse well-shod, and he was not waylaid by
murderous rovers. A knight, slowed by a squire
leading a heavily-burdened packhorse, would be lucky
to make the same trip in four days.

Ivanhoe was not a courier. Neither was he a
knight willing to delay his arrival by an hour - much
less four days.

"Where shall I leave it?" said Gurth, referring
to the admirable - but weighty -- tournament armor
paid for by Isaac, now sorely taxing the packhorse.

"I don't care," said Ivanhoe. "Under a tree,
down a well."

"What about your lances?" said Gurth. They had
ridden hard for two hours, until Ivanhoe had suddenly
reined in, furious. He should have known at once that
the very idea of taking along a squire, with heavy
armor, three lances, two battle axes, and a mace, was
useless.

"If you care so much about my almighty weapons,
turn around and take them back to Torquilstone," said

Ivanhoe. "They might be useful when my father and my king decide to finally rouse themselves."

"I cannot return to Torquilstone," said Gurth. "As you surely have need of my services."

Ivanhoe held back from commenting on the squire's usual presumption. "Strip the packhorse of everything it bears," said Ivanhoe. "Then set it free."

"A wise decision, Master," said Gurth.

Five minutes later they had resumed their travel. Ivanhoe wore only light mail and a sword. Gurth wore a leather vest, a battle axe thrust in his belt. They rode fast, eyes on the road.

"A wise decision," thought Ivanhoe, echoing Gurth's last words with bitter irony. He tried to think calmly and reasonably. But there was nothing reasonable about how he had left Torquilstone, about how he was traveling to Ashby, about what he would do when he arrived.

Even if Rebecca was not a captive -- even if Prince John and Sir Brian and their infernal army were not surrounding her -- even if Richard Lion-heart sat on the throne of England -- nothing would be reasonable.

He remembered the last time he had spoken with her. Sharply, covering any sign of the passion he had felt. Dismissively, as if the reason he didn't care to look into her green-gold eyes was because they held no fascination for him. The truth was just the opposite! He had to turn from her beauty before it swallowed him, like quicksand.

When he had been about to leave Rebecca and Isaac in the woods, to fight the men who had assaulted a group of Saxons, Rebecca had begged him not to go. Not because she feared for herself. But because she had feared for him: "A dozen men!" she had said. "Why must you fight a battle that can't be won?"

He understood it now. She had showed concern, compassion. And how had he responded?

His every word, his every action on that now distant day had been to separate himself from Rebecca. To protect himself from feelings that threatened to overwhelm his life. "Surely a woman as versed in holy matters as yourself understands that it is not up to me where and when I fight," he had said to her. Not just the words, but the tone dripped with contempt. "Even your 'Master of the Universe' couldn't send a clearer sign of my obligations."

She must imagine he hated her.

He could have pressed her hand to his lips and promised he would return to protect her. Instead, he had spoken like a fool. A vainglorious warrior, instead of a man feeling an irrepressible passion.

What could Rebecca possibly think of him? A knight who had broken his promises. A knight who had abandoned her when she most needed him.

More confounded than ever, Ivanhoe spurred his tired warhorse. On the road to Ashby, only one thing was clear: He must get to the trial before Prince John could pass sentence on Rebecca.

Because that sentence would be death.

How -- and whether -- he would stop John from killing Rebecca would be revealed only after he arrived. Whether he would have to face some heavily armored champion, or six warriors at the same time, or a fire-breathing dragon made no difference. Rebecca and her father had been under his protection. It had been his decision to obey Cedric and leave Rebecca to Sir Brian's mercies.

Now Isaac was dead, and Rebecca was in mortal peril.

Ivanhoe's honor was at stake. The lust for righteous battle ran through his blood. He would not risk arriving to Ashby late.

Gurth kept his silence for hours. He hoped his master would be thinking, and perhaps come up with a plan to penetrate John's defenses. Surely, Sir Ivanhoe did not intend to just throw himself at Prince John's warriors. If he did, Gurth would of course ride at his side, swinging his battle axe, fighting till his last breath.

But what good would that do Lady Rebecca?

The oppressive silence between the two men continued. Ivanhoe never once looked at his squire. He is deep in thought, thought Gurth. But as the day darkened, Gurth could feel that Ivanhoe's thoughts were darker still.

"Master?" said Gurth, finally breaking into speech. The moon had risen in a dark blue sky. Ivanhoe didn't turn to him. "Do you think there will be many soldiers outside Prince John's palace?"

It took a while for Ivanhoe to respond. And when he did, he responded with asperity. As if the question was annoying, the answer irrelevant. "It is not a palace," said Ivanhoe. "Neither is it a castle.

John has taken a merchant's home, and fitted it out with stolen riches."

"Whatever you call it, Master, my question remains. How many soldiers?"

"Such questions are useless, Gurth," said Ivanhoe. "Follow my lead, and try not to fall off your horse."

Ivanhoe spurred his horse faster. Gurth followed. His question had been answered, Gurth thought. Ivanhoe had no plan.

Without the packhorse, the two men made excellent time. At midnight, Ivanhoe reined in, and began to remove his horse's saddle. "What are you waiting for, Gurth?" They were his first words in many hours.

Gurth dismounted, and attended to both horses with care. It was some minutes before he lay himself on the ground, head on his saddle. There was not a cloud in the starry sky. Sleep beckoned. But Ivanhoe spoke again, anger and confusion in his tone.

"We will rest but briefly," said Ivanhoe. "I intend to see Ashby before daybreak."

Gurth held his tongue. Perhaps his master had thought of some way to sneak into Prince John's quarters. Perhaps he was about to reveal his plan.

Perhaps the plan was dangerous and desperate, and the anger was directed at himself and not his squire. As for his master's confusion, that could have been for many reasons.

Ivanhoe lay down alongside Gurth, looking at the same starry sky. "Gurth, listen to me," he said. "If I have treated you harshly, it is because I am so vexed. You left your beautiful Ethelreda in exchange for mortal danger, and I have not expressed even a morsel of gratitude."

"You think Ethelreda beautiful, Master?"

"Yes, I do," said Ivanhoe.

"Because there are some who do not appreciate redheaded beauty," said Gurth. "Of course, her red hair is nothing like mine, dull, coarse, and thick enough to deflect a sword blade. Hers is bright, touched with gold, like finest silk."

"Enough talk, Gurth. Ethelreda is beautiful. I congratulate you." Thinking of beauty, Ivanhoe's thoughts drifted back to Rebecca's face, looking down at him as he slowly woke from a drugged sleep.

"Smart too," said Gurth. "High-spirited, even for a redhead. It is a good sign for our future happiness that I miss her so much."

Gurth paused, waiting for an interruption that didn't come. It was time for weightier talk. "Master, you must not bother yourself with thanking me. Before you returned to Rotherwood, bringing Lord Isaac and Lady Rebecca, I was nothing but a churl. Now I am a great knight's squire, betrothed to a beauty, with two gold coins in my wallet. Even if I did not love adventure more than a man of my station should, I would endure any rough treatment to help save Lady Rebecca."

Gurth turned to look at Ivanhoe. "Surely," said the squire, "my obligation to her is as great as yours."

"Silence, oaf!" said Ivanhoe, sitting up.

Gurth remained lying flat, eyes on the stars, waiting for the tempest to pass. "Your 'obligation!' What 'obligation?' I am a knight, sworn to a code. I am the only one of us with obligations."

Gurth sat up. He spoke calmly. "Lord Isaac and Lady Rebecca treated me kindly. I could have tried to save Lord Isaac from death, and Lady Rebecca from dishonor -- but you held me back."

"Yes," said Ivanhoe. "You were braver than myself or my father." He remembered the moment he had butted his helmet-clad head into Gurth's skull. "If I had not driven you senseless, you would surely have killed many Normans that day."

"You meant well, said Gurth. "I have forgiven you long ago."

Ivanhoe nearly blew up again. But everything Gurth had said was true. "I should not have called you 'oaf.'"

"You are not the only one, Master," said Gurth. "Perhaps it is my size."

"Gurth," said Ivanhoe, insisting on a more serious tone. "When we approach Ashby, there is no need for you to leave the surrounding forest. You will hear what happens to me, and be able to ride back to Torquilstone with the news."

So his master still had no plan, thought Gurth, other than to die heroically. A plan that would leave Rebecca to her fate, and Prince John on his throne.

But how kind of Ivanhoe, thought Gurth. At so confused a time, to be worrying about his squire's fate.

"Gurth, are you listening?"

"Do you know the Abbey at Ashby?" said Gurth.

"Did you hear what I said? There is no reason for you to leave the forest. I do not need you to dress me in my armor, as I have none. Nor are you necessary to hand me weapons. All I will be using is the sword on my belt. And because you will be safe in the forest, you will be able to bring back news of my fate to my father and the King."

Gurth continued as if Ivanhoe had not even spoken. "The Abbot had a Saxon mother," said Gurth. "And has been entertained by your father at Rotherwood."

"Why this talk of abbots and fathers?"

"Listen, and you shall understand."

"You are the one who must listen, churl!" said Ivanhoe. "I have thought this over carefully. This is an order. You must and will obey. Tomorrow morning, you will remain safe in the forest and wait for news."

"No, Master," said Gurth. "I don't think so."

"You 'don't think so!." said Ivanhoe, rising to his feet, furious. "Of all the irritating, disputatious slaves in the world, I have to be saddled with you."

"I have never heard that word before. 'Disputatious.' I suppose it means that I am disputing you."

"I will not allow you to dispute anything further! I have decided. I know what I am doing, and ─"

"No, Master. You do not know what you are doing."

"I 'do not know--!'"

"Or you would see that your plan will lead not only to your death, but to Lady Rebecca's as well. I do not intend to let that happen."

"You 'do not intend!' Oaf, churl, slave!"

Gurth continued to look at his master calmly, waiting for a better response. Finally, Ivanhoe said: "I imagine you have a plan."

"Yes," said Gurth. "Would you like to hear it?"

An hour later, Ivanhoe and Gurth began to saddle their restive horses. The horses had but little rest. Gurth and Ivanhoe had none.

It had taken that hour for Gurth to explain his plan, a plan that would not only enable them surreptitious entry to the place of Rebecca's imprisonment, but would give them ecclesiastical authority for demanding a trial-by-combat.

Gurth had often overhead the Abbot in conversation with Lord Cedric. The Abbot, he insisted, was sympathetic to King Richard's cause. He would not only give Ivanhoe and Gurth monks' dress to cover their identities, but would follow them to the trial with a dozen real monks. The presence of abbot and monks would ensure that Prince John follow precedent. It would be nearly impossible for John to refuse Sir Ivanhoe's challenge.

"You believe this abbot will do us so great a favor," said Ivanhoe, "simply because his mother was a Saxon?"

"Not just that, Master," said Gurth. "It will be because of his love for King Richard, and his gratitude for your father's hospitality."

Ivanhoe was less sanguine. "What if that will not be enough? What if he refuses to help, or worse – raises an alarm about our arrival?"

"He won't refuse to help, Master," said Gurth. "Times are hard. I intend to make them easier for the Abbot of Ashby."

Gurth held out the two gold coins given him by Isaac of York. The gold glittered in the moonlight.

CHAPTER THIRTY-THREE

Inside John's throne room, Ivanhoe reflected on the success of his squire's plan. There were a dozen fat-bellied monks and one very tall and austere abbot just outside the door. These holy men had made it possible for Ivanhoe and Gurth, dressed like monks, to interrupt Rebecca's trial for witchcraft. Perhaps Gurth was right, and the very presence of abbot and monks would keep any additional Norman knights at bay, until John had agreed to Ivanhoe's demand for a trial-by-combat.

It was thanks to Gurth that he no longer had to face Prince John, five swordsmen, and Sir Brian. Perhaps one day he'd thank the disobedient churl. He was beginning to love him like a brother.

Ivanhoe had only to face the Prince and three swordsmen. Face them with Gurth and Brian at his side.

Anyone who had seen Sir Brian fight - or Gurth for that matter - would not be anxious to clash with the trio. Ivanhoe expected the Prince and his men to simply sheath their swords, and listen to what Ivanhoe had come to say.

"Yes. The same thing," Brian had said, repeating Gurth's words: "We all want the same thing. Justice for Lady Rebecca."

Rebecca, sitting in the chair below Prince John's throne, watched Sir Brian step alongside Sir Ivanhoe and Gurth, creating a solid line facing the Prince and his three swordsmen.

While Gurth and Ivanhoe kept their eyes on their adversaries, Brian's eyes were on her alone. His blade was as firmly held as Ivanhoe's sword and Gurth's battle axe, but she could see that his thoughts hadn't narrowed to the task at hand.

She had heard Brian's words clearly, and wondered if they could possibly be true.

Justice for Rebecca meant exoneration, freedom, a chance to leave England forever. Brian did not want her to die, but neither did he want her free. Rebecca was not a witch, and had done nothing to beguile Brian. Yet in his wild eyes there was ample evidence of a man who had lost all control of his fate. A Christian knight, of distinguished lineage, who had offered a Jewess marriage, could not be in his right mind.

Perhaps Prince John was right: Sir Brian was bewitched, enthralled, spellbound.

Therefore Brian's words were not true. He did not want "the same thing" as Ivanhoe and Gurth. More than "justice" for Rebecca, he wanted her to accept his passion. His obsession had nothing to do with justice. If Brian would be her champion in a trial-by-combat, he would be fighting to make her his own, body and soul.

One of John's two unconscious knights bloodying the stone floor stirred, groaning. Gurth, barely stepping out of line, silenced him with a kick to his head.

"Go ahead, Master," said Gurth, glancing from Ivanhoe to John. "You won't be interrupted."

"Prince John," said Ivanhoe. "The Abbot of Ashby waits outside your door. As your supposed witch has not confessed to any crimes, the Abbot agrees that a trial-by-combat is the best way to settle this trial."

John hesitated to respond.

In the sudden silence, pulled by an irrepressible impulse, Ivanhoe turned from John to Rebecca. Only for a moment, but long enough to set his mind reeling. Rebecca sat less than two steps from him, enervated

and pale, intelligence and concern in her wonderful
eyes. He forced himself to turn away.

Ivanhoe knew he must speak, but had lost his
train of thought. All he could think of was that
Rebecca was near. Rebecca was near, and he must show
her nothing of what he felt.

Just then Hunter stood, indifferent to the
unconscious men lying on the floor, stretching too-old
muscles. The great dog made a piteous growl, more
like a plea than a threat, then walked from the foot
of the throne to where Rebecca sat.

"She has even bewitched my old dog," said John.

Hunter looked up at Rebecca through clouded eyes,
then suddenly pressed his majestic head against her
leg in a show of affection.

"Animals always sense good from bad," said Gurth.
"That hound is better than any judge." Garth gripped
his heavy weapon, eager to swing it.

"Prince John," said Ivanhoe, forcing his
attention where it belonged. "I am more than happy to
settle our differences in this room."

"They are more than differences, Saxon," said
John. "You are a treasonous rebel."

"You are a usurper. I am a loyal subject of the rightful King."

"The King you dream of is dead and buried. You support a demon, raised by witchcraft, and will die a traitor's death."

"You cannot talk me to death," said Ivanhoe.

Gurth laughed, appreciating his master's wit. Eager to get on with the battle, he said: "You shouldn't have any trouble killing the Prince, Master. Sir Brian and I can take care of his boys."

Gurth raised his battle axe, grinning. Ivanhoe and Brian both raised their swords.

Prince John decided to sheath his blade. His swordsmen, as well as Ivanhoe and Brian did the same. Gurth slowly lowered his weapon, not quite ready to stick it back in his belt.

"Have you forgotten where your loyalty lies, Sir Knight?" said Prince John to Sir Brian. "How can you stand with a Saxon?"

"Because you refuse my just request for a trial-by-combat," said Brian.

"I refuse because you are bewitched," said John.

"If you care to have the Abbot of Ashby's opinion on the matter, I will be glad to call for him," said

Ivanhoe. "He has explained the law quite clearly: In a trial-by-combat, it is our Lord Jesus who sits in judgment."

"Your Richard-loving abbot is full of clever notions," said Prince John. "But the fact remains that you, and not any divinity, is eager to be this witch's champion."

"Not only Ivanhoe," said Brian forcefully. "I have already demanded that right. I demanded it before he walked into this room."

The spark of jealousy was ignited for all to see. John could detect a crack in the defiant wall – Ivanhoe, Brian, and Gurth -- before him.

"The knights who fight on either side of the conflict have no say in the matter," said Ivanhoe. "They are merely pawns of our Savior. Whoever wins in such a battle has not won by the strength of his hand, but by the actions of our God. A midget could best a giant in such a contest, if such is the will of the Lord."

John thought fast. He needed not only to survive this encounter in his throne room, but to survive his brother's plans to take back the throne. "Indeed," he said. "If what the Abbot says is true – and how could it be otherwise, since he speaks with the wisdom of the Holy Spirit — then I may appoint whoever I like to attest to this witch's guilt."

"Yes," said Ivanhoe.

"And if my knight succeeds," continued John, "that success will be due to one thing only: The will of God."

Rebecca feared where Prince John was leading this theological argument. Sir Brian's jealous spark could be easily set ablaze.

"And if her knight succeeds," said Ivanhoe, "that will also be due to the will of God, and not to any knight's special prowess."

"That is very modest of you to say," said Prince John. "Seeing as you intend to be Rebecca's champion."

Sir Brian interrupted: "No. Not Ivanhoe. No one but me will be her champion."

"You are confused, Sir Brian," said Prince John. "Understandably so, as this Jewess has you enthralled. If you were able to think clearly, you would realize what everyone else in this room does — that Lady Rebecca has chosen her champion. Your beautiful Jewess has chosen Sir Ivanhoe."

"That is a lie, said Brian. "She has not chosen anyone."

"Look at her, Sir Brian," said Prince John. "Look deeply and you will see which of you two knights she prefers."

Brian turned to Rebecca, distraught. What John said could not be true. Brian had risked his life, saving her from certain death. He was prepared to throw away privilege, title, dignity, all because of his love. She knew she could have no greater champion. But looking at her, desperate for her eyes to yield to his passion, he saw nothing but pity.

Rebecca spoke: "I want no trial-by-combat. I ask for no champion."

"What she means," said John to Brian, "is that you cannot be her champion, as she loves someone else."

"That is not true," said Brian.

"What is true, is that she has no love for you at all," said John.

"You know nothing of Rebecca's heart," said Brian, horrified. "I know better. I know that she will learn to love me."

"You cannot learn to love anyone," said Prince John, enjoying his insinuations. "No one taught the witch to love Ivanhoe. Look at her, look at him, and you will know why she wants him to be her champion."

Brian couldn't help look from Rebecca's horrified face, desperate to cover her feelings; to Ivanhoe, equally unequal to the task of disguising his passion. Beyond Ivanhoe's enforced grimness, something wondrous threatened to bloom. Anyone could see it, thought Brian. A sense of joy was waiting to burst forth from Ivanhoe. While Brian's own heart was heavy with resentful despair. Brian looked back to Rebecca, accusingly.

"So that is why you reject me," said Brian. "Because you love this Saxon."

"No," said Rebecca.

"A man already betrothed, a man who will do nothing for you," he said. Furious, he stepped away from Ivanhoe, one step closer to Rebecca. "Admit it," said Brian. "Tell me the truth. Tell him, tell everyone. You love one Christian knight in this room, and his name is Ivanhoe."

"I love no knight," said Rebecca. "I have no champion. I want no champion."

"Silence," said John. Somehow his authority had been returned to him. "You have heard Ivanhoe express the Abbot's interpretation of our law. The two knights who will fight to settle this matter are but pawns of our Lord Jesus. Their bravery, their strength at arms matter not a whit."

John stepped close to Sir Brian, his tone pitying. "You are convinced that Lady Rebecca is innocent, are you not?"

"Yes," said Brian. Brian turned away and took sudden hold of Rebecca's hand. "Please, let me be your champion. I will not fail you."

"No," she said, pulling her hand free. Whatever pity he had found in her voice and manner had disappeared. Rebecca said: "You will never be my champion."

"All right," said John, smiling at the look in Sir Brian's face. "I agree to a trial-by-combat. The witch's champion will be Sir Ivanhoe."

"I want no champion," said Rebecca. "Just let me be."

"Silence, Jewess. You are in a Christian country, and must abide by Christian law. Ivanhoe has offered to champion your innocence. I hereby appoint him to that unholy task. As I have passed sentence on you, it is my right to choose the court's champion."

John paused, looking around the room, enjoying the damage wrought by his cleverness. "To prove Lady Rebecca's guilt in a trial-by-combat," he said, "the court chooses Sir Brian de Bois Gilbert"

Brian took a step back, appalled.

He was still reeling from John's insinuations, and from Rebecca's spurning of his help and his love. Perhaps she didn't realize that if he, as the court's champion, bested Ivanhoe in combat, she would be burnt at the stake.

"The trial-by-combat will take place in two days," said Prince John. "The combat will be to the death."

CHAPTER THIRTY-FOUR

The trial-by-combat would be a divine test of guilt or innocence. Agreeing to it gave Prince John license to take control. He was not a usurper, but a ruler following heaven's dictates. He was not fabricating lies to suit his politics, but acknowledging God's Will.

Now that Sir Brian - firmly rejected by Rebecca - had been named the court's champion, the Prince called in his warriors. Two dozen rushed past a phalanx of Abbot and monks, crowding the throne room, surrounding Ivanhoe and Gurth.

Ivanhoe understood there was no need to fight. He would save his strength for the trial-by-combat. First Ivanhoe, then Gurth, surrendered their weapons.

"What about Sir Brian?" one of Prince John's knights asked. "Shall we take away his sword?"

"To attempt that would be foolish," John said. "Sir Brian is not only a loyal Norman - he is the court's champion."

As if to prove his point about Brian's return to loyalty, the Prince ordered Rebecca's wrists to be again bound behind her back. Brian didn't protest, by word or action.

Ivanhoe restrained Gurth from intervening against an overwhelming force. But Gurth would have broken free from his master's grip, had not Rebecca spoken.

"No, please. Do not fight these men," she said. "For my sake, dear Gurth."

The squire met her beseeching eyes, and stopped resisting. "And do me one more kindness," she continued. "Go away with your master to a safe place."

"There will be no safe place in this world until you are free, my lady," Gurth said.

Brian saw Rebecca avoid Ivanhoe's gaze, but that gave him little comfort.

"I want no champion, Gurth," she insisted. "Neither you nor Sir Ivanhoe must come to harm on my behalf."

"See that she is treated properly," Ivanhoe said, turning to Prince John. "You have sworn to allow her fate to be judged by trial-by-combat. Until then, she is innocent."

"Get the damned Jewess out of here," the Prince said. "And these Saxon dogs as well."

As Rebecca was led away, Brian's feelings were overwhelmed: Not by anger for her treatment, but by jealousy.

It was Ivanhoe who had ridden to Ashby to rescue her, Ivanhoe who would be her champion.

Brian, Ivanhoe, and Gurth would not see Rebecca for two days.

In Prince John's dungeon, an old woman prisoner glared at a jailor, chaining one of Rebecca's ankles to the wall. "Why do you do that?" the old woman said.

"Because she is a witch," the jailor said.

"If she is a witch," the old woman said, "that chain won't stop her." When the jailor left, the old woman urged Rebecca to break free and fly to safety. "If you are a witch, they will burn you," she said.

"I am not a witch," Rebecca said. "I cannot break chains, and I cannot fly. But if they burn me, perhaps our Heavenly Father will grant me consolation in the World-to-Come."

"If you are not a witch, why have they brought you to this place?" said the old woman.

"Because they hate me," said Rebecca.

"Why do they hate you?"

"Because I am a Jewess."

This statement surprised the old woman. "But then you can easily free yourself! Jews practice black arts. Not just witchcraft, but alchemy. That is why you never get sick, why you always have gold in your pockets."

"None of that is true," said Rebecca.

The old woman looked at her closely. "You have a kind face," she said. "As troubled as it is beautiful. Even from a distance, I can see that Prince John is dishonest. Greed and ambition have made him evil."

"Why are you here?" said Rebecca.

"For stealing bread from the Prince's kitchen, I am to be flogged," she said. "But I am not like you. Though I am a Christian, I don't ask Lord Jesus for consolation. I am a Saxon, and ask my old gods – Mista, Skogula, and Zernebock -- for vengeance."

The old woman suddenly took firm hold of Rebecca's hands. Her compassion stirred Rebecca profoundly.

What did Rebecca want from her God? she thought. Not vengeance, but understanding. Had she wanted Ivanhoe to come for her, or had she hoped he would stay away? Had his appearance brought joy, or foreboding? Why must there be a trial-by-combat, when Rebecca didn't even know if she wanted to live or die?

So much had happened so quickly, events spinning and twisting in maddening coils of confusion. Still mourning her mother, her father had been murdered. How could God have allowed Brian - her father's murderer -- to be driven mad by lust for her? If not for Lady Rowena, Brian would have raped or killed her. But Rowena, so dear to Rebecca, was Ivanhoe's betrothed.

Was Rebecca fated to fall in love with the man Rowena was to marry?

And what about Ivanhoe? What did he want from Rebecca? What did she want from him?

"To find peace, you must go to Spain as soon as you are able," Isaac had said to her. "Because I can see beyond all the terrors of this place, that you have a greater fear." His strength fading, he had paused for breath. "That he will find you. Come for you. Ivanhoe."

That is why her father had insisted on extracting her promise: That she would leave England, find her way to her mother's family, to Zaragoza.

"Give me your word," her father had said. "That you will never abandon your faith and your people."

But Rebecca had not given her word.

Instead, she had answered her father's plea with a protestation: "Why do you ask that of me? Ivanhoe means nothing to me! Nothing," she had said, a moment before the life faded from his eyes.

"Father, no! Don't go. Please. Only a moment longer. Only a moment." She had held him close, muttering prayers, rocking back and forth, back and forth.

But all her prayers could not bring Isaac back to life. Neither could they atone for the sin of lying to one's dying parent.

Despite their differences, despite his betrothal to a woman she loved, Ivanhoe meant something to Rebecca. Something beyond words, beyond rational thought. Isaac had felt her terrible fear: That he would find her. That he would come for her.

"What is wrong?" said the old woman, hours later. Rebecca had been shivering violently, that she had broken her from sleep.

"So much is wrong," said Rebecca. "That you were hungry enough to steal bread from a tyrant. That men would flog you for trying to live."

"I watched you sleep, and you were at peace," said the old woman. "Until a shadow passed over you. What was it?"

"A nightmare," said Rebecca. Rebecca's mind had retrieved fragments of her dream, a vision of Sir

Ivanhoe as she had first met him, standing behind the wooden cross marking the crossroads.

She faced the old woman, but her eyes saw nothing of her. Remembering how Ivanhoe's tattered chain mail was marked with another cross, the cross of the Crusader. Blue eyes shined in his filthy face. She recalled feeling he must be a warrior returning from murder, pillage, and rape.

But the dream told her otherwise. Ivanhoe was not evil, but good. Not a murderer, but a man of noble intent. Their paths had crossed that day, their eyes had met, and nothing would ever be the same for either one of them.

Now, at Ashby, their paths had crossed again. Their eyes had met in Prince John's throne room. Some great event was pressing on her, on both of them, something greater than the terrible trial-by-combat.

Something inevitable, something that could not be escaped. That is why she had woken.

Rebecca could see the old woman clearly now, looking at her with concern. "Dreams have much to tell us," said the old woman. "Would you like to tell me about yours?"

"No," said Rebecca. "I want my dreams to vanish. I don't want them to plague my waking life." Feeling the old woman's disappointment at being rebuffed, Rebecca added: "But you are very kind to offer your help."

In place of being secured in John's dungeon, Ivanhoe and Gurth were sent to a filthy pallet in the servants' quarters. The servants kept as far from them as possible. Knight and squire were champions of a witch, and the servants feared what dark powers they might possess.

Gurth insisted that his master sleep and eat. He would need his strength for the combat to come. "You must think of nothing else, Master," said Gurth. "Nothing but the battle with Sir Brian."

It was clear to Gurth that Ivanhoe's thoughts were elsewhere. That the battle was within his own heart.

Was it possible, thought Gurth, that the knight could not see what was evident to his squire? That more than honor and justice were at stake for Ivanhoe.

That the woman he championed was the woman he loved.

CHAPTER THIRTY-FIVE

Sir Brian was given a bed draped in silk, close to Prince John's rooms. Servants brought him fine foods, a resplendent tunic, chain mail imported from Spain. Knights showed him a choice of weapons he would have at his disposal for the battle with Ivanhoe.

But like Ivanhoe, Brian's mind was not on that battle. Unlike that knight, Brian had been spurned.

Brian's thoughts about Rebecca were neither joyful nor fearful, but offended and aggrieved. It was not only Prince John who had refused to let him be her champion. She had refused him. As she had once refused to accept the crown of beauty he had offered her at the tournament, she now refused to let him defend her with his life.

Not because she feared for what harm might come to him. No, not at all! It was because, he thought, she detested him. Brian felt her detestation as a sting, an insult that would never end.

Prince John, believing Brian would do his bidding, decided to take no chances with the outcome of the trial-by-combat. While Ivanhoe's armor had been left behind on the journey to Ashby, Brian's armor was readied, polished to a magnificent sheen.

When the Abbot of Ashby dared question a combat fought without fairness, John responded with casuistry: "It is not a question of fairness. It is a question of what God has provided to each of these men. As God will determine the trial-by-combat, so He has determined how these knights will be dressed and armed."

Ivanhoe would only be wearing chain mail, carrying a sword. He would not even have a helmet or shield. Brian would be encased head-to-toe in impenetrable metal, with shield and lance in hand. Prince could talk all he wanted about the will of God, but he had little faith in the supernatural. His faith was in arms and armor, and the strength of his champion.

John spent the best part of two days ensuring that his champion remained committed to besting his rival. He filled Brian with dispiriting tales of witchcraft and duplicity. The Prince wanted to turn Brian from the weakness of despair to the violence of rage.

So John told Brian fanciful legends: Men driven to madness by hags whose black magic allowed them an illusion of beauty. Tales of love potions and will-breaking poisons, of noxious herbs wafting salacious dreams into sleeping knights.

Did not Brian remember how he had been assaulted by Ivanhoe, weakened from injury, in Isaac's home? Could he not understand that even then Brian had been bewitched, his powers impaired? If not for witchcraft, surely Brian would have already killed both Ivanhoe and the Jewess.

Insisting that Brian's love was nothing but Satan-sent deception, Prince John rubbed the wound of Brian's jealousy with yet more terrible salt. He told Brian, in lubricious detail, of the Jewess's liaison with Ivanhoe during the days and nights she had treated his tournament injuries. How Ivanhoe and Rebecca had made love, again and again, not twice or three times, but ten times a night.

Only a succubus could make mortal man that insatiable, John said. Only a witch could arouse that much passion.

The Prince forced Brian to conjure the terrible scene: Rebecca stripping Ivanhoe of his clothes, bringing him to her naked body. Flesh against flesh, her mouth pressed to his as she pulled him inside her body with desperate hunger.

Ivanhoe's eyes must have been closed, or he would have seen hellfire burning in hers.

"Think of it," John said. "Imagine it."

And Brian did. In his mind's eye, the woman he loved possessed Ivanhoe completely. A fallen angel enveloping him with enormous wings.

Yet still Brian hesitated to believe it completely. "You were not there with them. How can you possibly know?" he said.

"Rebecca will not be the first witch burned in England," said John. "The marks of witchcraft are evident. Evident in her face and manner. Even more evident in the passion she creates in her lovers."

"But if she has made unholy love to Ivanhoe, then he is bewitched," said Brian. "And should not be allowed to champion her."

"You are mistaken," said Prince John. "You are the only one she has bewitched. Ivanhoe is the one she has chosen to adore."

Brian could no longer repel the terrible words. Twisting and turning in his silk-draped bed, waiting for the morning of the trial-by-combat to arrive, he finally accepted the truth.

He would never have Rebecca's love.

No matter what he said, what he offered, what he suffered, she would never want him as he wanted her. And far worse, she wanted someone else. Ivanhoe.

Brian's sorrow spoiled like old milk.

Exactly as Prince John desired, wild rage stirred his blood. A rage that swept all before it.

Prince John had made him understand that Rebecca was indeed a witch. That Brian had been the victim of her sorcery. That just as she had never loved him, he had never loved her. Whatever love he had felt must have been false, as false as black magic.

He could almost believe that he no longer felt anything for her.

Rebecca had a champion - Ivanhoe. Ivanhoe, the man the witch made love to. The court had a champion - Brian. Brian, the man the witch rejected.

The only way to prove the woman he had loved was inhuman, that the love he had felt was an illusion cast by demonic force, was for Brian to win the trial-by-combat.

That would be simple, Brian thought. Imagining the pleasure of his victory, Brian was finally able to sleep through the night.

On the morning of the trial-by-combat, he rose from his bed with confidence. He knew what he must do.

Brian must kill Ivanhoe, proving the witch's guilt.

Then Rebecca would burn.

Burn until decisions she had made in her life would rush past her shut eyes. Burn until she would remember what Brian had offered, what she had refused. Burn until she would know that she could have had honor instead of disgrace, eternal love instead of unbearable pain.

Brian imagined it: Rebecca at the stake, her beauty consumed by ravenous flames.

She would burn until there would be nothing left of her to torment him.

CHAPTER THIRTY-SIX

Two days had been time enough to send tidings of the trial-by-combat to every corner of the realm, though hardly enough to bring all those concerned to Ashby. News of the great event had reached Torquilstone only hours before the combat was to take place.

By that time, Lord Cedric and Lady Rowena were no longer present in the castle.

King Richard was likewise nowhere to be found.

Minutes before the combat was to begin, Hunter sat at Prince John's feet, assaulted by the smells and sounds of hundreds of strangers.

It was no wonder the mastiff was restless. Hunter kept stirring, rising to his shaky full height until the Prince would slap him sharply on his enormous head. The Prince wanted him still, on display, and for nothing else. John cared nothing for Richard's old dog - for dogs in general - but the once powerful beast, with his great size and distinctive markings, was a symbol of royal privilege. Prince John cared a great deal for symbols.

The Prince sat on brightly colored cushions at the top of the reviewing stand, flanked by strapping knights, richly dressed nobles, and the austere Abbot of Ashby. Two trumpeters in red and green costume stood at either end of the stand, waiting for John's signal. An honor guard of fifteen tournament knights in beautiful new chain mail, carrying spears -- more ceremonial than lethal -- stood at attention beneath John's stand. Their polished helmets reflected bright sun.

The old dog at John's feet was simply one more element in a tapestry of power. The Prince knew that every regal sign, every mark of kingly rank must be exhibited this day.

Even without the chance to ogle a captive Jewess, a combat to the death was enticing enough to crowd the perimeter of the tilting field with local nobles, freemen, and serfs. Everyone knew this deathly contest was to settle not only whether a beautiful woman was a witch, but more importantly, which of two brothers was to rule their nation.

The Prince had proclaimed the real King Richard dead; that he, John, was the only legitimate ruler of

England. But more than a proclamation was needed to solidify his rule. John needed the consent of the clergy, the support of the nobility, the trust of common people.

Looking over the heads of the privileged audience below his chair, past his young knights standing at attention, across to the lesser gentry and merchants on their benches, to the horde of serfs and free peasants standing and sitting on the hard-packed earth, John understood that the trial-by-combat forced on him by Ivanhoe was a blessing in disguise.

Had he simply had the Jewess executed at the end of her trial, there might have been whispers of expediency, corruption. There might have been gossip as to the validity of the verdict. Such talk could have led to doubts about John's proclamations about Richard.

Now there would be no doubts.

One man would win the trial-by-combat, and the verdict would be clear and just to everyone assembled here.

The Prince had no need of an army to enforce his plan. His fifteen tournament knights, though young and inexperienced with war, were expertly trained, and eager to prove their worth. An additional knight stood ready to torch Rebecca at John's command. Sir Brian would kill Sir Ivanhoe, and all England would know that the Jewess was a witch.

Everyone would accept that the impostor who had arrived at Torquilstone was nothing but the witch's unearthly creation. The Richard they had loved – the true Richard Lion-heart -- was rotting in an Austrian grave.

Rebecca stood immobile, tied to a stake below where the Prince sat, separated from him by the narrow tilting range. In this fashion, John could watch her face as Brian and Ivanhoe clashed. He would enjoy himself, knowing that the accused witch was seeing the same unequal conquest, watching the heavily armed and armored Brian hack her useless champion to death.

Surely dread would overcome her, not merely for Ivanhoe, but for herself. As Ivanhoe would be struck down, impaled, the Jewess might shut her eyes. But she would know what would be coming next. She would fear it, thought John. The fire.

Rebecca's enormous eyes stared back at the world. If there were comments from the crowd about her lustrous hair and pale skin, her defiant posture, her uncanny beauty, she could not hear them. Wood was piled around her, as high as her chest. Fire blazed in a bronze cauldron to one side, where John's knight stood ready to ignite a torch.

A torch that would set the pile of wood flaming, for a slow and merciless death.

But the Prince had no entry to Rebecca's thoughts. He could not know that her dread had nothing to do with being burned alive. She didn't know how or why, but she sensed she would not leave the world today. Her fear was not that she would die hideously, but that she would live; in sin, filled with shame.

John had made sure to bring out Rebecca only after the contesting knights were within their two pavilions, set up at either end of the tilting range, without a view of the witch's stake. Sir Brian would do his bidding, thought John, but there was no reason to weaken the knight's resolve. Brian must remember the trial was not to rescue a fair damsel, but to condemn a repugnant witch.

The Prince's pennant flew over Brian's pavilion. Inside, hidden from the view of the crowd, were Sir Brian, three attendants, and his skittish warhorse.

One side of the pavilion was open, so Brian could look across to the other pavilion. But without stepping out beyond the mouth of the pavilion, Brian could not turn his head and see the dancing flames in the cauldron, and the silent woman tied to its adjacent stake.

It took Brian enormous effort to stay within his pavilion, and allow his men to finish dressing him in his heavy armor. He tried to keep his mind on the battle to come. It must be quick, decisive. He didn't want to linger on that field, watched by Rebecca. He thought of battle strategy. How he would rise in his stirrups, and drive his lance into his rival's chest.

Looking to the second pavilion, Brian wondered whether Ivanhoe felt any fear. He wondered whether the Prince was wrong, and that Ivanhoe was as bewitched as himself. That neither love nor honor was impelling the Saxon to his fate, but sorcery.

He wondered whether Ivanhoe had the same desire he had: To look one last time into Rebecca's green and gold eyes.

Ivanhoe's pavilion had no pennant. From this distance, Brian could see Ivanhoe in his inadequate chain mail, attended only by the redheaded, truculent Gurth. Ivanhoe looked across to Brian, meeting his eyes calmly, without enmity. Brian looked back, trying to turn jealousy to hatred.

Suddenly, all Brian could feel was a terrible longing he had thought gone forever.

Gurth stepped outside their pavilion, and turned his head. Brian knew the squire was looking at Rebecca, tied to the stake. But he could not hear what he was reporting to Ivanhoe.

"Lady Rebecca is quiet, Master," said Gurth. "Looking neither right nor left, head held high." Returning to the pavilion, Gurth added: "She didn't see me, but she knows we are here."

Brian turned away from Ivanhoe's pavilion. Longing turned to deep sadness. He knew he was bewitched. He knew the witch must die, or he would be forever in her thrall. But still, in his heart of hearts, he knew that such logic was false.

What he felt was not stronger than reason, stronger than enchantment.

If only I could look at her, thought Brian.

Not from a distance. To go close enough to feel her breath of life in his face.

To feel the possibility of joy.

Overcome with emotion, Brian began to unfasten his heavy breast plate.

"How can she know anything?" said Ivanhoe, inside his pavilion. Ivanhoe's warhorse snorted violently. Whether as a reproof to Ivanhoe or in anticipation of combat was impossible to say.

"She knows a great deal," said Gurth. "Very wise she is, and not just in the healing arts. She knows you are about to fight for her life, and she is grateful."

"I doubt it."

"More than grateful."

"What is 'more than grateful,' oaf?" said Ivanhoe, unable to keep affection for the squire from his tone.

"Grateful is one thing, but this, what she feels for you, that is something else," said Gurth.

"She feels nothing for me, and rightly so," said Ivanhoe. "As I feel nothing for her. Nothing but a sense of duty. Nothing but a chance to honor my commitments."

"That's a great deal of nothings, Master," said Gurth. "Perhaps you should take a look at her face before the trumpets sound. It might give you confidence."

"Her face will not give me confidence. Her face will only remind me of how I have failed her, repeatedly, to my shame."

"It would be best, Master," said Gurth, "to gallop directly past him."

"And I don't need her to give me confidence," said Ivanhoe. "The rightness of my cause gives me all the confidence I need."

"Did you not hear me, Master? Gallop past Sir Brian," said Gurth. "So you may come at him from behind."

"You dare advise a veteran of the Holy Crusade how to battle?"

"As you have neither shield nor armor, you are lighter and quicker, and can easily get behind Sir Brian."

"Spoken like a churl," said Ivanhoe.

"In his heavy armor and armor, he might not see you at first. Then, as he starts to turn to your, you can hack into his neck."

"Spoken like a serf who knows nothing of knightly honor," said Ivanhoe.

"You are about to meet a Norman who is even more ignorant of knightly honor, or he would not be fighting a man deprived of proper arms and armor."

"I thought you were a believer, Gurth," said Ivanhoe. "Men do not decide a trial-by-combat. The decision comes from God, and God is just."

"I am a believer," said Gurth. "I believe that men have no idea what their God intends."

"I am also a believer," said Ivanhoe. "I believe that whether I live or die, the trial-by-combat will free Rebecca."

"A man in chain mail cannot win against a man with a full suit of armor - unless he is willing to fight any way he can." Ivanhoe quieted his restive horse. "And remember who this Brian is," Gurth insisted. "The man who not only killed Lord Isaac, who not only abused Lady Rebecca, but also imprisoned your betrothed."

"I know who he is," said Ivanhoe.

"If Lady Rowena were in your place, she would not hesitate to kill Brian any way she could."

"Do not talk about Lady Rowena!" said Ivanhoe. "She is so far beyond your lowly station, you could never imagine what she might think."

"All right, Master," said Gurth. "I will not talk about Lady Rowena."

There was a moment's mutual silence. Ivanhoe broke it, speaking in a conciliatory tone: "You, an untrained slave, have bested warriors again and again."

"I was never a slave."

"No, Gurth. I meant only that, despite your birth, God has given you strength and passion enough to overcome your enemies. I trust He will do the same for me."

Gurth had no such trust.

Wildly frustrated, Gurth stepped out of the pavilion to look once more at the proud Lady Rebecca. As before, she didn't look at him. But Gurth believed she was aware of his presence. He hoped that gave her solace at this terrible time.

Gurth knew was that if Ivanhoe was killed by Brian, a torch would set the pile of wood around Rebecca on fire. She would be engulfed by flames that would burn her flesh, crack her bones, reduce her to smoldering ashes. Even if she was one of the very few who would be able to hold back her screams, death would come slowly, hideously, inescapably.

Yes, Ivanhoe was right. Death would free Rebecca. But that was not the sort of freedom for her that Gurth wanted.

Gurth turned from Rebecca, about to step back into the pavilion to renew his argument with his master. But a strange sight caught his eye.

Ivanhoe, from inside the pavilion, saw the same thing.

So did Prince John, rising from his seat on the reviewing stand.

John was furious.

"What are you doing?" John shouted. "Go back!" His high-pitched voice ran higher still. "We have not yet started."

The Prince held back further questions, each one perfectly obvious: Why was his champion Sir Brian not wearing armor? Not on his horse? Not waiting for the trumpeters to sound the beginning of the combat?

And why was Richard's damn dog standing again, looking below through nearly blind eyes. Hunter could not see what the others saw, but neither could they sense what the old dog felt.

Something or someone that could not yet be seen, nor smelled, nor tasted. The mastiff's body shook violently.

But Prince John's attention remained on Sir Brian. The court's champion no longer had the advantage of arms and armor. Brian wore only chain mail and sword belt, walking along the tilting range toward Ivanhoe's pavilion.

Ivanhoe had thrust past Gurth, and was walking directly toward Brian. Like Brian, Ivanhoe wore his sword belt. He walked as fast as he could without running. Ivanhoe wanted to meet Brian before he could get to the center of the tilting range.

Because the center of the tilting range was where Rebecca stood, tied to the stake.

"They are bewitched, both of them," said John. "This trial cannot go on." He turned to the Abbot, to the nobles waiting for his decision, then to the knights on either side of him. There was no time for debate or discussion.

"Go," said Prince John to his eager knights.
"Kill Ivanhoe and Brian, kill them both. Make certain
the witch is put on fire."

Rebecca saw Ivanhoe and Brian arrive in front of
her at the same moment. The men's eyes were locked on
each other, as if mutually refusing to look at the
woman they both loved.

"I will draw my sword," said Brian. "You do the
same. Then you must kill me, and set Rebecca free."

CHAPTER THIRTY-SEVEN

Richard Lion-heart traveled without retinue.
That had been the case since his release from an
Austrian prison; since his group of supporters had
arranged to bring him, incognito, across treacherous
borders on land and sea. Since the moment he had
arrived at Torquilstone and revealed his familiar face
to Lord Cedric.

When Richard had ruled Britain, there had always
been men around him. When he woke, when he went to
sleep. When he sat at table, when he hunted.
Courtiers, warriors, statesmen. Doctors, priests,
scholars. Anxious to teach, to counsel, to protect.

The King was more than a man, he was Britain made
flesh. The country must be kept whole, inviolate.
Even in the Holy Land, Richard had little respite.
Even in the heat of battle, he had been surrounded by
Crusaders eager to lay down their lives for his
safety.

That was not what Richard had wanted.

He had wanted to make his own decisions. He did
not need counselors to teach him wrong from right. He
did not need soldiers to put their bodies between him

and enemy blades. He wanted to fight on his own. Not only to best Saracen warriors with his strong arm, but to choose England's path forward with his own heart's counsel.

Now Richard was back in England. Some knew the Lion had returned. Others disbelieved that fact, or pretended that it was not true. Richard would have to regain control from his usurper brother. More than loyal warriors were on the way to Torquilstone. Advisers were also on their way: Norman grandees, Saxon overlords, veterans of the Crusade, even Papal emissaries. Each with their particular plans for how best to take back the throne. For how best to rule.

Perhaps one day, Richard would try and listen to them.
Perhaps one day, wearing royal robes, the King would tolerate a new retinue. But not today.

Today he had no retinue. He had his strong arm, and his strong will. The will that had driven him to leave Torquilstone, and follow Ivanhoe to Ashby.

In place of an armed escort, he had old Lord Cedric, and two young women, all of whom had refused to stay behind.

"We should stop here, my Liege," said Lord Cedric, slowing down. It was not his first suggestion on the long ride to Ashby, and it was met in the usual way.

"I will stop when I am ready to stop," said Richard. But he slowed down, gentling his overworked horse.

"Once we get to the top of the hill," said Cedric, "we will be visible from the tilting grounds."

"Do you think I don't know that?" said Richard. He reined to a stop alongside Cedric. "Old friend, you worry like a woman."

"Some women, perhaps," said Cedric. "But not our companions."

Like Richard, Cedric wore a hooded cloak, covering his chain mail and sword belt. Behind them, the women were also cloaked, disguising their rank. But their hoods were off, revealing their sex and their bright hair. One, Lady Rowena, was blonde. The other, Ethelreda, was redheaded.

Cedric called to them to stop, but the two women did not heed him. Indeed, Rowena spurred her horse faster, intending to be the first up the hill. Ethelreda raced after her.

The women crested the hill, side by side, then disappeared down the other side.

Neither woman was there when Richard removed his cloak, revealing chain mail over a tunic of azure and gold. The royal colors. The mail over his chest was marked with a rampant Lion; as famous in the distant Holy Land as in England itself.

"Only follow me to the top of the hill," said Richard. "That will be a good place to watch. In case I die, you will be a worthy witness to my combat."

Lord Cedric protested, but the King wasn't listening. Richard Lion-heart grinned, happy to be without retinue, happy to charge up the hill on his own.

Fire burned in the cauldron beside Rebecca. The noise of the crowd swelled. A dog, not far from where she stood, barked. The Prince was shouting out orders. Rebecca's heart beat like a minstrel's drum.

But she had heard Sir Brian clearly. "I will draw my sword," Brian had said. "You do the same. Then you must kill me, and set Rebecca free."

"No," said Rebecca. "That is not what I want."

Ivanhoe and Brian finally turned to her, hands on the hilts of their sheathed swords. Tied to the stake, she was unable to turn her head, to look from one to the other. She saw both men at the same time. Equally passionate, equally conflicted. Neither knew what course to take, how to save Rebecca without violating their honor. But their confusion remained for only a few moments.

Suddenly there was no need for Ivanhoe to agree to Brian's selfless offer.

"Draw your swords!" said Rebecca. "Save yourselves!"

Staring past Ivanhoe and Brian, she could see John's tournament knights approaching from below the reviewing stand, crossing the tilting field, spear points dancing in sunlight.

Ivanhoe and Brian drew their swords. They would not fight each other. They would fight together.

Obeying John's command, the knight at Rebecca's side dipped his torch into the flaming cauldron. Before he could touch his blazing torch to the pile of wood around Rebecca, Ivanhoe hacked through his arm, and Brian thrust through his chest.

Prince John's knight fell dead over his fiery torch.

Rebecca steeled herself. She had foreseen a momentous event, some unknown, inescapable force that would sweep her away from everything she had ever known. But not this. Not the sudden union of the two knights who loved her. Not the certainty that they would be killed along with her, against the cacophony of a jeering mob.

Ivanhoe and Brian remained shoulder to shoulder, backs to Rebecca, facing the steady approach of fifteen knights. John's trumpeters added to the noise, sounding an alarm that would bring more warriors to the field.

"That was honorable," said Ivanhoe to Brian. "To offer your life to save an innocent."

"It was not honor that drove my action," said Brian.

Both men watched the tournament knights grow near.

"It will be an honor to die by your side," said Ivanhoe.

But as the tournament knights prepared to charge, leveling their spears, all heard the sound of hoofbeats, and a ferocious war cry.

Gurth, on Ivanhoe's warhorse, galloped across the tiltfield, charging directly into the line of spearmen. Having no weapon, the squire bent low, and ripped a spear from one knight's grasp. Other young knights scurried away from the fast moving charger.

Rebecca could see Ivanhoe and Brian ward off the first group of young knights, her champions slashing with quickly bloodied blades, shouting fiercely. She was too tightly bound to see Gurth wheel about, his spear thrusting and whirling, spear point and shaft wreaking terrible damage.

Rebecca knew all three men would fight to their last breaths. She wanted them to live, all three, even Sir Brian, but she was powerless to help them. There was no confession she could make, no surrender that would stop the killing.

All the blood spilled on her behalf was useless. There were too many knights. And more would come, she thought. Dozens, hundreds if Prince John needed them.

Ivanhoe, Brian, even dear Gurth - all would die. Because of her.

Rebecca shut her eyes, not wanting to see the moment when the line of spears would tear apart her defenders. She forgot to ask God for his mercy, to beseech Heaven for a miracle.

But still, the miracle arrived.

No angels descended, no lightning bolts shattered the enemy, no earthquakes opened to swallow evil.

What came was an utterly uncanny cessation of crowd noise.

It was as if everyone watching had shut their mouths, barely breathing, standing still. As if a thick blanket had muffled everything but the sound of clashing steel, the hoofbeats of horses…and the barking of a dog.

Rebecca opened her eyes.

Hunter, Richard's old dog, a dog hardly able to stand, a somnolent, silent, dying dog… was running past her. Running like a puppy, barking like a hound chasing deer.

Tied to the stake, Rebecca could not turn her head to see where the dog was going, could not see what the crowd saw. But she was certain of one thing: She was not dreaming.

Rebecca could not fathom what the barking dog meant, nor what it had to do with the silence of the crowd.

Meanwhile, the fight continued, eliciting other sounds. Steel rang against steel, warriors cried out in pain or exultation. Ivanhoe ducked under a spear, and thrust his sword into a tournament knight's belly. Gurth, on horseback, pulled out his spear from where he had driven it into another young knight's back.

But she had lost sight of Brian.

This was a blessing, as Rebecca did not see him struck. When she caught sight him, Brian was already falling to his knees, a spear lodged in his chest.

Sir Brian de Bois Gilbert stared up at Rebecca, amazed to find himself at the end of life's journey, his face white with pain. His eyes shined with regret.

Rebecca could not understand why he was so easy to hear, why the noise had stopped. Not just the jeers and shouts of the crowd; the clamor of clashing weapons had ceased as well. Nothing interfered with his words.

"May God protect you, Rebecca," said Brian. "I am sorry to have failed you."

"You have not failed me, Sir Knight," said Rebecca. "You have shown courage and honor. And goodness."

"I tried to show you more," said Brian. "That even a man like me can love a woman like you." Before she could answer, or he could say any more, an obliterating force swept away his terrible pain.

Brian fell over, dead.

Rebecca was surprised by a wave of grief for the man who had killed her own father.

Ivanhoe, his fury renewed by Brian's death, charged forward. The half dozen men he faced had stepped back and away, refusing to engage him. Ivanhoe shouted his war cry into the strange stillness.

But John's knights didn't take up his challenge. Even if their numbers were overwhelming. Even if other warriors, called by the trumpets, were already hurrying to join them. They stepped further away, looking past where Ivanhoe stood.

The tournament knights had never experienced war, but they had been raised on tales of valorous battle outside the walls of Jerusalem. Of a Holy Crusade led by a great British king, a ferocious fighter of huge size.

A very large man had galloped down the hill, onto the field. Most had never seen the true king of England, but all knew the symbol marking his chain mail.

Everyone could see the Lion adorning the large man's chest.

Gurth, yards away, reined in his excited horse, looking past Ivanhoe with wonder.

"What is it, Gurth?" said Ivanhoe. Two steps from Rebecca, bloody sword in hand, Ivanhoe didn't turn, still waiting for another attack.

"Justice," said Gurth, lowering his bloody speak.

Before Ivanhoe could make any sense of this, the sound of hoofbeats approaching from behind his back led him to whirl round, his blade extended to another source of potential danger for Rebecca.

But no danger was approaching.

Two women, riding fast, side by side. Beautiful and young, fearless and wild. One with red hair. The other the blonde beauty to whom Ivanhoe was betrothed.

It was not the women who had stopped the noise of the crowd, who had held back the tournament knights, who had brought everyone in the stands and on the ground to their feet, caps in hand, eyes filled with deep respect.

It was Hunter, the King's old mastiff, running across the field to meet his master.

Prince John had come with steadfast knights and well-dressed nobles, with trumpeters and bright pennants, with clergymen and merchants and serfs eager to see a witch burned before their eyes. These symbols of John's authority, these signs of his power, paled in comparison to the faithful dog knowing his master. Leaping and jumping, tongue out, trying to fly into Richard's arms.

Anyone could see that Hunter was not greeting some creature brought back to life by a cunning Jewess. Hunter was living proof that the true King of England had returned.

Feeling the adulation of the crowd, Richard Lion-heart knew he would not be drawing his sword that day.

He dismounted, directly across from where Prince John stood on the reviewing stand. Grasping his dog's head in both hands, Richard turned to meet his brother's desperate eyes.

PART FIVE: ZARAGOZA

CHAPTER THIRTY-EIGHT

Rebecca had seen Sir Brian die.

After that, little made sense. Not Ivanhoe's unanswered challenge to the tournament knights, not the snorting of Gurth's restrained warhorse, not the cessation of crowd noise and martial hostilities. Not her memories of Rotherwood, where, on the day she had met Ivanhoe, she had been confronted by Brian's arrogance and contempt.

Not how her hate for Brian had only grown with each new mark of his obsession for her, until, on this day, tied to this stake, it had evaporated to nothing.

Lack of sleep and sustenance had left her weak, but it was the absence of meaning, the inability of logic to deal with feelings, the confusion of memories, that had left her on the verge of collapse. Only the ropes tying her to the stake kept her standing.

Rebecca tried to prepare herself. To make sense of her life before it must end.

Ivanhoe and Gurth would die, she thought. Just like Sir Brian. She would burn alive, intoning God's Name. Until her defiant voice would fail, until even in her mind she would no longer be able to hear the Holy Name. At that moment, her soul would flee her tortured body.

But the Will of God is mysterious.

That Will, that Divine Intelligence, could not be understood by His creations. To try and fathom why good men and women suffered, why evil flourished, could lead to sinful doubts.

All she knew was that she was alive, and that her preservation was His doing, His desire.

The approach of Lady Rowena, slipping from horseback, her blue eyes filled with rage, was real, not an apparition fabricated from longing; only because He had brought her to where Rebecca was tied to the stake.

As to why the Lord wanted Rebecca to live, as to how He had predestined the rest of her days, these were unknowable to mortal minds.

Lady Rowena hurried closer, poniard in hand.

Lady Rowena, her friend and protector, beloved of Sir Ivanhoe. Could Rowena know what ran through her mind? Could she possibly forgive Rebecca's hopeless attraction to her betrothed?

Rowena's blade flashed, cutting through knotted rope. This was God's work. Of all the angels and saviors He could have sent, He had sent Lady Rowena.

Rebecca fell to the ground.

Fatigue and terror had taken its toll. The hard ground beneath her body was like a soft embrace. Instantly, she let go of the turmoil of thought. For a moment, only feelings assailed her; until blissful stillness came.

Rebecca lay motionless.

She did not know that it was Gurth who picked her up, carrying her body in his blood-stained arms. That Rowena, Ivanhoe, and Gurth's beloved Ethelreda followed them.

When Rebecca's eyes blinked open, she was being conveyed in a rattling horse-drawn cart. All she could see was the sky above where she lay. She could hear the rush of words around her; English words, anxious voices.

Then a glimpse of Gurth, staring at her with blunt alarm. Behind the burly squire, Sir Ivanhoe, pale with more complex worrying.

Sir Ivanhoe was deeply troubled, she thought.

Rebecca again felt her strength fading, as if the life force was eager to leave her bodily frame. As if a better existence called to her from the World-to-Come. A world in which Sir Ivanhoe did not exist. Where the fears he prompted in her heart could no longer flourish.

Lady Rowena's anxious face came into view, hovering between her and the sky. She spoke Rebecca's name, she took Rebecca's hand, then pressed it tightly. As if insisting that Rebecca must remain in this world. That she must live.

"He did terrible things," said Rebecca, too softly for Rowena to hear. "But he repented. And he loved me." Then even more softly, confessionally, Rebecca added: "I didn't want him to die."

Even if Rowena could have heard, she wouldn't have known Rebecca was speaking of Sir Brian. Even if Rowena had heard and understood, she would have recoiled at Rebecca's forgiveness.

"I didn't want him to die," repeated Rebecca, more softly still. As if speaking to herself. Insisting that she was guilty of inadequate vengefulness. Brian was responsible for her father's death, and yet she forgave him, she felt for him, she practically mourned for him.

"But I didn't love him," said Rebecca, suddenly louder. Loud enough for Rowena to hear, if not to comprehend.

"Don't talk, dear friend," said Rowena. "Your ordeal is at an end, but you must rest. We will care for you, as you have cared for us."

I didn't love him, thought Rebecca, making certain that she was silent. Looking into Rowena's eyes, Rebecca thought out the words she could never tell her: I love someone else. **I love the man you love before all others.**

Rebecca pressed back on Rowena's hand, pressed with all her strength. Soon Rebecca let go, let her eyes close, and let sleep take hold.

When Rebecca woke, she was in a luxurious bed. On her right, sunlight came through a window covered with real glass. On her left, a silver menorah stood on an oak chest. Glass, silver, and oak were goodly objects, but Rebecca doubted that she had passed into the World-to-Come.

She sat up, and came face to face with Gurth, sleeping in a chair at the foot of the bed. Distracted as she was, she couldn't help but notice that the burly squire was wearing an embroidered tunic of azure and gold – the royal colors – clothing far above his station.

"Where am I?" said Rebecca.

Gurth woke at once, got out of the chair, and came to the head of the bed. "My lady," he said. "Thank God we kept the doctor away!"

"What doctor?"

"At Ashby. The Abbot's doctor, he wanted to bleed you, but Ethelreda didn't like the looks of him. And then Lady Rowena, she is quick to make wise judgment, and her wise judgment is to agree with whatever my Ethelreda has to say, as she has proven herself worthy on many occasions – I speak of Ethelreda, though Lady Rowena is very wise as well. You must meet her. Ethelreda!"

Gurth hurried to the door, flung it open, and called again: "Ethelreda!"

The redheaded Ethelreda entered, a stranger to Rebecca. She could not know that the servant girl was wearing a lady's costume for the first time. Neither could she know that Gurth had been dubbed into knighthood by the flat of King Richard's sword.

"Do not make so much noise, Gurth," said Ethelreda. "Lady Rebecca is resting."

Where am I? thought Rebecca. How much time has passed? Where is Ivanhoe? Suddenly another question came to her, and she asked it plainly, and aloud. "Sir Brian," said Rebecca. "Is he dead?"

"Yes, my lady," said Gurth. "A valiant death, the death of a worthy knight."

"And Sir Ivanhoe?" said Rebecca.

"My master is alive and well," said Gurth. "Honored by King and country for his courage and skill in fighting the usurper's knights."

"And Lady Rowena?" said Rebecca. As if to ask about her friend would banish thoughts of her betrothed.

"Lady Rowena has been with you all week," said Gurth. It was the first inkling she had of how long she had been in bed.

"And the King? Has Richard Lion-heart really returned?" said Rebecca, still trying to separate dreams from memories.

"Indeed, my lady," said Gurth. "Returned, and grateful for the sacrifice of your father Isaac."

"And grateful for your daring," said Ethelreda to him, before addressing Rebecca: "Gurth galloped unarmed into a group of fifteen warriors, my lady. Scattering them like rabbits." Ethelreda had wet a cloth with fragrant water, and now pressed it against Rebecca's hot forehead. "Sir Brian and Sir Ivanhoe would not have fared half so well if not for mighty Gurth."

"Enough, woman," said Gurth, unable to cover his pleasure at her praise.

"Another thing: You must no longer call Sir Ivanhoe 'Master,'" continued Ethelreda. "Now that you are a knight, you are his companion in arms."

Could it be true that dear Gurth had become a knight? This lovely redhead seemed to have a clear sense of everything before her, thought Rebecca. It must be wonderful to be without confusion, to be so at ease in the world.

The wet cloth was cool and pleasant on Rebecca's forehead. She inhaled its fragrance, staring up at Ethelreda's vibrant face. "Are you are a healer?"

"I know enough to cool a hot head," said Ethelreda. "But I can do little to remove feverish thoughts."

"Ethelreda is my wife," said Gurth.

Rebecca tried to take in everything Gurth was saying. King Richard on the throne, Prince John running off to parts unknown. Her fever, her long sleep. Doctors consulted, then sent away. Lord Cedric, the King's new Counselor, inquiring after Rebecca from Ashby. Cedric's son, Sir Ivanhoe, also at Ashby, marshalling the armed forces arriving there daily.

But Lady Rowena was right here, here at Sheffield. Her friend had been up half the night with Rebecca, holding her hand, hoping she'd awake.

"She will be so happy to hear you are sitting up," said Gurth. He explained more: How they were in Sheffield, in the home of her kinsman Naftali. How he was indeed married, and happy for it! How marriage vows had been exchanged before the Abbot of Ashby.

Still foggy, Rebecca asked a question.

"No, my lady," said Gurth. "The marriage was not between my master and Lady Rowena. It was between myself and Ethelreda!"

The return of Richard would have been the ideal time for Sir Ivanhoe and Lady Rowena to marry, thought Rebecca. But they were not married. The married couple was Gurth and Ethelreda. If she was to believe everything Gurth had just said. If she was not now dreaming.

Sir Gurth, thought Rebecca. Rebecca said it aloud: "Sir Gurth."

Gurth beamed. "My Ethelreda used to be a scullery worker, but now she is a lady," said Gurth.

A week had indeed passed, an eventful week.

Rebecca was awake, she was listening, but it was difficult to absorb new thoughts, when other concerns pressed on her mind. Sir Ivanhoe and Lady Rowena were not yet married. Sir Ivanhoe was in Ashby. Lady Rowena was here.

Ethelreda was talking: "A scullery maid become a lady! As good as any fairy tale! My husband used to be a serf, but now he is a knight, wearing the Lionheart's colors."

Gurth a knight, and married, thought Rebecca. His wife, a scullery maid, suddenly a lady. A lady who could sense that Rebecca's forehead burned from feverish thoughts. Rebecca tried to still her mind, taking comfort from Ethelreda's scented cloth.

"I think you are a healer," said Rebecca, looking gratefully at Ethelreda.

Saved from burning at the stake, thought Rebecca. Now in a comfortable bed in a Jewish home, the home of her kinsman, Naftali. Brian dead, Ivanhoe alive, Rowena with her all week. Naftali would be certain to help her. He would know what she must do, and would make it possible.

The long and difficult voyage, away from England, to a new life.

A servant entered the room with hot soup and bread. Ethelreda had propped her up with a wealth of pillows, and was talking about how the benefits of broth were wasted if not eaten while hot. The bowl of soup wafted its delicious aroma her way. Ethelreda tried to spoon-feed her.

"No, thank you," said Rebecca.

"But you must," said Ethelreda.

Gurth had said something to her, and she asked him to repeat his words.

"What is Zaragoza, my lady?" said Gurth, the name of the Spanish city sending a shiver of fear through her body. But why should she fear a city filled with family, a city she had longed to go for so long a time? "I heard you speak out the word many times, while you slept in this bed."

"It is a foreign place," said Rebecca.

"A city?" said Gurth.

"Yes," said Rebecca. "In Spain. Zaragoza is the place where I must go." Ethelreda brought a spoonful of soup to her lips, but Rebecca wanted none of it.

"Why must you go anywhere, my lady?" said Ethelreda.

"I have family and friends in Zaragoza who will give me refuge," she said.

"Have you not friends in England?" said Gurth. "Why cannot our country be your home and your refuge?"

How could she explain to Gurth how she felt? To Rebecca the world had become "without form and void," just as the Torah described, in the days before God created light. She was in darkness, in a place without beginning or end, a land without boundaries, where there was neither sky, nor land, nor sea.

The only glimmer in the blackness was to escape to Spain before it was too late, before the turmoil in her heart would lead to the destruction of her soul.

She must fulfill her father's dying wish that she join her family and her people in that distant city.

Before Rebecca could bring herself to answer Gurth, Lady Rowena hurried into the room, her eyes shining.

"Rebecca," she said. "They just woke me with the news! Dear friend, how happy I am to see you awake."

Two steps behind Rowena stood her betrothed, Sir Ivanhoe. His face shaved, his tunic fresh, his handsome face showing every sign of emotional exhaustion.

Why was he not in Ashby? thought Rebecca. That is what Gurth had told her. Ivanhoe was supposed to be in Ashby, with his King and his father, performing his military duties.

"Why are you here?" she said. The tone was neither grateful nor repelling. It was almost possible to believe the words were without meaning, that they were simply the confused utterance of a woman too long asleep. Almost possible to believe the words were not directed at Ivanhoe at all, but at Rowena, who stood between him and Rebecca.

Why must you be here, dear Rowena? thought Rebecca.

"I sent for Ivanhoe last night," said Rowena. "Your fever had lessened, and I hoped you would wake today. I thought you would want to see him."

"No," said Rebecca. "Thank you. But no. I don't want to see him."

Violent anger crossed Ivanhoe's face. Rebecca shut her eyes, as if that could make their problem disappear.

Soon God would explain all. There would be light. Light enough to show what path God intended her to follow.

CHAPTER THIRTY-NINE

Ivanhoe returned to Ashby.

Eight days passed, and Rebecca strengthened. In
Sheffield, she was able to eat, to sleep, to walk in
Naftali's early spring garden. Ethelreda cooked for
her, Gurth watched over her. Lady Rowena walked with
her, sat by her side, kept her company without
belaboring her with questions. A faint blush had
returned to Rebecca's cheeks, though her eyes retained
their haunted look.

Naftali had sent couriers to the coast, where a
boat would take Rebecca and two servants across the
Channel to Normandy. The servants were a married
couple of Saxon descent, chosen by Naftali for their
honesty, loyalty, and physical strength. Urgent
letters in Hebrew and French had been dispatched to
relatives, friends and clients; to Anjou, Poitiers,
Guienne, and Gascony. Other letters, in Castilian,
Spanish, and Ladino, had been sent farther; to
Aquitaine, Aragon, and to Rebecca's solicitous family
in Zaragoza.

Naftali was taking no chances. Many years
cultivating relationships in a dozen countries would

be repaid by Rebecca's safety. Overland travel from Normandy to Spain was arranged at considerable cost. Great lords were not only offered large sums for protecting the daughter of Isaac of York on her passage. They were offered vital trade from the East, and the latest in weaponry from North and South. Guides, guards, and guarantees of safety would be waiting at every border crossing from dukedom to principality to kingdom. Naftali had every reason to expect his kinsman would arrive healthy and whole in Zaragoza.

But the merchant's belief in contracts and letters of credit did little to assuage Gurth's fears. The new knight had ridden to Ashby, asking his former masters – one, Lord Cedric, the new King's Counselor, and the other, the newly brooding Sir Ivanhoe – for permission to accompany Rebecca to the British coast.

Sir Ivanhoe had said as far as he was concerned Gurth could accompany Rebecca to the gates of hell. Lord Cedric was less flowery to his former serf. "Permission granted," he had said. "But if you let any harm come to her in England, churl, you will answer to me."

Gurth had wanted to go much farther, but Rebecca had put a stop to his wishes. "If you care for me, dear Gurth," she had said, "you will stay in England, with your knightly obligations -- and your beautiful bride."

It was early morning, but Rebecca had already embraced Naftali, kissed Ethelreda, and thanked the servants who had attended to her so carefully. She would have ample opportunity to shower grateful blessings on Gurth when they reached the Channel coast.

Rebecca would be setting out in an hour. But first she must say the most difficult farewell of all -- to Lady Rowena. That farewell could not be complete without a confession of all Rebecca had suppressed in eight days of silence.

Rowena had been watching the servants load a wagon with provisions and warm clothing for the voyage. Rebecca approached, and asked if she'd come with her to the garden.

"Gladly," said Rowena. Soon the two friends were sitting in mutual silence, holding goblets of sweet mead. The sun had chased away a morning mist. Rebecca was wondering whether to say something about the buds threatening to burst forth all around them. Rowena wondered whether to mention that there was not a cloud in the sky.

Eight days had passed without mention of Sir Ivanhoe.

Rowena spoke first: "Forgive me, I almost forgot." Rowena took out a folded parchment from inside her cloak. "A scroll came for you last night. From the King."

Rebecca took the small scroll from a satin pouch, and began to unroll it. "Is it difficult to read?" said Rowena.

"No. The writing is very clear."

"What I meant, is it difficult to learn how to read? Because I have asked the Abbot if he would let me study reading and writing with one of his scribes."

"It might be difficult for some, but not for you," said Rebecca. "Not only because you are wise, but because you are someone who cannot be stopped."

"That is what I told the Abbot," said Rowena. "When he suggested reading was not woman's work."

"You might remind him that beheading Holofernes did not seem like woman's work either," said Rebecca. Rowena didn't bother to ask who this was, as she watched Rebecca roll up the scroll, and replace it in its pouch.

"What does it say?" said Rowena.

"It is written in Latin, by the Abbot of Ashby on Richard's behalf. The King's seal is at the end of it. Demanding safe passage for me, promising Heavenly rewards for those who help along the way, and earthly punishments for those who would hinder my path."

"You read Latin as well as English?" said Rowena.

"Yes."

"French and Spanish, and what else?" Before Rebecca could answer, Rowena plunged ahead: "The reason I will learn to read and write, is that I may send you letters. If you like, you may write to me as well."

"I do not deserve your friendship, my lady."

Rowena put aside their goblets, and took hold of Rebecca's hands. "Today of all days, you must not call me 'my lady.'"

Rebecca pulled her hands free and stood. She turned away, trying to find the words she needed to say. Rowena stood, and gently turned her friend around. When they were face to face, Rowena said: "I know you have something to tell me."

"Yes," said Rebecca. "In being rude to Ivanhoe, I have been rude to you, his betrothed."

"You have never been rude. Not to either one of us."

"I said I didn't want to see him. He had ridden from Ashby in hopes that I would be no longer asleep. And when he found me awake, and looked at me, I demanded that he go away." Rowena continued listening, her face showing nothing but understanding. "Is that not rude to the man who saved my life?"

"Do not forget that Ivanhoe owes his life to you, my dear," said Rowena.

"I have been ungrateful."

"No."

"Hateful."

"You can never be hateful," said Rowena. "It is not in your nature."

"I have been hateful to you!" said Rebecca, her eyes wild with guilt.

"All I have ever felt from you was love and devotion," said Rowena.

"Even now?" said Rebecca, as harshly as she could. She let a moment pass, so that what had been allusion and suspicion might become clear. "When you

have seen evidence of what I feel? When you must
suspect me of the vilest treachery."

"Now more than ever," said Rowena. "Though what
I suspect of you is not treachery, but its opposite.
Despite your deepest feelings, you have been loyal to
me."

"No," said Rebecca. "I should have spoken of my
feelings. Told you long ago. That would have been
loyal."

"I could have spoken long ago as well," said
Rowena. "Matters of the heart are difficult. But
time can and will resolve them."

"Not all of them."

"We were children together," said Rowena. "I
loved Ivanhoe like a brother. When he went away, that
love changed to something else. I imagined him a
great warrior, fighting in the service of Lord Jesus.
I loved him the way a damsel is meant to love a
knight. I imagined him a hero."

"He is a hero," said Rebecca

"Yes. A hero who often gets in his own way."

Rebecca could hold back no longer: "I am in love
with him," she said.

"I know," said Rowena. "I am glad you acknowledge it."

"Why should you be glad of a feeling so wicked?" said Rebecca. "To love another woman's betrothed! And that woman her dearest friend!"

Rowena pulled Rebecca into her arms.

"Thank God, I am going away," said Rebecca. "Thank God, I will never have to look at him again."

Rowena held her close, until she – but not Rebecca -- could see Sir Ivanhoe quietly approach, coming to within a few feet of where they embraced.

Rowena said: "It is nearly time to go."

Then Rowena let go, and Rebecca raised her head.

Rebecca saw the impossible: Sir Ivanhoe standing in the garden in a shaft of sunlight between two great trees.

"I didn't want him here," she said to Rowena. Then Rebecca addressed Ivanhoe directly: "I didn't want you here."

"That is true," said Ivanhoe. "But after consultation with my father, my former squire, and Rowena, I have decided to ignore your request."

"What does he mean?" said Rebecca to Rowena.

"I will let him explain," said Rowena.   She kissed Rebecca's cheek with tenderness.   "Goodbye, dear friend," she said.   "I will learn to read and write.   I promise you will hear from me one day."

Rowena smiled briefly at Ivanhoe, then walked away, not looking back.

The earth seemed to open beneath her feet.   "Why are you here?" said Rebecca.

"Richard Lion-heart has sent me along with the scroll demanding your safe passage."

"Why did he send a knight, instead of a simple courier?"

"Because the King wants a knight to guard you on your voyage.   A knight with experience of foreign shores.   A knight who will protect you all the way to Zaragoza."

Rebecca didn't answer this, instead speaking out what she needed to say: "Go after her.   Lady Rowena loves you."

"As I love her," said Ivanhoe.   "But I have not come here for Rowena.   I have come here for you."

"Stop it," said Rebecca.   "I will not listen —"

The bravura speech had lessened the anxious lines in his handsome face.   He stepped close to her, close enough to touch. "Rowena has released me from my vow."

"Because she imagines I love you," said Rebecca.

"I will never abandon Lord Jesus, nor King Richard," said Ivanhoe. "I will always remain loyal to Britain, even in distant Spain."

"Why speak of things that do not concern me?"

"That is hardly fair, Rebecca," said Ivanhoe. "When everything you say or do concerns me."

She could not bear to look at his ardent face, and turned away. Ivanhoe placed a hand on her cheek, the gentlest of touches, demanding nothing but that she know he was there.

She turned to him, struck by the love in his eyes.

"I am sorry," said Rebecca. "My behavior to you has been unforgiveable."

"I have killed men, and you have healed them. We come from different people, different traditions. There is so much you know that is foreign to me. Languages, remedies, gold transmuted into parchment that can travel the world. But I can be helpful on a long voyage. Set up nightly campfires, entertain you with stories of the Holy Land, and see that no harm comes to you. No harm along the way, nor ever again."

He waited for her to say something. Finally, she spoke: "Is it really true what you say? Has King Richard actually given you the task of accompanying me to Spain?"

"Richard Lion-heart has given me no task," said Ivanhoe. "He has given me permission to follow my heart."

"But I have given you no such permission!" said Rebecca. For a moment, she thought he might have finally lost patience. But then he smiled, allowing himself to be pleased by her words.

"No such permission," he said. "At least not yet."

"Just as you will never give up your faith or your people, neither will I," said Rebecca.

"Yes."

"What can you hope to accomplish by accompanying me on a journey that must end with you returning to England alone?"

"I am not thinking of accomplishments," said Ivanhoe. "Or ends of journeys. Or problems that may prevent our forming a bond of holy matrimony."

"You're not thinking at all," said Rebecca. There was no querulousness in her tone, but rather a new understanding.

"I love you, Rebecca," said Ivanhoe.

She wanted to answer in kind. But it was too much, too fast, to do more than acknowledge her feelings with silent joy.

When she finally spoke, it was not about love, at least not directly. "I will stop thinking as well," said Rebecca.

They would be sharing a lengthy voyage. She could not imagine how it might end. But just as sunshine dispels dark night, Rebecca knew she would one day speak the words he longed to hear.

THE END

Made in the USA
Middletown, DE
26 December 2022

20381272R00307